One More Lie

CATE TAYLER

ELEPHANT SHOES PRESS

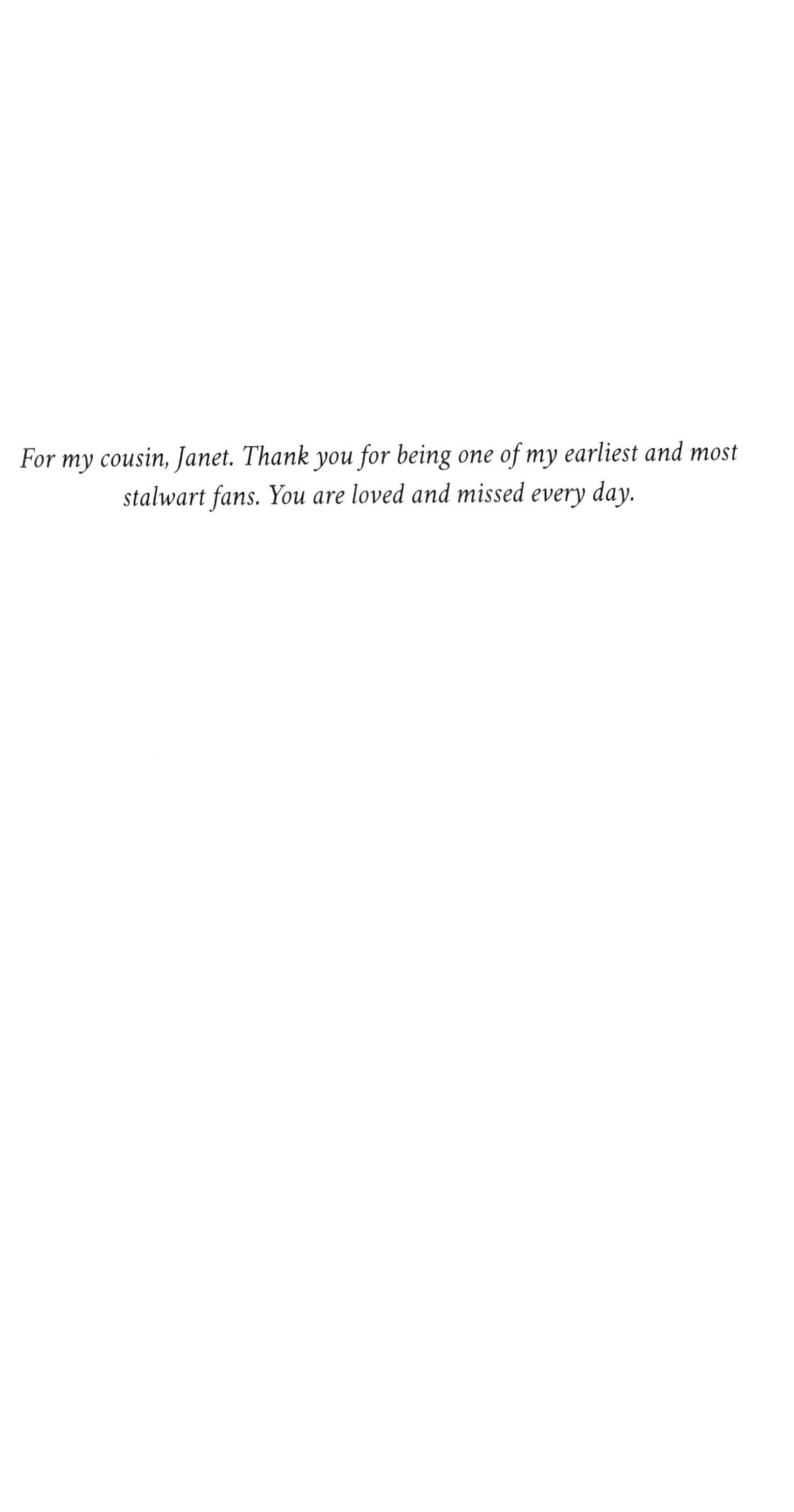

For my cousin, Janet. Thank you for being one of my earliest and most stalwart fans. You are loved and missed every day.

One

Piper

Three Months Ago

The somber graveside service complete, most of the mourners drift away. I barely register the platitudes, the squeezes of my arm or pats on my shoulder as they walk past. It's unseasonably warm today, but I'm so cold from the inside out I'm shivering. Some people think it's a good sign for the sun to shine during a funeral, but I think it's a damn insult the weather should be so nice when you're putting your best friend in the ground. Especially when it's the middle of December and only a week ago it was snowing so hard, it caused a multi-car pile-up on I-95. The same pile-up that brought us here.

The tiny baby in my arms squirms, and I sway to calm her. Violet is only two months old and she has no idea what's going on, no idea we're standing at the foot of her mother's grave, and —like me—no clue as to what comes next.

Laura's parents stand to my right, Denny's face wet from tears as he stands stoic, arms around his wife. Lulu weeps openly against his chest and I long to have that kind of comfort. Unfortunately, I have never felt that and doubt I ever will. But I have Violet and I have Tessa, who stands on my left with an arm around my waist. She, Laura, and I were a team, the best of friends, sisters. Under the tree at home, there are three identical gift-wrapped boxes, each containing a Powerpuff Girl charm. Now I wonder if I should return them or set Laura's Blossom charm aside for Violet. It's one of the many details that I am now responsible for but will leave for another day.

"I'm going to head to the cafe and see if I can help Bette set up." Tessa adjusts Violet's little knit cap and kisses her head.

"I'll be there shortly."

Bette arranged for a small lunch for Laura's parents and closest friends at her cafe. I don't really want to go. I want to curl up on the couch under a blanket and not come out again until March. Winter's for hibernation, right? It's the time for everything to die, for the earth to prepare for new growth in the spring. Sounds like a good time to mourn my best friend.

Violet squeaks, and I'm reminded it can't be only about me anymore. I look down at her and smile. Her eyes are closed, little bow mouth moving like she's suckling. She's getting hungry.

"Piper." Laura's mother's voice shakes. "Denny and I are going to pass on the lunch and go home. Do you want us to take the baby or might you be able to take care of her, just for a little while?"

"I've got her," I say. Even though custody passed to Lulu and Denny upon Laura's death, they're not set up yet to take over her care.

"Thank you," Lulu says, her voice watery. "Please give our apologies to Bette."

"She'll understand."

She strokes the baby's cheek before turning to take her husband's arm and walk away. I stand there over the open grave,

Laura's pearl-gray casket covered in a few ceremonial shovels of dirt and the roses tossed down by her mourners. Tears are cold on my cheeks as a breeze kicks up and brushes its icy tentacles across my exposed face.

"What am I supposed to do, Laura? You were the one who always had the answers." I look down at Violet, who stares up at me with her now-open dark brown eyes. I trace her button nose, her cheeks that are already filling out, the little dark curl poking out from under the cap, and I know the answer as sure as if Laura spoke it to me. And maybe she did, in the way some people say God speaks to them.

"I promise you, I will look after your daughter. I will protect her and love her and make sure she grows up knowing all about you," I say. "I promise to do whatever it takes to give her a happy life."

I blow a final kiss to Laura, holding her daughter tight and repeating the promises I mean to keep. No matter what.

TWO

Piper

There is no justice in this universe.

He's still the most gorgeous human male specimen to have walked the earth since Cary Grant. Thick waves of dark blond hair frame his square, scruffy jaw and curl behind his ears down the nape of his neck. His eyes are the color of my dad's old army jacket—the one I refuse to throw away despite there not being one original button or zipper left, the one currently hanging off the hook by the back door of my confectionery. Wide shoulders, sinewy muscles flexing under a salmon-colored button-down, long thick legs, and pillowy lips that've launched a million dirty fantasies. He ambles in, his quick perusal of the store relaxed, but the way he carries himself is simply—commanding. He's a sauntering, sexy wet dream.

I despise every square inch of him.

His gaze lands on me and the corners of his mouth curl up in a devastating smile. Except for the tiny lines that crinkle at the corner of his eyes, and the angles of his face that have sharpened with age, he looks the same as when I last saw him fifteen years ago at our college graduation. *He couldn't have put on fifty pounds,*

lost some hair, broken that perfectly patrician nose of his? Like I said...
no fucking justice in the universe.

I steel my spine and lift my chin, prepared to face the man who broke my heart. Who broke *me*.

"Pip Poincelot. God, it's been so long."

I grit my teeth. "Not long enough. And it's Piper PONS-low. 'Points-a-lot' is a tired joke."

If he hears the edge in my voice, he's ignoring it. He leans against the counter and I'm grateful for the foot-and-a-half of purple quartz between us as his voice drops a notch when he tells me I look great. It's not my fault his voice can still hit me right between the legs. It's only science, a chemical reaction no different from when you heat sugar and cream to make caramel.

"Why are you here, Webb?" I'm happy—and surprised—my voice is so steady. I even sound bored. Twenty-two-year-old me could never pull off being so casual around Webb Duncan. That version of me had silly romantic notions about white knights on noble steeds and a naiveté when it came to what love really is. When it came to Webb.

"Didn't Hayes tell you?" He quirks an eyebrow. "I'm moving here. Opening a new practice just down the way." He jerks his head toward the beach. "Hayes said the Isle used to have a full-time dentist until he retired. Figured I can be his replacement."

My brain stumbles over his announcement. "You're moving here? To Sandcastle Isle?"

He chuckles. "I am."

I'm trying to process the news, but I'm unable to reconcile Thomas Webber Duncan, of the wealthy Weston, Massachusetts Duncans, moving to a place whose unofficial motto is "Poor Man's Nantucket." We're a blip of an island located just off the southeastern tip of Rhode Island, accessible only by ferry and sea plane. It's a small, homey community with fewer than ten-thousand year-round residents, give or take. There is one fine-dining restaurant and no night clubs or golf courses. We're salt-of-the-earth people here. What reason could he have to move to such a remote place, where his pedigree and pretty face won't get him far?

He laughs at my befuddlement, causing my face to heat with embarrassment. "I'm setting up a full-service dental practice with two partners. Pam is DDS, Trev does orthodontics, and I specialize in oral surgery."

My stomach does a weird flippy thing when he says *oral*. I sneak a glance at his left hand and clock the absence of a ring, though that means nothing. "Your wife is okay moving here with you? We're not exactly a booming metropolis."

For the first time since he walked in, he looks uneasy. "She's staying in Weston. We've divorced."

This is where I should say, "I'm sorry to hear that." But I'm petty. He left me to marry his on-again, off-again college girlfriend. I hope he's hurting.

Like I said, I'm petty. Sue me.

I busy myself by wiping down the already-clean counter, cursing my luck. I should be in the back creating confections and Mara should be out here. I could've avoided this whole awkward situation. But her husband Drew, my ex-boyfriend-turned-business partner, had to sneak her away for a mini-vacation before their baby comes. "So you're on the Isle because you've moved here, but why are you here? At Sugarbreakers?"

"I didn't have a chance to talk to you at Laura's funeral. I wanted to tell you how sorry I was."

"You were there?" My voice is scratchy, the way it always gets when I think about my best friend. It's been three months since she slipped on the ice coming out of the library and died, but some days it feels like yesterday. Other times I can make it the whole day without crying. The whole funeral is a blur. Prince Harry could've been there, and I wouldn't have noticed.

"Of course. She was my friend, too. Once."

I swallow past the small lump in my throat. "She would've

appreciated it," I say and mean it. Laura was a better person than almost everyone I know, including me.

"She has a daughter now, right?"

"Yep." Thinking of the infant chases away the wisps of grief and makes me smile. "Violet."

"Is she with her father?" Webb asks.

"Her grandparents." I check my Fitbit for the time. It's April 1st—how fitting since this is like one giant cosmic joke—and outside peak tourist season, so it's not busy in the shop and I keep limited hours. "Look, I have things I need to do before I close up for the day. Unless you'd like to pick up some candy or something?"

He pulls a face, as if I've just suggested he jump naked into the frigid Rhode Island Bay. "I don't eat candy."

"That's crazy. Who doesn't eat candy?"

He shrugs a shoulder. "I like a piece of chocolate now and then, but candy is usually too sugary for my taste. Not to mention the havoc it wreaks on your teeth."

"Taffy is our signature product," I inform him, miffed.

His expression is horrified. "Caramels, taffy—those are the worst. I always advise my patients to avoid those and the hard candies, like jawbreakers. You know, parents worry about their kids getting addicted to drugs, but they should really worry about sugar addictions. Not only can it lead to obesity but it can cause tooth decay, periodontal disease, edentulism—that's tooth loss. And most people don't know this, but your overall health is directly tied to your oral health. They say marijuana is a gateway drug. I'd add Jolly Ranchers to the list."

I gape at him. "You realize you're in a candy shop—my candy shop."

He looks around and nods. "It's nice. Very colorful."

"Well," I start, jamming my hands on my hips. "I hate dentists."

He regards me with a slight grin, looking more amused than offended. "Most people do."

He's baiting me. It's what we used to do back then. But this is now, and I'm not into fun and flirty banter, not with him. Ten minutes and already he's twisting me up inside. He must sense the change from the polite indifference I've been trying to exude because his grin fades, and his eyes turn serious. "I'm sorry—"

"'Bout what?" I counter. "For comparing me to a drug dealer?" *Maybe breaking my heart? Almost ruining my life?*

"I didn't say that," he protests.

"You called Jolly Ranchers a gateway drug." I gesture to the display behind him. "I carry ten different flavors."

For the first time he looks abashed, his infamous swagger wavering. "Could we talk?"

"Like I said, I have things to do. See you around, Webb."

I turn and walk through the doors leading to the back of the shop. I listen for the telltale sound of the door opening, the bell jingling, and the door shutting again before I breathe easy again. A part of me was afraid he'd follow. I ignore the teeny, tiny part of me disappointed he didn't.

It took me years to get Webb out of my system and out of my head. I won't let him get a hold again.

⊹⊱⊰⊹

I'M BRUSHING MY TEETH WHEN THERE'S A KNOCK ON MY FRONT door and a voice calls out, "Piper, hey! Where are you?"

"Bah-rum," I call back with a mouthful of toothpaste. I spit and rinse, then walk out to meet Tessa. She's plopped on my couch with the remote, flipping through the channels. She's already in her flannel pajama set, the one with the dancing bunnies I mock her for but secretly love. I can't pull off cutesy, so I'm in my worn light blue URI sweatshirt and gray fleece leggings.

"You need to lock your door," Tessa says, clicking on the next episode of *You*. It's our Friday night tradition, when she isn't traveling, to binge a series and scarf down a pint of ice cream. "We just finished bingeing the latest season of *Fear They Neighbor*. Did you not learn anything?"

"Uh, you're my neighbor," I remind her, heading to the kitchen for our respective pints of Ben & Jerry's—hers Brownie Batter Core, mine Phish Food. Dairy-free because it seems the closer I get to forty, the less food tolerant I become.

I've known Tessa Brandt since college and had invited her out to Sandcastle Isle a few years ago after she divorced her asshat husband. Originally, she lived with Laura and me, but when Laura got pregnant, Hayes—the same Hayes Rutherford who brought Webb back into my life—offered her his spare room. How Tessa and Hayes could share the house without either killing or boning one another was beyond me. But both were insistent they were friends, only friends, and nothing but friends so help them God. And help the rest of us that have to witness their elaborate self-denials.

"I can only do one episode tonight," I say, picking up the remote. "I have to take the early ferry to pick up Violet tomorrow. Lulu and Denny have some church thing they need to attend."

"Are they any closer to signing over custody?"

"They said they've been in touch with their lawyer. It's only a matter of drawing up the papers."

The Rosellis took custody of Violet after the accident that killed Laura, but they are both in their early seventies and at their own admittance not prepared to raise another child. Laura and I grew up together, and with no siblings and the baby's father unknown, we'd agreed I should be the one to raise her.

I'm excited about the prospect of becoming a mother, but

any happiness will always be tempered by the pain of it coming at the expense of my best friend's life. I had my chance years ago and I lost it; this was Laura's chance and she deserved to be able to raise her daughter.

"Laura would want you to have her." Tessa smiles at me as if she knows what I was thinking.

I lean my head on her shoulder, swallowing back my jumble of emotions. They're always close to the surface, but seeing Webb today brought my regrets into the open.

"Hey," Tess says, patting my head. "What's going on with you?"

I sit up. "I saw Webb today."

"What? How?"

"He lives here now. Apparently, Hayes invited him." I give her a brief recap of the afternoon. "Hayes didn't say anything?"

Tessa shook her head. "I haven't been home much."

I jam my spoon into the ice cream to dig out a bite. "He looks good. Great, actually."

"Asshole."

I grin at her. "I love you."

She nudges me with her arm. "How do you feel about this?"

"Well, Dr. Brant," I say, "If I'm being honest, I'm shook."

"Is he here alone?"

"I guess so. He said he's divorced." I run my spoon around the edges of the pint. "He came in and talked to me like nothing ever happened. Like I was simply an old friend he ran into."

Tessa shakes her head. "I can't believe you didn't punch him in the balls."

"I was too stunned." The last time I saw Webb Duncan, he was leaving my bed after a weekend of marathon sex. We were supposed to meet up the next day at the Kinney Azalea Gardens. He never showed; a few days later, I received a text breaking things off. Shortly after that, he and Carolynn were engaged.

"Maybe this could be a good thing." She bumps my shoulder

when I give her a dark look. "Hear me out. I know how badly he hurt you, but honey—don't you think you should tell him what happened? Give him a chance to apologize and make it up to you?"

"No, I'm not going to tell him shit," I snap. "There's nothing he could do now to make what he did back then okay."

She puts her arm around me and holds me close. "Honey, if we learn anything from Laura's accident, it's that life is too damn short to hold on to regrets."

"I'll think about it," I say, setting my half-eaten pint to the side and picking up the remote to start the series. I need to clear my head. Tomorrow, I'm seeing Violet, and she's all that matters now.

THREE

Webb

"Welcome to Sandcastle Isle. A little spot of paradise in New England."

Hayes and I clink our beer bottles together. We're sitting out on his deck in a pair of white Adirondack loungers with a tabletop fire pit going and a cooler with more beers between us. The night is cool but warm enough to subsist in only a sweatshirt and jeans. Except for Hayes. He's wearing a pair of cargo shorts. I've known the guy for almost twenty years and one thing that hasn't changed is his style.

I take a slug of the beer, a porter from a local microbrewery that's a bit heavy. "Have to admit, it's a pretty place. I wasn't sure at first, it being so small. But it's just what I needed."

"I'm glad. Though the population doubles between June and September."

I shrug. "Still not the same as living in the city. It's much better."

"Have you explored any? Been to the other villages on the Isle?"

Sandcastle Isle is its own municipality, but it's divided into four separate villages. The townhome I'm renting is in Sakonnet

Village on the western side of the Isle. The dental office will be located in The Shoals at the southern tip, where Piper has her shop and where she and Hayes live. "Just here and Sakonnet. Haven't had much time."

"Not missing much. North Village houses all the summer mansions, and the Isle's only Dunkin', so it has that going for it. Eastshore has the best waves and it has a Del's, but not much else."

"Can't remember the last time I had a frozen lemonade. Probably URI."

"When do you think you'll be ready to open the practice?"

"By June 1st, if all goes well," I tell him. "My contract with DDS gives a 90-day deadline for new offices to open and if we don't make it by then, the CEO will sue us for breach."

Hayes's eyebrows shoot up. "Isn't your mother the CEO?"

"Yes. Yes, she is." I swig my beer.

DDS is Duncan Dental Services LLC—the family business of which I, son of both the founder and the current CEO, am only a part of as a franchisee. They buy dental practices, sometimes acquiring them from retiring dentists, sometimes taking over an existing office. Then DDS sells franchising licenses to dentists who might want to practice on their own but don't want the hassle from the business side and who lack the capital to start from scratch. They get to concentrate on their patients while DDS does all the background work. Dad retired leaving Mom as current CEO, my best friend Graeme is Vice-President of Acquisitions, and my ex-wife the VP of Marketing.

I'd been expected to take on an executive role, the one my brother, Philip, would've held had he not died, but I'd invested too much time into my schooling to not put my degrees to use. For the past five years, I'd been working at a group practice near the homestead in Weston, where I had purpose and was valued for my contributions far more than I'd be as my mother's office monkey. But when the divorce happened and this opportunity to start over outside of Massachusetts came up, I had to jump on it. I had to get distance from my family, from my ex-wife, from the constant reminders of how I was put on this earth for one reason only, and I'd failed at it. I'll forever owe Hayes for suggesting it, and Graeme for convincing my mother to add the dental office on Sandcastle Isle to our list of locations, since my partners and I couldn't afford to buy it outright on our own. I'm not independently wealthy, and I don't plan on ever claiming the trust fund that passed on to me after Philip's death.

"Have you met SASBO yet?" Hayes asked.

"Saz-bo? What the hell is that?"

"The Shoals Association of Small-Business Owners. They run The Pier and surrounding neighborhood. If you want your business to succeed, you'll need them. You already know who their leader is."

"I'm guessing the older lady who owns the cafe on the corner of the pier. I heard her the other day ordering folks around like a platoon commander."

"Who, Bette?" Hayes laughs and shakes his head. "She can be a dragon if you get on her bad side, I'll give you that. But she's really a softie. No, it's Piper."

The beer I swallow goes down the wrong pipe. "Piper?" I choke out. "Shit."

"So long as Piper is on your side, you've got nothing to worry about. She's the unofficial mayor of the Isle. Everyone loves her."

Well, fuck. "I went by her store earlier. Pretty sure she hasn't forgiven me for going back to Carolynn."

I'd hoped fifteen years would've been enough time to smooth out the hurt. The way I ended things back then was shitty, no two ways about it. The first words out of my mouth should've been an apology, followed by heavy groveling. Instead, I reverted to my old self-defense mechanism—charm—and crashed spectacularly.

"It didn't help when I swallowed my foot by telling her how awful her taffy was," I add. "Not that I meant hers personally. All sticky candy in general. I did a rotation in a low-income, rural clinic and the amount of dead and decayed teeth I had to take out of kids whose diet included a steady stream of high-fructose corn syrup turned me off to most sweets."

"Unfortunate," he says. He tips his bottle at me. "Like I told you back then, you were an idiot."

"I know."

"A class-A asshole."

"Yeah, I get it," I grumble.

"You pulled some douchebaggery in the first degree."

"All right." I kick him under the table. "You made your point."

Hayes chuckles and I'd punch him, but he's not wrong. He hasn't called me anything worse than I've called myself over the years. I chose the wrong woman, and I'm paying the price.

"At least you don't have Carolynn to contend with anymore. Even if she took everything you had, it's worth the price to be free." He raises his drink.

Despite how acrimonious the divorce was, the urge to defend my ex-wife to my friends is second nature. "She didn't take anything. I gave it to her freely. It's not entirely her fault we didn't work out. I wasn't the right man for her. I knew it back then, but I was trying to do the right thing."

"I know," Hayes says with a surprising gentleness. "But I'm glad you finally realized sacrificing your happiness to make up for something that wasn't your fault—they're called accidents for a reason—was stupid before you got too old to play the field again. Still, you wasted what, thirteen years?"

We'd gotten married right before my second year of dentistry school. The first few years weren't too bad, but that was only because we were so busy. We were both in grad school, then I had my residency. It wasn't until she went to work for my parents and we moved near them that everything started going to shit.

"I guess I hoped she'd be on my side when it came to Mom and Dad, but it was more like she was the daughter and I was the in-law. Or outlaw, as they probably saw it." I never fit in with my own family, but Carolynn did.

"Do they know she cheated on you?"

I grunted and stared out at the yard. "I don't know. Doesn't matter. It was over before then. I was just dragging my feet. Walking in on her bent over our kitchen island was just the impetus I needed."

Hayes drops his empty bottle into a blue bucket with a clink and takes another one out of the cooler between us. "Took you long enough to come to your senses, but I'm glad you did."

"Might not have been soon enough." I tap the beer bottle against my leg. "If I can stop shooting myself in the foot, maybe I can get Piper to hear me out."

I was a fucking coward back then, convincing myself I owed it to Carolynn to give her one-hundred percent of myself, which meant cutting Piper out of my life entirely. Except I never was able to exorcise her from my thoughts. I was never able to give Carolynn one-hundred percent because I'd already given a piece of myself to Pip, and I never got it back.

"Women, man," Hayes says with a shake of his head. "Can't live with them, can't fuck them out of your system."

He's looking past me to where Tessa Brandt is walking across the short span of grass separating this house from Piper's. She was roommates with Piper and Laura at URI and part of our larger friend group. Now she's Hayes's roommate, which I already thought was interesting. Now I'm even more intrigued.

"All right, time to change the subject." He reaches beside him and holds up a deck of cards. "Hope you brought enough cash."

"Liar's Poker?"

"I'm ready to win my money back."

Hayes hasn't won since college, but he's optimistic. Or foolish. Either way, he owes me about $3500 from our yearly game at this point. Not that I'll ever actually collect; it's all in good fun. I'm ready to forget about Piper for the moment and add to my friend's IOU.

"Game on."

FOUR

Piper

"Look at this little darling," coos Bette Regules, who owns Beachcomber's Cafe a few doors down. "She has Laura's cute little nose."

"Mm." The baby is sleeping in the sling strapped across my body. I don't see it, but she's the third person today to comment on some feature of Violet's that reminds them of Laura. When I picked her up from Lulu's earlier this morning, Lulu had commented about her being the spitting image of Laura as a baby, only with darker coloring. Maybe it's a gene some people have that gives them that ability, like how only some of us can roll our tongues. I don't possess it. Violet, with her big brown eyes and wispy nut-brown hair, looks like... Violet.

"What can I get for you today, Bette?" She's here for fudge, like she is every Sunday afternoon.

She taps her chin and hums, pretending to mull over the choices before deciding on the usual—one pound peanut butter fudge, one pound caramel pretzel, and one pound dark with sea salt flakes. "Oh, and can you wrap up an extra half pound of the peanut butter separately? Last week I didn't get to try a bite before Jonathan gobbled it all up. I'll give him his own so he keeps his filthy fingers off mine."

I chuckle. "Sure thing. How's the restaurant?"

"Oh, you know." She waves her hand in the air. "It's off-season so not too busy. But did you hear about Dana King and Vic Guerra?"

She lowers her voice and leans forward, a wicked gleam in her eye. Gossip is oxygen on the Isle and Bette is the main tank. "They were caught playing *tickle the pickle* on the dunes the other night."

My eyes widen. Yes, I'm a guilty consumer of gossip. "But isn't Dana dating some guy on the mainland?"

Bette shakes her head. "Not since he decided taking the ferry was too much trouble. But Vic has been after Dana forever. Now he's finally got her."

"Yay for Vic."

"We'll see. You know what they say—the chase is often better than the catch."

"I say good for them." I wrap Bette's fudge in wax paper and place it in individual boxes before sliding over to the register to ring it up. At least someone on this Isle is getting some because it's sure not me.

The bell over the door jangles, startling Violet. I soothe her as the new customer walks in. Bette makes a throaty noise and when I look up, I scowl. Was I not unwelcoming enough the other day?

Webb smiles at us and walks up to Bette with his hand extended. "Hello, I'm Webb Duncan, new dentist in town. You own the cafe, right?"

I catch the roses blooming in her cheeks when she shakes his hand, surprised she doesn't do the whole swoon and faint. "Bette Regules. I don't believe I've seen you in there. I'm sure I would've noticed."

He dips his head briefly in an *aw shucks* kind of move. "I was in on Saturday morning with Hayes and not looking my best, I'm sure. I had your chocolate-chip banana pancakes and can I tell you, they are the best pancakes I have ever eaten. Hayes says they're second only to your croissants. I can't wait to try them."

Bette titters—fucking titters—and touches his arm. Her eyes blaze and she lingers a little longer than necessary. "That is so sweet of you."

"Oh, brother," I mutter under my breath, poking the iPad touchscreen a little harder than I probably should. I flip the tablet over to face Bette so she can pay. "$24.05, Bette."

Bette barely looks at me or the tablet as she taps her card to pay, still focused on Webb. "Next time you come in, ask for me, and I'll be sure you get a complimentary pastry. To welcome you to the Isle."

"That's awfully nice of you, Mrs. Regules."

"It's Ms., but please, call me Bette." She scribbles her signature and plucks the bag off the counter.

He smiles again all wide and bright. "Bette. It's lovely to meet you."

She waves her fingers at me and sweeps toward the door, turning back once to waggle her eyebrows behind Webb's back before leaving. I resist the urge to roll my eyes. Like my dad always said, "Keep it up and they'll roll right out of your head."

"What can I get you, Webb? Unfortunately, the ice cream machine is on the fritz so I have no dairy-free, sugar-free, gluten-free sorbet on hand and that's the healthiest thing I sell." I lean one hand on the counter, the other patting Violet's rump through the sling.

He leans over the counter to stare at the baby. "Is that Violet in there? Can I see?"

I pull the edge of the pouch away so he can see her face. "She's lovely," he says. His face alights with another smile not as bright as the one he turns on for everyone else, but warmer. He looks up at me still smiling, and it's way more disarming than his other one. A feathery lightness fills my chest, but then I remember what happened the last time Webb made me feel like this, and the feathers turn to pie weights.

"Apparently she looks just like Laura."

His forehead wrinkles. "Eh, I don't see it."

"See? Me neither. I was beginning to think there was something wrong with me." I'm about to smile, but I cut that shit off. I don't need to encourage him.

"Pip," he begins.

"Stop calling me that. It's Piper."

He continues like I haven't spoken. "I know I did a shitty thing to you in college. But I'd like a chance to make it right. Can we talk about it? Maybe over dinner?"

I start to shake my head, but his pleading voice stops me. "Please, Piper?"

Maybe Tessa is right and I should get this over with, let him apologize to me, accept it, and move on. Finally. Only I'm not sure that will be enough to stop the aching I feel down to my bones, to assuage the guilt and regret I will carry the rest of my life.

I draw in a breath and meet his wary gaze. "I have Violet until tomorrow."

"I can pick up a pizza and bring it by your house? Help you babysit?"

"No," I reply quickly. The last thing I need is Webb's presence to taint my sanctuary. "My house isn't really guest-ready. Besides, I'm not babysitting; I'm in the process of adopting Violet."

"Oh, wow. That's—congratulations." He sounds sincere and the earnest look on his face shakes something loose.

With a sigh, I relent. "If you want, we can grab a slice after I close up. Il Pomodoro Dolce has great pizza."

"Sounds like a date." He grins, a glint in his eye.

I frown. "Sounds like a slice. I can give you thirty minutes."

Violet lets out a squeak, letting me know she's awake and ready for a bottle. I take her out of her cozy pouch and place her against my shoulder. "There, there, jellybean. I'll get your bottle in a sec."

"Can I hold her?"

Webb puts out his hands and I eye him for a moment before handing over this precious bundle. "I'll only be a minute. I need to warm her bottle."

He takes her and starts talking to her in a sing-song voice while he sways back and forth. My heart seizes at the sight. He looks like a natural and damn if my ovaries don't twitch, the traitorous bitches. For a microsecond, I think about our baby—the one I never got to hold, the one he never knew about. But it hurts too much and I will not go there again. I go to the kitchen to warm the bottle, using the time to remind myself that it doesn't matter how sexy Webb looks, or how cute he is holding a baby, he's still the same asshole who smashed my heart into oblivion. Fifteen years later and it still feels like it's only being held together by cheap dollar-store glue.

I return to find Violet cradled in his arms, Webb smiling down at her like it's no big deal she's chewing on what looks to be an expensive silk tie. She gurgles like she's answering him as he whispers to her. Great. He's even charmed Violet.

"I can take her now." I shake the bottle. "She's a messy eater. I would hate to see her damage more of your suit."

He looks at me, then down at his tie, and chuckles. "I can always buy another one. But I should get back to the office. We're interviewing prospective staff."

He hands Violet back to me and I settle her in my arms to feed. "You look good with her. A natural," he says, repeating the same thing I thought about him. My heart doesn't just seize then. It splinters, holding itself together by the barest of measures. I keep my face turned down so he can't see the pain I'm having a terrible time hiding.

"What time do you close up?"

"Five on Mondays. I'll meet you at the pizza place. It's near your office."

"See you later, then."

He leaves, and I finish feeding Violet. "Don't fall for that charm, jellybean. He cannot be trusted. He's a heartbreaker."

Violet's still drinking from the bottle, but she looks at me and gurgles, dribbling milk out of her mouth. I mop at it with the burp cloth and laugh. "You'll understand when you get older. Your heart is a precious organ, little one, and needs to be protected. Someday you'll find your Prince Charming, and he won't be anything like Webb Duncan."

FIVE

Webb

It's a little before five when I arrive at Il Pomodoro Dolce. The Sweet Tomato, if my high school Italian hasn't failed me, can be only generously called a hole-in-the-wall. The pizzeria occupied a tiny sliver of space a few steps off The Pier. If it weren't for the pink neon tomato in the window, I might have passed it by.

There is a short pink Formica counter with three stools abutting the front window. A bistro table for two is hidden in a corner just inside the door. A glass display showcases the Slices of the Day—a pepperoni, a cheese, a bacon-mushroom-meat-ball, and a Margherita with balls of mozzarella topping a red sauce and garnished with whole basil leaves. Adjacent to the case is another pink Formica counter where orders are obviously taken and rung up. A short older woman with a thick gray bun, deep-set wrinkles, and T-shirt depicting a cartoon slice of pizza wielding a light saber that reads "May the Sauce Be With You" has a phone pressed to her ear and is writing as quickly as she speaks. "Fifteen minutes," she says, hanging up the phone, which starts ringing again almost immediately. She picks it up and snaps, "Hold," before sliding the ticket onto a stainless steel table separating the front of the restaurant from the kitchen.

"Order in!" she shouts, then barely sparing me a glance she picks up the phone and proceeds to take another order. "You want chicken and barbecue sauce?" she asks the person on the other end of the line. "Sacrilege. Next you'll be asking for pineapple. No. I'll give you chicken with our house made smoky marinara, how's that? Fine. Fifteen minutes."

She hangs up and scribbles out another ticket, slaps it on the table behind her, and yells out again. Finally she addresses me. "What can I getcha'?"

"I'm waiting for someone, actually," I say, gesturing out the door. "I'll order for us both when she gets here."

She purses her lips and looks me up and down. "Who?"

"Excuse me?"

"Who? Who are ya waitin' for?" She makes a hurry-up gesture with her hands. "Only locals would make a date to meet here, so it must be someone I know. Who is it?"

"Uh—Piper Poincelot?"

She nods once. "Piper gets the same thing every time. Bacon, olives, and pineapple. You want to share that or get your own?"

I nod at the phone. "It didn't sound like you offered pineapple."

She shrugs. "It's not normal. But Piper wants pineapple, Piper gets pineapple. She's a sweet girl."

"That she is," I murmur.

Her eyes narrow. "What are you doing with Piper? Who are you?"

I turn my sixty-watt smile on her. "I'm Webb Duncan. My partners and I are taking over the dental office and opening a new practice."

"Webb?" She scowls. "Like a spidah?"

I'm used to this reaction and give my customary chuckle. "Short for Webber."

"How do you know our Piper?"

"We went to college together."

Her scowl opens to a smile. "Well, why didn't you say so? Any friend of Piper's is a friend of ours. I'm Gina Donato. What would you like, sweetheart?"

I decide to have the same, although pineapples and olives isn't a combination I ever thought I'd be keen on. But when in Rome... Gina writes out a ticket and sends it to the back.

"We'll get that started for ya," she says, though it comes out sounding more like *staw-ted*. Damn, I've missed this state. Four years of college endeared me to the accent, which is not unlike back home, where "r"s tend to become "ah"s and are unceremoniously tacked on to the end of most words ending in vowels. Of course, my parents wouldn't dream of their children speaking so common-like. The Massachusetts accent was practically thrummed out of us from an early age. Maybe that's why I like this one. It's more real.

"Sorry, Nana." A young girl darts in from the back of the pizzeria and plants a peck on Gina's cheek. "I had to stay late for tutoring, and I missed the first ferry."

"S'alright." The woman beams at the girl and pats her cheek. She's glowing with pride when she looks at me. "This is my granddaughter, Jamie. Jamie, this is Piper's friend, Dr. Duncan. He's going to be the new dentist."

"Nice to meet you, Jamie."

"Uh, you, too." She doesn't meet my eyes, and her cheeks are turning as dark as the marinara sauce.

Gina doesn't seem to notice. "Jamie here is going to be a doctor."

"Nana, I don't think he cares—"

Gina squeezes the girl's shoulders and ignores her protest. "Won second place in the Rhode Island State Science Fair."

"That's amazing," I tell her. "What kind of doctor?"

Jamie is still red in the face, but she replies. "Immunology, maybe. Or virology. I haven't decided if I want to be a medical doctor or maybe a research scientist."

"I couldn't decide if I wanted to be a dentist or a medical doctor," I confess. "So I decided to do both. I became an oral surgeon, which required me to get my M.D. in addition to my D.D.S.—Doctor of Dental Science. You can do both, too."

"She can do anything she wants," Gina proclaims, giving her a smacking kiss on the cheek.

"Nana," Jamie scolds, but she's also pleased.

"You know, we'll have the practice up and running by June. If you ever want to come by and talk about a medical career, my door is always open."

Jamie's face lights up. "Really? Oh, Dr. Duncan, that would be wicked cool. Thank you."

"What's wicked?"

We all turn and see Piper pushing Violet in a stroller up to the counter. She looks at me with a brow raised, gaze narrow. Gina speaks up.

"Dr. Duncan here offered to give Jamie advice about becoming a doctor."

"Is that so?" Piper's tone is light, but I can sense an edge to her smile. She bats her lashes at me. "That really is wicked cool."

I know the mockery is meant for me and not the teenager, but I choose to ignore it. "Gina has our order started. She said you always get the same thing."

She squints. "I thought we agreed to a slice. I can make do with one of those," she says, pointing to the case containing the ready-to-go slices.

I lift my hands. "I'm hungry."

She shakes her head, but covers her obvious irritation with a genuine smile for Gina. The older woman comes around the counter and coos at Violet, who's wide awake and kicking her feet. She giggles at Gina's tickles. "Such a beauty. Like her mother."

Piper's smile quivers. My heart clenches, and I want to put my arm around her. But since I can't be sure she won't smack me if I touch her, I stuff my hands in my pockets instead.

The phone starts ringing again, prompting Jamie into action. Gina blows a kiss to Violet then excuses herself to help out in the kitchen. I gesture to the corner table. "Have a seat?"

The door opens and a few more patrons enter, leaving little room for the two of us and the stroller. She grimaces at the table, then heaves a sigh as if coming to a reluctant decision. "Your office is nearby, right? Can we take the pizza there? It's too chilly for Violet to sit outside, and it's too crowded in here."

"Absolutely." We only have to wait a few more minutes before Jamie calls that our pizza is ready. She hands me a bag with paper plates, napkins, and plasticware. I pay and leave a generous tip, which Jamie acknowledges with gratitude. Piper's shaking her head again when I open the door for her. "What?"

"You can't help yourself, can you?"

"What do you mean?"

She wrinkles her nose. "Making every female you meet fall in love with you."

There's no waiting for me as she pushes the stroller up the sidewalk toward my office. I laugh to myself.

Not every female.

SIX

Webb

At the office, I lead her into the kitchenette that will serve as a break room once we're open. I place the pizza on the table and drop the bag on top so I can help Piper out of her jacket. But she beats me to it, removing the old Army jacket and draping it across one of the chairs. She sits before I have another chance to be chivalrous and pull out the chair for her. I take the hint and back away to remove my own coat.

She glances at me. "I see you lost the tie. Sorry if Violet ruined it."

I laugh. "No you're not."

Her lips twitch. "You're right. I'm not. But I'm sure Violet is, or would be. She isn't petty."

I wash my hands while Piper makes Violet comfortable in the stroller, then we switch and I start plating slices of pizza while she washes up.

"Should I cut Violet's into small pieces or will she just gnaw on the crust?"

Piper whips toward me with a look that shouts, "What kind of idiot are you?"

"I'm kidding, Pip."

"I know," she says, a little on the defensive side.

I laugh again. "Liar." Her blush makes me laugh even harder.

"What is so funny?"

"I should be offended, but it's actually comical how little faith you have in me. I am a doctor, you know. Not just of teeth, either."

She scoots in her chair and picks up her slice, folding it over and blowing on it. I avert my gaze, because the way her lips purse into a perfect little O and her cheeks puff out are making inconvenient things happen in my pants. And that is not what tonight is about. Tonight is about groveling.

She takes a bite and chews, staring at Violet, who's contentedly babbling at the sea animals hanging from the mobile above her head. I take my own bite, surprised at how flavorful the combination of toppings is.

"I had my doubts," I say. "But this is actually really good."

"Right?" She says around another mouthful. "Gina promises she'll give me her sauce recipe someday, but I'm not sure I'd be able to do it justice even if I followed it to the letter."

"She lets you get pineapple on your pizza, which I understand not everyone gets to have. I heard her refuse to put barbecue sauce on for a customer, which is a pretty common topping nowadays."

She snorts. "Not around here. Gina and Tom would rather burn their place to the ground than sell out by making trendy pizzas."

"How come you rate so highly as to get whatever you want?"

"I've known them my whole life. When my dad was Mayor, he helped them with the permits and such to open the place. And I went to school with their oldest son, Geno. I think Gina hoped we'd end up marrying and making lots of babies."

"What happened?" I asked, holding back an irrational urge to find this Geno and extract his wisdom teeth without sedation.

"He married someone else more suited to him."

"The way Gina talks, you hang the moon for her. Who can be more suited for her son?"

"Mike Phillips," she deadpans.

My bite of pizza lodges in my throat when I laugh and I cough-choke it down. I stand and open the refrigerator. "I forgot to get drinks back at the pizzeria. But I have bottled water and a six-pack of Narragansett."

"Water."

I grab a can of beer and a bottle of water that I open and hand to her. "Thanks," she says, taking a small sip. She stares at my beer while I tap the top of the can then pop it open. A wistful smile plays at the corners of her mouth.

"I can get you one if you'd like," I say, tipping the can toward her.

She shakes her head. "No, sorry. I was just thinking of my dad. He used to do that—tap the top of the can before opening it."

I lean forward to capture her gaze. "Pip, I'm really sorry about your dad. I only met him that one time, when we all came here for Thanksgiving break, but he seemed like a great guy."

"He was," she says quietly, breaking eye contact. "You know what I miss most? He used to make these Hermit Cookies. They were like gingerbread but with raisins. It was his mother's recipe and he would make them whenever I was having a tough time, and sometimes just for the fun of it. Since he's been gone, I haven't had one."

"Why don't you make a batch?"

She shrugs. "He didn't have the recipe written down anywhere I could find. Anyway, it's just one of those things."

"I should've called when I heard. I'm sorry I didn't."

She dismisses my apology with a wave. "How is your family?"

"Same as ever." I grunt. "Dad's retired, Mom's taken over as the CEO, and both think I'm still as much a screw up as I ever was."

She stares at me thoughtfully while she chews. "You're a doctor. I'm going to assume you're not an alcoholic or a drug addict, or an ex-con. You're a productive and respectable member of society."

"So?" I tilt my head and peer at her, wondering what she's getting at.

"If all that still doesn't meet your parents' standards, it says more about them than about you." She raises and lowers her shoulders. "You're any normal parent's dream child. That's all I'm saying."

"My brother was their dream child," I say, lowering my gaze. In my thirty-eight years on this earth, they never failed to remind me of that. When he died from his leukemia over thirty-three years ago, so did all their hopes and dreams for a son worthy of carrying on the family name. "I was born to be his spare parts, but we know how that turned out. Marrying Carolynn was the only thing I ever did they were happy about, but now I've divorced her."

Instinctively I know I've stepped in it by mentioning Carolynn. Piper goes very still, then she sets her pizza down and wipes her mouth.

"Piper, I need to say something." I put down my own slice. Here goes nothing. "I'm sorry for hurting you. I should've handled things better."

"Webb—"

"No, please. Let me finish." I reach across the table and miraculously she lets me take her hand. "The night I was supposed to meet you at the Gardens, I was on my way. But I got a call from Carolynn. She'd gone out drinking with her friends and they abandoned her, so she called me for a ride. I would've said no; we'd broken up and I figured this was a ploy to get me alone. But she started crying and she sounded off. I was only going to drop her at her sorority house. I thought I'd only be a few minutes late to meet you."

"But you got into the accident." She tried to pull her hand out of my grasp, but I clung to it. "I know all that. Then you decided Carolynn was the one, not me. End of story."

A wave of pain crosses her features before she schools her face into a placid expression. But that glimpse of pain was all I needed to see to feel like total shit. She has to understand the truth. Carolynn wasn't the one, she was never the one.

"It's not as simple as that, Pip."

She jerks her hand away and this time I let her. There's a fire in her eyes when she glares at me and stands. "This was a mistake. I need to get Violet home. She's going to want to eat soon."

Fuck. Her porcupine quills are standing at attention again. "Wait. We need to talk about this."

She's closing the pizza box and gathering the small mess she made into a pile. "No, we don't. We managed not to talk for fifteen years, I think we can keep up the streak."

I huff out a breath, exasperated and pissed. Mostly at myself, though that's not how it comes out. "You don't understand."

She plants her hands on her hips. "I understand perfectly, Webb. I don't need you to spell it out for me. The text you sent was quite enough."

My chair scrapes against the linoleum as I stand. "That's not fair. I tried to talk to you in person, but you wouldn't take my calls."

"Fair?" She laughs but it's without any warmth. "Like it was fair of you to stand me up, to let me learn from some random chick the reason was because you were with your ex-girlfriend? Fair to let me come to the hospital looking for you, sick with worry because after an entire night and half a day, you still hadn't found the time to call and let me know you were okay, only to discover you holding your ex in your arms and kissing her all over?"

My gut clenches. "I didn't know you'd been there."

She blinks her shiny eyes quickly and sniffs. "Well, I was. I got to see for myself, so when you did send me a text telling me it was over, I already knew why."

I try again, my voice pleading. "Pip—"

"Stop calling me that!" She smacks the water bottle off the table. Red blotches mottle her cheeks. "You know what? I'm not having this conversation. I'd rather pretend none of it ever happened."

I can't help the flinch. It was the best time of my miserable life the past decade and a half and she wants to pretend it didn't happen. Can't say I blame her, but damn that stings.

Piper tucks a blanket around the baby and reaches for her jacket. This isn't how it's supposed to go. I swallow hard. "Wait. Pip—Piper—I'm sorry. I'm so damn sorry. I would rather cut off my own balls than hurt you. If I could do it all again—"

She slips the jacket around her and zips it. "It's too late. Look, we're not going to be friends again. But I recognize you're going to live here, and we'll inevitably see each other. So I promise to be civil. But I don't want to be friends again. I don't want to talk about whatever in the past. I've moved on."

"Would you please just listen—"

"No, I'm leaving." She grabs the pizza box and puts it on top of the stroller. "And I'm taking this."

She pushes toward the door. I want to chase after her, but my feet are stuck to the floor. I'm helpless when she turns her back on me and walks out of the building, taking the rest of my dinner with her along with any chance of making things right.

SEVEN

Piper

Drew is already at the shop when I arrive the next day. He's at the desk in the cramped office poring over a sheath of papers spread over the top. He wears a bright purple and electric teal sweatshirt with our Sugarbreakers logo on it. I wasn't sure about the sweatshirts and T-shirts Drew suggested we sell. "People pay us to advertise our business," Drew had said when he pitched the idea. God love him, he'd been right. Then again, he usually is. Not something I would ever tell him, though. My business partner's ego is already perfectly healthy, thank you very much.

"Hey." I drop into a chair across from him.

He barely spares me a glance. "First stage of horse manure."

I roll my eyes but smile at the old joke despite myself. "I see spreadsheets and a lot of red ink. Is that why your forehead has all those lines?"

He gives me a thoroughly unamused glare. "My forehead is not lined."

"Okay," I concede. "Striped then."

I laugh when he wads up a piece of paper and chucks it at

me. "Seriously, tell me how it's going. We'll make it through the year, right?"

He sighs and scrubs a hand down his face. "Barely, providing we maintain the same level of sales as last summer. We really need to nail that presentation to Hudson next week."

It'd taken weeks to finally score a meeting with the chief buyer at Hudson Consolidated Foods, which is the largest distributer of gourmet foods in New England and western New York. But finally, Drew and I had the chance to take Sugarbreakers' signature taffy and caramels to the next level and sell them throughout the region. The influx of revenue would mean turning all that red ink to black on Drew's precious spreadsheets.

"We will."

Drew looks up again and wrinkles his brow. "Why are you so chipper? You're never in this good a mood."

"Thanks a lot," I grumble. "You make it sound like I'm a curmudgeon."

He stares at me pointedly and I scoff. "Okay, maybe I'm feeling a little happier than usual."

Drew sits back and taps his lips with his pen. His blue eyes light with amusement. "Did someone get lucky last night?"

"What? No." Though my face flushes, because as much as I hate the man, I couldn't help but appreciate how well Webb has aged.

As if reading my mind, Drew says, "Heard you were at dinner with Webb Duncan. The same Webb Duncan who broke up with you via text, then married his ex a few months later."

I narrow my eyes. "Of course you heard. Half the Isle probably heard and are already planning a walk down the aisle. We shared a pizza, sort of, under the guise of burying the hatchet. But I was reminded pretty quickly why the only place I want to bury a hatchet is in his smug face."

Drew's shoulders relaxed. "If he keeps bothering you, tell me."

My heart swells. After the whole thing with Webb, I took myself off the market for a while. But when I was ready to move on again, I couldn't seem to keep a relationship going for more than a couple of months. Drew was the one who finally got through my defenses. We lasted a whole year during which I told him everything. Outside of Tessa and Laura, he's the only one who knows the truth. While it didn't work out romantically, we have a lifelong friendship and that is worth far more.

"I think I can handle myself, but I appreciate the offer." I sit forward on my chair and grin. "No, I'm in a good mood because I'm getting closer to becoming a mother."

Drew drops the pen and sits up fast. "Laura's folks signed the papers?"

"Not yet. But when I took Violet home this morning, Lulu told me that she and Denny were meeting with their lawyer this week about drawing up the adoption papers. By summer, I might be a mom."

My voice cracks and tears drip down my cheeks. Happy tears, mostly, although there's some regret mixed in there. I've accepted there always will be. Drew comes around the desk and lifts me out of the chair to grip me in a strong hug. "Oh, Piper—I'm so happy for you. You're going to be a great mom," he whispers in my ear, and his words go a long way toward banishing the bittersweetness in my heart.

"You think so?"

He draws back and holds me shoulders. "I know so."

"Well, then," I say, gesturing to the desk. "Now we really need to make sure we nail this. I'm going to have an extra mouth to feed."

I'VE BARELY BEEN ABLE TO EAT OR SLEEP THESE PAST FEW DAYS, but for once my anticipation comes from a place of excitement rather than anxiety. Tomorrow, I'm going over to Lulu and Denny's to look over the paperwork and discuss the next steps. I talk to Laura every night, just as I did before the accident and just as I have every day since. Maybe I'm projecting, but I feel her with me. I feel her approval. I promise her I will always take care of Violet. Her daughter will grow up knowing how much Laura loved and wanted her.

I'm in such a good mood I've barely thought about Webb this week, consciously at least. It appears my subconscious has its own agenda. He's been present in my dreams; sometimes he's the villain, sometimes the hero. Sometimes, like this morning, I wake up hours before my alarm, restless and sweaty, unable to go back to sleep until I've satisfied myself. Try as hard as I do to imagine Chris Pine or Chris Evans or Chris Hemsworth—hell even Chris Meloni though I'm not normally into the zaddy thing—it's Webb I finish to. My traitorous body can't seem to get the message that Webb Duncan is dead to us. D-E-A-D.

Which is why I fluster when he says my name at Beachcomber's. I'm a few minutes late opening the shop but if I don't have my coffee, customers are liable to get my cranky side. Plus I could smell Bette's fresh-baked croissants from the parking lot. My caffeine addiction and the promise of flaky, buttery goodness are the only things holding me in my place when Webb approaches me.

"Good morning, Piper." His voice is tentative, his eyes wary, but he still has the sexy, smoldering thing going on. I turn my attention to the giant chalk menu hanging over the counter, studying it as if it holds the secrets of the universe. *Well, it kind of does—have you had Bette's croissants?*

He tries again while I will the people in line in front of me to hurry up and order their damn coffee already. "I was about to walk over to your shop."

I inch forward. One down, one to go, and then I can place my order and get the hell away from Webb and his stupid scent, and his stupid scruff with the touch of gray. "Why? I sell candy. Isn't that like selling crack on the street corner?"

He chuckles under his breath. "I probably deserve that."

I look at him with my brow raised, and he has the grace to at least look like he feels bad. "I have a lot to apologize for, things I didn't even get to the other night before I screwed it all up. Will you please give me another chance to make things right?"

"If you want to be forgiven, then fine. I forgive you." My shoulders are practically up to my ears and I make an effort to relax them. "Now will you go away?"

"What if I want more than forgiveness?" he asks, his voice smooth and dark as the coffee I'm about to order, and it makes just as jittery. "Not that I believe for a minute you do forgive me."

The lady in front of me pays and steps to the side. Relieved, I smile at Bette's son, who's working the register. "Hey, Jonathan."

"Morning, Ms. Poincelot," Jonathan says. He pronounces my name correctly, though I'm always correcting him to just call me by my first name.

"It's Piper, Jonathan. I think we've known each other long enough. I used to change your diapers," I tease.

He shakes his head. "My mom is already mad at me for not being *professional* enough when I'm at work. Who cares if I wear a shirt while I'm cleaning the place after hours? I'm wearing one now, when it counts."

He tugs on the light green polo emblazoned with Beachcomber's logo. I hold back a laugh and click my tongue sympathetically. "Moms can be so tough. I'll have the usual, please, with an extra shot. Oh, and only six Splenda. I'm cutting back."

He moves to the counter behind him to begin making my coffee.

Webb chokes. "Six and you're cutting back?"

"I like it sweet," I bite out. "It used to be eight packets of regular sugar, not that it's any of your business."

"When the practice opens, you can have a complimentary cleaning." I slide him a look that makes him raise his hands, though one corner of his lip curls upward. "You can see my partner, Pam. I won't go anywhere near your mouth."

His eyes drift to my lips and when he looks up, they're darker, smokier. I turn my head and watch Jonathan cap my coffee, then pull a croissant out of the case and drop it in a bag. I place a ten on the counter, more than enough but Jonathan can use the tip, and I need to get the hell out of here. He slides the bag and drink to me, and I step to the side while I grab my cup. But before I can take the bag, Webb has it.

"Excuse me." I reach for it, but Webb holds it behind his back. His eyes are twinkling, but not so much in humor as in determination. I take a steadying breath and look around, hoping no one I know is witnessing this. No such luck. There's a reason Beachcomber's Cafe is the news hub for the whole Isle. I avoid the curious looks of the regulars sitting at the side counter behind Webb and lower my voice. "Give it to me, Webb."

My cheeks instantly heat and his lopsided grin grows wider. But he correctly reads my face and doesn't make a smart remark. Instead, he dips his chin and looks up at me through thick, golden eyelashes. Fuck, that's how he hooked me the first time I met him. His guileless hangdog look was enough to melt my panties then, and I hate that, despite our history, it still does. "Come on, Pip. Five minutes. Just give me five minutes to apologize for being a world-class ass. Then and now."

A part of me, a huge part of me, wants to forgive and forget. In fact, if it were only about his dumping me and going back to his ex, I might've. He doesn't know the real pain he caused when he dropped out of my life, and it's that pain holding me back. I can hear Laura in my head—*the reason you can't let it go is because you haven't let him go. Hear him out once and for all then MOVE ON.*

Laura was always the smarter one of us two. And the kindest.

I give a hard shake of my head. "Just give me my breakfast, Webb, and then leave me alone. It's a small Isle, but not so small we can't avoid each other if we try."

This time when I grab for the bag he doesn't resist. His gaze no longer simmers with amusement or attraction, or whatever the hell I thought I saw in them before. There's a glimpse of hurt and for a second I feel bad.

I retreat to my shop, once again half-hoping he doesn't follow me, half-hoping he does. I always was a bit of a masochist.

EIGHT

Webb

Ambushing Piper before she's had her morning coffee was a terrible idea. But when she walked into Beachcomber's yesterday, my body moved toward her of its own accord. After being hundreds of miles away from her all this time, you'd think her pull on me would've faded. Apparently, you'd be wrong. It's as though I'm in the desert, and she's an oasis beckoning me. But she's not giving me anything to quench my thirst for her. She's not even giving me the time of day. *How can I show her I'm not the asshole I was if she won't give me a chance?*

I'm still ruminating over my exchange with Piper this morning when Graeme calls. I pick up my cell, relieved for the distraction. But it doesn't last long.

"There's a slight hitch," he says by way of greeting.

I take my computer glasses off and rub my eyes. "What constitutes a slight hitch?"

"The marketing plan for Seaside is behind schedule."

"Fucking Carolynn." My ex-wife was in charge of the marketing department at DDS. Part of her job is to design and implement marketing plans for the individual practices based on their location and demographics. Apparently the other part of her job is screwing me over.

"Eileen said she'd handle it."

"Right," I scoff. "Probably by taking Carolynn out to celebrate. She doesn't want this place to succeed. If it weren't for you going to bat for us, she never would have agreed to this location."

"I knew you needed to get away and frankly, it's not a bad investment. We don't have many locations in southern New England," Graeme says. "How are things going down there otherwise?"

"We got about half the equipment we ordered in, with the rest scheduled for the next couple of weeks. The contractor has almost all the exam rooms framed out. Drywall guy should be here next week and then we can get the flooring in. It'll be tight, but we'll make the June 1st opening date." If it kills me we'll make it. "If the marketing materials aren't ready by then, I'll find a local printer to make our signs and stationery. Hell, I'll use a sharpie and poster board if I have to."

"Good to know," he says. "But I meant personally—how are things going personally? Did you meet up with the woman you used to date?"

"Piper?" I give a bitter laugh. "Yeah, I met up with her."

"How'd that go?"

"About as well as a double root canal. She hates my guts."

"You mean that famous Duncan charm isn't winning her over?" He's mocking me. Graeme knows what I did to her back in college. He thought my moving here was a bad idea strictly because it would mean living in close proximity to Piper, and if things ended up not working out, it'd be awkward at best. I fear he may have been right, although I'd never tell him that.

"It's going to take more than charm, believe me." I fill him in on our dinner the other night. "I don't know how to get her to listen to me."

"Maybe ease into it," he suggests. "Don't push too hard. Let her get used to the idea of you being around now."

"You're probably right." I exhale a frustrated breath.

"I usually am."

I laugh. "I doubt your wife would agree."

"Tish knows the truth—I'm always right, but she's never wrong."

We say our goodbyes and I toss my phone on the desktop. It's not surprising Carolynn is pulling shit like this, but I'm enraged nonetheless. This isn't just my livelihood—there are two other people counting on this location's success, not to mention the hygienists and admin waiting to start their new jobs. If Carolynn hasn't gotten the marketing off the ground, we may be opening to zero patients. So much should have already been done to promote our presence.

Then I remember what Hayes said the other day about SPASBO and an idea starts percolating. I go in search of my partners to let them know what's going on. They're in the break-room laughing and passing a small plastic bucket back and forth.

"Whatcha got there?"

"You wouldn't like it, Boss," Trev says, waving me off.

Pam's eyes glitter. "It's sugar. Pure sugar."

She holds up the container. Strawberry Cotton Candy from Sugarbreakers. I frown, pretending to be offended. "I like candy as much as the next person."

Pam and Trev exchange a look, then burst out laughing. Now I am offended. Pam shakes her head. "Sorry, Webb. But aside from the occasional chocolate protein bar you eat, I don't think I've ever seen you with a piece of candy. A cupcake, cook-ies, ice cream, flan—yes. Cotton candy? Caramels? Uh, no."

"I don't have a big sweet tooth," I say, a little defensive now. "Besides, I know you've seen what processed sugar can do to a person's health, starting with rotting their teeth."

"In excess, yes," Pam argues, rolling her eyes. "But if you brush soon after, or at least rinse your mouth, you can enjoy candy like a normal person without it causing the downfall of society."

She holds the bucket out to me, her brows dancing in a dare. I pluck off a piece of the fluffy confection and pop it in my mouth, where it melts on my tongue. Strawberry flavor bursts in my mouth, and I'm surprised by how much I like it. All right. Maybe they have a point.

Trev points at me, his lips curved in a cocksure grin. "See? You like it. Admit it."

"I admit nothing." I nod at the container. "So you went to Sugarbreakers. Did you see the owner there?"

Pam gives the bucket to Trev and wipes her hands on her pants. "There was a teenager working the register when I stopped in. I'll have to take Jeremy one of these days. My brother will flip over the variety of fudge they have."

"Isn't the owner a friend of yours?" Trev asks, stuffing another piece of cotton candy in his mouth.

I wince. "Once upon a time. She's not my biggest fan at the moment."

"Oh God, what did you do?" Pam shakes her head. "Please don't tell me you went all anti-sugar crusader on her."

She barks out a laugh at the look on my face. "Seriously?"

"It's not like I was picketing her shop," I say, though my defense sounds weak even to me. I give them a condensed version of our first meeting. "I stuck my foot in my mouth."

Trev is trying hard to keep it together while Pam gives me a look of sincere pity. My face heats. " "It's not that bad."

"You likened her to a drug dealer," Pam says flatly.

"Accidentally," I mumble.

Trev wipes at his eyes. "Oh, man. Thanks, I needed that laugh today."

I pull out a chair and sit. "Maybe I should've saved that story for after this. I need to let you guys know about a little hiccup."

"Don't tell me the contractor won't finish on time," Trev says, worry replacing his easy humor.

"Nothing like that. It's about the marketing. I guess Carolynn hasn't submitted a plan for our opening yet."

"What does that mean?"

"We might not get all the advertising we need in place before the grand opening. But Graeme is on it. In the meantime, we should probably have a back-up plan. What's the point of having a Grand Opening if no one knows about it."

"Yeah, but DDS was supposed to do all the heavy marketing. We can't afford to send out our own direct mailers or do media ads. That was in our contract." Trev folds his arms across his chest. "This is Carolynn trying to screw you over and us getting caught in the crossfire."

He's not wrong, and I'm embarrassed to put my partners in this situation. I roll back my shoulders. "It'll be all right. But I think we should see if we can get help from the other businesses around here. Hayes told me about this business group, kind of like a Chamber of Commerce. The Shoals Professional Association of Small Business Owners. We can join the group and see if we can do some cross-promotional advertising or something."

Pam considers this. "That's actually smart. This is a small community and word of mouth will probably be our best marketing."

"All right. So what do we need to do?" Trev asks.

"That's where it gets tricky. We need to talk to the head of the group." I rub at an imaginary spot on the table with my thumb.

"And that's tricky why?" Trev asks, his voice wary.

"It's, uh, Piper."

"The one you insulted. Figures." Pam snorts. "Why are you men so stupid?"

"Hey," Trev protests.

She points a finger at him. "Two words: Honey Potter."

At the mention of the stripper who conned him into giving her thousands of dollars in cosmetic dental work back during his horn-dog bachelor days, he slumps back in his chair grumbling. "Even my wife doesn't throw that in my face."

"That's because Lali's a better person," Pam says. She points at me. "And you—what you're going to do is march your cute little behind up to that candy shop and beg forgiveness for being such an idiot."

Inwardly, I laugh because that's exactly what I've been trying to do. But all I say to Pam, who doesn't know my history with Piper, is, "Yes, ma'am. I'll make nice with the candy lady."

Too bad I have no fucking clue how exactly.

NINE

Piper

I don't recognize the two other vehicles parked in front of Lulu and Denny's when Violet and I arrive. I think nothing of it as I unlatch the car seat and heft her to the door. Since starting solids, Violet has been putting on weight. "It may be time to move you into the convertible seat, jellybean."

The door swings open before I knock, and Lulu holds out her arms. "There you are. Just in time."

She gives me a quick squeeze and ushers me into the sitting room. "Everyone, this is Piper Poincelot. She and Laura grew up together."

An older man around Lulu's age stands and offers his hand. He's stout and bulky, his meaty hand flaccid in mine. "I'm Martin Rickford, the pastor at Lighthouse Christian Mission."

"Pastor Marty is a dear friend to us," Lulu explains. She gives him an affectionate smile. "I don't know what we would've done without him and the rest of our church family."

"Nice to meet you." I hold back the urge to wipe my palm on my jeans and look at the other man and woman in the room.

The woman, slim and poised, rises and leans in to air-kiss my cheeks.

"Piper, it's been so long," she exclaims, her apple-red lips spread in a smile phonier than my knockoff Coach bag. When my brow furrows, she puts a hand to her super sleek, platinum bob and laughs. "My hair was darker then. It lightened as I grew up."

With the help of her hairdresser, maybe. When I still don't recognize her, she clicks her tongue and playfully smacks my arm. "I'm Hollis, Laura's cousin. From Hartford."

Surprise jacks my brows upward. Hollis Smith, Lulu's sister's daughter, was a summertime fixture at Laura's house when we were kids. Or summertime pain-in-the-ass if you want to get specific. Her father was some big deal at an insurance company, and she was a spoiled brat who made our lives miserable for two weeks every year until we were twelve. I haven't seen her in twenty-five years and other than an occasional wedding or funeral, I don't think Laura had either. I'm almost positive she wasn't at the wake. So why was she here now?

I meet her smile with an artificial one of my own. "Hollis, wow. It's been so long. You look great."

"Thank you," she says. She turns to the man still sitting on the couch. "This is my husband, Aaron Whitley."

He has dark blond hair and wears gray tailored dress pants with a tucked black polo and expensive leather loafers. His bored blue eyes slither over me. I'm grateful he simply nods and doesn't extend his hand. The creep factor with this guy is high.

It doesn't go unnoticed by me that Hollis didn't return the nicety, but I'm not offended. That's her to a T. I set the car seat on an ottoman and offer a small wave. "Nice to meet you."

He nods before turning his attention to his phone. I unstrap Violet from the seat and I'm about to sit down in one of the armchairs with her when Hollis reaches out.

"May I?" Reluctantly, I transfer Violet to her. She looks unnatural holding the baby while wearing what is obviously a Chanel pantsuit. A cream-colored one. I offer a spit up rag to her, though it'd be kind of funny to see Violet spit up on her fancy outfit. Told you I was petty.

"I miss the baby years," she says, sniffing Violet's head. "I have two boys, but they're much older. Ten and twelve."

"How nice." I clasp my hands in my lap and look at Lulu expectantly. Denny isn't in the room with us, but I can hear him out in the garage. "So. I didn't realize it was a brunch party."

Lulu's smile is strained. "I thought this would be a good time to discuss Violet's future. Hollis wanted to visit, and Pastor Marty had an opening in his schedule. You were already coming back with Violet. It all worked out."

I look between Lulu and the others in puzzlement. "I'm not sure I understand what the Pastor and Hollis have to do with me adopting Violet."

Lulu doesn't meet my eyes, while the Pastor stares at me over a cup of tea. Hollis releases a strangled noise, part sympathetic and part mocking. She's watching me with pity on her face, her husband still so focused on his phone I'm not sure he knows what's going on.

"Piper, I know you and Lulu had talked about Violet coming to live with you, but that was before," Hollis says in an even voice.

Anxiety skitters along my skin. I try to catch Lulu's gaze, but she's still avoiding me. *Because she knows she's betraying me? Betraying Laura? Betraying Violet?* "Before what? Lulu, what's going on? I thought you'd already had the papers drawn up?"

"We were about to, but I talked to Pastor Marty, to make sure we were doing the right thing, and he suggested we make sure there wasn't any blood kin who might be willing to take Violet. When I mentioned it to my sister, Meryl, she suggested Hollis."

"Aaron and I wanted to have another child, but it wasn't to be," Hollis interrupts to explain. "Violet is a sign from God."

Pastor Marty's face lights up at this pronouncement, but I

am sure deep down to my bones that the only God Hollis worships can be found in her husband's paycheck. My throat goes dry. My heart is about to leap out of my chest and fall battered, bruised, and bleeding on the beige Turkish carpet. This can't be happening.

It takes a couple of tries to get words to come out. "This is, um—it's a shock, really. No offense, Hollis, but you and Laura were never close. Did you even know she had a daughter?"

Hollis stiffens, all traces of faux friendliness evaporating. "Of course."

I turn to Lulu, not caring how desperate I sound. "Lulu, Hollis may share DNA, but you know me. You practically helped raise me after my mother left. Laura was my sister, and I promised her I would always take care of Violet. I've kept that promise."

"I know, Piper, but—" She trails off, the distress on her face evident. She looks to the Pastor, who sets his teacup down and clears his throat.

"Lulu has told me a great deal about you, Piper, and it sounds like you are a fine woman. But let's look at what's in the baby's best interest. If you were to raise her, it would be in a single parent home. You own your business, but as I understand it's seasonal and not without risk. Not to mention the time you have to put into it. How could you expect to give your undivided attention to Violet? How will you be able to support her? Children cost a lot of money to raise."

I open my mouth to protest, but he puts a hand up. "Hollis and Aaron have a family they provide well for. Don't you think Violet deserves to be raised in a loving, God-fearing family environment, with a mother who can stay at home with her?"

I fist my hands in my lap and fight to keep my voice steady. "With all due respect, Pastor, I believe Violet should be raised by people who love her and who will make sure she grows up knowing all about her mother and how much she loved her. I don't believe the size of a person's bank account, or what they do for a living, or whether they are married is an accurate measure of how well they can raise a child."

"Piper, no one is saying you wouldn't be a good guardian for Violet," Lulu says. "But perhaps you aren't the best choice. Violet needs a mother and a father."

"Laura was raising her on her own," I point out.

Aaron has pocketed the phone and is watching the proceedings with the same dispassion as someone waiting for a traffic light to turn green. Hollis doesn't let his lack of enthusiasm stop her from pleading their case. "The fact is, we are experienced, involved, dedicated parents. Violet would go to the best schools, have all she ever needed and wanted. She'll have two doting older brothers to look after her. I mean, it really isn't a contest here."

"No, it's not a contest," I snap. "It's a child's life."

Violet's face turns purple and a moment later, the smell of death reaches us. Aaron's face turns to disgust, and he backs further into the corner of the sofa, while Hollis simply looks horrified, and Lulu embarrassed. Pastor Marty remains unflappable.

I jump up and Hollis hands Violet to me without argument. She's going to need a complete outfit change. For that matter, so does Hollis. I hide my smirk at the brown stain on her pants.

I use this as an excuse to escape the room, only briefly considering running out of the house and taking Violet far away. Instead, I grab the diaper bag and head to the nursery. "Good job, jellybean," I whisper against her head.

In the nursery, I focus on tending to Violet to stave off the tears threatening to fall. Once they do, I don't know if they'll stop. My heart is breaking, even more so than it did the night three months ago when Sheriff Alvarez knocked on my door to tell me there'd been an accident. But I need to hold it together. I won't back down, I won't stop fighting for her, and I won't show them any weakness. Laura and Violet are depending on me.

I give the baby a quick washdown in the bathroom sink, then dry her off and take her back into the nursery to dress her. Lulu stands there, playing with a figurine of a cardinal she keeps on top of the dresser. She holds it up with a wistful smile. "Do you know the legend of the cardinal? It says that when you see a cardinal, it's the soul of a loved one coming by to say hello. It makes me feel better to know Laura is watching over her daughter."

I shake my head at her. "Then you must know this isn't what Laura would want. Hollis is practically—no, not practically—Hollis is a stranger."

Lulu sighs. "Laura didn't always make the best choices. Becoming a single mother, for one. So I'm not inclined to consider what she would want. I am only thinking about what is best for Violet."

I slide a new onesie and a sleeper patterned with tiny koalas on Violet in record time. "I can take care of Violet. I am more than capable of giving her everything she needs."

"You can't give her a father. Hollis can."

I whirl on Lulu and pull up short when I see the pain on her face. She's staring at Violet with hurt in her eyes, and I know in my heart she truly does have what she thinks is Violet's best interest in mind. I can't argue with a grandmother wanting her granddaughter to have two parents, not after she's already lost a mother. But while I may not be married and my family is down to one selfish mother who lives across the country, I have a village of friends who will be there for Violet the way they were for me. People who already treat her like their own.

I hold Violet close and breathe her in. "You promised me," I say weakly.

Lulu drops her gaze. "Hollis and Aaron rented a house nearby for the week. They're going to take Violet for overnights, become acclimated with her before they take her home to meet the boys."

"This is so fast, Lulu." Sheer panic is the only thing to explain what happens next. I open my mouth and blurt out, "You should know, I've been seeing someone seriously for a little while now."

Surprise flashes across Lulu's face. "You are? You never mentioned you had a beau."

"I would've told you sooner, but I didn't think it mattered." The fibs are sliding off my tongue like chocolate meltaways.

"We've talked about having a future together, I mean"--I try to laugh past the frog in my throat--"I'm pushing forty here. It's about time."

"Give me a chance to talk to him. I'll let my guy know our timetable needs to move up some, that's all. If that will make a difference."

Her brow wrinkles. "I don't know. This is something I'll need to talk to Pastor Marty about, but is there really a possibility you could give Violet a home with two parents?"

She looks so hopeful over the news, which in turn emboldens me. I swallow. "Absolutely."

"What's his name?"

I rack my brain for a name, any name, and go with the first one to come to mind. "It's, uh, Bill."

"Bill knows you were going to adopt Violet, and he wanted to be a part of that?" she asks.

"Yes, definitely. Like I said, we've been talking about it."

"Then why didn't you ever say anything to us?" Lulu sounds more than a little hurt and guilt grabs hold of my chest in a vise-like grip.

"We wanted to be sure." Oh my God, what am I saying? I just made up a pretend almost-fiancé. There's no way this can't backfire on me, but I'm desperate. I can't lose Violet, but I need time come up with some sort of solution. And maybe a fiancé.

There's a dating app for every lifestyle out there. Maybe there's one for fake relationships.

"Lulu, I'm just asking you not to rush this. Give me a chance to show you that your first instincts were right. I know Violet belongs with me. Let me prove it."

Lulu murmurs. "It has been a while since I've seen my niece. Maybe Denny and I should get to know her a little better, too."

I breathe out a sigh of relief. I bought myself time. Too bad I don't have a freaking clue how I'm going to get myself out of this.

I look up at the ceiling in silent prayer. *Laura, I'm going to need your help.*

TEN

Piper

Before I leave, we agree Violet will spend the week with Hollis and her husband, but more consideration will be given to who should get the baby. My careless lie worked to buy me time. I let myself cry once I got on the ferry. Saying goodbye to Violet was the hardest thing I've done in a long time. I drive off the ferry and park on the dock. I'm in no hurry to go back to my empty house. I'll only sit and worry and overthink. I'd rather do that over a glass of Whiskey Sour. My hands are buried in my pockets and my head is down as I head toward The Seahorse, a dive bar only a local could love. I don't see Webb until I bump into him.

"Excuse me," I mutter, glancing up. He towers over me, a look of contrition on his face, and it's apparent he stood in my path on purpose. I sigh. "Excuse me," I repeat, more pointedly, stepping to the side.

He matches my step, forcing me to stop. "Not in the mood, Webb."

"Are you heading to the bar?" He jerks a thumb over his shoulder.

I sigh. "Yes. If you'll get out of my way. There's a Whiskey Sour with my name on it."

His eyes shift between mine, a glimmer of worry in his gaze. "Are you okay?"

I tug the end of my braid. "I'm fine."

He steps closer. "Sorry. It's just… you don't look okay."

My throat stings. I try to swallow against it, but it won't stop hurting. Webb is not the person I need to confide in, though. He's already proven he can't be trusted with my heart. I'm not about to open myself and show him all the cracks in it now.

"How about you let me buy you that Whiskey Sour?" he offers. "You don't have to talk to me and I won't force you to listen to an apology. You just look like you shouldn't be alone right now."

I look off to the side and feel my defenses crumbling. I push past him, but against my better judgment find myself beckoning him to follow. "I'm going to hold you to it."

AN HOUR LATER, I'M FINISHING MY SECOND SOUR AND reminiscing with Webb about the better times back in school. "Whatever happened to that other guy you and Hayes roomed with? The one who took two girls to a frat party and convinced both of them the other was his cousin?"

Webb smiles into his beer. "Paul. Last I heard, he was married and with four kids. All girls."

I snicker. "Serves him right. Now he has to worry about assholes like himself sniffing around his daughters."

He laughs. "Yeah. Pretty sure that's why he's already bald."

I laugh and finish the last of my drink. We're sitting at the bar, so I catch Tony the bartender's attention and hold the empty glass up.

"You sure you want another?" Webb asks. He holds his hands

up and chuckles when I give him a look. "Hey, I just don't want you to add me not stopping you from getting wasted to my list of transgressions. I think the list is long enough."

"You have no idea," I mutter, turning away from him.

If he heard me, he doesn't acknowledge it. "So you never married? Never got close?"

"Nope." I pull the end of my braid over my shoulder and watch Tony mix my drink.

"Ever think you will?"

"Nope. I've seen what happens when you marry the wrong person. Not looking for that kind of life-destroying commitment."

Out of the corner of my eye, I see his flinch. Tony hands me my drink and I eagerly take a sip. My buzz is swiftly heading into drunken territory, but it's just what I need. So is talking to Webb, strangely enough. The revelation leaves me unsettled.

"Why did you decide move here?" I ask.

"I needed a fresh start."

"Away from Carolynn?"

He tips the bottle to his lips and takes a drink before answering. "Her, yeah. My parents, too. My life, if that's what you could call it."

"Is this a permanent move for you, or do you think you'll go back?" My voice is even as I ask the question, but I think he picks up on what I'm really asking. He and Carolynn were always on-again/off-again. Even when he swore it was over for good, I shouldn't have trusted him. I was only a little surprised when he dumped me to go back to her.

He spins on his stool to face me. "I'm never going back."

I choke out a laugh that's more bitter than I intended. "Heard that before."

"Piper."

He says it so pleadingly and in that gravelly tone that gets to me. I turn on my stool, my knees brushing against his. It's innocent contact and through the denim of my jeans, it's not like I can feel much. Still, warmth spreads through my body and it's not only from the whiskey.

His look is intensely serious, like he's staring into my soul. "Never."

I nod once, then turn away, still feeling the lingering burn of his gaze, of the touch of his body to mine.

"I think it's great you're adopting Violet," he says, leaning an elbow against the bar and resting his head on his fist. Normally I'd appreciate the change of subject, but it brings back to mind my current predicament, which was floating blissfully outside the reach of my brain thanks to the alcohol.

"Yeah, well. Not everyone thinks so."

"Want to talk about it?"

I bite my lip. My resolve to keep it to myself weakens. "Adopting Violet may not be the certainty I thought it was. Laura's cousin wants custody, too."

"Fuck."

"My sentiments exactly." I take a long pull on my straw. "But she's married, with kids already, and now Lulu has to think about who would be best for Violet."

"Shit." He runs his fingers through his hair and my hand twitches with the need to do the same. *Is his hair as soft as it used to be?* Looks like it. Golden and perfect and soft...

"Is there anything I can do?" His question snaps my eyes off his hair. "Write a character reference or something?"

"Know anyone named Bill?"

"Uh." His forehead creases. "A few, why?"

I wave my hand in dismissal. "Never mind."

"Well, if there's anything I can do to help, let me know."

I give him a sidelong glance, assessing his sincerity. "Thanks."

"I was wondering," he asks, one side of his lips quirked up. "Since you don't seem to hate me anymore--"

"As much," I correct him. "I still hate you, just not as much. Considering you're buying my drinks, seems only fair."

"Since you don't seem to hate me *as much*, could I ask a favor?"

I squint at him. "What sort of favor?"

"We're launching our practice in just under two months, and our marketing plans have gotten delayed. Do you think you and the other SASBO members might help us promote ourselves? We'd even love to join the group, if you have room for new members."

"What were your marketing plans supposed to be?"

"Direct mail adverts, television and radio ads, a billboard." He uses his fingers to tick off the items. "Website, fliers, business cards."

"Why are those all delayed?"

He hesitates. "Carolynn was in charge of all that. I guess she's feeling spiteful."

"Why would you trust your ex-wife to get those things done for you?" I scoff. "That seems like asking for trouble."

"It was part of the contract." He raises his empty bottle. Tony switches it out for a fresh one. "Seaside Dental is kind of like a franchise. My family's company, DDS, oversees a bunch of smaller locations up and down the East Coast. For a relatively small buy-in, they help set up the office and run the back end— marketing, legal, financial, insurance, all that. The provider only has to worry about managing their local staff and taking care of patients."

"Sounds like a good deal, but I still don't see what Carolynn has to do with this."

"She's the Marketing VP."

I stir my drink with the straw. "Ah. I see. Well, I can ask at our next meeting, which happens to be tomorrow." I was going to beg off, but now I guess I need to go. "Membership takes a while to be approved. You have to show solvency and longevity."

"How long does that take?"

I shrug. "There's no real timetable, though a year is usually the minimum you'd have to be in business. But I can talk to them about helping you guys with advertising."

He lets out a breath. "My partners and I would appreciate it. You know, they stopped by Sugarbreakers the other day. Couldn't say enough good things about it."

"Really? They don't think I'm corrupting the children of the world with my Devil treats?"

He lets out a loud gust of laughter. "I deserve that. No, they aren't as sanctimonious about nutrition as I am."

"At least you recognize you have a problem."

"I used to care for children in a rural clinic. Kids whose diet included a steady stream of high-fructose corn syrup. The problems they ended up with—well, it turned me off to sweets. Sometimes I get carried away when the subject comes up, and I let my passions take over."

I lift an eyebrow. "Is this an apology?"

"Hell, no." He smirks. "You told me I couldn't apologize."

I roll my eyes. "About abandoning me. You can apologize for insulting me."

His Adam's apple bobs and his face pinches. "Then, I'm sorry."

Our gazes lock and I know he's apologizing for more than his big mouth, but I pretend I don't. "I will accept your apology... for insulting me," I add, just to be clear.

His lips tighten, but then he dips his head at me in thanks. Something's shifted between us tonight, a truce of sorts I guess. But I'm not ready to forgive him just yet. Because if I accept his apology, the right thing would be to follow up with my own. Which would mean telling him something I had thought I'd never have to confess, and I'm not ready to open that can of worms. Not yet. Maybe not ever.

WE ENDED UP STAYING AT THE SEAHORSE SEVERAL MORE HOURS, until we were both sober enough to drive to our respective homes. We shot some pool, talked about a lot of superficial shit, and blatantly ignored the sparks and shouts of unfinished business between us. A few times, I caught him staring at my lips. And there might have been a moment or two when I found myself appreciating the way his ass looked, especially when he was bent over the pool table to line up a shot.

But in the end, it was just a welcome distraction from my worries over Violet. Once I was home, all those anxieties came roaring back. It was after ten here, but only eight where Tessa was on her business trip. Her job as an investigator for an insurance firm takes her around the country a few weeks every month and this is one of them. I wish she were here in person, but I'll have to settle for a video call.

"Hey, Pippi. To what do I owe the pleasure?" She peers at me through the screen, her gaze sharp with alarm. "Oh no. What's wrong?"

I sigh, my voice filling with tears. "It's Violet."

Tessa frowns. "Is she okay? What happened?"

"I may not get to adopt her."

I spend the next few minutes filling her in on what happened earlier. "As if DNA is all that matters. I was closer to Laura and her parents than Hollis ever was. She didn't even come down for Laura's funeral for God's sake."

"That is so unfair," Tessa agrees. "And who is this pastor to give any opinion? He didn't know Laura or what she'd want, and he doesn't know you. What are you going to do? Are you going to call a lawyer?"

I shake my head. "I couldn't do that to Lulu and Denny. Besides, I don't have any claim."

"Do you want me to investigate this Hollis and her husband, maybe find something you can take to the Rosellis to convince them not to go through with this?"

I start to shake my head no, but then I consider the offer. It wouldn't be a terrible idea to check Hollis and Aaron out and make sure there isn't anything in their life that could harm Violet. If they end up adopting her—the thought nauseates me —it would at least be a small comfort to know she was going to a safe home.

"Could you do that?"

"Of course I can. I'm very good at my job and I have connections."

I take a steadying breath, ready to reveal the stupidity making this situation worse. "They were going to go on Monday to start the proceedings for Hollis to adopt her. But I convinced Lulu to think about it some more."

"Well that's good, at least. It's got to mean something if they're willing to think about it some more."

"That might be because," I draw in a long breath, then let it all out in a rush of words. "I told them I was in a committed relationship with a guy named Bill."

"Okay--"

My leg bounces up and down, my voice jittery as I continue. "And that we'd been talking about marriage and that Bill wants kids, and is open to adopting Violet, and I didn't tell them because I didn't know it would matter."

Tessa blinks once, twice, then she leans into the camera. "I never should've lent you my Pippa Grant collection. How could you lie like that? Do you know how it's going to make you look when they discover the truth? This isn't a romantic comedy where some handsome stranger shows up out of the blue to save you."

I lean on my elbows and cover my eyes, unable to look my friend in the eye. "I know, I know. I panicked and it just came tumbling out."

"Oh, honey. What are you going to do if—when—they find out it's not true?"

"I'll come up with something." I swipe at the wetness under my eyes. "How soon can you start checking out Hollis? If you can find anything that would prove they are all wrong for adopting Violet, then my little white lie won't matter."

"I get home in a couple of days. In the meantime, I'll reach out to my contacts and start a background check—credit, criminal, the basics. Text me what you know about them."

"Thank you, thank you, thank you."

She gives me a lopsided grin. "It's what friends are for. I love you, Pippi. Hang in there."

"Love you, too, Tessie."

She blows me a kiss and signs off. I don't know if it's wrong to pray Tessa finds dirt on the Whitleys, but since it all comes down to making sure Violet is taken care of, I figure it's okay. If they don't have anything to hide, then there's nothing to worry about.

ELEVEN

Piper

Bette turns the sign on the cafe's door to "closed" and checks the lock. Ben and Rudy Berger, brothers who own the tackle and boat rental shop, push two tables together to accommodate our group. The cold drizzle and gunmetal sky mirror my mood and I would rather be home, wearing my fuzzy slippers and curled up on the couch with a book while I wallow in self-pity. Instead, I'm here at our monthly meeting of The Shoals Association of Small-Business Owners.

Not wanting to drag this meeting out any longer than necessary, I clear my throat before calling the meeting to order. Paloma Henriquez, the florist, reads the minutes from the last meeting and we discuss approving them. It should be a quick process but as usual turns more towards town gossip. Usually, this wouldn't bother me but all I can think about is the favor Webb asked of me.

"I have a request from a non-member asking if their business might be considered for membership. I explained our criteria. They'll hold off on submitting an official application until next year, but they did ask if we could promote their grand opening."

"Is this about that hot guy who wants to open a dentist office?" asks Maisie Wayne, who operates The Inked Butterfly tattoo and piercing parlor. She blows a curl of pink-dyed hair out of her eyes. "Because if it's not, I'd like to add him to the agenda. I'm dying to know his story."

"Such a hottie, isn't he?" Bette says, fanning her face. "If I were a few years younger, I'd give all you young ladies a run for your money."

"Ew, Mom," Jonathan pipes up from where he's wiping down tables on the other side of the room.

"Hush and put a shirt on."

He rolls his eyes and pulls a tank top from where it hangs from the back pocket of his cargo shorts. Bette sighs while he dresses. "You know, he used to love running around naked when he was a toddler. Everything on display, flapping away in the wind. I should be grateful he at least wears pants now."

I bite my lip and clear my throat again. "Maisie is right. This is about Dr. Duncan, or rather, about Seaside Dental."

Ben lifts his ball cap to scratch his forehead. "Why does a dental office need advertising?"

"We haven't had a dentist on the Isle since Dr. Don retired. People won't know they're there until after they've opened, but I assume they'd like to have some patients already lined up," Henry Reyes points out. Henry owns Waveriders next door to Sugarbreakers, which sells and rents jet skis, surfboards, body boards, and other equipment to use for water activities. He also owns a second shop that sells skateboards and bicycles, and it's located next door to the dentist office.

"Hayes told me you had some sort of falling out after college," Jordan Brown offers. She owns the salon on the other side of The Shoals. "But now you're helping him?"

"It was nothing and it was a long time ago. It shouldn't be a consideration."

"We heard you arguing here the other day." Rudy whistled through his teeth. "Hoo boy, if looks could kill he'd have been a pile of ashes on the floor."

"It was a spat. Again, nothing."

"Then what was Friday night?" Bette slides me a sly look. "I hear you were having dinner together at his new office, but then you stormed out like your pants were on fire. Doesn't sound like nothin'."

I glare at Henry, who at least has the decency to look somewhat ashamed. He shrugs a shoulder.

My head is beginning to throb. The perk of living on an island is that everyone knows one another and we all look out for each other. We are all family and can be relied upon on to have each other's backs. Even when their protectiveness is misguided and they act without having all the information. But the downside of island life is that everyone knows each other's business and they have no problem sharing that knowledge.

I try a smile. "Thank you for looking out for me, but there's no need. Dr. Duncan and I may not see eye-to-eye on everything, but he's bringing a good and useful service to the Isle. I think it would be neighborly for us to help him out."

"What do they need from us?" interjects Sascha Burowski. Her mother and father are the ones who technically own the little jewelry shop on the pier, but they've been traveling all winter, leaving their middle daughter in charge.

"I think they just want to spread the word that they're here and opening."

"We can do that," Maisie says. The others murmur in agreement. All except Mr. Beasley, the curmudgeon who owns the nearby package store.

"I don't think it's our responsibility to advertise for every

Tom, Dick, and Harry who sets up shop around here," he grouses. "What about our reputations? Our credibility?"

"Rod, it's a dentist office," Bette says patiently. "Not a sex shop."

"Too bad," Maisie mutters under her breath. Henry gives her a speculative look.

"I'm just sayin', we're not an advertising agency." He folds his arms and presses his lips together.

Bette sighs and looks at me. "Piper, I think the majority is on board with helping our new neighbors promote their very valuable service."

"Great. I'll let Webb—er, Dr. Duncan—know." I adjourn the meeting, say my goodbyes, and quickly head to the door. Unfortunately, I can't always make a clean exit without someone tracking me down. This time it is Bette who follows.

"What about you, honey?" Bette says, placing a hand on my arm. "You know we all promised your dad to look after you. I don't think he'd like it too much if we took the side of someone you're feuding with."

I hold back another groan. "I'm not feuding with Webb or anyone else. I'm here on his behalf asking for help."

"Because you have a good heart and you always do your best by the rest of us, even if it means sacrificing your own comfort. Like staying here after your father died."

I put my hand over hers. "I wanted to stay, Bette. This is my home."

"You shouldn't have to worry about letting the devil into your home." She gives me a knowing smile, a twinkle in her gray eyes. "I know that man did more than just simply break your heart once. Does he know?"

"About?"

"The baby and what happened?"

I inhale sharply, darting my gaze around to make sure no one is in earshot. "How do you know?"

"Your dad needed someone to talk to about it. He swore me to secrecy and as you can tell, I've kept it a secret. After seeing you and the doctor together, then finding out you were a thing back in college, I put two-and-two together. Since you're not denying it, I guess I assumed correctly?"

"He doesn't know." I grasp her hand. "He can't know. It was so long ago and there's no point in bringing it all back up."

She squeezes my hand back. "He'll never learn from me. You just let me know if you want me to put a few drops of laxative in his coffee."

Impulsively, I kiss her cheek. She's the closest to a mother I have despite there only being a fifteen-year difference between us. "It's fine, Bette, really. I was thrown at first, but he and I are fine. Totally fine. I'll see you tomorrow morning."

The drizzle has turned to rain. I dodge between the drops to my car, cursing under my breath the whole way. Now I've told one more lie, because it sure as hell is not fine.

TWELVE

Webb

Not sure I've ever had a week suck so badly. Discovered the hard way that when it rains, a three-inch deep puddle forms in front of the back door of the practice. Henry, the guy who owns the skateboard shop next door, recommended a cleanser on the next block. I had to dig deep into my memories from college to understand he was talking about a dry cleaner. They can save my Todd Snyder suit, but the Tom Ford loafers Carolynn bought me two Christmases ago are toast.

The painters we hired to paint the exam rooms used the wrong damn color. I don't know how the hell you can confuse slate with coral, but they did. Now it has to be redone, and the equipment that was to be delivered and installed has to be delayed until next week, putting us that much behind schedule.

Meanwhile, we're still waiting for the final exam room to get drywall. The contractor had an emergency and can't get to us until later in the week. There goes the flooring timetable. The hits just kept coming.

I didn't think the day could have gotten any worse—until my mother's name flashed on my phone screen.

My mother got wind of all our construction woes and called to remind me we were under contract to open no later than June 1st. No mention of the marketing delays that would put DDS in breach, but no surprise there.

"I knew this was a bad idea," she said to me first thing.

"Hello to you, too, Mom."

"Don't be a smartass, Thomas. You asked for this. You wanted to run away to a Podunk little island in the middle of the ocean and open a DDS office. You convinced me to put this company's money and resources behind you, and now I hear you couldn't even hire a competent contractor?"

"It's only a small glitch," I gritted out. "I'm handling it."

My mother scoffed. "Thomas, do you know how this will look? We have never failed to open a practice."

"And we won't now, Mom."

"If you can't open by the projected date, I will recommend we pull the license. You will be on your own, and I will expect this company to be repaid. Am I clear?"

"As Swarovski." She didn't hang up right away, so I asked, "Was there something else?"

"Carolynn doesn't seem to be doing well."

"I know she doesn't seem to be doing her job."

"Thomas," my mother said, her voice softer than usual. "At least call her. You blindsided her with the divorce and then moved away. It's awfully cold to completely cut her out of your life after you've spent nearly twenty years together."

I wondered how Mom would take it if I told her Carolynn might not have been blindsided if she hadn't been so busy fucking the company CFO. "She wasn't blindsided, Mom. She chose to ignore the facts until they bit her in the ass."

I released a weary sigh. "Look, it's really not your concern. I'm sorry she isn't taking it well, but I did everything I could to make it work. It was a mistake to begin with and one I let stand for too long. It's time we all move on."

"Fine." CEO-Mom returns in her crisp, no-nonsense voice. "And I've spoken with Carolynn about the marketing issue. She said she'd tried to reach you to discuss but you won't take her calls, and that's why the delay."

I snort. "She has my email."

"Some things need an immediate response. So when she calls you this week, I expect you to answer. If you don't and the marketing plan is delayed any further, we will not be held responsible."

"Fine."

"Get yourself together. You're on notice. I won't hesitate to pull the contract when you breach it." It doesn't escape my notice she said *when*, not *if*.

It's Friday night and I should be out shaking off the misery of this day. But it's after eight and I'm still waiting for Carolynn to call so I can put the marketing plan fiasco to rest. I also haven't had time to check in with Piper about getting help from the locals, but I figure I'll call her tomorrow. I'm alone in my apartment relaxing in my boxer briefs and my favorite worn URI T-shirt with Thai takeout, an icy cold beer, and the Bruins on the flatscreen getting their asses pummeled by Tampa Bay. Not that my team getting beat is ever a good thing, but at least if it were a thrashing by Canadians, or at least a team where ice naturally occurs, it would seem more honorable. I'm about to call it a night, get this miserable suck of a week over with, when someone knocks at my door. I debate throwing on a pair of sweats but only for a heartbeat. Fuck it. They're the ones who've come to my door unannounced, whoever they are. They get what they get.

I fling the door open and everything stops. Time, my heart, even the action on the ice as the second period comes to a close. Piper stands there looking every bit as beautiful as the first time I ever saw her. She's in black jeans that hug her curves closer than a Porsche driving a switchback up the mountain and a baby blue cropped sweater clinging to a pair of the most stellar breasts I've ever seen. Her face is flushed and if she's wearing more than lip gloss I can't tell. Her cavernous eyes are open wide and with one step forward, one blink, I would happily fall deep down into those eyes and lose myself.

I don't know how long we stand there staring at each other or who's more surprised by this snap of electricity. Finally, in a soft but strong voice she asks, "Can I come in?"

Oxygen returns to my brain. I step back, holding the door open for her. "Sorry, yeah. Of course."

She walks past, careful not to touch me and that's probably a good thing right now. It doesn't matter how pissed off I am or how frustrated she makes me—the plain and simple truth is I want her. I've never stopped. I close my door and take a moment before turning to face her.

She's looking around the place at the artwork, the furniture, the stainless steel appliances—everywhere but at me. Her gaze comes to rest on the TV where highlights from the last period play. I use her distraction to watch her, waiting for some clue to help me solve the mystery of Piper Poincelot.

"I know I showed up unexpectedly at your place, but do you think you could put some pants on?" she asks, her focus still on the screen.

Right. I'm half-naked and heading toward half-mast. "Just give me a sec."

I rush to my room and throw on a pair of shorts. When I return, Piper's standing at the balcony doors looking out. The nighttime view doesn't offer much, a sprinkling of lights over a thick black emptiness. She turns her head, and her eyes are as dark as the water is.

I gesture to the sofa. "Would you like to sit? Can I get you something to drink?"

She sits in the armchair. "I'll have one of those, if you have another," she says, pointing at the half-drunk bottle of Allagash Tripel on the coffee table.

I snag one out of the fridge, pop the top, and bring it to her. "I'm guessing you're here to talk about SASBO? I didn't get a chance this week to follow up with you. Are the other owners willing to help us out?"

She takes a long pull from the bottle before answering. "There was a little discussion about whether they should."

I chuckle a little nervously. "People hate dentists that much?"

"Not dentists, per se. They don't care for your business model."

"What the hell does that mean?"

"It means"--she picks at the label--"they don't want to trust their health to a corporation. They want healthcare professionals who are independent and not beholden to a faceless entity."

I take a drink. "The corporation, as you put it, only concerns itself with the business side of things. Freeing my partners and me up to focus on patient care. That's a good thing."

"You don't need to convince me," she says, setting the bottle aside. "We agreed to give you a chance. Let us know how we can help."

"Thank you, Piper. My partners and I will put together some ideas."

She nods, but she's barely looking at me, instead staring just past me. Her eyes are a bottomless well of sadness. I wish I could put a smile on her face. "Pip, what's going on?"

Her eyes turn shiny as she drops her head in her hands. "I'm sorry. Tessa is still away and with Mara pregnant, I didn't want to bother her or Drew so late. But I didn't want to be home right now."

She stands quickly. "I should go. I really just meant to tell you about the meeting."

I reach out a hand and snag her wrist, pulling her to a stop in front of me. I slowly rise, tugging her toward me, and put a finger under her chin to raise her face to mine. Her features are screwed up in worry, and she looks desperate to talk. "Come on, tell me what's going on."

She releases a shuddering breath, then breaks. I put my arms around her and hold her while she lets it all out. I rub her back and whisper that it will be all right, whatever it is.

After a few minutes, she sniffles and steps out of my embrace. "I'm sorry. I didn't mean to snot all over you."

"That's what friends are for, right?" I ask lightly. "Want to talk about it?"

She gives a shaky laugh. "It's just been a rough week. I miss Violet, and I'm so worried about what's going to happen, but I don't really have anyone else to talk to who knows what's going on."

I'm fourth on her list, but I'll take it considering a week ago I wouldn't have even made the cut. "Come on."

I guide her to sit down again, this time next to me on the couch. "Talk to me."

She rakes her fingers down her ponytail. "I...I might have done something stupid and if Lulu finds out, it may ruin my chances to get Violet. And I can't figure a way out of it."

"It can't be that bad."

She laughs mirthlessly. "Oh, it is." She chews on her bottom lip, and I track the movement, desperately wishing I could be the one to nibble on the plump flesh. She almost catches me staring, but I manage to cut my eyes to hers just in time.

"I told Lulu my boyfriend and I were talking about marriage, and that we could get married sooner if it would make a difference in adopting Violet. Since that seemed to be the biggest issue, that I was single. They—and by they, I mean that pastor and Hollis—also had concerns about my financial status, but as soon as we sign the deal with Hudson Foods to distribute our candy across their network, that will be resolved.

It's really the whole two parent thing that's a major sticking point."

She takes a breath and I try to catch up, my brain stumbling on one big thing. "Wait, you have a boyfriend?"

"No," she says, tossing her hands up. "That's the problem. I made someone up, and once Lulu finds out, I'm screwed."

"Wow." I let out a whistle. "Okay, that is a big deal."

The look she gives me says, *duh*. I press the spot between my brows where I know my stress divot is forming. "Okay. Let's think about this. What if you sat her down and explained? She's reasonable, right? She'll understand you were distressed when you told her that. Maybe she won't hold it against you."

"She will." Piper groans, dropping her head in her hands. "What have I done?"

I put my hand on her back, pleased she doesn't flinch at the contact. A thought occurs to me. "Wait, I have an idea."

She lifts her head, hope and skepticism warring across her face. "What? Tell me."

"What if I pretend to be the boyfriend?"

She jolts away causing my hand to drop. Her expression is almost insulting. No, wait, it *is* insulting. You'd think I'd just asked her if I could lick her grandmother's toes. She shakes her head furiously. "No. No way."

"Why not?" My pride is wounded. "I know you said you still hate me, but maybe you let me do this for you as my penance. Let me make up for what I did to you in the past."

She sucks in a breath through her teeth at the mention of the giant elephant in the room. Maybe this will give us a chance to address it, since not talking about it really doesn't work for me. And I don't think it does for her, either.

"Pretend we're going to get married?" she repeats.

"Just for a little while," I suggest. "Until you convince Lulu you're the right choice to raise Violet—with or without a husband."

She no longer looks terrified, which I count as a point. "Think it over," I tell her.

"You would do that for me?" she asks.

"I'd do anything for you, Piper," I say. "If you give me the chance."

We stare at each other for a long moment. I'm trying to remain calm, taking in very quiet breaths, afraid with one wrong move she'll bolt. Then I decide to take a chance. I reach out and touch her cheek. "Anything."

Her eyes flutter and she sways toward me. My hand slips behind her head and I angle mine as I move in closer, ready to taste the sweet, soft mouth I've been craving for so long. But just before I can reach her, so close our breath mingles, my phone buzzes and knocks us both out of our stupor.

We both look down at the table where the screen is identifying the caller and curse. "I have to take this. I'm sorry, it's work."

She scrambles to her feet, muttering under her breath. "I'm such an idiot."

"Pip, wait," I reach for her but she shakes me off. I'm torn between answering the call from Carolynn or ignoring it and risking my mother's wrath. I could always call her back.

But before I decide that's the best course of action, Piper is out my door in a blink and I can't blame her. I'm an asshole. I kick the table, then pick up my phone and swipe to answer it, girding myself for the battle I know my ex-wife is going to give me and wishing like hell I'd just turned my phone off.

THIRTEEN

Piper

I'm so stupid. Stupid, stupid, stupid.

I chant the mantra all the way to my car and all the way home. Not only did I confess to Webb the idiotic lie I told Lulu, but I actually entertained the idea of using him as my pretend fiancé. Worse—I almost kissed him.

My hands go to my lips, which are tingling despite not having actually touched Webb. We were so close though, and I know—I just know—if he had kissed me, I would have burst into flames. I don't know if I could've stopped myself. And if I let him back into my life, back into my body, it's going to open a whole Pandora's Box I'm not ready to open. It was a lucky thing Carolynn called when she did.

Carolynn. Seeing her name come up on his phone was bad enough, but then he was going to answer it. Talk to her. While he was sitting next to me! Maybe it was work-related and only work-related, but can I really trust him? Dump me by text for a woman, shame on you; dump me again for the same woman, shame on me. Ugh. I will not go down that path again.

I spend a restless weekend avoiding Webb and trying to come up with some scenario in which my little lie doesn't fuck me over. Monday morning, I arrive at the shop in the foulest mood I think Drew has ever seen. After kicking a guy out for telling me I should smile more, Drew pulls me off the front register and makes me sit in the office.

"I feel like I'm being called into the principal's office," I try to joke, but it comes out more petulant than funny.

"What going on, Piper? I've never seen you like this." Drew's concerned voice prickles, mostly because I'm embarrassed.

I tell him what's been going on with the adoption, leaving out the part where I lied about having a fake fiancé. I also skipped over Webb's offer to pose as the fake fiancé. Drew would go into a tailspin if he knew I was talking to Webb, let alone letting him get close again. But he never has to know, because I am putting an end to whatever might have been starting again.

"That's the stupidest thing I ever heard." Drew throws his pen onto the desk. He curses, shaking his head. "It's the twenty-first century. Have the Rosellis forgotten?"

"They're ultraconservative. It's why Laura didn't speak to them all that much, especially after deciding to have Violet out of wedlock."

"They're morons," he mutters. "No one would be a better mother to that little girl than you."

Tears prick my eyes. I put a hand to my heart. "Thank you. I needed to hear that."

He leans back in the chair. "So what can we do?"

You want to be my pretend fiancé? Your wife wouldn't mind, right?

"I'm going to continue to plead my case. The deal with Hudson will eliminate any doubt as to my financial abilities. And Tessa is helping me, er, vet Hollis and her family. Maybe she'll find something the Rosellis don't know about."

He cocks an eyebrow, the corner of his mouth turning up in a sly grin. "Digging up dirt. I like it."

I wince. "I don't want to, but desperate times and all that."

"Piper, can you give me a hand?" Mara, Drew's wife and my co-confectioner in the shop, calls out. I duck out of the office and cross the hall to the kitchen.

"What do you need?" I ask, pulling a polka-dot apron off a hook and tying it on.

Mara holds up fistfuls of fresh taffy. "It needs to be pulled but the alien inside me has decided it's a good time to use my bladder as a trampoline."

I chuckle and move to take her place. She's due with their first child in August and I'm not too proud to admit I'm a little jealous. They're creating a family, one I might've had if things had gone differently. A familiar ache radiates from the barren-ness of my womb. Over the years, the pain's dulled, but every now and then the wound is poked—like when Laura told me she was pregnant and when Drew broke the news about Mara. Both were extremely sensitive about it, two of the only people who knew what happened, reminding me why I love them so much.

Webb's presence has dredged up all the bad memories. It's more than a poke to the wound, it's a slice. But I've got more pressing, more timely issues to worry about, so I push it all out of my mind and lose myself in candy making. Pulling taffy is freaking cathartic. I work it until it's shiny and stiff enough to be rolled and cut. By the time Mara comes back, I've done half the batch.

"Sorry," she says, oiling her hands in preparation to take over.

"No biggie. Pulling taffy relaxes me. Quiet upfront?" I feel guilty my attitude is costing Drew office time, since he has to be out front to catch customers.

"Far as I can tell. It's still wet outside, but the clouds seem to be moving out." She settles on a stool and resumes the task. "Do you want me to do caramels, too?"

"No, we have enough for now. I was going to stay late to do

some more batches of fudge to freeze, though, so you can leave the sweetened condensed milk out."

I leave her and head out to the front to relieve Drew. I promise to paste a big fat smile on my face and be nice.

"You sure?" he asks, not convinced in the slightest.

I push him toward the back. "I'm sure. I will not run off any other customers."

He returns to the office and I start working on making room for the Mother's Day displays. It's less than a month away, and we need to get the gift displays set up so people have time to browse and buy. I dig under the counter for the box of pastel tablecloths and heft them to the counter.

Movement at the front door catches my attention. Webb is standing with another man, his shaved head and warm-bronze skin a contrast to Webb's thick, blond locks and lighter complexion. I'm not in the mood to deal with him, but apparently this week is not the week Piper gets anything she wants. Webb's companion opens the door and walks in, the blast of cool air a welcome touch to the fire that marches across my skin when Webb looks at me.

"Hello." My voice is froggy so I clear my throat and try again. "Welcome to Sugarbreakers. Let me know if you need anything."

My smile is barely a flicker on my face, and I try to look busy by taking the tablecloths out of the box and shaking them out. But the guy with Webb wants to talk.

"Hi, I'm Trevor Glass," he says, putting out his hand. I give it a quick, firm shake. "And you know my partner, Webb." He cocks his head at Webb, who looks unusually uncomfortable. Good. Maybe he won't stay long.

"Piper Poincelot," I say. "Nice to meet you."

"Webb said you talked to the other members on your business council and asked them to help us promote our dental clinic opening," he says. "I wanted to thank you for that. We've visited most of the shops on The Pier and everyone has been so gracious about letting us leave some fliers."

I shoot a glance at Webb standing off to the side, staring at me with brows drawn together and a gentle gaze that makes me want to burrow my head into his chest and cry it all out. I snap back to Trevor and do my best to offer a warmer, steadier smile.

"You're welcome. And if I can hang a flier for you or anything else, let me know."

"Actually, we were talking," he gestures at Webb, "and we thought it might be a good idea to offer all the business owners a free cleaning. You can come in, check us out, and then spread the word about how great we are."

I smile. "That would be really nice, thank you."

When I don't offer more than a tight smile, Trevor gets the hint and straightens. "We'll let you get back to your day."

"Nice to meet you," I repeat, forcing a brighter smile. I turn my back and let out a breath when I hear the jingle of the bell over the door indicating they've gone.

A throat clears and I startle, dropping the tablecloths. My head whips up to find Webb standing in the middle of the shop. "What the hell, Webb. I thought you left. You scared the crap out of me."

He moves to the counter. "I wanted to make sure you were okay."

"Peachy. Never better," I reply, flashing my teeth.

The grimace on his face tells me he doesn't buy it. "Can we talk about the other night?"

I fold my arms. "No."

He barks out a laugh. "I forgot how direct you can be."

I raise my shoulders and drop them again in an exaggerated shrug. "That's okay. For a moment there, I forgot you were an asshole."

"Pip, come on."

"No, Webb, you come on. Offer to be my knight in shining

armor? Try to kiss me? But oh, then your precious Carolynn calls and once again you drop me to run to her. You know what, I learned my lesson last time. I'm not going to go through this again. Thanks for listening to me, thanks for comforting me, and thanks for the drinks the other night. But this, you and me? It's not going to happen again. So"--I wave my hand toward the door--"You know the way out."

He waits a beat, his lips pursing like he wants argue, but his eyes catch on something behind me. His jaw twitches before he turns around and leaves.

"That's him?" Drew asks.

I look over my shoulder and catch the steel in his expression. "That's him."

He frowns. "You okay?"

I lift one shoulder. "When it comes to Webb? Yeah, I'm fine."

Only I'm not entirely sure if I'm lying to Drew or myself.

FOURTEEN

Piper

"Nothing? How can there be nothing?"

I flop back in my seat and stare at the ceiling, Tess's news spoiling my appetite and turning the sweetness floating on the air from Bette's delicious pastries into a cloying annoyance instead of their usual welcome tickle to my taste buds. She reaches out and puts her hand on mine.

"It's only preliminary," she says. "I only had time to run the basic backgrounders. Their finances and credit are solid, and they have no criminal records—save for a few speeding tickets Aaron Whitley has racked up in the past year. But I don't have a current case, so I'll be home for a few weeks at least. I'll keep looking."

Tessa is great at her investigator job. I have every confidence she'll find something to prove Hollis and her husband would be unfit caretakers for Violet, if there's anything to be found. But it will have to be something big to convince Laura's parents that a wealthy married couple with children are a worse bet than a single woman living a comfortable, though not extravagant, life.

"I have to tell them the truth, soon. We have to find a

smoking gun, something—anything—that will make them look worse than me for lying."

"There's bound to be a skeleton or two buried in the yard," Tessa assures me. "Trust me to dig them up. Just hang on another week."

"I'll try." I pick up my coffee and gesture at her with the mug. "Enough about my problems. Tell me what's going on with you? How do you not have a case to work on?" For as long as she's had this job, I've never known her to have more than a day or two in between cases and now she's talking weeks.

Tessa rolls her eyes and finishes the last bite of carrot-chia muffin. "I'm burnt out. I've been constantly traveling for the past three years. So I'll only be providing support for a little while out of the office in Woonsocket. It'll be nice to sleep in my own bed at night and eat out of my own kitchen."

"Or mine?" When Tessa was home, we shared more meals at my house than hers. She says my pantry is stocked better.

"Or yours." She laughs and sips her own drink.

"Hello, ladies."

My mouth poises on the croissant I'm about to bite into. Webb stands next to the table with a friendly smile on his face and a to-go cup in his hand. I take a small bite, conscious of crumbs falling on my shirt, and set the croissant down before brushing off the specks of bread.

"Hey Webb," Tessa says, her face lighting up. *Traitor.* "Join us. I was just filling Piper in on the nothing I've found on Hollis."

"Tessa," I hiss.

"What? You told me he knows what's going on."

I also told her what almost happened between us, and still she invites him to join us. *Traitor,* my brain repeats.

He turns to me, frowning. "I'm sorry to hear that. Have you seen Violet lately?"

"Not lately. Hollis has her still, but she's supposed to bring her back tomorrow." I can feel crumbs on my lips and lick at them. Webb's eyes darken when his gaze lands on my mouth, but it's only for a fraction of a second before he looks back at Tessa.

As much as I'm over Webb, his voice still does things to my most sensitive parts, and they twinge when he speaks to Tessa. "I rarely ever see you."

"I travel a lot for my job."

"Before you leave again, let's try to get together," he suggests. My hands clench around the cup I'm holding. Tessa casts a sidelong glance at me and there's a curious twinkle in her eye I don't care for.

"Why don't you take a seat now?" she says, motioning to the empty chair next to me. Her bag is occupying the chair next to hers, so it makes sense to offer this one but the look in her eyes and the slight pursing of her lips tells me there's an ulterior motive to her offer.

Webb glances my way, his relaxed demeanor stiffening. "I won't interrupt your meal. I only wanted to say a quick hello."

Relief loosens my shoulders, which have unconsciously risen to my ears. Until I spy Henry, Ben, and Rudy staring at our little group and realize what happens now will only fuel the gossip mill. It's the last thing I need. I force a smile and pat the empty seat. "You're not interrupting anything. Sit."

The surprise on Tess's face almost makes me laugh, but it's the stark shock on Webb's that has me hiding behind my coffee cup. After his surprising re-entry into my life, it's about time I have the opportunity to leave him speechless. After a momentary hesitation, he sits. "Thank you."

I'm very conscious of his presence, and not only because the width of his shoulders puts him squarely into my personal bubble. While he and Tessa talk, I eat my breakfast and pretend to listen. But each time he lifts his cup to his mouth, his arm brushes mine and sparks skitter across my skin. I glance at him out of the corner of my eye to see if it affects him, too, if there's any indication he's doing it on purpose. But his eye contact with Tessa as she speaks is solid. His lips are slightly parted and his head nods almost imperceptibly. He really is a good listener. He also smells incredible—a spicy contrast to the sugary sweetness of the cafe, all black licorice, ginger, and midnight fantasies. His thigh grazes mine as he shifts in the chair, but he moves away and I want to weep at the loss of contact. I should kick my own ass for feeling this way.

Tess's voice brings me back from my dark thoughts. She points at my cup. "Want a refill?"

She doesn't wait for my reply and scoops up the cup. "Be right back. Want anything, Webb?"

"Nah, I'm good," he says, raising his cup.

I think she gives me a wink before walking away, but it's so surreptitious I could be wrong. Webb sips from his cup while I finish off my croissant.

"You didn't have to invite me to sit," he says finally, just low enough for me to hear. "I came over to say hello to Tessa, not bother you."

I swallow the last bite. "I did. Henry and the Berger boys were watching us."

He cocks his head. "Can sixty-something-year-old men really be considered *boys*?"

I laugh. "My entire life I've never heard them called anything else. But they mentioned the other day at the meeting how they saw us arguing here last week, and I really hate to be the subject of gossip."

His gaze drops to my mouth once again and the wariness in his eyes gives way to something else. He reaches out and brushes my bottom lip with his thumb. My mouth parts, and his own lips twist up on one side. "You had a few crumbs there."

My heart pounds, so hard and so loud I'm sure they can hear it on the other side of the cafe. "Webb—"

"Piper, we need to talk. Once and for all. I don't think either of us is going to be able to move on until we do."

"Speak for yourself," I mumble.

He turns toward me, draping his arm across the back of my chair and pinning me with a dark gaze. "You forgive me, then?"

His silky voice wraps around me, clenching my heart on its way to settling between my thighs. We're in the middle of a crowded cafe and my body is reacting like an orgasm-deprived nymph. Attempting another private conversation can't be a good idea. I don't get the chance to answer before Tessa returns.

"Here you go." Her cheery voice yanks me out of Webb's orbital pull. She puts my cup down and drops a bag in front of Webb before retaking her seat and setting her cup down. "I know you said you didn't want anything, but the cheese Danish was fresh out of the oven."

She looks at us, her smile becoming a saucy grin. "Did I interrupt something?"

"No," Webb says, standing. "I have to go, though. Thanks for the Danish."

"Wait," I say before I can second-guess myself. "I'll be at the shop tomorrow. Come by after three; I'll be able to talk then."

His posture relaxes and an easy grin takes over his face. "I'll see you then."

He nods at Tessa and leaves. She jerks a thumb at his retreating back. "What was that?"

I continue to stare, long after he's left my line of sight, my lips still trembling from his brief touch. "I don't know, Tessa. I don't know."

FIFTEEN

Piper

There's a bump in the Sugarbreakers's sales thanks to most of the region's schools enjoying spring break at the same time. It helps that March has gone out like the proverbial lamb, and a warm front has displaced the storm clouds with clear blue sky. We normally wait until Memorial Day weekend to begin selling our homemade ice cream, but it would be a crime to miss this prime opportunity for sales to all the families traipsing through. Even The Inked Butterfly is doing a brisk business among the college students who are home for the Passover/Easter/Ramadan holiday weekend, a holy trifecta that only happens every few decades or so. This pre-season bump is good for all of us, but I'm too stressed to enjoy.

I haven't seen Violet in over a week, the longest I've gone without seeing her since she was born, and it's eating me up inside. Hollis is supposed to bring her to me this evening, but she hasn't agreed to a specific time or location. I'm having my doubts she'll hand the baby over and my stomach churns thinking of the possibility. *What recourse would I have, really?*

Ruby and Pearl, the twin teenage sisters I employ, arrive after school lets out. I put them to work up front, intending to put some time in the kitchen. I get through a batch of peanut brittle before Webb shows up. I'd hoped he'd forgotten; once I had time to sleep on it—or not sleep, as it went—I immediately regretted agreeing to this *talk*.

What's there to say, really? Is there anything he could say that would change what happened?

I make quick introductions, inwardly groaning at the stars popping out of both girls' eyes. To my surprise, Webb doesn't engage them in platitudes or small talk, but merely says a quick hello before turning all his attention to me.

"Are you still good to talk?"

"I can take a short break." I untie my apron, trying to sound normal even with my insides churning. "Girls, I'll be out back if you need anything."

I beckon Webb to the back door and lead him to the small alcove that houses the dumpster and recycle bin we share with Henry's shop. We sit on opposite sides of the small square picnic table out there and he jumps right in.

"Look, I know you don't want to talk about the past," he begins. "And I'm not trying to hurt you by bringing it up. But, I strongly feel we need to do this."

He folds his hands on top of the table and stares at me with an intensity that pins me in place. "I care about you, Pip. I didn't set out to cause you pain. I don't deserve your forgiveness, I get that. All I ask for is a few minutes to explain what really happened."

My cheeks flame and my breaths shallow, but I don't flinch. I want to look away, to bury my head and hide my face so he can't see how these simple words are undoing me. His sincerity, his earnestness, his total lack of guile—it's both a salve on the gash in my heart and kindling for the guilt burning within.

"I explained before how she was drunk, her friends had

skipped out on her, and she was alone at a bar downtown. She sounded scared, and I couldn't leave her, too."

My back stiffens. He couldn't leave her, so he left me instead.

"I was only going to drop her off at the house, then meet you. But we had the accident." His face contorts like he's reliving the memory. "It was my fault. The accident. I was driving too fast because I wanted to get her out of my car and get back to you. When the deer ran out in front of us, I couldn't control the swerve."

His voice shakes and he breaks eye contact. "Carolynn took the brunt of the impact when we hit the tree. Her pelvis was crushed which ruptured her uterus."

"Oh my God. That's awful." I put a hand to my heart. I don't particularly like Carolynn, but this is a tragedy I wouldn't wish on my worst enemy. "But, why didn't you tell me what happened? I would've come running."

He stares down at the table top and traces a knot in the pine with his thumb while he talks. "I couldn't at first. We were both being treated. Then after I was released with minor injuries, I didn't have my phone. I went to check on Carolynn, and that's when they told me she had to have emergency surgery. Her parents were traveling in Europe and couldn't get a flight home right away, and her sisters were useless as always. I had to be with her. She had no one."

"It still doesn't explain why the next time I heard from you was by text days later."

He raises his head, and I ache at his stricken expression. "They had to give her a hysterectomy. She couldn't—can't— have children. Because of me. I was the one driving. She was inconsolable. I had to do what I thought was right."

That must have been when I saw him with her at the hospital. There are so many conflicting emotions whirling inside me, competing for attention, I don't know which one to hold on to. I close my eyes, which begin burning.

"I was weak," he continues. "I should've been strong enough to tell you to your face, but I think a part of me knew if I saw you, I wouldn't be able to go through with it. I'm sorry I did that to you, more sorry than you can imagine."

I draw in a shaky breath and let it out slowly, opening my eyes. "I was so angry with you, I didn't want to see you. I gave you no chance to explain. That's on me."

He reaches out to clasp both my hands in his. "You had every right."

I waver about telling him my side of things, but I need to know one more thing first. "I understand you felt responsible, but I don't understand why you thought you had to marry her. Staying with her through her recovery—okay, maybe. But marriage, Webb? That's what broke me. When I heard you were engaged, that's when I think I gave up on any lingering hope I had for us."

His grip on my hands tightens. "I felt I owed it to her, since I was the reason she couldn't have children. How could I go off and live my life, possibly have my own children, knowing what I did to her? And when she decided early on in our marriage she didn't want to adopt, I accepted it. To me, it was my penance."

"Webb, please tell me you know now it wasn't your fault," I say, my throat thick with emotion.

He gives a small smile. "I know. Took years of working on myself, but I finally believe it. It's one of the reasons I finally stopped putting up with her bullshit and left. I didn't owe Carolynn anything, not anymore. But you—at the very least I owed you an explanation and apology."

I pull back, needing to put a touch of distance between us. What if I had told him about my pregnancy, like I'd planned to that night? There were choices to discuss, decisions to be made, and I needed him by my side. But would he have insisted we keep the baby, would he have married me out of obligation? Would I be the one he was leaving now, instead of back then?

Laura always thought I should tell him, while Tessa didn't see any point after the fact. He'd made his choice when he broke up with me to be with Carolynn and I made mine. It doesn't matter now how it came to be, what happened, happened. As much as I wish I could change things, I can't.

There's a quiet tension broken only by the cawing seagulls flying overhead. My mind races with thoughts and memories, but most of all with regrets.

"Piper. Talk to me. What are you thinking?"

There's one thing I know I can do. "I wish you had come to me before you did anything. I wish you'd given me a chance to change your mind. I wish—I wish we had both done a lot of things differently. But I understand."

"Do you really?" Webb looks hopeful for the first time. "Because Piper, I want nothing more than to make everything up to you. If you'll forgive me, maybe we can... maybe we can pick up where we left off? Or start over? Whatever you want, as long as I get to keep you in my life this time."

His hands reach across the table for mine again, but I pull them away and set them in my lap. "I forgive you, Webb. And yeah, I think we can be friends again. But that's all I can give you. There's too much water under this very rickety bridge of ours."

I think about the other night. And there's still Carolynn between us.

He lets out a resigned sigh. "I understand."

We stand and move toward the back door. There's still awkwardness, but less tension. I put a hand on his arm, the muscle there flexing under my palm. His eyes flicker over my face and the magnetism between us begins growing again. I think I surprise him when I put my arms around his neck, because he hesitates a half second before returning the embrace. My nose nestles next to his throat and I hope he doesn't notice I'm breathing him in.

I release him before he gets the wrong idea—or the right one, depending on your perspective. I've decided I won't tell him about the pregnancy, which solidifies friendship as the only thing I can offer. Anything deeper would require the whole truth and I can't.

"All right, well. Now that's settled, I need to get back to work. I've got a few trays of truffles in the freezer I need to dip."

"Being a confectioner sounds much more fun than what I do."

"You mean rotting teeth as opposed to fixing them?" I hold the door open for him.

He looks at me with chagrin. "You're never going to let me live that down, are you?"

I pretend to think on it. "Um, nope."

He laughs. "Do you have a bathroom?"

I point to a door behind him. "Right in there. Feel free to let yourself out the back or through the front when you're done. I'll be in the kitchen."

I snag my apron off the hook and head out front to let the girls know I'll be hands deep in chocolate—literally—for the next hour and pull up short.

Hollis is here, finally. She stands alone, dressed head to toe in soft, pink cashmere, her platinum bun pinned perfectly above the nape of her neck. Not a hair out of place, not a smudge of her rose lipstick anywhere but on her inflated lips stretched taut in disdain and on the straw peeking out of the iced to-go cup from Beachcomber's.

"Hollis." I look behind her. "Where is Violet?"

"She's at my aunt's house. Aaron and I have to go back to Hartford for a couple of weeks to take care of some business, but we'll be back as soon as school lets out." She takes a sip from the drink and makes a little noise of pleasure. "We'll definitely have to come back here. This vanilla latte is to die for."

I fold my arms. "You were supposed to bring Violet here."

Hollis shakes the ice in the cup. "That wasn't going to happen. She's with Lulu. See, Piper… I'm on to you. My private investigator has been doing some digging, and your whole story about being practically engaged is one huge lie. Once I tell Lulu, you can forget about adopting Violet. That baby is mine."

Webb

I catch myself humming while I wash up in Piper's bathroom. Can't help it—all the guilt hanging around my neck over how I treated Piper has dissolved, leaving me lighter than I've been in years. It was no easy feat to reclaim our friendship, and honestly, I was prepared to do a lot more groveling, but it's worth it. She's back in my life. While Piper insists friendship is all she's willing to give me, I'm not ready to give up on something more. I just need to take it slow. Not too slow, since I've already wasted more than fifteen years, but I've got to be cautious.

"Don't fuck this up," I say to my reflection.

I poke my head in the kitchen to say goodbye, but it's empty. I hear raised voices coming from the front of the shop and push my way through the door. Piper has her back to me. She's facing a tall, Scandinavian-like woman whose sneer ruins any attractiveness she might've possessed.

"Did you really think you'd get away with it?" the woman is asking.

Piper's shoulders lower, but she keeps her head up. The woman continues to berate, each barb visibly landing. But my girl stays locked in place. I'm trying to understand what the woman is so smug about when her words start to penetrate the fog of anger rolling over me.

"It's pathetic you felt you needed to lie about having a boyfriend, let alone lie about being engaged. Didn't you think it reeked of desperation?" She berates Piper. "It's so obvious you made it up."

It registers that this must be Laura's cousin, the one competing to adopt Violet. The married one. Piper's shoulders rise and fall, her distress evident in the way she's beginning to collapse in on herself. I don't even need to think about it. I step up behind Piper, my arms instinctively moving around her middle to hold her. She stiffens and I hug her tighter before putting on my brightest smile.

"Hello. You must be Laura's cousin. I'm Webb, Piper's fiancé."

Piper stills, but hopefully her face isn't registering the same level of shock as the cousin's. After a few seconds, she reaches up to put her hands on my arms.

"Webb," Piper says, her voice surprisingly steady and strong. "This is Laura's cousin, Hollis Whitley."

"Smith-Whitley," the woman says as if on autopilot. Hollis looks from Piper to me, her eyes narrowing. "Piper's fiancé, you say?"

I kiss the top of Piper's head. "Also known as the luckiest man on earth."

"That can't be true," she says, putting a hand on her hip.

"It is," I say, my gaze never leaving Hollis's face. My arms are a protective barrier around Piper and I tug her in closer.

"My PI asked around and no one said you were dating."

Piper speaks up, and I breathe a sigh of relief she's game to play along. "Maybe your PI owes you a refund. Apparently he got bad information."

"It's inconvenient you didn't bring Violet with you, as

promised," I tell Hollis. "But we'll call Lulu and arrange to pick her up. I've been wanting to meet Lulu and Denny, anyway. Laura was also a good friend of mine back in college."

Hollis hikes the strap of her Coach hobo onto her shoulder. "This isn't over, Piper. This little stunt"--she waves a finger at Piper and me--"won't last. You can bet on it."

She stalks out, letting the door slam shut behind her. Piper scrambles from my grasp and whirls on me. "What are you doing?" she growls.

I glance over my shoulder at the teenagers behind the counter, pretending not to be absorbed by this whole exchange. Putting my mouth to her ear, I whisper, "Keeping you from losing Violet."

She shivers, moves a step away, and jerks her head toward the back. "Come on."

Once we're outside again, she begins laying into me. "You realize that stunt you pulled will be all over the Isle by nightfall. Ruby and Pearl are friends with Bette's son, Jonathan. They're probably in there now texting him about my engagement."

"Good." I can't help the self-satisfied smirk I sport.

"Good?" Her eyes are practically popping out of their sockets. "How so? How the hell do I explain this?"

I scratch my head. "Weren't you the one who made up the story about a fiancé?"

"Yes, but—"

"And," I speak over her. "Were you not just playing along with it? If you wanted to come clean, Piper, you could've told her I was only kidding."

She makes a noise of frustration and moves away from me, muttering to herself. "I can't believe this. I just made everything worse."

I rest against the picnic table and fold my arms, watching her stress pace. "You didn't. This is much, much better."

She stops pacing and looks at me, her big brown eyes incredulous. "How do you figure?"

"I've only met Hollis this one time, but I can tell, you are by far the better person to raise Violet. If this little—ploy—makes that happen, it's much better than letting that harpy get her claws into that baby."

Her gaze flickers, the gears in her head obviously turning as she considers this. "So you're willing to play my fiancé until the adoption goes through?"

"I told you I was the other night."

She runs a hand down her ponytail. "Oh my God. This is crazy. I can't believe you did that. I can't believe I'm considering running with it!"

I spread my hands out. "It came out in the moment. She was acting so superior and once I realized what was going on, my first instinct was to knock her off that high horse of hers."

I smile, recalling the stark shock on Hollis's face. Her smooth ivory skin turned red and blotchy. "It was worth it."

She purses her lips. A tiny wrinkle I never noticed before forms at the corner of her mouth. "What do you get out of this?"

I can pretend you're mine while I work on making it real. "I get a chance to prove to you I'm not the same asshole I was."

"I already know that. You're a completely different asshole now."

I snicker. "I missed that sass."

"This is crazy, Webb. So crazy. This will never work."

She drops her head into her hands. "And I was going to tell them the truth, beg them to understand my desperation. I might have had a chance at them forgiving me. But God, I'm so stupid. I'll be humiliated if this comes out, but worst of all, I'll never see Violet again. If this blows up, Lulu and Denny will never forgive me for lying to them."

I pull her hands away to hold them in mine. "I won't let that happen, Pip. Besides, what's the alternative?"

She stares, frowning, at two seagulls fighting over a piece of chocolate. I caress her hands with my thumbs. "What are you thinking, Pip?"

She cuts her gaze to me and I'm bolstered by the spark flashing in her eyes. "First, I'm thinking you need to stop calling me Pip. But also—if we're going to do this, we need to tell Tessa and Hayes. And I have to tell my partner, Drew, and of course his wife. I can't lie to them."

I nod. "I'll tell my partners. They can be trusted, of course. Maybe Graeme, my best friend. I don't know yet."

"You don't trust him? I thought you two were really close."

"We are, but he would feel obligated to tell Tish—his wife— and she's not so good with the secret keeping." I give a wry smile. It's an understatement.

"What about your parents?" She asks, the little wrinkle making a reappearance.

My brows draw down. "The less they know, the better."

"Maybe they won't find out," she offers.

"They will." I snort. "They have their ways."

She's quiet as she regards me. Letting go of my hands, she steps to the side. "And Carolynn? What will she say?"

"Doesn't matter. It's over." I duck my head so I can look her straight in the eye and she can see my sincerity. "It's really over."

She holds my gaze another moment, then looks away. "If we're really going to do this, we should get together and hammer out the ground rules."

"Ground rules?"

"Yes. If this is going to work, we need to be on the same page. I'm calling Lulu to arrange to pick up Violet. Come to my place for a late dinner. We can talk about it then."

"Just dinner?" I tease.

"Webb, I'm serious about us only being friends."

"Okay. But Pip?"

She sighs. "Yes?"

I tug her ponytail. "I reserve the right to try to change your mind."

SEVENTEEN

Piper

Webb shows up at seven p.m. on the dot holding a bottle of Chardonnay. "I realized about halfway here I should have asked what dinner was. You might've preferred a red."

I take the bottle and usher him in. "The white will do. Hope you like coq au vin."

"Love it," he says. "Is Violet here?"

"I talked to Lulu earlier. She's invited us to lunch on Saturday. I'll pick up Violet then."

The oven timer buzzes. "Could you get the salad out of the fridge while I get this?"

Webb finds the dressings next to the salad and puts it all out. I take the chicken out of the oven and set it on a trivet on the kitchen table to begin dishing it out, while he plates the salads. We move as if we've been doing this together forever, like it's the most natural thing in the world. He pops the cork on the wine and pours us each a glass, then sets them at our places before pulling my chair out for me. I sit before I swoon and make a fool of myself. His smile dazzles, crinkling the corners of his eyes as he picks up a fork. "This looks delicious."

"Thanks. Hope it lives up to its appearance." I watch him from under my eyelashes while he samples the dish. When he hums his approval, I relax—about the food at least. The noises of appreciation coming out of his mouth vibrate through me. I take a long sip of wine, the chilled liquid doing little to douse the fiery arousal he's ignited against my inner protests. I take a bite of chicken and let out my own happy moan.

We ease into comfortable conversation while we eat, and once finished, I nod my chin at him. "Before we start setting ground rules, I need to make sure you're really okay with this. With lying to almost everyone."

"What we each want is inherently good," he says. "You'll provide a more loving home for Violet, and I'll provide much needed health services for the Isle. Win-win."

"The end justifies the means." I take in a breath. "Awfully Machiavellian."

"I only scored a 56 on the Machiavellian scale," he says, puffing out his chest. "I'm actually not that evil."

"49." He deflates some, and I smirk into my glass.

"Guess you're a better person than me." He tilts his glass to me in a mock toast.

"It just means, on the whole, I'm not comfortable with deceit. I've been on the shitty end of it enough in my life."

Webb stretches across the table and rests his hand on my arm, electrifying my skin. I resist the urge to melt in a puddle under the soft warmth of his touch. "Hey," he says, his voice low and intense. "I promise to always be honest with you. I want you to know I will never lie to you. You can trust me."

I flinch, not at his touch, though I'm sure it's what he thinks. He sits back and stares at me. I clear my throat and gulp the rest of my wine. "We should talk about what's going to happen—or not going to happen—between us."

"All right." An amused gleam dances in his eyes. "Let's start with what's going to happen."

I finish my wine and stand to refill it. "We're going to have to sell it, especially to Lulu and Denny. Which means we'll have to act all lovey-dovey, at least in public."

"What do you see that entailing?"

I stare at my wine, a heated flush creeping up my neck. "Holding hands, sweet talk, kissing," I mumble this last one into my glass.

When he doesn't say anything, I glance up to gauge his reaction. He's looking much too smug. I scowl. "What?"

He stands and walks over to me. Before I can react, he takes the glass out of my hand and sets it on the counter, then pulls me into his arms. With a finger under my chin, he tilts my face up then leans slowly in. My eyes flutter closed as his lips lightly brush against mine. Holding my chin between his thumb and forefinger, he deepens the kiss, tongue sweeping against mine. His other hand comes to rest on my hip. My body arches into him without my permission, but as my brain screams, *this is a bad idea!* and my heart trembles with uncertainty, my pussy is shouting *Yes! Yes! Yes!*

I melt into him, my arms moving around his neck. His thick ridge presses against my stomach, and one of us—I think it might be me—moans. And then...

It's over.

He steps back, taking all the heat with him. Maybe not all of it, since my panties still may scorch right off me, but enough to leave me standing confused and cold. My breath rasps. The only indication he's affected at all by what just happened is the way his fists clench at his sides.

I touch my lips and steady my breaths. "What was that?"

Something flickers across his face but is just as quickly replaced by an impassive expression. "If we're going to kiss in public, I figured we should get the initial awkwardness out of the way."

I huff out a short laugh. "Mission accomplished. Now it's not awkward at all."

He drops his head a moment, then lifts it and flashes a grin. "Sorry, it got away from me."

I pick up my wine and down it in one long swallow. I refill my glass with the rest of the bottle and do a mental inventory of what else I have on hand, because I'm pretty sure this won't be my last glass. "Maybe we should talk about what is not going to happen."

He picks up his wine glass and follows me into the living room. I take up position in the center of my sofa and tuck my legs under me. He gets the message and sits in the overstuffed chair with the end table between us. "First," I begin. "What just happened can't happen again."

The corners of his eyes twitch like he's about to be a smart ass, but he only nods in agreement. "We'll keep any kissing chaste."

"Obviously, kissing isn't the only thing we should keep chaste. Hand-holding, hugging when necessary, a touch to the hand or shoulder or cheek now and then—but nowhere else. This"--I circle my hand in front of my chest and pelvic area--"is off-limits."

He mimics my gesture in front of his crotch and deadpans, "Same here."

I ignore him and continue. "We'll keep our story simple— reconnected at the funeral and you moved here to open a dental office and see if we had a chance."

He leans forward. "I couldn't keep my eyes off you. It was like the past fifteen years didn't happen and it was just us, young and stupid and hopeful again."

I can feel his stare, but I keep mine firmly on the wine in my glass. "I gave you a hard time at first. But you won me over."

"I'm irresistable."

I trace the rim of my glass with my finger and look up at him, my eyes drawn back to his mouth, to those thick lips that felt so good pressed to mine, even better than I remember. My breath quickens, desire building like a storm cloud in my gut. I look away, my lips parting as I draw in more air, but my gaze lands back on his eyes, now a dark, piney green, and I'm transfixed. The years fall away and for the first time in forever the yearning in the pit of my stomach doesn't pull and ache the same lonely way. His eyelids half-close and his Adam's apple bobs.

"Pip," he says, his voice coming out part-groan, part-whisper.

"Webb."

"I'd really like to kiss you again."

I don't answer right away, because I don't know what the right thing is to say. I want him to kiss me again. I want him to do more than kiss me, the thought causing me to draw my knees in and press my thighs together in a feeble attempt to hold myself together. I want to feel his lips, his tongue, his teeth on me. All over me. *I want, I want, I want...*

But no. This arrangement we're agreeing to can't include these sorts of extracurriculars. Not with so much at stake.

I set my glass on the table next to me. "I think I've had a little too much wine. I'm going to get some water. Want any?"

I stand but before I can move away he reaches across the gap between us and grasps my wrist. "Pip—"

I pull out of his grasp, not in a harsh way, but decidedly. "It's Piper." I need to keep things formal. We can't go back to how it used to be or there's no chance I'll come out of this with my heart intact. "This is a bad idea. We need to stick to doing the bare minimum, okay?"

He stares at me for a long half-minute, then sits back with a sigh. "Okay."

I take extra time in the kitchen to gather myself. This is an arrangement, a deal between two friends, that's all. To pretend otherwise is courting disaster. Until I'm willing to tell him everything, this can't go further, and I will never be willing to do that. I need to keep a wall up between us.

But that kiss… my fingers linger against my mouth, and I let myself swim in the feelings he stirred up for a moment before I lock it all down. Our relationship is a fictional construct and once the adoption goes through, we'll carefully deconstruct it.

The mental pep talk works and I stroll back into the living room a little more sober, a little more confident, a little more steadfast. Webb is standing, facing the fireplace with an arm resting on the mantle. Shoulders back, chin up, I plaster a smile on my face that freezes when he turns around. His generous mouth is cocked up on one side, the smattering of soft scruff along his jaw begging to be stroked—and I know right then and there that no matter how hard I try to resist this magnetism between us, I am fucked.

Well and truly fucked.

EIGHTEEN

Webb

Piper's nerves are palpable, practically shedding off her body and onto me. I grasp her hand and tug her around so she's facing me, not the door to the Rosellis. "Pip—"

"It's Piper," she growls, eliciting a grin from me.

"Today it's Pip. Engaged couples have pet names, and that's always been mine for you so it's easy to remember." I squeeze her hand and duck my head to make eye contact. "Take a breath. It's going to be fine."

"How do you know? How do you know they won't see through us right away?" Her eyes flicker back and forth between mine, and I do my best to project the reassurance I know she's looking for.

I raise her hand to my lips and brush a light kiss across her knuckles. Her shudder is subtle. Try as she might, I know I'm affecting her. After the other night, all I can think about is claiming her rosebud of a mouth again. But she's been working —and succeeding—at keeping her distance. I should respect that, and I would, except the glances I catch when she thinks I'm not looking, the tiny tremors when I touch her, the way her eyes blaze in the first second she sees me—it contradicts everything coming out of her mouth.

"I love you and you love me." Her eyes widen almost comically, and I chuckle. "Sell it to yourself and we'll sell it to them."

She snorts. "You sound like Barney the Purple Dinosaur."

My smile spreads. "Oh, wait." I reach into my pocket and take out a ring. It's a peridot, her birthstone, in a vintage white gold setting. I found it at an antique store near my condo. Not as big and flashy as the one I gave Carolynn, but that's not Piper. At least I hope it's not.

I lift her hand and slide it on her left ring finger. "There. Now it's official."

She looks at the ring, her mouth open in a little O. "Webb, it's beautiful. You didn't have to—I mean, I have costume jewelry that would've sufficed."

"You wound me." I clutch my heart. "You think I'd give my fiancée something fake? This may not be a diamond, but it's a precious gem." Like you, I want to say, but I know that'd be too much.

She swallows and looks up at me through her lashes, her mocha eyes filled with some unnamable emotion. "It matches your eyes."

I blink. "Does it? I didn't notice. I just know it's your birthstone."

She laughs. "Peridot isn't my birthstone. I was born in July; it's ruby."

"Ah, shit." I slap my forehead. "I'm sorry. I can find a replacement—"

"Don't you dare. I love it." She leans up on tiptoes and pecks my cheek. I'm smiling like a fool.

"I saw movement in the front window," she murmurs, taking my hand. "Think that'll help sell it?"

And just like that, my heart sinks. It's still only an act to her.

I hold her hand until we reach the door, when she lets go

and rings the bell. The door swings open immediately, startling Piper into stepping back. She bumps into my chest and I put my hands around her arms to steady her.

"Piper!" A short, older woman with chin-length gray hair and sky-blue eyes holds out her arms and engulfs Piper in a hug, forcing me to drop my hands. Piper lets out a quiet *oof*, then pats the woman on the back. I assume this is Laura's mother. The eyes are a dead giveaway.

"You must be Bill," Laura's mother wraps her arms around me, but she's a small woman and can barely get around my chest. She's also shorter than Piper, so I have to bend to return the awkward embrace.

I cock an eyebrow at Piper. "Nice to meet you, Mrs. Roselli. You can call me Webb."

"Oh, I thought you said his name was Bill?" Lulu asks Piper.

"Webb is his nickname," she replies.

"Call me Lulu. Come in, come in," she says, ushering us into the house. She closes the door behind us and motions for us to follow her. "Everyone is in the sunroom. It's so sunny out, such a nice break from all the nasty storms we've been hit with."

Piper looks puzzled. "Everyone? I thought we were having lunch with only you and Denny."

"Pastor Marty was so excited when I told him about your engagement. He wanted to meet Bi—Webb." Lulu's cheerful voice belies obvious discomfort. The smile fixed on her face is just that—fixed. Her gaze shifts to the side, her heart-shaped face—another nod to Laura—tinged with pink. I slide Piper a questioning look, but she only shrugs. Her jaw is tight, though, and I know she's not happy about this development.

"Where is Violet?" Piper asks, looking up the stairs.

"Napping. She had a rough night." Lulu wrings her hands. "I'm afraid she kept us up most of the night. Denny might not be at his best, but I convinced him to have lunch with us."

We follow Lulu down a short hallway and through the

kitchen to a room with three walls of windows. The sunlight streams through, muted by a light tint on the windows that doesn't disrupt the view of a lush, narrow yard leading to a wooded area. Two men are sitting on wicker furniture I think I last saw in a rerun of The Golden Girls. The heavier, balding man stands and instinctively I know this is Pastor Marty. He wears a lightweight, beige suit with a mint-green collared shirt that does nothing for his ruddy complexion. Against the peach-and-tan furniture he could have easily been camouflaged. He extends a pudgy hand. "Pastor Marty Rickford. You must be Piper's fiancé, Bill."

"You can call me Webb. It's short for my middle name—Webber," I add at his puzzled expression.

It's curious he introduces himself to me before Laura's father. I shake his hand and turn toward Mr. Roselli, who remains seated. He's broad-shouldered, his hulking frame fitting incongruously on the floral furniture, salt-and-pepper hair cropped close to his head. He looks at me, but I'm not sure he sees much with all the sorrow swimming in his eyes. He looks much older than his wife, his rough tanned face marred with deep creases, especially around his mouth.

"Mr. Roselli, it's a pleasure to meet you," I say, reaching my hand toward him. He grunts before giving me a quick hand-shake, then nods his head at one of the empty seats.

"Hi Denny," Piper says, bending over to kiss his cheek. For a moment when he looks at her, his eyes clear and his lips turn up. "It's good to see you."

"You, too, dear heart," he says, speaking in a strained, grav-elly voice. He pats the chair on his other side, placing himself between Piper and me. She raises her brows at me in an apolo-getic glance. I give her a quick wink. He's protective of her, and he hasn't made his mind up about me, yet. I can respect that.

Laura's mother sits on the other side of Piper while Pastor Marty claims the seat next to me. On the coffee table in front of us are a stack of small tea plates, a platter of egg salad sandwiches cut into fours, cheeses and crackers, and an antipasto tray. On a side table is a pitcher of lemonade and a carafe of what I assume is coffee. I'm proven right when Lulu pours a cup and passes it to the Pastor. "Would you like a drink? I have lemonade and coffee here, but Piper knows where the water is if that's what you'd prefer."

"Lemonade would be great, thanks," I say.

"We have beer, too," Mr. Roselli says, picking up a brown glass bottle of Sam Adams. "Considering the inquisition you have planned for the young man, I think he might need something a little stronger than lemonade."

Lulu's lips tighten, but she pours me a glass and hands it over without saying anything.

Pastor Marty chortles like it was a joke, but he's annoyed. "Now, Denny. It's not the Spanish Inquisition. There are no torture devices."

"Not even a comfy chair?" I murmur into my glass. Piper scolds me with a look, but Mr. Roselli chuckles.

"I'm sorry?" Pastor Marty says, either not hearing me or understanding the Monty Python reference. My money is on the latter.

"We simply want to get to know the man who's won over our Piper," Lulu says, jumping in. "It was a surprise, but a happy one. Laura always worried you wouldn't find the right man."

Piper's lips flatten. She takes a cup of coffee from Lulu. "Did she now?"

"Of course," Lulu answers. She passes a cup to Pastor Marty and pours herself a lemonade. "Please help yourself. This is a casual get-to-know-you lunch. Not an inquisition," she says with a pointed look at her husband.

"We want to make sure if Piper were to adopt Violet, that she'd be going to a safe and loving environment," Pastor Marty says, piling cheese and crackers on his plate.

"Even if I wasn't marrying Piper, Violet would still be going to a safe and loving environment," I say with a smile, but there's a sharpness in my voice. Who the fuck is this guy again? A foot nudges mine under the table and Piper glares at me. I take a sandwich from the platter.

"Didn't mean to imply otherwise," Pastor Marty says. "It's simply a fact that children who grow up in a home with a mother and a father are happier, better adjusted, and more likely to be successful members of society."

I'm about to ask where exactly he got that fact from, but Lulu jumps in, possibly sensing the tension building. "Piper, tell us how Webb proposed."

Piper's face is creased in panic. We hadn't practiced a proposal story. But it just so happens I have one I can tell.

"Pip," I say, "Why don't I tell the story, darling?"

Relief wars with curiosity across her face, but she nods. "Of course. You tell it so much better."

"I'd planned on proposing to her on her birthday, but after she told me of your hesitation about letting her adopt Violet without being married, I knew I'd have to do it sooner. Had the ring—"

Piper holds out her hand for Lulu to ooh and ahh over it. "Not a diamond?" Lulu asks.

"Peridot. It matches his eyes," Piper replies with a wink at me.

"So I had the ring and she knew it was coming, but I still wanted to make it a surprise. We took a drive up the coast and spent an overnight at a little bed and breakfast right on the beach. I woke her at dawn for a sunrise walk and as we strolled along the sand, I collected bits of sea glass, stowing them in my pocket. When we reached a dune, we stopped to enjoy the colors and light coming over the horizon. I took the pile of sea glass out of my pocket and held it out so the sunlight glittered off all the pieces—greens and blues and amber. 'Look,' I said, 'doesn't the sun make these sparkle?'"

The room is quiet and Lulu is staring at me with a soft expression. I feel Pastor Marty studying me, while Piper watches intently, leaning forward on her seat. Mr. Roselli is slumped back in his chair wearing a faraway look. I clear my throat and continue the story.

"She humored me with a look, but she was all about the sunrise. So I prodded her again. 'Really, you need to see this sparkle.' This time when she turned around, I'd picked the ring out of the pile of sea glass and dropped to one knee. I said, 'Pip, will you allow me the privilege of loving you with all I have for the rest of our lives?

"And she said, 'Yes. Now get up before you ruin that very expensive pair of pants.'"

Everyone laughs. I take a drink of my lemonade and look over at Piper who's biting back a smile.

"Such a charming story," Lulu gushes. She rubs Piper's arm. "You're so lucky."

"No, I'm the lucky one," I say. Piper gives me a subtle roll of the eyes, but I mean every word. Wish I could make her believe it.

NINETEEN

Webb

We continue with lunch, everyone except Laura's father making polite conversation. He continues to sit and sip on another bottle of beer, leaving the plate Lulu fixed for him mostly untouched. Each time I try to pull him into conversation, Pastor Marty comes up with some idiotic question to ask me. So far I've told him about my family, my career, the practice I'm opening—even about my brother's death from childhood leukemia. I've stayed away from any mention of my ex-wife. But that doesn't last long.

"Tell me, Webb. You're about the same age as Piper. How is it you haven't been married yet?"

"Actually, Pastor, I'm divorced."

Lulu is cleaning up the plates, but she stops and whips her head up. She looks between Piper and me. "You've been married before."

It's not a question or a statement. It's an accusation. My spine stiffens and I take a sip of my drink before responding. "Yes. My ex-wife, Carolynn, and I were married for about thirteen years. We divorced last year."

"No children in all that time?" The question is innocent

enough, and logical. But there's a glee about Pastor Marty, like he's about to catch me in something.

Here's the other thing about the question—it hurts. After a few years, I thought we might talk about adopting or trying surrogacy. But Carolynn could only put off the discussion so many times before she finally admitted to me that she'd never seen herself as having children, even before the accident. Talk about a kick to the nuts. But all I tell the Pastor is how we were unable to have our own, which is still more than he deserves to know.

He digests this information, filing it away, for what reason I couldn't say. Before his line of questioning can resume, there's a squawk from the monitor on the side table.

"Violet's awake," Lulu says.

Piper jumps up like her ass was pinched, joy softening the tension in her features. "I'll get her."

She dashes out of the room at the same time Mr. Roselli stands and collects his empty bottles. "I need to get back to work. I want to get that lawnmower working so I can mow tomorrow."

I also start to stand, but he waves me down. "It was good meeting you, Webb. You take good care of our Piper."

"I will, Mr. Roselli."

"Denny." He pats me on the shoulder. "We'll be seein' ya."

Lulu stares after her husband until he disappears through a door to what I assume is the garage. "He can't bear to be in the same room as Violet," she says quietly.

Pastor Marty puts his hand on her knee, a little too high to be proper. "Give him, time, Lulu. He's a proud man who needs to work out his grief on his own time. We need to keep praying for him."

She pats his hand and gives him a little smile. Thank God Piper returns before things become more uncomfortable, or I give in to the urge to smack Pastor Marty's hand off Lulu's knee on behalf of Denny.

A smile takes over my face when I see Violet snuggled in Piper's arms, but it's no rival for the light radiating off Piper. The baby is clutching Piper's blouse in one tiny fist and with her dark curls, Violet could be Piper's biological child. They look so natural together. I can't imagine the cold woman I'd met the other day taking Piper's place. I won't allow it.

I kiss Piper on the cheek and smooth a hand over Violet's head. "There are my girls."

Piper raises her brows at me and I try to communicate with a subtle shrug. Got to sell it.

"Thanks for lunch, Lulu. I think we're going to take this little one home." I notice the diaper bag slung over Piper's shoulder for the first time.

"It was a very nice meeting you," I say, squeezing Lulu's hand. "Laura was a good friend, and I'm happy to get to know her family."

Lulu gives a small nod of her head. Pastor Marty claps me on the back. "Good to meet you, Webb. Why don't I walk you two out?"

"That's not nece—"

He cuts Piper off. "It's no trouble. It will give us a moment to talk," he adds in a low voice.

He accompanies us all the way out of the house and stands by while Piper settles Violet into the car seat in the back of my car. I use the opportunity to go on the offensive.

"What exactly is your role in all of this, Pastor?"

"I'm providing my counsel to ensure Violet ends up with the right family."

I fold my arms. "I see. But it's ultimately the Rosellis' decision."

"It's an emotional time. Lulu and Denny are clouded by emotion, understandably, so I am here to be an objective advocate for Violet. Lulu cares deeply for Piper, but she has a responsibility to her daughter and her granddaughter. I'll be frank with you, Webb. I'm not convinced I can recommend Violet be adopted by you and Piper."

Something scary must show on my face because he takes a step back. Good. He should be scared. "And why is that?" I growl.

"This is all very convenient—your reunion and engagement. Hollis and her husband have been married for ten years, have two boys together. A solid, tangible commitment. What's to say that after living together for a while, you and Piper decide marriage doesn't work for you two? Where would that leave Violet? Fatherless, once again. Growing up without a positive, permanent male role model or worse—a series of men coming in and out of her mother's bedroom." He looks over my shoulder and smirks. "As I understand it, that's not dissimilar to how the young women were living these past few years."

The sharp intake of breath from behind me tells me Piper is listening. I step into the man's personal space and give him a wolfish grin. "Marty, I don't care if Jesus Christ himself comes down and crowns you the new Messiah. If you ever, ever, disparage my fiancée or cast aspersions on her character again, I will rip your tongue out and shove it so far down your throat you'll be speaking your sermons out of your ass. Though I suspect that's probably where they come from anyway."

He turns red, his jowls vibrating as he sputters. "How dare you—"

"How dare you," I snarl.

I turn my back on him and help a stunned Piper into my car before walking around and getting in on the driver's side. Without looking back, I pull out of the Rosellis' driveway and wordlessly head to the ferry.

"Oh my God," Piper moans. She covers her eyes and leans her head against the window. "What did you just do?"

I snap a quick look at her. "What did I do? I defended your honor. I put that pompous ass in his place."

She laughs then, but there's not a trace of amusement in it. "You put him in his—God, Webb. You just provoked him. He'll go back to Lulu and tell her you threatened him. I need him on my side."

"He's never going to be on your side, Pip." I grip the wheel tightly, imagining it's the Pastor's neck. "He thinks this—you and me—is all for show."

"It is."

"But he doesn't know that for sure. And as long as he suspects we're not on the level, he's going to work against us. In the meantime, I'm not letting him call you—or Laura, in case you didn't catch the innuendo—whores."

She's quiet the rest of the way to the ferry. I show my ticket and pull onto the ramp to park when she speaks again. "Thank you. For defending me, but mostly for defending Laura. I think he's the reason her parents were so cold to her when she told them she was pregnant. Her mother is very religious, always has been, but it's been more intense since they retired."

I take her hand and tug so she's facing me. She tucks a long strand of taffy brown hair behind her ear. Her pale coral lips turn down at the corners. "It's going to be fine. We just need to remove any doubt in Lulu and Denny's minds about us. Then it won't matter what that blowhard says."

"And how are we going to do that?"

I lift my shoulders. "We get married."

Piper

"No. Absolutely not."

I carry Violet in her seat into the house. Webb follows close behind carrying her bag. "It would remove all doubt."

I set Violet down and spin on him. "Are you fu"--I dart a quick guilty glance at the baby--"flipping kidding me? We can't get married."

He shrugs. "Why not? As of last week, it's been 120 days since my divorce was declared final. Under Massachusetts law I am free to marry anyone I choose. Do you have a secret husband or something that would keep you from marrying me?"

"How about the fact I don't love you."

I unstrap Violet and take her out of her seat. She grabs on the ends of my hair and puts them in her mouth. I try to tug them out of her grasp, but it only results in her pulling even harder. "Ouch."

"Here, let me." Webb reaches over and carefully extricates my hair—most of it, anyway—from her little fists.

"Thank you," I say, readjusting her so she's facing out and can't as easily grab hold of me again. "She's probably hungry. She didn't finish her bottle on the ferry."

"I got it." Webb takes a fresh bottle out of the bag and goes into the kitchen. While he readies the formula, I sit on the sofa with the baby on my knees and mutter to myself. "Marry him. Is he crazy?"

Violet responds by blowing bubbles. I nod. "Exactly."

"Hear me out," he says, coming into the room and handing me the bottle. I position Violet in my arms and nod my chin at him.

"Fine. I'll hear you out before I say no again."

He sits on the coffee table facing me, our knees brushing together. "We can have a quickie marriage at the courthouse. We'll say we didn't want to put it off, especially for Violet's sake. By the end of the year, we'll split up, blaming getting married too fast as the reason."

It makes a perverted sort of sense, but there's no way I can marry Webb. I may not see marriage in the future for me, but I still believe it's a sacred institution and this would be mocking it. Not to mention how it would complicate this already convoluted lie we have going. "If we married, even for pretend, they would expect both our names on the adoption paperwork. Staying engaged, I can probably convince them not to add you since we're not legally together yet. What happens in six months when we split up. Share custody?"

He stares at Violet with a wistful smile and plays with her toes. "Of course not. She'd be yours. I'd sign over my rights."

I stare at Violet drinking from her bottle, and she stops sucking to smile at me. I would do anything for this little girl, but marrying Webb? It might be a step too far.

"I can't, Webb," I say, meeting his gaze. "It's very sweet of you to offer, but I can't make this lie worse."

He pushes up from the table. "I understand. You're probably right. It would only complicate everything even more. We'll find another way to get past Pastor Dick's reservations."

"His name's Marty."

"I said what I said." He winks at me. "When she's done eating, you want to take a walk downtown—hand-in-hand? No time like the present to go public with our, uh, engagement."

God, I'd almost forgotten we've involved the entire Isle in our little deception. At least the important people know—Tessa, Drew and Mara, Hayes. Drew is not happy with me. When I called to tell him last night, before Ruby or Pearl had a chance to fill him in, I had to hold the phone away from my ear. Webb had already gone back to his place and my windows were shut, so I was saved from the humiliation. I cringe thinking about how we left things. He's never been so angry with me and frankly, I'm pissed at him, too. He doesn't have to agree with what I'm doing, but he also doesn't have to make it sound like I'm committing felony murder. Mara assured me he just needed time, but I don't know. I have this sense I may have caused an irreparable rift in our friendship.

"Hey, Earth to Piper." Webb chuckles. "Where did you go?"

I shake my head. "Just thinking. Um, yeah. Let's take a walk."

Later, we're walking up the sidewalk leading to The Pier. I take a deep breath and clutch the stroller handle. "All right. Let's do this."

"Where to first?" Webb asks, peering around. There's a stiff breeze coming off the water, blowing his thick hair around his face. With his sunglasses and serious expression, he looks like a cologne model. I peek at his body. Maybe an underwear model.

"Beachcomber's Cafe," I say, bringing my attention back around. "It'll save us time—five minutes in there and the entire Isle will know. Even the hermits on Eastshore who keep to themselves."

He opens the door to the cafe and sweeps his hand, motioning me inside. The entire place stills as every head turns to look at us.

Bette taps the bell on the counter and shouts, "Congratulations, ya sneaky devils!"

Everyone claps, much to my mortification. I hadn't expected this much attention. Webb leans in close and whispers in my ear, "Guess the cat's out of the bag."

My teeth are clenched in what I hope is a believable smile. "You think?"

He guides us to a corner table where the umbrella stroller will be out of the way, his hand resting low on my back. Once I'm settled in my chair, he goes to the counter to place an order for us. I field half a dozen congratulatory greetings before he returns with our coffees and two pieces of banana bread, warmed and glistening with melted butter. Butter, sugar, and bananas make for a heady fragrance and I breathe it all in. My stomach grumbles. I hadn't eaten much at lunch thanks to nerves.

He nods at the bread. "On the house."

"Bette is too sweet," I say, breaking off a piece and popping it in my mouth. I sip my coffee while Webb makes sure Violet has her pacifier and blankie. My brows lift. "Six Splendas?"

His smile sparks a buzz in my stomach. "I was going to go with five since you said you were trying to cut it back, but I figured this was a six Splenda day."

"You remembered," I murmur.

"Of course."

A few other locals stop by our table to coo at the baby and offer us more congratulations. At one point, Webb takes my hand, and I lose myself in the sensation of his warmth, in the tingles from the tiny circles he's drawing on it with his thumb.

When Maisie jokes about how much we'll probably enjoy the

wedding night, Webb and I exchange a glance that stokes the heat growing between my thighs. His eyes darken, making the gold ring around his pupils more intense.

An older couple tells us their story about reconnecting and never forgetting the love of your life, and Webb shoots me a knowing look. I'm almost convinced of his sincerity and it strengthens the desperate need building inside. I don't know how platonic our arrangement will stay if this keeps up.

When we're left alone, I bring up the question that's been on my mind since lunch. "How did you come up with the proposal story so quickly?"

He wipes his mouth and shrugs. "It's a variation on how I proposed to Carolynn."

The fire goes out, leaving me cold and ashy inside. "Oh."

Stupid, stupid woman. For a few minutes I forgot this wasn't real.

"Hey," Webb whispers, leaning toward me and looking at me with concern. "What's wrong? I'm sorry. Is it because I mentioned Carolynn? Fuck, Piper, I didn't mean to—"

I wave him off and force a laugh. "No, it's fine. I was surprised because it sounded very romantic, perfect. I should've guessed it's because you'd actually done it before."

My face is hot, entering the hard crack stage, and I fuss with Violet to hide my embarrassment. It doesn't matter. It shouldn't matter. We're putting on an act, telling stories. It's a bonus he has some real-life experience to draw from. It's just that he's so good at making me forget it's fake.

"Pip," Webb says. "You should know the actual proposal wasn't nearly as romantic as you think. I only used the basics of it for our story. In reality, she was mad at me for waking her up so early to see the sunrise, and for suggesting the walk on the beach because the wind messed her hair. And the ring wasn't what she would've chosen for herself—at least not until I explained it'd been my grandmother's. Then of course its status as an heirloom superseded the old-fashioned cut and setting."

He tries to laugh it off and hide behind his cup, but it's plain to see the memory hurts and my own chipped ego is forgotten as I reach out to touch him. There's a zing, but unlike before, this one goes straight to my heart.

TWENTY-ONE

Piper

Lulu said Violet hadn't slept well the previous night, but she went down without a fuss and slept until six o'clock this morning. After accepting congratulations from nearly everyone it seemed, Webb and I walked the baby around the beach, making sure to share a peck on the lips whenever someone could be watching. If Hollis's PI was lurking around taking photos, we gave him a show. We were selling this new development in our relationship hard. By the time the sun began to set and we headed home, our bellies full of complimentary pizza from Gina and carrying a bottle of congratulatory champagne from cranky Mr. Beasley of all people, my mouth ached from keeping a delirious grin on my face all night.

Webb spent the night at his condo, which is a good thing because I'm quickly discovering my body can't be trusted. The last thing I need is to complicate this further with sex, no matter how good it promises to be.

Violet and I are dressed and breakfasted, and she's playing on the floor while I go over the proposal for Hudson Foods Drew emailed to me yesterday. There's a knock on my door and I expect to see Webb. But I'm not disappointed it's Tessa.

"Your door is locked," she says in lieu of a greeting.

"Good morning to you, too."

She comes in and shuts the door behind her. "You never lock your door."

I point to the baby. "I'm more careful with Violet around. Besides, I don't feel like hearing another lecture from Webb."

"How is your fiancé?" The grin on her face is both lascivious and mocking. I stick my tongue out at her. She laughs.

"Coffee?" I ask, already knowing the answer.

"God, yes. Please." She takes a seat and lays a folder on the table. "I come bearing good news. Or bad. Depends on your perspective, I suppose."

I pop a pod in the coffee maker and take out the creamer she keeps in my fridge for our coffee mornings. "Hold up, let me get Violet and then you can tell me."

I scoop the baby up, along with her blankie. It's a half panda, half chenille blanket and fits in her chubby hand. She loves that thing and it'll occupy her while we talk.

"All right," I say, settling into a chair. "Hit me with it. What did you find out?"

She opens the folder and slides it over to me. I peruse the contents, not sure what I'm reading. "Is this a police report?"

"Uh huh." She sips her coffee and groans in approval. Then she taps the top page with an artfully manicured finger.

"That, my friend, is a police report about a fire that occurred in the Whitley's neighbor's garage about two months ago."

My eyes widen. "They think Hollis set the fire?"

"Not her," she says, hiding a sly smile behind her mug.

"Aaron?" I believe the guy is possibly a predator, a perv at least, but an arsonist? It would mean getting his own perfectly manicured nails dirty.

"Try the little Whitleys."

"No," I gasp. "The oldest is only twelve! How can that be?"

"They're little hoodlums." She sets her cup down. "That

camp they were at a couple of weeks ago? It was an outdoor boot camp for troubled youth. Participation in it was part of the plea deal, along with restitution that Mommy and Daddy will be paying."

I shake my head. "Wow. I thought maybe, given who their parents are, they might end up being assholes-in-training. But felons?"

"I'm still poking around. But this is a good start, right?"

"Yeah, it's a great start."

I kiss the top of Violet's head. "I don't know if this is enough to convince Lulu, especially if Pastor Marty has any sway—which he does. His influence runs deep, and he's obviously on Hollis's side. What if Violet ends up adopted by them? What might these kids do to her?"

"So you'll take this to the Rosellis?"

I reread the report and shake my head. "Not yet. I need more. But there is something I can do. I have the feeling Lulu and Denny's reservations about me adopting Violet are strictly on what they see are 'moral failings,' like not being married."

"Yeah, but the engagement to Webb should take care of that."

"I'm not so sure." I fill her in on what happened yesterday and Pastor Marty's clear bias toward Hollis. "He has their ear, Tessa. That's what I'm competing with."

She leans across the table. "So what are you thinking of doing?"

Violet chews on the panda head, little gurgling noises coming out of her mouth. "Whatever I have to do to keep her safe."

WEBB COMES OVER FOR A LATE DINNER. HE HAD A LONG DAY, starting with informing his partners of our engagement and ending with breaking the news to his best friend and parents. From the look on his face, it didn't go well.

"Where's the baby?" he says after we greet each other and he steps inside.

"Upstairs. She conked out right after her bottle."

"Oh," he says, sounding disappointed. He hangs his leather jacket on the rack in the entryway. He's dressed casually tonight, a sight I'm not used to but one I truly appreciate. Dark-wash denim jeans cling to his thick thighs and highlight how perfect his ass is. He's holding a plastic bag and wearing a black T-shirt with a cartoon slice of pizza in the center of the chest and the phrase, "...And I'm gonna keep it" written underneath. Il Pomodoro Dolce's logo is printed over his heart.

"Love the shirt," I say with a laugh. "Little weird, though."

"That's because it's supposed to go with this one." He tosses me the bag and I open it to find a similar shirt, this one with a whole pizza minus one slice in the center of it and the words, "He stole a pizza my heart..." emblazoned over it.

I put a hand to my mouth. "Aw, this is so sweet."

"They're from Gina. I stopped in earlier to grab a slice and she congratulated me. Well, us, I mean."

"You eat there an awful lot," I say, folding the shirt and hanging it over the stair railing so I'll remember to take it up later. "Those killer abs of yours are going to start to suffer."

He cocks an eyebrow. "Killer abs, huh?"

I roll my eyes. "It's an objective fact—you're hot. Doesn't mean anything more."

"Mm-hm." He pats his stomach, where I can attest his abs are not suffering—yet. "Well, I might love pizza more than I love having a six-pack."

"Can't say I blame you." I pat my own belly. "I love my pizza more than acquiring a six-pack."

He tugs on my braid. "You don't need a six-pack. You're perfect as you are."

My heart flutters and I forget what I am about to say. "Thank you," I say on a breath.

He meets my gaze again, and my heart trips once more at the goofy grin on his lips. "It's an objective fact."

Is it getting warm in here? I take a step back, out of the orbit of his spicy scent so I can drag in a normal breath. "Dinner isn't pizza, but it's Italian."

He lifts his nose. "Smells wonderful, whatever it is."

"Melanzane di Parmigiana." I lead him into the kitchen where the eggplant dish is warming in the oven. The table is already set, Mr. Beasley's champagne popped and chilling in an ice bucket off to the side, next to a bouquet of purple roses courtesy of Paloma.

Webb fingers one of the petals. I nod my chin at the arrangement. "Another congratulatory gift."

He laughs. "Boy, we're cleaning up here."

"I know. I feel bad." I bite the inside of my cheek. It's true, I hate lying to my friends.

"It's for a good cause."

"I know." I carry the dish to the table, reminding myself the end justifies the means. I suppose my Machiavelli score has gone up and after tonight, it'll get even higher.

Webb is uncharacteristically quiet as we eat. My pulse pounds in my ears, and I lay a hand on my knee to try to keep my leg from bouncing. "So, how did your phone calls go?"

"I told Graeme the truth. I couldn't keep this up without his help. He thinks I'm nuts, but he promised not to tell Tish or anyone else. He's on board so long as it helps the business."

"What about your partners? How did they take the news?"

"Very well. They know we have history, so it wasn't completely out of the blue. I'm sure they suspect something, but they didn't ask too many questions."

"And your parents?"

He stabs at the eggplant with a little more force than necessary. "As expected."

It's not hard to guess what he means. "I'm sure it's a shock to tell them you're engaged so soon after your divorce. And to someone they never met."

"Yeah, sure." There something in his tone saying there's more to it.

My curiosity gets the better of me. "What did they say?"

He refuses to meet my eyes. "It's not important."

I decide not to push it; his parents are a sore spot and poking it won't make what I'm about to say any easier. I push my plate away and take a fortifying breath. "I talked to Tessa today. She has more information about Hollis."

Briefly, I fill him in about the young arsonists. His face flushes with anger. "You have to tell the Rosellis. There's no way in hell Violet can go with those people."

"I don't know if it's enough," I say with a shrug. "Like I told Tessa, Pastor Marty has a lot of influence, and he's firmly in Hollis's court. I think you're right and we need to remove any doubt about the future."

"So what are you saying?"

"We should get married, officially." I lean across the table. "Only if you're still up to it. If your parents are giving you a hard time, I don't want to make it worse."

Webb grunts, one side of his mouth quirking into a rueful grin. "Can't possibly."

He stares down at his plate, obviously bothered. "What did your parents say, Webb?"

He inhales a long breath through his nose, then looks up at me. "They completely believe the engagement story, and they'll believe we're getting married for real."

"That's a bad thing?" I force a short laugh.

"They believe it because they also believe I must have been cheating on Carolynn, and I left her to be with you." He pinches the bridge of his nose. "Ironic. Of course, I never told them it was Carolynn who cheated and no way she ever would have mentioned it."

Guilt, or maybe shame, slices through me. It shouldn't matter what anyone thinks, but my stomach turns at the thought anyone considers me a homewrecker. Webb must read my face, because he scoots his chair closer and reaches out to touch my cheek.

"Hey," he says, his thumb sliding along the side of my face. "They don't matter, Pip. What they believe doesn't matter. Whatever we have to do for Violet, right?"

"But it's a huge deal, Webb. And it only serves my purposes, not yours." I put my hand over his. "If this risks your relationship with your family, we shouldn't do it."

"I don't have a relationship with them. They had me to save Philip, I failed. They wanted me to become Philip, and I failed there, too. As far as they're concerned, I've failed them at every turn. But I'm not going to fail you.

"Violet belongs with you. You're loving, loyal, protective. That's what Violet's going to need and no stranger, especially not that cousin of Laura's, can give that to her. Yes, I will do this for you, but it doesn't only serve you or me. I want to do whatever I can for that little girl and to honor Laura."

I blink back against the wetness filling my eyes. "Thank you, Webb."

When he smiles at me, the tension drains away, replaced by an unfamiliar hope and optimism...and something more dangerous. My pulse ratchets up. I can't go there again with him, no matter how badly my body wants it, not when there's still something so huge between us.

"If we go through with this, we will not be engaging in all the usual matrimonial duties."

"Matrimonial duties? You mean like divvying up the chores?" I'm glad to see his humor return.

"You know what I mean." I stab a tomato and point it at him. "Sex. We keep the ground rules intact."

"I can honestly say, in my experience, there's less sex to be had after marriage than before. Since we're having zero right now, I think it's safe to say it isn't a worry. Not for me at least."

He lifts his drink to his mouth, then pauses. "Of course, I've never been married to you, Pip."

TWENTY-TWO

Webb

It was an amazing meal. I'm still stealing bites while I help her clean up, and she smacks my hand with a laugh. Her nervous energy seems to have dissipated, maybe because of the champagne we finished or because taking this final step is a relief. Or maybe because this whole thing is absurd.

She brews us a couple cups of coffee, and we retire to her living room. I set my cup on a coaster and look around. I love this little cottage of hers. It's not much different in design from Hayes's house, but the decor is all Piper. Warm, neutral colors with pops of vibrant color in unexpected places. Like the bright scarlet sofa sitting amidst a palette of light slate blue walls and creamy white curtains. Throw pillows and blankets are tossed casually on the furniture and a low-rise built-in bookcase holds well-loved books and sundry tacky trinkets from far-flung places like Vegas and Kenosha. It's a home, vastly different from the sterile house I grew up in and the modern minimalist decor of the house I shared with Carolynn.

I'm drawn to the framed photos arranged on the ash wood mantle, particularly one of a small child holding a fish as big as she is, a grinning man crouched behind looking at her and not the camera. Had to be Piper and her dad. Another photo shows Piper and Laura with matching brace-filled smiles and decked out in ski gear, a stamp in the corner proclaiming the location as Stowe. There's a photo of Laura in a hospital bed holding a newborn Violet, Tessa on one side and Piper on the other, and I have to swallow against the lump in my throat. All three women beam at the camera, even Laura with her tired eyes. There are a few more photos, but my eye is drawn to the bi-fold frame on the end.

On one side, the three women in matching rose pink mini-dresses and covered in glitter hold up glasses of champagne or wine. On the other are the same three in graduation gowns, arms linked and laughing. I have my own photo, only with Hayes and Graeme; Piper hadn't even looked at me that day. I pick it up and stare down at the two photos, focus squarely on the short brunette. In the newer photo, her mocha eyes sparkle. Her graduation photo shows those same eyes to be flat, dull. I'd broken up with her less than a week prior. It sickens me knowing I took her sparkle away on what should've been one of the happiest days of her life. Right here and now, I vow to never disappoint her again.

"We were the Powerpuff Girls." Piper stands next to me and takes the photo from my hands, a slight sad curve to her mouth. "But Blossom is gone and now it's just Bubbles and me."

I'm not familiar with the show beyond knowing it's a cartoon starring three superhero girls. But I understand the bond she alludes to. I point to the newer photo of them. "What's going on here? You look like Vegas backup singers."

She laughs. "You got Vegas right, but it was for the wedding of a mutual friend. It was the last time all of us were together before Violet was born... about nine months later."

I whistle. "Is that where Laura met Violet's father?"

"Yes, but that's all she would say. She disappeared one night, texted us about some hot Air Force pilot she'd met, and said she'd see us later. She never talked about it, and she never confirmed she got pregnant on that trip, but it was kind of obvious."

I nod at the Vegas photo. "I always thought you'd be happily married with half a dozen children. Laura, too. Not Tessa, though."

The corner of her mouth tightens, then she chortles. "Irony of ironies… Tessa is the only one of us three to actually get hitched. It didn't last but a couple quick years, but it was intense. Laura and I joked we'd be spinsters together until Violet came along."

"Never met the right person?" I'm prying, probably far too curious for my own good.

The pinch to her features belies her casual shrug. "My mother settled for the first man to promise her the world, and even though he tried, she realized much too late it wasn't what she wanted. I was eight when she left, and I didn't understand it then, but I do now. If you settle for anything less than true happiness, you'll never be satisfied, and then you end up with heartaches all around. I especially never wanted to bring a child into the world if there was a chance of that happening."

Her voice breaks off. I wait for her to continue as she replaces the frame on the mantle. "I've had a few serious relationships, even one I could almost see going the distance. In the end, they always proved I was right to hold back. None of them stuck. It was hard to find anyone I believed in enough to make me really happy."

"There was no one?"

She lifts her chin and stares at me with dark pools of grief. "Maybe once," she whispers.

Loathing settles heavy in my chest, making it difficult to breathe. My throat is tight, and I strain to say something, but I can only squeeze out her name. Like a prayer, a plea for forgiveness.

She turns, her proud profile set in stone. "It's all turned out for the best. I'd rather be alone for the right reasons than with someone for the wrong ones."

Reflexively, I wrap my arms around her and bury my nose in her hair. She tenses, but thank God she lets me hold her because my knees are so weak at the moment, if I let go of her I'll fall to the ground. I inhale the heady scent of sugar and sweet pea as I cling to her.

"Piper, I never meant to hurt you," I murmur against her head. "I swear to God I thought I was doing the right thing. I thought you would move on, find someone a million times better than me. It wouldn't have been hard."

She doesn't speak, doesn't move, doesn't relax. I keep going, telling her everything I should've told her before. "You were— are—an amazing woman. Kind, smart, sexy as fuck…any man who can't recognize the treasure you are doesn't deserve you. And that includes me. I didn't deserve you back then, I don't think I deserve you now."

I kiss the top of her head lightly. "But I'd like the chance to try."

Her chest rises and falls in a rapid rhythm. Under my chin, her head moves back and forth. "I can't go there again, Webb. I —I just—I can't."

I close my eyes and breathe in one last time before I let go and step back. She spins to face me, her lips drawn down, her eyes full of apology. My mouth twists in a sad smile. "I get it."

"If you can't go through with our plan, I understand," she says, her voice wobbly.

"Oh, hell no," I assure her, curving my lips into a dazzler that's all show and no substance. I'm hoping she can't tell the difference. "This was never about you and me. It's about Violet and making sure she ends up where she's meant to be. With you."

I can't help but think how that's where I was meant to end up once upon a time, if I hadn't fucked it all up so royally. Maybe with a little time and patience and a hand from fate, I can fix this, once and for all. Whether I deserve it or not, I want a second chance with Piper. I need a second chance. Because she's it for me. I just need to persuade her to believe I'm it for her.

I jerk my head to the sofa. "Come on. Let's sit and work out the details."

AN AWKWARD HOUR LATER, WE'VE DECIDED ON A DATE THREE DAYS from now for the wedding, that only Hayes and Tessa will attend, and we'll tell everyone when they ask it's so sudden because we didn't want to waste any more time. I shoot Graeme a quick text with an update, then turn my phone off. I'll deal with him tomorrow.

Piper clears her throat. "Earlier, you said we'd probably need to stay married for at least six months so we don't raise suspicions. Do you think that's still a good timeline?"

Depends on how long it takes me to convince her to stay with me. "Let's plan on that as a minimum, but then play it by ear."

"I guess—," she chews on her bottom lip. "You'll have to be on the adoption papers."

I sit back. "I hadn't thought about that. It would look weird if I wasn't, and besides, the Rosellis may not agree to the adoption if it's not the both of us."

"Shit." She drops her head in her heads and growls. "I can't ask you to also take on fatherhood for the rest of your life."

"Why not?" I say lightly, though I'm seriously interested in the answer. Maybe she doesn't think I'd be a good father and damn… that hurts.

She lifts her head up and stares off to the side, playing with the ends of her hair. "I just pictured raising Violet on my own.

No offense, Webb, but I don't have much of a track record with reliable partners, and it started with you."

"Guess I can't argue with that." Regret punches me in the heart.

I put my hand on her leg. "What if I have my lawyer draw up a prenup that grants you all parental rights? No one but us needs to know about it. Would it give you peace of mind, knowing I can't take Violet away from you?"

Her face flushes. "When you put it like that, I sound like a total bitch."

I shake my head. "Not even. I understand, Piper. I've let you down before and while I promise I'm not going to hurt you again, if signing a prenup will ease your mind, I'll do it. I'll tattoo it on my ass if you want me to."

She laughs. "A prenup on your ass? Not sure that'd be legally binding."

"But it'd look good." I smile, grateful for the break in tension. "So what else needs to happen?"

We spend another half hour going over the logistics. It's nearly eleven by the time we finish. We agree to meet at the courthouse in the morning to get the license, and I begin making my exit. She follows me to the entryway, where I grab my jacket off the rack next to the door. "So I'll see you tomorrow."

"Webb," she says. I stop with my hand on the knob and lift a brow, waiting for her to continue. She darts her tongue out and licks her top lip, and I can't help but follow the movement. I can't help a lot of things when it comes to her.

Her eyes flick to the side and she's folded in on herself. "I need to tell you I'm sorry, too. And I'm more grateful than I can say for what you're doing for me now."

I drop my hand on the knob and face her. "There's nothing for you to apologize for, okay? And I've already told you, marrying you isn't a hardship. Violet needs you and this is no sacrifice to make sure she has you."

The lines around her mouth deepen, her eyes full of shadows. She closes them briefly and opens them again. "I wish…"

Her voice trails off. I swipe a loose bang off her forehead and tuck it behind her ear, tracing the outer edge with my finger before I pull it back. "I know," I whisper. I bend my head and kiss the side of her mouth. Her warm sigh fans out against my face as I linger there, lips ghosting above her mouth, drinking in her sugary scent, the taste of coffee on her breath. "I know," I repeat.

Reluctantly, I pull back, but not too far before she fists my shirt and drags me back to her. On tiptoes, she leans into me and crushes her mouth against mine. I drop my jacket and grasp her head in my hands, angling it to where I can get the deepest access. I'm not going to question this quick change of heart, and I sure as hell am going to enjoy it.

She opens her mouth to invite me in, her tongue tangoing with mine, both of us frenzied. Her hands wrap around my hips and pull me into her. The long, thick ridge of my dick presses against her stomach and I swallow her moan, releasing her face to slide my hands around her back and down to palm her high, round ass.

I squeeze, knead, rock against her while our mouths continue their dance…teeth nipping, lips sucking. Her heart beats in tune with my heart, her tongue swirls in time with my tongue, her need pulses in rhythm with my need. It's been so long, so fucking long, since I've felt this out of control, this hungry, this right. I nip at her ear, lick the salty-sweet skin under her jaw, suck on the curve of her neck, all while her hands roam across my chest and under my shirt, my cock growing with every breathy whimper.

I'm pushing us toward the living room, needing to lay her down so I can properly explore every delectable inch of her, when the baby monitor squawks to life. We freeze, our gazes locked as if we're both thinking the same thing; if we don't move, don't even breathe, she'll go back to sleep and we'll go back to—

A piercing wail cuts through the air. Piper wriggles out of my arms with an apologetic grimace. "I'm sorry."

I shoo at her, trying to calm my ragged breaths. "No, go. Don't worry about me."

She hesitates, but Violet's not having it and more crying comes through the speaker. She dashes up the stairs while I attempt to cool myself down. I lean on the wall and laugh to myself. Piper may insist on this marriage not being real, but it doesn't get any more real than when you're cockblocked by your infant.

TWENTY-THREE

Piper

When I dropped Violet off at the Rosellis, I let them know Webb and I were going to have a simple, private ceremony that Friday. Lulu was happier than I've seen her since the funeral. She insisted on hosting it in their backyard if we wouldn't mind moving it to Saturday to give Lulu more time to set it up. Lulu had offered for Pastor Marty to officiate, but that was a nonstarter. I don't even want the man to be there. Instead, I asked Letitia at the clerk's office if she would mind making the short trip to the mainland to do the deed. If I'd stopped to think about it for a hot minute, I would've found someone not on the Isle so the date of our wedding wouldn't become public knowledge. The less scrutiny, the better.

Webb and I haven't talked about the kiss since it happened. THE KISS. It feels as though any reference to it should be in all caps, because it was more than just the fusing of our lips together. It was the start of something that cannot happen. I'd like to be able to separate my heart and my libido, but it's not possible with Webb. It never was.

"Damn it," I mutter.

Tessa looks back at me. She's insisted on taking me out to buy a wedding dress, though I've told her there is no way in hell I am spending more than $100 and there will not be any crinoline, bows, trains, veils, or poufy sleeves. So here we are at a boutique in Newport, looking through racks of sundresses.

"Not finding anything?"

"What?" I answer, momentarily confused because I've only absently been browsing the shop. "Oh, no. I mean, honestly I've not been looking too hard. I have a perfectly serviceable dress in my closet, the one I wore to Drew and Mara's wedding."

She looks down her nose at me. "You are not wearing to your wedding the same dress you wore to your ex-boyfriend's wedding to another woman. It's bad luck. Besides, they were married in November. You can't wear jewel tones in the spring."

I sigh and half-heartedly flip through the hangers, but nothing catches my eye. Everything is either too frilly or too flowery or too beige. I like bold colors, hence the teal and electric purple logo for Sugarbreakers, but this shop screams coastal grandmother chic. Pretty, but not me.

We thank the saleswoman and exit the shop empty-handed. Tessa puts on her sunglasses for the walk up the block to the next store. "All right, spill it."

"Spill what?"

"I know you're nervous about this whole thing, which is understandable," she says, looping her arm through mine. "But your mind is a million miles away and you keep muttering to yourself. What did Webb do that has you all in knots?"

When I look at her in surprise, she laughs. "Oh, honey. This is how you were in college when a guy had you all twisted up. Granted, it was mostly Webb back then and this has his handiwork written all over it. So what did he do now?"

"He kissed me," I admit, my neck turning red at the memory. "I mean, kissed me-kissed me."

"Interesting."

"That's all you have to say? Interesting?"

She scoffs. "You are marrying the guy. Frankly, I expected a little more from you."

"More? I shouldn't have even gone that far. And if it weren't for Violet waking up, it might have gone even farther and I'd be more of a wreck."

"Why?" Tessa guides me off the sidewalk to sit on a small bench. "You said you guys talked things out and agreed to put the past behind you completely. I get it if you don't want to give him a second chance at a relationship, this upcoming marriage of convenience notwithstanding. But Piper, there's nothing wrong with having a little fun."

"There is when I haven't been completely honest with him." Another flush creeps up my neck, but for an entirely different reason. "There's no point in telling him about the baby if we're not going to be together for real. If we were to take this relationship seriously, I would have to. I couldn't keep something that big from him. And then if I told him, what's to say he wouldn't walk out on me? He might end up hating me for not telling him sooner, especially after everything that happened with Carolynn."

Tessa puts her arm around me. "The two of you made that baby together, it's not like you were on your own there. And what happened wasn't your fault."

"Wasn't it, though?" I had been so ambivalent about what to do the first few weeks and then even after I decided I was keeping it, I had a hard time enjoying it. I'd barely come to terms with the little bean sprouting inside of me before it was gone. Maybe I hadn't loved it soon enough. Laura said that was crazy talk, but what did she know? She loved Violet from the moment the second line appeared on the test.

"It wasn't," Tessa says in a firm voice. "I think you do need to tell Webb, though. You shouldn't have to bear this horrible memory on your own."

"And what if I tell him and you're right, he doesn't hate me for keeping this secret? But now he feels even guiltier for what he did and decides he owes it to me to stick around, like he did with Carolynn." I shake my head. "I don't want that. We've agreed to do this marriage thing for at least six months after the adoption is final and then go our separate ways. I just need to keep my lips and my hands and my thoughts to myself."

I stand, finished with this conversation lest I turn into a sopping, blubbery mess on the sidewalk. "Now, let's go find me a dress."

TESSA IS PUSHY, BUT THAT'S WHY I LOVE HER. SHE NIXED THE bright pink floral maxi dress I found, and I have to admit she was right because the one she came up with is spectacular. A strapless fitted A-line with a swing skirt in light-peach with a bright olive-green ribbon belt reminiscent of Webb's eyes. Best of all—it has pockets. I even find a dress in the same green with a white rosebud pattern for Violet.

We stop by Paloma's on the way home and compromise on a bouquet of wildflowers instead of fancy roses or lilies, even though my suggestion I carry a bouquet of flower-shaped lollipops is serious and, whether she likes it or not, still on the table.

"I guess that's everything," I say. I dart a glance at my shop door. Drew and Mara have been taking care of Sugarbreakers for me this week. Mara's been keeping me up to date with sales and inventory, not that there's much to say. I think she's trying to make up for the silent treatment I'm getting from Drew, who, aside from an email meeting reminder about the Hudson Foods proposal, hasn't acknowledged my existence since I broke the news about the impending wedding.

"Listen, do you mind dropping the dresses off at the house for me?" I ask Tessa. "I haven't been in the shop in a few days."

"Sure."

Pearl is at the register, while Mara is busy in the kitchen making her famous mint meltaways. "He's out back," she says by way of greeting, her sympathetic smile not giving me the warm fuzzies. He's sweeping up the little patio when I walk outside. I wait for him to acknowledge me, to say something, but he's focused solely on the task at hand. I rub my arms against the cold, even though it's not the air giving me a chill. Drew's freeze-out could give a penguin frostbite.

"Hey," I finally say when it becomes apparent he's not going to make the first move.

He dumps the sweepings into the dumpster through the side hatch and then looks at me. I point to the lid that has been secured with plastic zip ties. "Hope that keeps the damn sky rats out. They seem worse this year."

"It's the wind. Keeps flipping the lid up and inviting them to feast." As if summoned, a breeze kicks up, blowing his black curls into a tangled array around his head. But he doesn't move. He simply stares at me, clutching the broom and dustpan in one hand like a standard bearer, jaw muscles clenching and unclenching. The wind sets my ponytail swinging and I tug it back into place, trying to decide what to say next.

He takes the decision out of my hands. "What are you doing, Piper?"

I don't pretend not to know what he's talking about, but I do take umbrage at his gruff tone. "I'm doing what I have to for Violet."

He huffs out a breath and shakes his head. "Right. This is all for Violet. You're compromising your integrity, deceiving the people who love you, setting yourself up for another fall—and it's just for Violet."

I set my hands on my hips and lift my chin. "That's right. I will do anything to save her. I told you what Tessa discovered. If she goes to Hollis, she could be hurt, or worse."

He takes a step toward me. "So then go to Laura's parents and tell them. Show them what Tessa found. It's not too late to call off this bullshit."

"Shh." I look around, but I don't see anyone in earshot. Still, I move closer and lower my voice. "Hollis might have her own PI snooping around."

He tosses the broom down and tilts his head to the sky, muttering under his breath. I've never seen Drew look like this in the ten years I've known him. His face is a rolling thundercloud of emotion—anger, sadness, disappointment. It's the last one that has my eyes prickling.

"You're willfully putting your life in the hands of that son of a bitch who almost destroyed you once. What's going to happen when he does it again?"

My nostrils flare. "It's not like that. This is solely transactional. No feelings are involved."

Drew laughs, but there's not a trace of warmth or humor in it. "You really believe that?"

I lift a shoulder. "Why shouldn't I?"

"Because, Piper, he's manipulating you. God." He puts his hands on top of his head and stares at the ground. "I thought you were smarter than that."

"Excuse me?" I grind out from my clenched teeth.

His head whips up. "He used you once before until he got bored with you. He's doing it again and it pisses me off that you can't see it."

"First of all, we're using each other. Second, you don't know what you're talking about. He didn't leave me because he was bored."

"Oh no? Then why did he leave you pregnant and alone to go back to his ex-girlfriend?"

I'm so stunned he threw that in my face, all I can eke out is a meager, "He didn't know I was pregnant. Besides, it's none of your business."

"Right. Until you need me to pick up the pieces. Again." His lip curls in disgust. "I knew the moment you told me about him you still carried a torch. It may have dimmed over the years, but the second he set foot on this Isle, that motherfucker roared to life. You haven't fallen in love again. You're still in love. And you're about to play out your wildest fantasy."

I rear back from the slap of his words. "It's not true."

"I won't do it, Piper. I can't. If you go through with this sham of a marriage, don't expect me to be around when it all comes crashing down on you. When Webb Duncan stomps all over your heart again."

"It's not going to happen. I won't let it."

The look on his face is pure pity and I'd like to claw it right off him. He's one of my best friends, but right now I hate him— even more than I hated Webb back then. "You can't help it, Piper, and I can't stop you. But I can wash my hands of it. I have my own family, now, to take care of."

He walks past me. I jump when the door behind me slams shut, and another person I love abandons me.

TWENTY-FOUR

Webb

I can't stop thinking about Piper's body. It's softer, curvier, and even sexier than I remember. The other night when she was plastered against me, I could hardly breathe for the want coursing through me. When our lips joined, every nerve ending stood straight up, jolted by an electric prod—along with my cock. The way it nudged perfectly in the notch between her thighs has fueled my fantasies the past two nights. It was all I could do to keep my hands above her waist the last time I saw her at the town hall while we applied for our marriage license.

I'm glad Laura's mom convinced Piper to have the wedding in their backyard instead of at the town hall. Whatever the reasons behind the wedding, Piper deserves a special day. It won't be as grand as the one Carolynn and I shared, and that's a good thing. A hundred grand for a fancy party is ridiculous, and if I'm being honest, that wedding was no more real than this one. Less so, because how I feel about Piper is truer than I ever felt about Carolynn. If only Piper felt the same, it'd be the most perfect day.

My partners want to support me, so they'll be in attendance. Graeme, who still thinks I'm nuts, wants to come down with Tish. Hayes and Tessa will be there, but Piper hasn't said anything about her other friends. She hasn't mentioned her mother, but I assume she isn't flying in from L.A. Meanwhile, I did extend an invite to my parents, but as suspected, they have some made-up event they can't miss.

I'm leaving Beachcomber's after arranging a surprise from Bette when I see Piper scarpering down The Pier toward the beach. I call out to her.

She pauses on the steps leading to the sand and looks back at me, then continues on down. I take off at a run, horrified by what I see on her face. She's pale and shaky, her eyes rimmed with red. I gather her into my arms, tugging her off the main path to rest against the pilings holding the pier up.

Her arms wrap around my waist and she buries her face in my chest. I hold her like that until her quiet sobs subside, resting my cheek against the top of her head. "Do you want to talk about it?"

She sniffles and sucks in a breath, then another and another, until she's able to answer. "No. Just a stupid fight."

"With who?" I frown down at her. "Who made you cry, so I can go kick their ass?"

She huffs. "It's not important. Just a spat between friends."

"Was it Drew?" I put a finger under her chin and tilt her face up. Her eyes skitter to the side, before coming back to rest on mine. I grimace. "He doesn't like me."

"He and I dated a long time ago, before we decided we were better off as friends." She sniffles again. "He knows about—us—our history. He thinks I'm making a mistake by marrying you, even though I've tried to tell him it's just an arrangement. There's nothing more."

The pang from her pronouncement is fleeting but hurts all the same. It's also not sitting well with me that he's her ex-boyfriend and trying to warn her off of me. What's his ulterior motive?

"He doesn't matter," I say, ducking to catch Piper's eyes. "Only Violet matters. She's who we're doing this for and if he was a real friend, he'd understand."

"Don't," she says, shaking her head.

"Don't what?"

She draws in a shaky breath. "He's one of my closest friends. He was there for me…when I needed someone. He's always supported me, until now. So please don't say he doesn't matter or he's not a real friend."

"Okay," I say, chastened and irked at the same time.

Jealousy rips through me, but my breath remains even, and I pretend to be unbothered when I drape an arm across her shoulders and walk her onto the sand with me. She kicks off her sandals and I pause to slip off my loafers and socks. It gives me a chance to ask the question I've been pondering for two days without having to make eye contact.

"So, about the other night," I begin, tucking my socks into my shoes.

She folds her arms and looks out toward the water. Her voice is clear of tears, but still a touch raspy. "What about it?"

I straighten and attempt to put my arm across her shoulders again, but she's put too much distance between us now. I swallow back a silent oath and let my arm drop. *It was pretty fucking amazing, that's what.* "We let ourselves get carried away."

"Yeah."

I steal a glance at her profile. She continues to stare out at the water, her eyes reflecting the diamonds of light bouncing off the surface. Her cheeks are flushed, which could be because of her crying jag or it could be something else. I'm hoping like hell it's because she's thinking of our kiss the way I am.

"Do you think we could let ourselves get carried away again?" A corner of my mouth tips into a smirk.

She side-eyes me, her gaze dropping my mouth. "It's not a good idea."

"I don't know. Seemed like a fantastic idea the other night."

She unfolds her arms and flips her ponytail forward over her shoulder to play with the end. "Don't you think this is all complicated enough without adding sex into the mix?"

"No," I answer truthfully. "I don't think sex will make things worse, in fact, it'll probably make it better. I'm not being facetious," I quickly add when she rolls her eyes at me. "I mean it. Think about all this tension between us right now. We could relieve a lot of it."

"So, sex as stress relief? Is that what you're suggesting?"

"It's also fun. So yes, I'm suggesting we do it to relieve stress and have fun. Once we're married, Pip, I plan on staying faithful —for however long you'll have me. But I guess I shouldn't assume the same is true for you. Maybe you still want to be free to play the field?"

She laughs. "I'm not about to parade a bunch of men in and out of my bedroom after we say *I do*. Did you forget we live on a very small island?"

I reach for her hand and pull her to a stop. "Is that the only reason? Because nothing's stopping you from heading to the mainland to find a warm body."

Her eyes narrow. "Is that what you would do?"

A huff of frustration escapes my mouth. "I already said I wouldn't. I only want one woman, Piper. I want you. And I don't think I'm being presumptuous in thinking you want me, too. All I'm saying is—if we want each other, why don't we let ourselves have each other."

"It's not that simple," she murmurs.

I draw her into my body and bend my head to whisper in her ear. "But it is. Let me show you."

MY BLOOD IS THICK AND HOT, PULSING IN MY VEINS AND FILLING my cock to painful lengths. The door to her bungalow is barely closed before my arms wrap around her and my mouth finds her throat. Her skin vibrates under my lips from the breathy moans she makes, I swear on purpose, just to drive me crazy. I nip at her neck, my hands yank on her ponytail and when she squawks I freeze in place.

"Did I hurt you?" I smooth my hand down the back of her head.

She claws at my shoulders, her nails biting into me, even though my shirt. "Yes," she breathes. "Do it again."

With a growl, I slant my lips over hers and tug on her hair again, swallowing her gasps. I back her against the wall next to the foyer table, grinding against her as I take and take and take, her fingers clutching my hair, mouth as hungry as mine. She bites my ear; I suck on her neck. Her fingers start working the buttons on my shirt, my own sliding into the waistband of her pants, delighting when they skim across a bare ass. I can't wait to get her naked. I have to get her naked.

She opens half my shirt and presses her hot mouth against my skin, flicking a hard nipple with her tongue. I glide my hand to her front and finding her wet, I nearly lose it. With a low growl, I slide one finger into her heat. She bucks against me and I chuckle.

"You like that?" I lick the shell of her ear.

"More," she whimpers, digging her nails into my shoulders and arching under my touch.

I'm happy to comply. I slide a second finger into her, needing to remove the pants that are limiting my movement, but unwilling to take my hands off her. Another second or two, just a little more. She clenches around my fingers and I'm done for. These pants are coming off. I remove my hand and grin at her small moan of protest. "I'm not done with you yet. See what you do to me?"

Her eyes are dark as midnight as she watches me lick her taste off my fingers and press against her. A vibration rolls through me, then another, and when she reaches between us, I'm so ready for her to release my pulsating hardness and take me in her soft hands. But she doesn't reach for my fly or the bulge straining against her. She dips her hand into her pocket and removes her cell phone, going still at the sight of her screen.

Aria.

"It's my mother. I have to take this," she says, squeezing out from under me. I collapse into the empty space left by her, banging my head against the wall. I'm too breathless to argue, my ardor not yet getting the message we've taken a time-out. A painful, but hopefully short time-out.

She takes a deep breath and answers, though to my ears she still sounds out of breath. To her mother's, too, apparently.

"I was just, er, running," she says into the phone, drifting a quick guilty glance at me before ducking into the kitchen.

I stand there waiting for my pulse to normalize, trying to wrap my head around what just happened. Not the greedy way her body responded to my touch or the complete lack of control on my part. She answered her phone. She put a stop to things to talk to her mother, a woman she barely has a relationship with. *Where does that leave me if she'd rather take a call from her than make out with me?*

With a bruised ego and a raging case of blue balls, that's where.

TWENTY-FIVE

Piper

My mother wastes no time explaining the reason behind her call.

"You're getting married?"

I wince and check over my shoulder to see if Webb heard the shriek. His head rests against the wall with his eyes closed, chest heaving as hard as mine, and an impressive swell in his pants. Silently, I both curse and thank my mother for the interruption. I was on the verge of making a big mistake.

"Piper? Are you there? Why are you panting?"

"I was," I take a breath, "running"--she wouldn't know the only running I do is a tab at The Seahorse--"and how are you, Aria?"

"I was fine until I heard from a complete stranger that my own daughter is getting married!"

I walk through the kitchen and huddle with my phone by the side door. "It just happened a few days ago. I hadn't had the time to call you."

"You didn't have a minute to send a text?"

"It seemed impersonal." Of course, that was how she informed me of her last marriage. By text. After it had happened. The divorce, on the other hand, warranted a phone call and an hour-long one-sided bitch fest reminding me over and over again of the consequences of making a commitment without being a hundred percent certain of your own happiness.

Aria rolled right over my dig. "And you're adopting a baby? My God, Piper! Why wouldn't you discuss something so monumental with me?"

"When have I ever, Aria?" I sigh into the phone. "Besides, I told you after Laura died I was planning on taking care of Violet."

"I thought you meant like an aunt or something, not become a parent. This is a huge responsibility, Piper. It's life changing."

"I know," I snap. "But in every good way. Wait, you said you heard from a stranger?"

"Yes, a private investigator. Jim or John or something like that. He said he was working on behalf of Laura's cousin, that you were actually fighting her for custody, and everyone believes your marriage is simply a ploy to get the upper hand. God, I hope that's true."

"Sorry to burst your bubble, but it's not. Webb and I are very much in love."

"About this Webb—and really, what kind of name is that? The investigator told me some disturbing news. His divorce was final only a week ago, did he tell you that?"

I swallow. No, actually, he said it was four months ago. "I know all about his previous marriage."

"And did he tell you his parents have all but disowned him for divorcing this woman? Apparently, she's an executive in the family business but he's not. And she got everything of value in the divorce—the house, the cars, the stocks, the joint account. Are you making him sign a prenup?"

"No, there's no need—"

"You have a business of your own. You need to protect it."

I grind my teeth. "Webb isn't after what little money I have. Besides, how did you find all this out?"

"The investigator. I told you. He had a thick file on this man, including all his financials, a criminal background check, a credit report. He said as mother of the bride, I should be aware of who my daughter is marrying. It was embarrassing when he realized I didn't know anything going on in my own daughter's life."

"You haven't known anything about my life since I was a kid and it never bothered you before."

She continues as if I hadn't spoken. "He's not a criminal, and his credit score is very good. But, Piper, he's almost broke. Are you paying him to marry you so you can adopt Laura's baby?"

"What?" I nearly shout. "That's ridiculous. No, I'm not paying him. We're in love. I'm sorry if you can't believe it, but it's true."

"Fine, fine," she says. "You're in love. But," she continues in a more controlled voice, "what have I always told you? Never jump into something so permanent unless you can be absolutely, positively certain it's what you want. Sure, maybe with Laura's death and with forty breathing down your neck, you think adopting this baby will make you happy. But what if it doesn't? What if a few years down the road you meet your soulmate? Only now you're saddled with a baby and a husband you realize can't make you as happy as you deserve."

"I suppose I can leave them behind and start a new life. Worked out for you, didn't it?"

She makes a strangled noise and for a second I consider apologizing, even though I didn't say anything that wasn't true. But then she speaks again and for the first time in twenty-nine years there's a note of regret in her voice.

"I deserve that," she simply says. "But that's what I mean, Piper. You don't want to do that to the baby or to Webb, not if he loves you like you say he does."

I'm not so much a fool I honestly believe Webb loves me. He's doing me a favor, a huge one, but I'm not naive enough to think he's doing it for anything more than trying to make up for the awful way he treated me. And for Violet. But no, he doesn't actually love me, as nice as it might be. No—no, I don't want him to love me. Ugh. I shake my head as if I can throw the errant thought out of my head. And this is why I have to stop making out with him.

"I'm not settling, if that's what you're worried about."

"I am worried a little," she admits. "But you're a big girl and I have to trust you've learned from watching my mistakes. What really has me concerned is Webb. Why didn't he have any children with his first wife?"

"Guess the PI wasn't so thorough after all." I sigh. "She couldn't physically have children because of an accident. And she didn't want to adopt because she was fine not having any."

"And Webb? Did he want them?"

I check for where Webb is, but he's nowhere in sight. Did he leave? "It's not really any of your business."

"What I'm getting at, Piper—How can you be sure he isn't the one settling?"

My face grows hot. "Because that's the only way someone would want to be with me? If they were settling for second best?"

"That's not what I meant at all. I just want to make sure you go into this with your eyes wide open. Are you certain he's not interested in the insta-family you can give him? If that's his driving cause, then it doesn't matter how much you love him. He'll never be truly happy and eventually, you'll come to resent him for it or he'll decide it just isn't working anymore. What if he meets his soulmate?"

Then he'll leave. I wasn't enough to make my mother stay. Drew, the one man I felt I could love after Webb, married Mara less than a year after our breakup. Apparently I am not enough for someone to want forever with. And if this whole marriage thing were for real, eventually Webb would leave, too. I already know this, but hearing it confirmed by my mother drives the point home.

I say none of this to Aria. Instead, I tell her, "I don't believe in soulmates. So your scenario doesn't really compute."

Her sigh is so heavy and aggrieved I can almost feel her breath against my cheek. "I don't want to see you get hurt."

"No one's going to get hurt," I assure her. "Least of all me."

I'M NOT A LIAR. YOU PROBABLY THINK THAT'S A LIE ITSELF, BUT it's not. Other than the occasional feeling-sparing fib—my most common one being "Yeah, it was good for me, too"--I've always been an honest and straightforward sort of person.

But lately, I can't seem to stop the falsehoods falling from my lips one after another until I'm now at the point I don't know what is true anymore. It scares me how good I'm getting at this deception thing.

This last prevarication, however, is stuck in my chest like a butterscotch button swallowed down the wrong pipe.

No one's going to get hurt. Least of all me.

Webb isn't in the house when I go looking for him. I find him on the little patio out back, sitting in the bright green Adirondack, typing on his phone. For half a minute, I stand in the doorway and watch him. The tips of his thick lashes shimmer gold in the sunlight. A dusting of soft, light scruff dapples his jaw and his lips—delicious, firm, plump—quirk up at the corners when he catches sight of me. My chest is filled with hundreds of tiny flapping wings and I press against it to quiet them.

He beckons me outside with two long, thick fingers, the same ones that only minutes ago were coaxing pleasure out of me. Liquid heat pools between my thighs. I walk toward him and take the empty bright yellow chair next to him, crossing my legs in hopes the pressure will tamp down any remaining desire. Because now I've had a moment to collect myself and remember what a bad idea it would be to fall into bed with this man. A delicious idea, but bad nonetheless.

"So how is your mom?" he says.

"Aria is, well, Aria."

"You call her by her name?"

"Once in a while, I slip and call her Mom," I say with a shrug. "But I made a pact with myself a long time ago that she hadn't earned the title. She never seemed to care one way or the other."

"I can't imagine calling my mother Eileen. Even Carolynn didn't call her that. But then, my mother is about appearances." He turns so he's facing me. "What did she have to say?"

"Hollis's PI contacted her and told her all about the adoption and our engagement, and Hollis's suspicions about it being a scam. I had to assure her it wasn't."

"You hadn't told her, I guess."

"We don't talk much."

"Not even about adopting Violet?"

I lift my hands and drop them. "I did tell her, sort of, after Laura died. But she wasn't paying attention. And she hasn't checked in on me since then, so I didn't have the opportunity. Maybe I knew how she'd react, so I subconsciously avoided it, I don't know."

"Guess she isn't too happy?"

"Not for the reasons you might think, though." I give him a wry smile. "She doesn't want me to make a mistake I can't live with, like the one she made when she married my dad and had me."

His eyes fill with concern. "I'm sorry she makes you feel like a mistake. I know how it feels."

I give him a sad smile. "I know you do."

We hold each other's gaze for a long moment, then I break contact by nodding at the phone in his lap. "Everything all right?"

"Apparently, your mother isn't the only one the PI has tried to contact. Graeme said some guy was skulking around the office complex, asking a bunch of questions about me, Carolynn, my parents. Graeme put security on notice, and he hasn't been around since."

My shoulders slump. "It's only a matter of time."

He reaches out to take my hand and interlaces his fingers with mine. "Hey. They can think whatever they want. After Saturday, we're going to be husband and wife, and no one can prove it's for any reason other than love."

I shift in my seat so now I'm facing him, too. "My mother said the PI told her your divorce was only recently final. Like, last week. Is that true?"

He grimaces. "Not exactly. Our divorce was final four months ago. But Massachusetts law has a 120-day waiting period before you can remarry. I don't know why, to make sure it takes?" He shrugs. "Last week, or it might have been week before last, was the milestone."

A flutter of relief passes through me. "Good. I mean, not that it should matter."

"But it does." He lifts my hand and brushes a kiss across my knuckles. "Pip, I was free and clear before I got here. Before I came to the shop. Before I asked you to dinner."

I smile at him. "Okay."

He stares at me, his thumb stroking the back of my hand. Every caress sends a shiver up my spine, and tiny sparks go off in my stomach…and lower. I squeeze my thighs together, a new warmth joining the dampness from earlier. My gaze drifts to his mouth, his lips parting. If I lean over, if he meets me halfway—

Abruptly I stand, yanking my hand out of his. "I have to go. I have things to take care of."

He sighs and stands, casting a rueful glance down. "I guess I do, too."

I blush, then burst out laughing. He cocks an eyebrow. "It's funny?"

"It's ridiculous, is what it is."

"Just what a man wants to hear about his erection."

I cover my eyes. "God, I'm sorry. I'm not laughing at you, just this whole situation—"

He grasps my wrist and pulls my hands away. "Piper, I'm going to be completely honest. I want you. I've never stopped wanting you, whether you believe it or not. But if having a physical relationship is causing you this much distress, then I'm fine going without. I can't promise to stop wanting you, but I won't push you. If and when you're ready, just know I'll be here."

He kisses me, a light touch on my lips, then lets me go. "Go do what you have to do. I'll finish setting up my new room."

I nod and walk away. He's made the decision all mine and I know he means it. I should be happy to have the control, and I am. I'd be happier if I could trust myself to exercise any self-control, but I have a sinking feeling that keeping this faux marriage non-sexual is going to take all my restraint.

TWENTY-SIX

Piper

Friday morning, I wake to a message from Webb asking me to meet him at Beachcomber's. We've decided he won't move in until after the wedding, so I haven't seen him since our somewhat awkward parting yesterday. I made myself scarce while he finished moving in the rest of his things, except for toiletries and a couple changes of clothes. Tess thinks I'm being an idiot, and maybe I am. But after Saturday, I'm going to be living with the man. I need this time to shore up my resistance, to remind myself why I can't keep making out with him. Because it will lead to sex, and sex with Webb... well, that will lead to feelings and I can't catch feeling for him again.

I find him waiting for me at a table tucked in the corner with two cups of coffee. He rises and kisses my cheek. "You look beautiful."

"Thank you." I take in his forest green formfitting LaCoste polo and tailored khakis, the styled coif he sports, and his ropey forearms with appreciation. "So do you."

"Before we get to the reason I wanted to meet this morning," he says, looking over my shoulder, "I have a surprise for you."

He raises his finger and smiles. I look behind me and see

Jonathan coming out from behind the counter carrying a wrapped platter.

"You didn't have to get me anything," I say. "I didn't think to get you anything."

"This is something we can share, although I won't make you." There's a twinkle in his eye as Jonathan sets the platter on the table and removes the foil wrapping.

I gasp. In front of me is something I haven't seen in forever. "Are these Hermit Cookies?" I look at Webb curiously.

A flush of pink tinges his cheeks. "You mentioned this was a favorite of yours that your dad used to make you, especially at times when you needed comfort. I figured this was one of those times. I have never had these before, so I asked Bette about it. She tracked down the recipe your dad used to use. Turns out, his grandmother and Bette's were friends, and this happened to be one Bette's grandmother kept in her recipe journals. I asked her to make a batch."

My eyes water, the lightly browned cookies blurring together. He nudges the plate toward me. "Go ahead. Try one. I don't know if they'll be exactly like your dad's, but as close as I could find."

I blink the moisture away and reach for one of the rectangles. They're warm and fragrant, the ginger and cinnamon transporting me back to Dad's kitchen table. I take a bite, chewing slowly as the taste fills my mouth, and the memories threaten to overwhelm me. I look at Webb in wonder as he watches me expectantly.

"They're perfect," I whisper.

His features smooth out and his smile covers his face, crinkling the corners of his sparkling eyes. "I'm glad. May I?"

I hold another cookie out to him. He takes it and bites into it, his eyes widening as he chews. "Wow. These are amazing. Not too sweet, with just the right amount of spice. I even like the raisins."

We each finish another cookie and then wrap them up again to take home. I lean across the table and grasp his hands. "Thank you. This might be the kindest gift anyone has ever given me."

He raises our joined hands to his lips and places a tender kiss on my knuckles. "I have something else for you."

I sit back and groan. "I didn't even get you a card."

He chuckles and reaches into his back pocket to pull out an envelope, which he passes to me.

"What's this?" I open it and unfold the blue-backed paper inside. "Oh. The prenup."

"I signed it," he says. "I know Violet's security is most important to you. Just needs your signature. I'll have my lawyer make copies for us and keep it on file at her office."

"Doesn't it need to be notarized?"

"Not technically, though it'd be good practice. But I figured if we wanted to keep this quiet, we should keep the number of people who know about it to as few as possible."

He holds out a pen. "Unless you want to find a notary—"

I take the proffered pen and shake my head. "No, it's fine." I sign and refold the paper, then hand it back to him. "Now your millions are safe."

He scoffs. "Even if I had millions, I wouldn't have been worried." He returns the blue back to his pocket and gives me an assessing look. "I have to get back to the practice. Are you going to be okay? I can cut out early. I mean, I am getting married tomorrow. I don't think Pam and Trev would begrudge me the day off."

"No, go. Do what you have to do. I have a lot of things to take care of myself." Like freak out in private.

"Lunch later? Dinner?"

"No," I say, shaking my head. "Don't take this the wrong way, but I need some space today."

He's quiet for a long moment, and I think I've offended him, but then he throws me that dazzler of his. "Hayes wants to take me out and get me drunk."

"Tess wants to do the same," I confess.

"So I guess I'll see you tomorrow?"

"I'll be the one holding a bouquet."

His lips curve. "I'll be the one who can't keep his eyes off you."

⊱━━━⊰

IT'S A SHAME THIS IS WEDDING ISN'T REAL, BECAUSE SATURDAY morning has dawned with clear blue skies and sunshine so pure, so warm, you might think it's already June, not April. Tess and I ride the ferry together and drive to the Rosellis. It's been almost a week since I've seen Violet. I'm excited to see her in the little dress I bought for her. But my excitement is tempered by nerves. I can't stop fiddling with my hair, which I left loose and wavy just for this reason. Tess smacks my hand for the hundredth time on the drive between the dock and the house.

"You need to chill, babe," she says.

"Easy for you to say," I grumble. "You're not the one getting fake married today."

"First of all," she holds up one manicured finger. "Stop saying fake married. Letitia is an honest-to-God sworn officer of the court. You are getting hitched for real today." She pauses.

"It's a sham."

"Fine, then it's a shmarriage, but it's not fake."

"Semantics."

She holds up a second finger. "Second, it's a wedding, not a firing squad. It's not the end of the world."

"It's the end of mine as I know it." I blow my bangs out of my eyes. "Tessie, what if this doesn't work? What if we get married and I still don't get custody of Violet?"

"It's not going to happen." Her voice is calm, reassuring. I draw strength from her steely confidence.

"You're right," I say, flattening my palms against the garment bag on my lap. "If I seem at all unsure, that Pastor will pounce."

"Will Hollis be there?"

"I didn't invite her." My shoulders bunch around my ears. "But I wouldn't be surprised. Maybe I should ask Letitia if she can skip the whole speak now or forever hold your peace bit."

Lulu greets us in the driveway and ushers us around back. "Webb is in the first-level guest room. It's bad luck to see the bride before the wedding, so I'm not walking you past him."

"I'm not even in my dress, yet" I protest, but she's not having it.

"You use the guest room next to the nursery to get changed. The guests should be arriving soon. Tessa, watch over Piper and I'll handle everyone else."

"What about Violet?" I ask.

Lulu hesitates and my stomach sinks. Is Violet not here?

"Hollis has her," she answers.

My mouth drops open. "But I wanted Violet to be a part of today."

"She will be," Lulu assures, squeezing my arm. "Hollis is here. She's going to watch over Violet during the service."

My relief is laced with annoyance. Hollis was most definitely not invited to this wedding. But I suppose it wouldn't look good for me to throw a tantrum about it. So I grit my teeth and smile. "I brought a dress for Violet to wear."

I take it out of the garment bag and hand it to Lulu. "It's lovely," she says.

She gives me a tight hug. Wetness on her cheeks passes to mine when she presses me close. "I wish Laura was here. She'd be so happy for you."

Tears sting my eyes and I don't bother holding them back. "I miss her so much."

"I know."

We cling to each other for a long moment. She pulls back and fixes me with a watery smile. "She'd be the first to scold us for being so maudlin on such a happy day. Go get ready. I'll see you downstairs. Wait by the back door for me."

She gives Tessa a quick squeeze and shuts the door behind her. I take a deep breath and sniffle. Tessa hands me a tissue.

"Dry up the snot, Pippi," she commands. She pulls out a makeup bag filled to the brim. "I've got work to do."

I SMOOTH THE BODICE OF MY DRESS, LIKE THE MOTION WILL QUELL the flutters in my stomach. I feel ill. Like physically ill. "Tessa, I don't know if I can go through with this. I don't want to lie to Lulu and Denny. And I still haven't told Webb about the baby. About what happened. How can I marry him if I haven't told him?"

"It's going to be fine, Piper. Just remember—you're doing this to save Violet, okay?"

I nod, but my chest is still tight and drawing in air is getting harder to do. Tessa presses a glass of water into my hand. "Drink," she orders me. "Drink and breathe."

"If I do that at the same time, I'll drown."

She clicks her tongue. "Drink, then breathe."

I do as she says, taking small sips so I don't smear the lip stain she's painted on me. I take several slow, deep breaths and my heart begins to slow from a gallop to a trot. "What's taking so long?" I ask.

I want to peek out the window, but Lulu gave us explicit instructions to stay out of sight. I nudge Tessa. "Take a look. There's no weird superstition about maids of honor seeing the groom or whatever."

She peers between two slats in the blinds on the window next to the door. She gasps. "Fucking hell?"

"What?" I race to her side. "What is it?"

She straightens and turns her back to the window, the slats closing back up. "Nothing. It's nothing at all. Everything looks very nice out there. I was just surprised by all the—the flowers."

I narrow my eyes. "Flowers? What the hell is going on Tessa? What did you see?"

She doesn't get a chance to tell me. The back door opens, and Denny strolls in wearing a charcoal gray suit, white shirt, and dark gray tie with peach-colored pinstripes. He pauses in the doorway, his eyes shimmering as he stares at me. "You look beautiful, Piper."

I flush. "Thank you, Denny. Is it time? Did you come here to get us moving?"

He doesn't answer at first, his lower lip quivering ever so slightly. He clears his throat. "Everyone is ready if you are."

I glance at Tessa, who gives me an encouraging smile. "I'm ready."

He pops his elbow up. "If you're okay with it, I'd be honored to walk you down the aisle."

I blink my eyes rapidly and breathe in through my mouth. Tessa will kill me if I ruin her makeup job before I've even gotten to the ceremony. Not trusting myself to speak, I nod and smile as I take his arm. I can't go through with this charade. I can't keep lying to these people I love so much. My chest tightens and I rub at it, as if that can loosen the tension.

A violin begins playing a classical piece from a speaker somewhere and Tessa walks out ahead of us. "You okay?" Denny asks.

I nod and take a few calming breaths. From somewhere out back I hear a squeal and I know it's Violet. That centers me. I have to do this. I can do this. For her. "Nervous. But okay."

The music changes and I laugh to myself. It had to be Tessa

who chose "Marry You" by Bruno Mars. Denny pats my hand. "Ready?"

We step around the corner together and I realize quickly what Tessa was hiding from me. Smart move, because I might have fled out the front door if I'd seen this for myself.

The backyard is filled with flowers. Overflowing planters surround the perimeter and garlands are draped along the fence line and the back row of chairs—which is packed with people. My mouth drops open and warmth spreads through my chest. It was only supposed to be a few of us, an intimate ceremony. But it feels like half the Isle is there. Bette, Paloma, and the rest of the members of SASBO; Jonathan, wearing a Hawaiian shirt and bowtie; Ruby and Pearl, standing with Mara. A twinge of hurt pierces through my gratitude when I don't see Drew, but I don't dwell. I'm humbled, amazed, and feeling a big heap of guilt to see all these people standing up for me. If only this weren't a giant fraud, it'd be a pretty damn near perfect day.

Webb's partners are there—Trev with his wife and Pam with a young man I assume is her brother. There are a number of other people in the audience I don't recognize, although one woman looks familiar. I quickly forget about these strangers when I walk past Hollis and Violet. I reach out to shake the baby's hand, studiously ignoring the woman holding her and the two fidgety blond boys sitting next to her. Pastor Marty has a seat in front—gag—and then all of a sudden I'm standing in front of everyone, clutching the bouquet of wildflowers and violets in my hand while I stare at Webb. The sun picks up the golden highlights in his hair, casting an aura about him that's almost magical. His eyes are as lush and green as the grass we're standing on, his smile bigger than I've ever seen it. A real smile, not the controlled one he uses in public but the one that deepens the crow's feet around the corners of his eyes.

It's hard to look away, so I don't. I swallow hard, barely acknowledging the light kiss to my cheek from Laura's father.

Webb takes my hand and dips his head to whisper, "You are so beautiful."

I melt right into the ground, a puddle of peach and green at his feet. A gentle nudge from Tessa refocuses me and I face Letitia, the clerk, who's wearing an amused smile. When she begins to speak, I'm acutely aware of Webb, but everything else fades into the background. Letitia's voice is a low hum barely distinguishable over the pounding of my heart. It's a wonder I can follow along, but I say the right words at the right time and though it's almost a whisper, I manage to say the two most important ones.

"I do."

Webb is looking into my eyes and when he repeats his vow, a wave of calm settles over me. Everything is going to be all right now. This was the hard part and it's done. No more second-guessing the plan, no more doubting it will work, no more wrestling with guilt and fear. This is for Violet. All for Violet.

"You may now kiss your bride."

Webb cups my cheek with one hand, the other wrapping around my waist as he pulls me in, dipping his head to press a gentle kiss to my lips. My eyes flutter shut and I open under him, steadying myself with a hand to his arm. He tastes of mint and promises. Whistles and catcalls signal the end of our embrace. We part, breathless, and there's one salient fact I can't deny.

That kiss had nothing to do with Violet.

TWENTY-SEVEN

Webb

Lulu has outdone herself with the wedding preparations. With only a few days' notice, she's put together a top-notch event. Flowers are everywhere, the yard bursting with color and fragrance. Neither Piper nor I expected this much fanfare, or the buffet being served under a large canopy festooned with flowers and twinkle lights in the side yard. Nor did we expect so many people.

I especially didn't expect to see my parents—or my ex-wife.

They were already seated when I took my place with Hayes in front. I noticed Graeme and Tish first, and it was the chagrined glance to his left that alerted me to their presence. The nerves tumbling inside me became a roiling ball of acid.

"Fuck, dude. Why is Carolynn here?" Hayes gives voice to the exact thought in my head.

"I don't know," I mutter.

"You didn't invite her, did you?"

I glare at him, not bothering to dignify him with an answer. I look back and my ex-wife is staring at me with a cool, indifferent look in her eyes. I haven't seen her in over four months, the longest I've ever gone in twenty years, and I feel nothing looking at her. I don't hate her, I don't despise her—she's not a bad person, and she wasn't a bad wife. Other than the brief affair she had, I mean. But I couldn't really blame her for that. We simply weren't good together.

A man in a slate gray Thom Browne suit takes the seat next to Carolynn, and she breaks eye contact with me to smile at him. My grinding teeth catches Hayes's notice. He frowns in their direction and tilts his head toward me.

"Who's the suit?"

"Darren Wiggstaff." I practically spit the name out of my mouth. "He's the CFO. Total douchebag. And the guy who fucked my ex-wife." Maybe I don't blame Carolynn, but I can blame him.

Darren crosses his legs and drapes his arm casually across the back of Carolynn's chair. He leans across to say something to my parents and the four of them share a chuckle. Judging by the smirk on his face when he glances up at me, I'd say it was at my expense.

"Gotta admit," Hayes says. "Takes some brass cajónes to bring a date when you crash your ex-husband's wedding."

"She brought him to rile me up." I grin at Hayes. "Joke's on her. I care even less about him than I do her."

But I do care if it disrupts this day for Piper. That's what has me tense and fidgety. I adjust the sleeves of my shirt and stone-colored suit jacket. Tessa advised me to wear a light color, which meant buying a new suit since I tend to gravitate toward charcoal, black, and navy for my professional wear. It's straight off the rack, and with no time for tailoring, doesn't fit as well as the other suits in my closet.

"Chill, dude." Hayes places a hand on my shoulder and steadies me. "It's just some words and a piece of paper. Not like it's the real deal."

I growl and he moves his hand away with a snort. "Or maybe it is."

"It's for show," I concede. "But it doesn't mean I'm not going to take this seriously. For however long we end up staying together, I'm going to play my part."

"You guys decide how long that's going to be?"

"Not really." Piper says six months, but I'm not going to press for an end date. Piper wants me, it's been obvious. But she doesn't trust me and the longer we do this thing, the more time I have to convince her to give me a real second chance.

Letitia says hello to us and takes her place. Hayes and I turn to face the back of the yard as classical string music begins to play. Tessa comes from around the corner of the house looking like a 1950s pin up in a short light green dress, her hair teased into a high twist with a fall of blonde curls framing her face. A soft *wow* escapes Hayes's mouth, and I sneak a look at him.

"Stop drooling," I mutter out of the side of my mouth.

"Fuck off," he replies, but then he closes his mouth.

She makes her way to where we stand, giving me a wink. The music changes, moving from the quiet violin melody to an upbeat pop song, and everyone stands. Bruno Mars begins singing about looking for something dumb to do just as Piper, escorted by Denny, rounds the corner of the house and begins the short walk up the aisle. She hasn't looked at me yet, her attention caught by the sight of all her friends—and a few strangers—standing for her. Her mouth is open in a small *o* and even from here, I can see the bright shimmer in her eyes. I can tell she's overwhelmed and even more surprised than I was, but it doesn't stop my face from splitting in an ear-to-ear smile. Holy shit. She's so fucking beautiful. And when she stops for a second to take Violet's hand, something inside me cracks open and fills me with a desperate need. Everything is suddenly crystal fucking clear.

I want Piper. I want Violet. I want this family. I want it all—for real.

Piper looks bewildered, her expression mirroring the

emotions flailing about inside me. I desperately want to know what she's thinking, because the way she's looking at me makes me think there might be a chance she's feeling what I'm feeling. Or something close to it. Maybe it's wishful thinking on my part, but when she repeats the vows, I can tell it's in earnest.

We are not breaking up in six months. It's okay if she doesn't love me now. I can be patient. But I'm going to have to go back on my word not to press for more with her. Starting...

"You may kiss the bride," Letitia announces.

...now.

I put my palm to her soft cheek and with my other hand on her waist, draw her into me. Her face tilts up to meet mine, our lips making a tender connection. Then her eyes close and her mouth parts, granting me permission to go deeper. *Don't mind if I do.*

Our lips are fused, our tongues doing all the work, dancing and tangling. She grips my arm, I dig my fingers into her hip, and if it weren't for all the raucous whistling reminding me we have an audience, I'd already have lowered her to the grass to taste every inch of her.

With reluctance, I loosen my grip and pull away to a respectable distance. Her cheeks are flushed and rosy, her chest heaving as rapidly my own. The music starts again and I take her hand to lead her back down the aisle. We smile at the guests, who are all clapping. Well, almost all. My parents and my ex-wife and her date stand, hands clasped in front of them. Except for Darren, who has one hand in his pocket and the other resting on Carolynn's shoulder. I pay them only a second or two of attention, squeezing Piper's hand as the song playing finally penetrates my thoughts.

"Wait, is this—?" I turn to Piper, who is giggling.

"Yes, yes it is," she says, looking up at me. "It's Queen."

"Hayes," I grumble.

And so we completed our walk back down the aisle as a married couple to "Another One Bites the Dust."

THERE'S NOT A FORMAL RECEIVING LINE. LULU MEETS US AT THE end of the aisle and has Denny usher everyone to the side yard so we can do pictures. Hollis tries to sneak away with Violet, but my wife isn't having any of it and practically rips the baby from her arms.

My wife. She's holding Violet and I put an arm around her to keep them both close to me while Lulu directs the photographer, a member of her church who apparently does amateur portraiture as a hobby. We're done in about fifteen minutes since Piper nixed many of the artsy poses one typically gets and I declined any with my folks. Carolynn and I had about a dozen of those, along with the traditional family and wedding party photos. I kept one after the divorce because it's the only photo I have of my parents and me where they look genuinely happy. I hired a guy on Fiverr to Photoshop Carolynn out of it.

"I know you said not to do anything big," Lulu says. "So it's only a simple champagne brunch, buffet-style."

"Lulu, half of Sandcastle Isle is here," Piper says with a laugh. "I think that renders all of this anything but simple."

Lulu strokes Violet's hair and sniffs. "I never got the chance to do this for Laura. I'm grateful you gave me the chance to do this for you."

Piper's eyes water and she embraces Lulu, Violet crushed between them. Damn it, my own eyes begin to water, but I blink back the tears. With Eileen and Stephen Duncan lurking, it would not do to look weak. The women part and Lulu gestures for us to move to the tent.

"Go on ahead," I say to her. "We'll be right there."

This is the first chance I've had all morning to be alone with my new bride. When Lulu walks away, I take Piper by the elbow and lead her and the baby to one of the folding chairs still set up. "Let's sit and catch our breath for a minute," I suggest.

Violet blows bubbles and plays with Piper's beads, keeping up a steady patter in the suddenly awkward silence that descends between us. "So," I say.

"So," Piper answers.

"So much for small and private, eh?" I say with a laugh.

Piper chuckles. "Yeah, but I can't even be mad about it. Lulu has a big heart, even if she's misguided at times. And you heard her... about Laura."

"Yeah." I clear my throat. "How are you feeling? About this." I tap the slim gold band on my finger.

She looks down at the matching one on her finger that sits against her engagement ring. "Surreal," she finally says. "At first, I felt so guilty that everyone was here to witness our deception, but then I think I got caught up in the moment because it started to feel real. Too real."

She's looking away from me when she says this, so I put my hand on the back her head and gently prod her to turn to me. Her gaze slips to my mouth before meeting my eyes, which I take as a good sign. "To me, too," I confess. "Pip, I—"

"There you are!" We're interrupted by Tessa walking toward us. "Everyone is waiting for you to make your grand entrance as Mr. and Mrs. Duncan."

"Poincelot-Duncan," Piper amends and stands.

Tessa's nose scrunches. "Yeah, no. That's a mouthful we're not going to entertain. Suck it up, Mrs. Duncan."

Mrs. Duncan. I like the sound of it, though by the set of Piper's shoulders she isn't pleased with the moniker. We'll work on it.

"By the way, Tessa," Piper says. "The musical choices for the ceremony were... interesting. Know anything about it?"

Tessa snorts. "Thought a song about getting married for the

fun of it was the perfect song to kick things off. Hayes chose the Queen song."

"I knew it," I say with a groan. "Ass."

"We're just heading up. I don't suppose you noticed if an older, sour couple is still hanging around?"

"Your parents, I presume," Tessa says drily. "Sorry, they're still here."

Piper turns to me. "I saw them in the crowd and wondered. But you said they weren't coming."

"They weren't." I shrug. "Guess they changed their mind."

"Did you actually invite Carolynn, too?" Tessa folds her arms and lifts an eyebrow at me.

Piper gasps. "I thought that woman looked familiar. The one with hair the color of Merlot?"

I lift my hands, palms out. "I did not invite my ex-wife. Or the douche nozzle she brought."

"The cute guy with the close cut?" Tessa hums her approval. "He looks like a tasty snack."

I grunt. Piper narrows her eyes at me and asks why they're here. I shrug again. "I assume my parents invited them along. Why? I don't know. Probably to annoy me."

The four of us start walking toward the tent. I take Piper's hand in mine and squeeze. She looks up at me and gives me a small smile. Already I feel the tension radiating off her and I hate my parents for causing her more anxiety on what is already a fraught day. Pastor Marty and Hollis in attendance is bad enough; Piper doesn't need the added stress of meeting my parents and seeing my ex-wife. In fact, I'm going to keep it from happening by asking them to leave, quietly I hope.

TWENTY-EIGHT

Piper

Violet is perched on my hip and Webb holds my hand when we walk under the giant canopy. Our guests start clapping and I'm grateful for Webb's steady presence. I cling to his hand like it's a life preserver. Someone taps silverware against glass and soon a clinking cacophony rises, until Webb leans down and kisses me.

"I'm so happy for you, too," Bette says, kissing us both on the cheeks.

"Thanks for coming, Bette," I say. "It was quite a surprise seeing all of you here."

"We wouldn't miss this for the world," she says.

Webb looks over my head and draws in a breath. "Excuse us, Bette. There's some people Piper should meet."

He guides me out of the tent to a partly secluded spot under Lulu's big weeping willow where a small group of people stand —an older couple I assume are his parents, Carolynn and her date, and another couple I don't recognize. The man is about our age and sports a thick dark beard and mustache, a thick mass of braids gathered at the nape of his neck and held together in a leather band. His light brown eyes are filled with warmth and friendliness when he looks at me. His companion gives us a congenial smile, but her nostrils have a slight flare and her pretty onyx eyes keep darting between Carolynn and me.

"Piper, these are my parents, Eileen and Stephen Duncan. This is my friend, Graeme St. John, and his wife, Tish. You remember Carolynn."

I switch Violet to the other side and hold my hand out to each person as introduced. Cold fish is the best way to describe Webb's father; indifferent fits his mother. Graeme and Tish are both friendly in their greetings. I skip over Carolynn entirely, just give a small smile, and turn my attention to her date.

"This is Darren Wiggstaff. He's the Chief Financial Officer at Duncan Dental LLC." Webb's tone is frostier than the soft serve at the confectionery.

He extends his hand and I shake it. "It's a pleasure," he all but purrs, his gaze raking down my body.

"Everyone," Webb continues, gesturing to me, "this is my wife, Piper, and our soon-to-be—we hope—daughter, Violet."

Only Graeme is not surprised, since he knows the truth behind all of this. His parents merely raise their eyebrows, like he'd just shown them a new car he was planning to buy. Carolynn, on the other hand, has fire in her eyes.

"You can't be serious," she hisses. "My God, Webb. Marrying on the rebound is one thing, but adopting a child?"

Her words are directed at Webb, but they slap me in the face full force and I rear back. I open my mouth to ask her where the hell she gets off insulting me—us—at our wedding, but Webb interjects.

"I don't believe I asked your opinion," he snaps back. "And I sure as hell didn't invite you to my wedding. Or him." He says the latter like a curse word.

"I needed to see for myself the mistake you're making." She looks me up and down, then sniffs.

"This is all very sudden, Thomas," his mother says. She gives me a tight smile. "I'm sure you're a lovely woman, but I hope you can understand the shock this has been to us. To hear about our only son's engagement and marriage to a woman we've never even heard of before and now to learn this marriage comes with fatherhood?"

"You realize Webb doesn't have any money of his own," his father says, directing his statement at me.

"Dad, enough," Webb growls. "I know what you're thinking, and it isn't true. Now, this is not the time or place to discuss any of this. I will not have you ruining our celebration. You can either shut your mouths and eat, drink, and pretend to be merry, or you can leave. Piper and Violet are my family, and you can accept it and be a part of it. Or you can leave—for good."

His mother flinches, hurt flashing across her face before she once again schools her features into a cool mask. "Very well, Thomas. We wish you good luck with your new family."

"Webb," I plead, horrified he could dismiss his parents so callously. I mean, I get how cruel they can be, but did he not see the pain on his mother's face?

"Don't bother," Stephen says, taking his wife's arm. "When you're ready to talk about this like an adult, you know where we'll be. Come along, Eileen."

The rest of us are rooted to the ground while they walk away. Violet blabbers on, oblivious to the tension of the situation. Oh, to be a child again.

Webb turns on Carolynn and Darren. "Neither of you were invited. I suggest you leave, as well."

"Webb," Carolynn begins, but he gives her his back and faces Graeme and Tish.

"My partners are here. I'd like to introduce you."

Graeme smiles, then takes his wife's hand. "I'd like to meet them."

Webb settles his hand on my lower back and starts to guide

me away, but stops short and turns back to Carolynn. "I mean it. I won't have you ruining Piper's day. Leave."

He continues to lead me back to the tent. I hear Darren say, "Come on, Caro. He's not worth it." My stomach rolls over. This is not what I ever imagined my wedding would be like. I don't think any little girl fantasizes about a tense, awkward show-down between the groom, his parents, and his ex-wife.

I need a drink and to be with people I know, people who like me. I push Webb toward his friend and point to the buffet. "You go on, I'll catch up."

He tilts his head, the little worry divot making an appear-ance between his brows. "You okay? Listen, let me introduce Graeme to Pam and Trev, then we can go somewhere and talk about what happened."

I shake my head and give him a wry smile. "It was pretty self-explanatory. Anyway, it's over. I just need to get a drink, say hi to some of my friends."

He stares at me for a beat longer, like he's trying to decide if it's okay to let me go. Then he kisses the top of my head and starts to walk away, but Violet chooses that moment to whine. Webb turns back. "What's wrong pretty girl?" he coos to her.

Violet holds out her arms and Webb scoops her into his. A real smile lights up his face as she nuzzles into his neck. Tish says, "Aww," and puts a hand to her heart.

"Oh my God, Webb. You're a natural with her."

He truly is. He holds her like an adoring father, all smiles and snuggles. For her part, Violet seems as entranced, especially with his nose, which she's grasped.

An old but too familiar pain lances through me. My chest squeezes and I need air even more than a drink. I need air right now. They're already walking away and don't notice me slip out an opening. I look around for Tessa, but she must be in the house or somewhere under the canopy. The pain is growing heavier, the elephant sitting on my lungs and stealing my breath away. I walk around the other side of the house into the smaller side yard where the Rosellis keep their trash and recycle cans and put my back against the house. Huddled in the shade, out of sight, I drag in deep breaths.

"Are you okay?"

I jump, clutching at my chest. "Holy fuck. You scared me."

Carolynn steps further into the side area. "Sorry. I saw you walking over here and saw my chance to talk to you."

Great. Of all the people to witness one of my panic attacks, she's the third worst person I'd want to see. Pastor Marty and Hollis are ahead of her on the list. "I thought you left."

"I'm about to. Darren is calling his driver to come get us."

I'm still trying to regulate my breathing, but being subtle about it is making it take longer. I can only hope she doesn't notice my shakiness, or if she does, that she doesn't think it's because she intimidates me. I mean, she does, but I don't want her to know it. "What do you want, Carolynn?"

"I want Webb back," she says, and I laugh at her flat-out pronouncement.

"I think the ship has sailed," I say, finally regaining some calm.

"Come on, Piper," she says, dropping her voice as if we're sharing a secret. "You were there in college. You know we could never stay apart for long. He'll come back to me. He always does."

"He divorced you," I remind her. "He's married me. This isn't like—"

"The last time? When he was with you?" She smiles at my surprise, but it's not cruel. "I knew all about it. I also knew it was destined to be a fling. I figured he'd get it out of his system."

"Get it out of his system?"

"He had a huge crush on you. I wasn't blind, I could see it. But you were Miss Perfect, Miss Pure, Miss... Poor Girl. You were a novelty, and I knew it wasn't something that would ever last. That hasn't changed."

My heart starts racing again as heat floods my body. I clench my hands into fists. "You need to leave, Carolynn."

"I will," she says, putting her hands up. "I'm not trying to hurt you, Piper. In fact, that's why I came back. To talk to you and warn you."

This woman is so full of shit. But my curiosity is piqued. "Warn me about what? Webb? Webb wouldn't hurt me. He couldn't hurt a fly."

"Not physically, no," she agrees. She takes a step closer and lowers her gaze to the ground. "You know I can't have children, right?"

"Webb told me." A tiny bit of sympathy has me relaxing my hands. "I'm sorry about that."

She raises her head. "Don't be. I never wanted kids. I want to be the best in my career, and I can't do that with children. Besides, I've never really had that maternal instinct, you know? But I made a mistake when I underestimated how much Webb wanted a kid. That's really why he left me. He wanted to create a family. Well, now he has."

She jerks her head in the direction of the tent. "Adopting that baby will mean everything to Webb. He'll get to be a father, and he'll probably be a good one. But you see, once that happens, once he gets to experience having a child, he's going to remember he loves me. He's going to come back to me. Except, he'll be able to come home to me and still be a father. I assume you're not the vindictive sort that'd keep him from his child. Even an adopted one."

Inwardly I wince, because once upon a time that was exactly what I was on my way to doing. I shake my head, then stop when I realize it looks like I'm buying this fantasy. "He's not going back to you, Carolynn."

She gives me a pitying glance. "He always has and thanks to

you, and that baby, he will again. I have nothing against you, Piper. I truly don't. That's why I want to give you this heads-up. If you love Webb even a fraction of how much I love him, it's going to blow your heart up when he finally leaves. I'd really hate to see that happen. Maybe it would be best if, after the adoption goes through, you go ahead and call it quits. It might hurt less.

"Think about it." She turns around and disappears around the corner. I slump down to the ground, vaguely aware I'm sitting in my dress on a patch of dry grass, and try to process every bit of bullshit she just spewed. Because that's what it all was. Bullshit.

Right?

TWENTY-NINE

Piper

I look for Webb as soon as I return to the tent and find him easily. He's standing in a corner talking to his friends, still holding Violet. I hold up my hand, gesturing to give me a minute, and move to the drinks table. I really want a whiskey sour, but I settle for what's available and pour myself a chardonnay. A suffocating cloud of gardenia settles around me and my back stiffens. Hollis is beside me.

"Bravo," she says, a wolfish glint in her eye. "I didn't think you'd go through with this charade."

I sip my wine and barely spare her a look. "I have no idea what you mean. Excuse me, I need to go stand with my husband."

I give her a pointed look as I draw out the word. But when I go to walk away, she grasps my arm, digging her claws in and causing me to wince. I shake off her clutch and round on her, the hand not holding the glass fisted at my side.

"You think you've won, but you haven't," she hisses. "How long do you plan on keeping up this pretense? A couple of months? A year?"

"The vows mentioned 'til death do us part'," I reply with a

shrug. Technically I'm not lying. I'm just not fully answering her question. It hits a little too close to home.

"My PI is already gathering proof that you're only doing this to get a hold of Violet. You don't have her best interest in mind."

"You're the one who isn't thinking about Violet. And you're not the only one with a PI, sweetheart."

Her eyes round and I smirk. "Surprised? Didn't think I had it in me to investigate you? Trust me, what I've already found out is more than enough to sway Lulu and Denny's mind about who the better parent would be."

Her frosty blue eyes narrow. "We'll see about that."

Lulu and Pastor Marty approach. Laura's mother gives me a hug, but thankfully the Pastor keeps his distance. He stands next to Hollis, looking down his bulbous nose at me. I ignore him, refusing to shrink under his judgment.

"Lulu, everything is so beautiful," I say, genuinely appreciative. "You really didn't have to go to all this trouble, but I'm grateful. Webb and I both are."

"It's no trouble. You're like a daughter to us," she says.

"I was telling Lulu how generous it is of her and Denny to host this wedding," Pastor Marty says. "Especially since as close as you are, you're not technically family. The Bible does tell us, *you are acting faithfully in whatever you accomplish for the brethren, and especially when they are strangers.* It's a kindness they've given to someone not of their blood."

I shift uncomfortably on my feet. One point to Marty for reminding Lulu of my non-familial status. I'm eager to change the subject. "Where's Denny?"

Lulu's smile is strained. "It was getting to be a little much for him. He went inside. Are your boys enjoying themselves?"

Hollis waves her hand toward one of the tables where the two tow-headed boys are devouring cupcakes. "They are. You should have seen them playing with Violet earlier. They adore her..."

We watch as the younger boy picks up Violet's panda blankie that she must have dropped and runs it over to Webb. He takes it from the little boy with a smile and gives it to Violet, then turns and catches my eye, giving me a quizzical look.

Lulu puts a hand to her heart. "Oh, that's so precious. Jett made sure Violet had her lovey."

Pastor Marty points a finger at them. "They're going to be good big brothers."

Hollis sighs. "Aaron and I have wanted another child, but after complications with Jett's birth, it wasn't in the cards for us. Bringing Violet home would be a dream come true."

"And what about you, Piper?" Pastor Marty asks. "Do you and your new husband plan on having children of your own?"

My heart stutters, but I force myself to hold the anxiety at bay. I lift my chin and try to sound breezy. "If we had Violet, that would be more than enough. But I guess time will tell."

A firm hand settles on my back, its warmth radiating through me. I stare up at Webb, who's still holding Violet and smiling down at me like I hang the moon. It's bolstering and unnerving at the same time.

"I would make a dozen babies with Piper," Webb says, his eyes fixed on me. A sharp pain flares in my stomach. "But right now, our number one priority is Violet. If we are given the gift of adopting her, we would take into consideration her needs first."

"But siblings are such an integral part of growing up," Hollis says. "My sisters enhanced my childhood and they are my life-long friends. It's good to know once our parents are gone, we'll still have each other."

"Being an only child isn't terrible, either," I argue. "I had plenty of friends. My dad made sure I never wanted for anything."

"But—"

"My parents favor my brother over me," Webb says in a quiet

voice, silencing Hollis. He makes funny faces at Violet while he speaks, sending her into a fit of giggles incongruous with the subject matter at hand. "It's intentional and obvious, and even though it's not my brother's fault I can't help but resent him. For years, I bent over backwards trying to be as good as my brother but nothing was ever good enough. In the process I hurt people I cared about and wasted years of my life. All because my parents loved Philip more—and he was my blood brother.

"Because of my experience, I know if Piper and I do have children of our own, we won't let anything like that happen with Violet. We can promise she will have all the love, attention, and... wholeness... she needs."

No one speaks when Webb finishes his statement. I look up at him in awe. There's a slight lift to the side of his mouth, a glimmer of vulnerability shining in his eyes. He just told a group of strangers a painful personal truth, opening himself to gossip and pity—and he did it for me.

His hand moves to my shoulder and he pulls me into him. The uncomfortable silence stretches another beat until Lulu speaks. "Now you have family who loves you."

An expression flits across his face but it's gone before I can analyze it. He swallows. "Thank you, Lulu."

"I'm going to bring Denny a plate," she announces. She gestures to the food. "Please, eat! There's plenty and we can't possibly eat all these leftovers."

Hollis holds out her arms. "May I have a turn with Violet?"

I can tell Webb wants to say no, but I give him an imperceptible nudge. It's a reasonable request and we're the ones who'd look like jerks if we denied her. With reluctance, from both him and Violet, he passes the baby to Hollis. She fusses for a moment until Hollis bounces her and walks away, chattering about playing with her brothers. Pastor Marty narrows his eyes at us, then follows Hollis. Finally we're alone.

"Thank you," I put my arms around his waist, "for coming to my defense."

"Always."

I tilt my chin up. "I can't lose her to Hollis."

He stares down at me, brushes his thumb across my cheek. "Don't worry, she's not going to live with them. She's going to be ours."

He kisses me to the delight of our friends, and while I melt into him, I think about what he said. Ours. An hour ago, that might've sent a warm shock to my heart. But Carolynn's confident prediction, that if Webb adopts Violet with me there won't be anything stopping him from going back to her, puts a chill on everything. I have to remind myself that if it were true, he wouldn't have signed the prenup. Although, I only have his word it's a legal document; I should have had my own lawyer advise me.

He draws back, a tiny furrow appearing between his eyes. "I won't let anything happen to Violet. Or you."

I nod and smile, letting him think that's what was worrying me.

THIRTY

Piper

Webb doesn't leave my side for the rest of the afternoon. He introduces me to his friends, Graeme and Tish, and after some initial awkwardness we have a nice conversation. Even though Tish is Carolynn's friend, she is nothing but gracious and friendly. Webb is having his own conversation with Graeme and Hayes, while Tessa joins our conversation.

"Graeme told me you all went to college together," Tish says. "That's where you met?"

"Tessa, Laura—Violet's mother—and I roomed together," I explain. "Webb roomed with Hayes and another friend of theirs, Paul. The six of us used to hang out a lot."

"So you knew Carolynn back then, too," Tish continues.

I squirm and give her a tight smile. "Sort of. We knew her through Webb."

"She was in a sorority," Tessa adds. "She mostly hung around that crowd."

Hayes walks over and whispers something in Tessa's ear. She grins at me. "We'll be back. There's something we need to take care of."

"Do I want to know?" I ask dryly.

"Nope." Hayes takes Tessa by the hand and pulls her way.

I laugh in spite of the mischief they're obviously intent on making for us. "Those two normally can't be in the same time zone without bickering, so the fact they're conspiring together makes me a little nervous."

Tish laughs. "Reminds me of when Graeme and I were married. Webb and Carolynn took it upon themselves to fill our car with balloons. Made a quick escape from our reception an impossibility."

"I can imagine." I hope Tessa and Hayes aren't doing the same. When we can finally leave here, I want to bolt as quick as possible.

"You wouldn't know it to see them now, but Carolynn and Webb were quite the team once. They had their fights—boy did they fight—but it always seemed to blow over just as quickly as it began." She looks thoughtfully over at Webb. "It didn't surprise me when they separated, but I was surprised when Webb actually filed for divorce. It just seemed they always found their way back to one another. Carolynn once said they chose 'Whatever It Takes' by Lifehouse as their wedding song for exactly that reason."

I'm familiar with the ballad. It's even on one of my playlists, though as soon as I get the chance, I will be deleting that sucker. I'll never be able to listen to it without thinking of Webb and Carolynn. It was a good choice for them—a song about doing whatever it takes to stay together. Maybe it still is.

I'm not sure what expression is on my face, but suddenly Tish startles and puts a hand to her mouth.

"Oh, crap. That was totally inappropriate. I am so sorry. I-I didn't mean--"

I muster up a warm smile and lightly touch her arm. "No, it's fine. Don't worry about it. I know they have a history, I mean, I was there for the beginning of it." Ain't that the truth. "But I need to check on Violet, so if you'll excuse me. It was lovely meeting you, though. I'm sure we'll get together again."

Probably not, which is too bad because I do like Tish. But her loyalties are with Carolynn, I get it, and even though I know deep down she didn't mean any harm, I'm not sure we can ever be close. Besides, it's not like this marriage is meant for the long haul anyway.

I rush away, looking for Hollis and Violet. Lulu stops me as I head toward the house. "Oh, there you are. Listen, I wanted to let you know—Hollis is going to take Violet for the weekend."

She puts a hand up to quell my protest. "I know you said you weren't taking a honeymoon right now, but you and Webb deserve some time alone as newlyweds. She'll bring Violet back to your house on Monday."

"It's really not necessary, Lulu," I say, though it's futile.

"Nonsense," she says. "Besides, Hollis wants to take her to their home, to see how it all goes. She's been visiting with her in a rental house the past few weeks, but it seems silly for her to keep spending all that money."

"To Hartford? That's so—far away." My heart sinks to the floor. Not only did I want the time with Violet, but she would also be a perfect buffer between Webb and me. And after Carolynn's words earlier and Tish's reminder about the bond between the exes, I can use it.

"It's not that far and it's only for a few days. I know it's your week to take her."

I squeeze my eyes closed and take a calming breath before opening them again and looking directly at Lulu. "Give it to me straight, Lulu. Do you still think Violet would be better off with Hollis than me?"

She twists her hands together. "Pastor Marty and I are still weighing the options. I know it's not the answer you're hoping for, but I need to keep my emotions out of this decision, which is why I asked Marty to mediate. Of course you would do a wonderful job with Violet. We trust you. But Hollis and Aaron can provide more and maybe that should be a bigger consideration. I don't know, Piper. I'm doing the best I can."

I nod and give her a weak smile, trying and failing to hide my disappointment, the frustration at this whole silly situation. Laura would be apoplectic, but I keep that opinion to myself. She excuses herself and I dash inside the house to hide out for a little while.

※

AN HOUR LATER, I REJOIN THE PARTY IN TIME TO SAY GOODBYE and thank everyone for coming. When the last guest leaves, Webb pulls me aside. "Where did you go for so long? I was getting worried."

"I had a headache," I tell him refusing to meet his eyes. "I needed to rest a bit so I checked in on Violet and then laid down in one of the guest rooms." It's partly true. I had a headache. I checked in on Violet. And while I didn't lay down in one of the guest rooms, I did lock myself in one until I felt strong enough to face everyone again. And by everyone, I mean Webb.

I can't get Tish's words out of my head and it's so stupid, because she didn't really say anything I didn't already know firsthand. I guess hearing it from someone else, though, lends credibility to my fears. I'm right to keep my distance from Webb. No matter what he says, things between him and Carolynn will never truly be over. As his fake wife, I can live with that. As anything more than a casual friend, it will hurt too much. I'm so glad I didn't tell him about our baby. That's just one more emotional minefield that would complicate everything. It's in the past, just like we are. What we have now is simply an arrangement and in the future, when he decides to go back to Carolynn, I will be fine because I'm already expecting it. No more blindsides for me.

"Are you okay?" Webb is staring at me with concern etched across his face.

"Sorry, I zoned out. I'm fine, really. But I'm going to help Tessa with the decorations."

The caterers are packing up the dishes and station equipment. I start taking down decorations in the tent with Tessa and Hayes. I don't know what Webb is doing because I am pointedly ignoring him.

Lulu comes back from talking with the caterers. "We can handle the rest of this, Piper," she says. "Right, team?"

"Absolutely," Tessa says with a wink.

"Don't worry, we'll bring the extra cupcakes home," Hayes says around a mouthful of said dessert.

Tessa elbows him. A spray of crumbs flies out of his mouth with an "oof". "If he leaves you any. What is that, your tenth?"

"Children, behave." Lulu wags her finger at them. "Why don't you go find Webb and get going."

"If you're sure." I ball up the crepe streamers I took down and drop them in a recycle box. "Where is Denny? I'd like to say goodbye first."

"In the garage, tinkering as usual," she says, annoyance clear in her tone.

I slip around the front of the house and find the garage door cracked open. I lift and duck under it, finding Denny at his worktable with some piece of machinery and a screwdriver. He's lost the jacket and tie and wears a grease-stained, oilskin apron over the rest of his suit. With bifocals perched on the end of his nose, hands smudged with grease and lips pursed in concentration, he reminds me of Dad. A wave of nostalgia overwhelms me and my eyes prick with tears.

He jerks his head up and smiles when he sees me. "Well, here comes the bride. Where's your groom?"

"Collecting our things, I think." I pick my way over the cluttered floor. "I came to say goodbye and thank you. Everything was beautiful."

"That was all Lulu. I just shut up, pay up, and show up."

I laugh, then swallow hard to dislodge the lump sticking in my throat. "Thank you for walking me down the aisle, Denny."

His grin fades into a soft smile. "It was my honor. Clint Poincelot was one of the best friends I ever had. If the situation were reversed—"

He clears his throat and goes back to tinkering. I watch for a few seconds, screwing up the courage to ask the question on my mind.

"Denny?"

"Mmm?"

I take a breath and let it out. "Why did you guys change your mind about me adopting Violet?"

His hands still and he sets the tool down. "Lulu's just trying to make the best decision for our granddaughter."

"She's your granddaughter, too, Denny. Maybe I'm wrong, but it doesn't look like you care all that much for Pastor Marty. Why are you letting him influence who raises Violet?"

"It's complicated, Piper," he says in a low voice, turning the metal piece over in his hands.

"Explain it to me," I plead, leaning on the worktable. "Please. I'm trying to understand how one day I'm good enough to raise her and the next, I seem to lack the morals and character to be her mother because there's not a ring on my finger."

I raise my hand, the one with the slim gold band Webb slipped on there a few short hours ago. "Well there's a ring on there now. Am I now good enough?"

His face reddens and he squeezes his eyes closed. "Damn it, Piper. You don't understand—"

"Because it doesn't make sense."

He jerks back his stool and with a roar, throws the piece

across the garage. It strikes a tool chest against the far wall, landing in a metallic crash to the cement floor. My shoulders lift to my ears. Denny breathes heavily and I don't move while I wait him out, praying I didn't just fuck everything up for myself.

After an eternity, he cusses under his breath. "I'm sorry. I shouldn't have done that."

I swallow, still nervous to talk. "N-no. I shouldn't have pushed you."

He makes eye contact with me again and my heart leaps into my throat. He's not angry, he's simply… broken. With a strained voice, he says, "I called almost all the shots when Laura was growing up and I got it wrong. She ended up wasting her college education… broke, unmarried, and pregnant by 36. Dead at 37, coming home from a dead-end stripper job."

Indignation burns in my gut for my friend. "First of all, she wasn't a stripper—she managed the club and regardless of what you think of those places, it was successful. She earned a good living. Second of all, her education wasn't a waste—psychology just wasn't her passion. As for being unmarried and pregnant, well, so what? This isn't the 1950s, or even the 1980s. We don't need men to fulfil us, and we are more than capable of raising children on our own. Laura was a great person, a great friend, and she was on her way to being a great mom. If you think that's because you 'got it wrong', then I'm glad as hell you didn't get it 'right.'"

I back away from the table, fury and frustration tightening my chest. Denny stares back at me with a ravaged expression, then lifts his shoulders and lets them drop. "She's dead. My baby girl is dead, Piper, because I failed her. If I had been stronger with her, maybe she wouldn't be dead."

"But maybe Violet wouldn't be here," I counter.

His face crumples, but smooths out after only a moment. "But my baby would be. That's why Lulu will make the decision and I won't interfere. If she needs Pastor Marty to guide her," he swallows hard, "so be it. But like I said, my job right now is to shut up, pay up, and show up. And that's all."

He nods toward the garage door. "Roll that down all the way, will ya?"

He turns his back on me. Defeated in every way now, I leave and pull the door down behind me.

THIRTY-ONE

Webb

Piper is disappointed Violet isn't coming home with us, but I'm having a hard time believing her whiplash change of mood all comes down to that. Something changed, but I don't know what. When we said our vows earlier and sealed them with that kiss, I thought we might have turned a corner. There's nothing I want more than to turn this into a real relationship and until an hour or so ago, I thought we might have a good shot. Now it's like I'm back at square one, where she hates me again. She's avoiding me and it's bugging the hell out of me not knowing why.

She rests her chin on her hand and stares out the passenger window when we leave the Rosellis'. It takes her a few minutes to realize I've turned in the opposite direction of the ferry. Her head pops up and she turns to me with a frown.

"The ferry's back that way," she says, pointing her thumb over her shoulder.

"We're not going to the ferry."

She folds her arms. "Where are we going then?"

I grin at her. "It's a surprise."

She barks out a laugh. "I think I've had enough surprises today."

We both have, so maybe I reveal this one a little early. "I booked us a cabin in the White Mountains for two nights. Don't worry, it has all the amenities—running water, electricity, Wi-Fi."

"Like a honeymoon?" She looks horrified and I try not to take offense. "Does Lulu know? Is that why she sent Violet home with Hollis?"

I shift in my seat. "Technically a honeymoon, but really you can think of it as a simple getaway. I think there's still a lot more we need to learn about each other and it's easier to do that when there's nothing to distract us."

She glowers at me. "Oh, I already know enough about you."

I cock my head and glance at her. "What's that supposed to mean?"

Something flashes across her face, but it's gone as quickly as it came. She turns her head and faces out the passenger window again. "Nothing. Forget it."

At the risk of having my hand bitten off, I reach over and place it on her knee. "Hey. What's going on? Everything was going all right, at least after my parents left, then you disappear for an hour and come back as pissed off as the first day I saw you again. What could I have possibly done?"

She doesn't speak for a while and just as I'm about to give up on getting any answers, she hits me with a question. "What was yours and Carolynn's song?"

It's so out of left field, I fluster. "I--what?"

"What was your song?" She turns back to face me. "The one you probably danced to at your wedding?"

I can't imagine what relevance that has to us, but the look on her face has me racking my brain. "Uh, let me see--I think it was 'Hanging by a Moment'? No, another Lifehouse song. 'Whatever it Takes.' Carolynn chose it. Why?"

She stares out the windshield and twirls one of her loose curls around her finger. "Forget it. It doesn't matter."

"Obviously, it does. I just don't know why."

She won't look at me, so I find a lay-by and pull off the road. I put the car in park and throw an arm over the steering wheel as I turn to face her. "Pip. Look at me. What's this all about?"

She sucks in her bottom lip and looks at me, a million different emotions swimming in her eyes. Finally, she lets out a little huff and shakes her head. "It's--it's nothing. It's me being stupid."

"About what?" I sigh when she doesn't answer. "Come on, talk to me. Please."

She looks down at her lap and keeps twisting the ends of her hair, but she finally speaks. "Tish mentioned how she was surprised when you guys divorced, because she expected you'd get back together like you always did. She said your wedding song was 'Whatever it Takes' and how it was perfect because that was the two of you—doing whatever it took to find your way back together, like two star-crossed lovers. I was a little—I don't know, put out? Which is stupid, like I said, because it's not like this thing between us is real. It's a plan. An arrangement. A deal. Nothing more, and I have no right to feel jealous."

I rub my forehead. "Why was Tish telling you this?" I growl.

"Don't be mad at her," Piper implores. "It just came out in the course of conversation. I don't think she meant any harm."

Knowing Tish, that's probably true. Still, I would be having a talk with her and Graeme about keeping Carolynn's name out of future conversations. Then what else Piper said registers. "You were jealous?"

"Stupid, I know." She breathes out a laugh.

"Pip." I wait for her to look at me. "It's not stupid. And it's also not what it sounds like. Do you know why Carolynn and I always got back together after we fought?"

She shakes her head. I shift myself closer to her. "Because I always gave in. Whatever she wanted, whatever the problem, I gave in. She always got her way because I didn't care enough to fight about it. I just wanted to stop fighting. I didn't care enough about our relationship, even our marriage after the first few years, to fight to make it work with us both on equal ground. I took the path of least resistance. That's not some great love story. It's a fucking tragedy."

I reach out and cup the side of her face, caressing her cheek with my thumb. "That kiss we shared after we said our vows—that was the start of a great love story. Don't tell me you didn't feel it, too, because I know you did. You keep saying none of this is real, but that kiss was real. What I feel for you is real. And you, right here—this is real."

I thread my fingers through her silky hair and gently tug her closer. Her eyes blink closed and I press my lips against hers. I hold myself there, lips to lips, and let the sparks passing between us speak for themselves. When I pull back, her face is flushed an adorable rose color and her eyes are cloudy with lust. I slant her a grin. "Shall we keep going?"

Her eyes drift to my mouth and her tongue peeks out to moisten her top lip. I chuckle. "I mean to the cabin."

Her flush deepens as she settles back in her seat. "Right. Except I don't have an overnight bag. I'll need a toothbrush at least. Some deodorant. Change of underwear."

I don't think she needs the underwear, but I'm not going to press my luck by saying so. "Tessa packed what she thought you'd want. It's in the trunk."

"Is that what she and Hayes were doing when they snuck off?" I laugh.

"Probably. Although I wouldn't be surprised if they were doing other things."

"Me neither." She scoffs. "I wish they'd admit they're crazy for each other."

I pull back onto the road. "Right? Kind of silly not to admit your feelings when it's so damn obvious."

She understands I'm talking about more than Tessa and Hayes, but she lets it go. We continue to the cabin, the farther we get from Rhode Island, the more Piper relaxes. By the time we cross into New Hampshire and into the White Mountains, she is full on singing along with the radio at the top of her lungs. If I didn't find her so endearing, I might've kicked her out somewhere around Concord when she started belting out 'NSync songs.

The cabin I rented is tiny but its location more than makes up for any cramped quarters. I gulp in a long breath of fresh cool air. Critters rustle in the underbrush nearby, birds chirp from the treetops, and somewhere close, a brook babbles its way past. This is the kind of place where you can hear yourself think and after the whirlwind week Piper and I have had, it is exactly what we need.

She stops against a tree and tilts her chin up, a huge smile chasing away the shadows on her face. "Wow," she breathes out. "It's so quiet here."

I unlock the cabin door, then walk back to where she stands, squatting and scooping her off her feet. She whoops then bats my chest. "What the hell are you doing?"

"Carrying my bride over the threshold," I answer with a wink.

I nudge the door open and stride into the small space, an open-plan great room. "Home sweet home, for the next two nights at least."

The furnishings are sparse—a well-worn loveseat and coffee table surrounding a wood pellet stove making up the seating area; a small, scratched wood table with two mismatched chairs, a half-size refrigerator, microwave, and electric hot plate comprising the kitchen; and a double-size Murphy bed installed in the far corner. I set Piper on her feet in the middle of the room. The first thing she takes in is, of course, the bed.

"There's only one of those," she says, pointing at it.

"So there is." I rock back on my feet.

She eyes it, then says in a dry tone, "Well. I guess it doesn't get any more real than that."

THIRTY-TWO

Piper

Webb had arranged for the cabin to be stocked with food supplies, so after a quick dinner of cheese, crackers, veggies, and hummus, he and I relax on the loveseat together. It's seen better days and the middle bows, so we end up sliding into each other in the center. I pass him a glass of wine and he puts an arm around my shoulders. "You were radiant, today, Pip. I couldn't take my eyes off of you."

I twist the stem of my wineglass, a wave of heat rolling over my skin. "You weren't so bad yourself."

"High praise indeed."

I know we need to continue the conversation from the car. But this is nice and the wine has me feeling good. I don't want to ruin the happy buzz.

Unfortunately, he hasn't gotten the message. "Pip, we need to talk about us."

I sip my wine. "What about us?"

He takes the glass from my hand and sets it on the table next to his, then turns so he has to bend his leg to face me on the loveseat. This close, I can see the light gold rings around his pupils. I can feel the invisible tie between us, holding us together. This close it's hard to keep denying my feelings, but by God, I am going to try.

"What I said about this thing between us being real... I meant it," he says. "I want to give us a go. You, me, and eventually Violet."

I stiffen and he notices, because he grimaces. "You and me, at least. Although I love that little girl, Pip, you should know that. But I signed the papers and if things end between us, I will not pursue parental rights."

I relax a little, though for the first time, I also feel guilty and not just a little selfish for wanting to keep Violet to myself. "Look, Webb, I can't say I haven't felt things changing between us. But this thing, this marriage, is a means to an end. We agreed."

"I know what we agreed to, but do you think you can trust me to try for a little more? Pip, I'm crazy about you. You have to know that."

Shit. My eyes are beginning to burn, and crying is the last thing I want to do right now. I have to stay strong. "It's a matter of trust, more than belief. I believe you, but what does it really mean? What happens when you wake up one day and realize this is not what you want? That I'm not what you want?"

"It's not going to happen," he says with so much conviction, I almost believe him. I want to believe him.

"It already has once."

He rears back and closes his eyes, the look of anguish on his face so stark if takes my breath away. When he opens his eyes again, they're watery. He tucks a loose strand of hair behind my ear. "I'm not the same man except in one way—I still want you. I want you to be mine."

I push myself up and move out of his reach. "I do forgive you, Webb," I say quietly. "And I want you, too. But I don't know how much I can give you without risking my heart again."

His throat ripples, then he nods his head. "I said before I

wouldn't push you, and I will keep that promise. I'll follow your lead, Pip. But I needed you to know where I stand."

I stare at him a moment longer, then point back toward the bathroom. "I'm going to take a quick shower."

I grab toiletries and a change, then lock myself in the bathroom so I can cry under the shower stream in peace.

THE SHOWER HELPS, BUT I'M STILL LEFT WITH A STOMACH FULL OF cheese and apprehension. Neither of which is good for someone with my intolerance for dairy and guilt. I want to tell myself what's between us is nothing more than sexual awareness, nothing more than us giving into the attraction that's never gone away. I want to tell myself it's one-sided, but it's not.

I want him, damn it. All of him. But I can't, not with so much still left unresolved between us. Enjoying mutual orgasms would be so fucking great, but I don't think I can go down that road again and not fall right back in love with the man.

And if that happened, it would mean telling him everything. Slicing myself open and revisiting the old wounds. It would mean telling him about the baby. Once he finds out I kept that from him, that I'd considered never telling him even if the baby had been born, it wouldn't matter if I forgave him. He would never forgive me.

"How did I get in this mess?" I ask my reflection.

Tessa had packed a short, satiny white teddy for me to wear. It's not mine; I'm a flannel shorts and ratty t-shirt kind of girl when it comes to pajamas. She must have figured, rightly, I'd not put it on if I had something more comfortable to wear to bed because she didn't pack me anything sleepworthy besides this and a few t-shirts, which I'd have to wear without pants. Wearing my stiff jeans to bed was not going to happen.

I braid my wet hair, talking myself into a plan of action for the night. Maybe I can run to the bed and get under the covers before he notices what I'm wearing. We'll be sharing the bed, but if I ask him not to touch me, he'll respect that. Maybe if we wait long enough to retire, we'll be so tired it won't even be an issue. Then tomorrow—tomorrow, we'll hang out, take a hike, scroll through TikTok. Normal friend things. I can do this. I can keep this from moving into dangerous territory.

I step out of the bathroom and blink. It's dim in the cabin, the only light coming from a few lit candles placed around the room. The pellet stove is on and has warmed the space, but a frisson of awareness snakes up my spine, sending shivers through my body. Webb is still wearing his suit, sans tie, the first few buttons of shirt undone to reveal a dusting of golden hair. He stands in the middle of the room, one hand in his pocket, a cautious smile on his face. He stares at me, eyes sparking in the candlelight. I swallow hard, clutching the dress and undergarments to my chest. My barely covered chest. He swaggers toward me and I'm caught, transfixed by his gaze like a deer in headlights.

He removes his hand from his pocket and takes the clothes out of my arms, tossing them on the nearby table. Without breaking eye contact, he takes my hand and pulls me closer to him. His other hand is holding a small remote, and after pressing a button, he tosses that on top of the pile of clothes.

The opening notes to an Ed Sheeran song begin to play from a hidden speaker. Webb puts a hand to my waist and with the other hand, interlaces his fingers with mine. In what feels like a natural move, I rest my free hand on his shoulder and we start to sway.

"What is this?" I ask, my voice barely above a whisper.

"It's our song," he says. "We didn't have a wedding song, so I thought I would choose one for us. I thought this one was perfect because, well, you look perfect tonight."

He bends his head and presses his cheek to mine. The

contact sends my nerves into hyperdrive. I move my head a little, just to feel the rub of his soft scruff against my freshly scrubbed and sensitive skin. A low chuckle vibrates through him and in turn, through me.

He pulls back to stare at me, his smile deepening the creases at the corners of his eyes. I never thought I'd be into something like that, but I love it on him. I love that it's a tell he's genuinely happy. I love that it happens almost always when he's smiling at me. I love—

Fuck. I love *him*.

We don't say any words, just sway to the music. I close my eyes and lay my head against his chest, listening to Ed sing in rhythm with Webb's heart, my own heart skipping in my chest. I didn't want this to happen. But I never could control my heart, not when it came to Webb. But this time, I'm not young and naive. If he walks away this time, I already know I'll survive it as long as I can hold back at least a little of my heart. It's the only way.

As the song draws to a close, Webb pushes me away and twirls me once, then brings me back into him with our hands between us. I stare up at him. He lowers his mouth to mine and I open under him, letting him explore and taste and bite. I'm half aware the song has changed, but we continue to move together, swaying as our tongues tangle together in a sweet, seductive dance of their own.

I push Webb's suit coat off his shoulders, he nips at my earlobe, his hands slip from my waist to my ass. I let my head fall back so he can trail kisses down the slope of my throat to the hollow above my chest. My fingers undo the rest of his buttons, opening his amazing body to me. I rake my nails across his hard chest and down the firm, chiseled abs his love of pizza has done nothing to soften. I moan as he sucks at the sensitive skin behind my ear.

"May I?" he lifts his head to ask, a finger under the thin strap of the teddy. I give him my assent and he pulls both straps off my shoulders and down my arms, revealing the swell of my breasts. His tongue traces the edge of the garment, licking a hot path along my cleavage. I moan, yanking his shirt off his arms and leaving him naked from the waist up. He returns to kneading my ass, his tongue flicking out to lave a nipple through the satin material.

I pull back a few inches, both of us panting, his eyes a lusty haze that probably mirror mine. His hands tighten on my ass and draw me closer to him. The thick ridge of his dick presses against me, igniting an entire forest fire within. I flip open the top button his pants and lower his zipper, slipping my hand inside to wrap around his steel. His head flops back and he lets out a low curse.

Webb's cock is bigger than I remember. I can't get my entire hand around it and that little factoid has me pushing him toward the bed. He doesn't fight me on it, just goes where I'm leading him until his knees hit the frame and he falls back onto the mattress. He grabs me at the last minute and tips me over on top of him. He yanks my teddy down, exposing the girls in all their big, swinging glory. With a grunt of appreciation, he puts his mouth on one, using his fingers to pluck at the nipple of the other. His teeth scrape across my nipple and I suck in a tight breath. He lifts his head a moment to say, "I can stop if it's too much."

"Don't you dare," I hiss between my teeth.

He continues his sensual assault on my tits, but I'm getting impatient. From the way he holds me, I can't reach his cock and God, do I want his cock in my hand. In my mouth. Between my legs.

I roll over and sit up so I can pull his pants off. He does it faster than me, whipping them off and revealing a stunning, smooth as velvet and hard as titanium cock nestled in a perfect manscape. A feral noise escapes my mouth, much to his delight.

"Make that noise again and I'm going to come all over myself."

"Okay," I breathe, a devilish grin on my face.

"Oh no," he says. "I'm not coming all over myself. That's for you. As soon as I make you come over me."

He flips over and holds himself above me. He kisses a path that starts at my lips and ends at my mons. My knees automatically drop for him and he blows a cool breath of air over my very heated center. I shudder at the sensation, then rock as his tongue pushes between my already wet lower lips. "Fuck, Webb."

He spreads me apart with his fingers, his shoulders holding my legs apart so he can settle in with that magic mouth of his. In minutes, he's sucking on my clit and sending me spiraling over the edge.

As I begin floating back to earth, I look down between my legs and meet his gaze. His lips glisten with my essence and when he licks them I almost shatter again. But he reaches to the floor and in seconds, I hear the crinkle of a foil wrapped.

"I have to be inside you, beautiful," he says with a hungry voice. "I need to feel that pussy of yours clamping down on my cock so tight, the way you did on my tongue."

His dirty talk inflames more need in me. He positions himself over me, holding himself in his hand and sliding the tip of his dick through my wetness. I put my hands behind his head and bring him down, tasting myself on his tongue. At that moment he plunges into me and between the beautiful friction and the way his tongue pumps in and out of my mouth, I'm quickly spiraling again. Everything in me tightens. My nails dig into his back, my legs wrapped around his waist as he thrusts into me. I'm so close to the edge again. "Webb, Webb," I chant.

He puts his hand between us and with his thumb, rubs a circle on my clit. That's all it takes to topple me again and I fall with a keening wail. He follows close behind, grunting his release before collapsing on me, keeping most of his weight on his forearms so as not to crush me. We gasp, our bodies sticking together with sweat. I don't care that I just showered. I don't want him to move off me.

"Wow," he pants in my ear.

I laugh. "Exactly."

He lifts himself up and draws in a few steadying breaths. Staring into my eyes, he brushes light kisses across my cheeks, my nose, my lips. "Are you okay?"

I brush a sweaty flop of hair off his forehead and take a few deep breaths of my own before I answer. "Yeah. More than."

"Good," he says with a wink. He pulls out of me and I moan at the loss, which makes him chuckle. "Just need to take care of this condom and grab another. You up for round two?"

"Already?" I raise up on my elbows and watch as he ties it up and drops it in the wastebasket before going into his bag and retrieving an entire box.

"We have fifteen years to make up for, Beautiful. I don't want to waste another minute."

True to his word, he wastes no time at all bringing me to heaven and back over and over and over again.

THIRTY-THREE

Piper

It's late morning when I finally open my eyes, the smell of fresh roasted beans perking me up. I sit up and spy Webb in the kitchenette wearing only a pair of boxer briefs, using a French press. I watch him quietly moving around, hard sinewy muscles bunching as he works the press with the same finesse he used on me last night. Multiple times last night. Webb promised to wring every last drop of pleasure out of me and the delicious soreness between my thighs proves his success.

I rake a hand through the tangled mess on my head. Webb turns his head and the smile he gives me sets me on fire. I can't help myself from marveling at what those smiling lips did to me last night. This man owns my body.

"Morning, Beautiful," he says.

"Is it still morning?" I squint at the bedside clock. "Ah, two minutes to spare."

He pours us coffee and brings it over, perching on the side of the bed next to me. I take it with a grateful groan, noting it has cream in it. I take a sip—it also has the right amount of sweetener. Something in my heart trips at the small, thoughtful gesture. But while he may own my body—and probably my soul, too, since I think it drifted out of me somewhere around orgasm number six and hasn't returned—it's my heart I need to hold back. "It's good."

"They stocked us premium beans. I'm definitely leaving them four-and-a-half stars."

"Why the half star off?"

"Shower's too small to make love to my beautiful wife." He winks at me and the fire in me blazes.

I pat the mattress. "Sturdy bed, though. I'd say that makes up for it. I've always found shower sex to be a little uncomfortable no matter how big the bathroom."

He raises his eyebrow as he takes a sip. "Maybe you haven't had shower sex with the right man."

Since I don't want to bring up my sexual history, nor listen to his, I change the subject. "So what are we doing today?"

He shrugs. "I was thinking we could take a hike? Forecast said it was supposed to rain, but all I see is blue sky."

"Did Tessa pack me the right shoes?"

"I think she packed your sneakers, which will work. I'm only proposing a walk in the woods, not a climb up the mountain."

He leans in and drops his voice, using the velvet tenor of his that can liquify my insides in a heartbeat. "Unless you're too sore to walk today. We can just hang out, watch movies, test out the strength of the loveseat."

I waggle my brows. "As tempting as that sounds, I think I'd like to get some fresh air first. We've got all night again, right? Besides," I glance over at the loveseat, "I'm telling you now, there is no way that thing is comfortable enough for sex."

⊰||||||⊱

I'M NOT TOO PROUD TO ADMIT WHEN I'M WRONG. AND BOY, WAS I wrong.

Before we left the cabin this afternoon, we discovered the

loveseat is, in fact, comfortable enough for sex. Though I still contend I was partly right; there'd be no fitting both our bodies horizontally on those broken-down cushions. It was, however, the right size for Webb to yank down my jeans and bend me over the arm while he took me from behind.

Now we're walking on a sun-dappled path through the woods, the red maples overhead beginning to bud with red blossoms. Webb takes my hand to help me over a fallen log and doesn't let go. It's peaceful. Only the sound of woodpeckers searching for food and occasional rustling in the underbrush break the silence. It's the kind of place where you can hear yourself think, whether you like the thoughts coming to you or not.

"You're awfully quiet over there." Webb nudges my shoulder. "What're you thinking?"

"Funny you should ask. I was literally thinking about thinking."

"Thinking about thinking," he repeats. "Better than what I was afraid you were thinking."

I look up at him. "What's that?"

He stares off into the distance and shrugs. "I was afraid you were going to second-guess being together. We're out in the fresh air, where it's quiet and prime for ruminations. Maybe you start thinking it's a bad idea we fell into bed again. You've been half-resistant to the idea."

I smooth a hand over my ponytail. "I'm sorry I've been giving out mixed signals. This whole situation—well, it's brought up a lot of shit I thought I'd already dealt with. Plus, with the adoption and this," I gesture between us, "all on the heels of Laura's death."

I let out a breathy laugh. "I guess you can say I've been overwhelmed."

He pulls me to a stop and turns me to face him. He ducks his head to look me square in the eye. "Hey. I bulldozed my way back into your life when I probably should've left you alone. I hurt you and I don't deserve your forgiveness. It was selfish of me to even ask for another chance."

I shake my head, but he grips the back of my neck, the warm, firm pressure sending spikes of electricity through me. His eyes shimmer and he swallows hard, his throat visibly working. When he speaks, there's a hoarseness to the quality of his voice that cracks my heart open a little further. "Thank you for giving me another chance to be with you. I get how hard it is for you to trust me and all I can say is, I will spend the rest of my life making up for what I did. Whatever happens between the two of us and this marriage, whether you decide six months is long enough or you want to take it day-by-day, I'm here for you."

He's so earnest, so sincere, and I so want to trust in him. I want to take this day-by-day, month-by-month, year-by-year. But it can't happen until I tell him the truth, as much as it will hurt. And I just don't know if I'm ready. We begin walking again, still hand-in-hand. "Can I ask you something?"

"Anything."

"It's about Carolynn," I say.

He slows, but says, "Go ahead."

"You said you married her because you felt guilty for the accident that left her unable to have kids. Then you said she didn't want children, anyway. But did you?"

He draws in a deep breath. "Carolynn seemed devastated by the news, but after a few years—once we were both out of grad school and in our chosen careers—I thought we should consider adoption. She kept putting me off until one day, she admitted the truth. She never really wanted children. She liked the freedom and she took a lot of pride in her career. I think my mother might have convinced her that having children was a mistake."

His laugh is bitter. I squeeze his hand, encouraging him to

continue and after a few minutes he does. "I did want children. I want them still."

"What if she changed her mind?" I ask. "What if she called you today and said she wanted to adopt or find a surrogate? Would you want to give it another shot with her?"

"Piper, I married you," he says with a frown. "Christ, we're on our honeymoon. And after last night, you think I'd drop you to go running back to her?"

We both tense. With the exception of the marriage thing, that's exactly what he did.

He gives a self-deprecating laugh. "Don't answer that."

We continue walking in silence, but the fun, easy vibe is gone. I want to believe Carolynn is wrong, but what's that saying? Those who forget history are doomed to repeat it?

I trip over a half-hidden tree root and Webb catches me. I stare into his eyes, those freaking warm, gorgeous, green eyes and I know it. I've never stopped loving this man and I think—I think I'm going to let him have my heart to potentially break again.

He hooks one corner of his mouth up, looking unsure. "Uh, Pip?"

I swallow. "I'm okay."

He starts moving along again, but I remain rooted in place. "Webb?"

He stops and turns. "Yeah?"

I take a deep breath. It's going to hurt whether he leaves today, tomorrow, or ten years from now, so what the hell? "I think—I want to take it day-by-day."

His lips curl upward ever so slowly into a smile whose radiance rivals the sun. "Really?"

"Truly." I beam back at him, though there's a hitch in my smile because what I say next could change everything. "But, there's something I need to tell you."

A flash lights up the sky and a few seconds later, thunder

crashes over us. We hadn't noticed the storm rolling in behind us, but it was here and any moment now the gray sky above was going to open up on us.

"Shit, even if we make a run for it, it's still going to take a while to get back to the cabin," Webb says, sheltering me in his arms as the first of the raindrops fall.

I scope out our surroundings and spot a dark opening in a nearby rockface. "There." I point to it. "Looks like a cave."

We dash to the opening just as the heavens open in earnest. Fortunately, it's a shallow cave, with enough space for us to shelter out of the storm but not enough to hide any critters. The wind kicks up and I shiver.

Webb whips off his sweatshirt and lays it on the hard dirt ground. He lowers himself, then pulls me down to sit between his legs as he wraps his arms around me from behind. His hot breath tickles my ear. "Guess I shouldn't have mocked the weather guys this morning."

"They're always right, you know," I remind him.

"How do you figure? Half the time they say snow and we end up with a heat wave. Sunshine and we get rain."

I twist in his arms to look at him. "They always give us a percentage of chance. I bet the forecast didn't say '100% chance of rain'. It probably said 'most likely' or '70%'."

"90%," he grumbles.

"See," I laugh. "Even if it didn't storm, that just means the 10% chance for sunshine won out. Which is what they said. Therefore, weather people are always right."

Water drips down the side of his face as he stares at me, an impish gleam in his eyes. I turn all the way around and sit on my knees, leaning forward to lick the errant drop off his jaw. His scruff is rough on my tongue and I moan at the memory of the beard burn he gave my thighs last night. So worth it.

He grabs hold of my ponytail and tugs my head back to suck on the water that's dripped down my own face and neck. His warm mouth heats my skin, sending fiery tingles across the surface.

"What do you think they'd say the chances were of me getting you off in this cave?" He pulls up on the hem of my sweatshirt and I lift my arms so he can yank it off. My nipples bead through the thin fabric of my shirt. Of course I'm not wearing a bra—seemed pointless since we are all alone out here.

I know the moment he realizes this. He can't seem to pull his glassy gaze away from my chest. His hands come around my back and I bow against him, letting him hold my weight as he lowers his head.

"Mmm," My eyes drift close as he clamps his mouth over my breast through my wet t-shirt. "I'd say 99%."

He lifts up, surprise lighting his face. "Only 99?"

"You never know," I say, threading my fingers into his hair and tugging him back to what he was doing. "Maybe your foreplay game won't do it for me out here."

"Somehow I doubt that, Beautiful." He lifts my t-shirt, exposing my hard peaks. His tongue swirls around first one, then the other before he sucks it between his lips. I squeal when he nips before releasing me.

He unbuttons my jeans and snakes his hand inside. I moan as he slides his fingers between my folds. I hold his head to my chest, every tug of my nipple, every nibble and lick taking me closer and closer. I rock against his hand, fucking his fingers, his palm putting pressure against my overly sensitive bundle of nerves. In no time at all, I'm peaking. He hooks his fingers, hitting that oh so glorious spot and fireworks go off. I cry out, my whole body quaking.

He kisses me, his tongue doing a poke and swirl thing in a close imitation of when his head was between my legs last night. But it's my turn today. "Lay back," I command.

"Yes, ma'am," he groans. He tries to pull me on top of him

but I wiggle until I'm at my destination. I quickly flip open his fly and pull out his cock. He hisses a breath through his teeth.

"What are you doing, Beautiful?"

I answer him by running my tongue up the length of his shaft, then swirling it around his head to taste the precum waiting there. I look up from under my lashes, his eyes hooded and lips parted as he watches me. He reaches down to cup my jaw as I open and take him. He strokes my jaw as I move up and down his shaft, taking him a little further each time until there's nowhere else for him to go.

He sucks in a breath, moving his grip to my ponytail with one hand. I suck as I draw my head back, swirling my tongue around his head as I almost pop off, then repeat the motion. I set the pace, but when his hips tilt forward, seeking more, I'm happy to give it to him. I swallow as I take him deep. He grunts and begins thrusting... gently at first, but his speed picks up and soon he's using my hair to guide me along. There's a new rush of dampness between my legs. I balance on his thick, muscular thighs and flatten my tongue as his thrusts become more frenetic.

"Fuck, fuck," he grinds out. "Baby, you gotta stop or I'm going to unload in your mouth."

I hum in satisfaction and resist his efforts to pull me off. I look up at him, trying to tell him with my eyes and the curve of my lips that I want this. I want him to lose control. I want him to finish down my throat.

With a roar, his cock pulses between my lips and he spills down my throat. I slide my mouth off and he pulls me over him, his lips crashing down on mine.

"Fuck, Pip," he growls against my lips. "You're amazing."

We lay together, breathing hard, exchanging passionate kisses until I feel him grow beneath me again. Outside our shelter, the rain continues to come down in sheets. When the lightning flashes, I'm not sure if it's the storm or the connection between us causing it. Without words, we undress from the waist down. He pulls a condom out of his pocket before discarding them to the side. I take it out of his hands and have it open and rolled down in seconds. He chuckles, but it dies on his lips as I raise up and lower myself onto him. I'm so wet for him he glides right in to the hilt. I flex my muscles and squeeze his cock as I raise myself up. He shudders underneath me. "F-f-fuck."

I set a steady rhythm, his hands roaming my body as I flex and clench over him. I tighten around him on the upstroke, grind my clit against him on the downstroke, and in minutes I have us both on the cusp. I ride him hard and fast. My skin is on fire and the edge is so near, so near. Neediness consumes me while he continues to buck inside me, fucking me until I can barely think. I'm so close... that's what I'm chanting when he reaches down between us and starts working my bud.

That does it. He sets me flying, his own release right behind. He holds me as I float back to earth, my body jolting with tiny aftershocks.

"So beautiful," he whispers.

We lay together, talking in whispers, breathing each other in, waiting for the storm to pass.

THIRTY-FOUR

Piper

I'm pouring boiled sugar into molds, trying a new flavor for our homemade lollipops, while Violet watches from her bouncy seat. Black licorice isn't one of our most popular flavors; it has a niche following. But since the wedding, I've spent every night in Webb's arms soaking up his scent and black licorice is the closest I can get to mimicking it. A few drops of licorice extract, a touch of mint—a nod to his career—and a splash of agave for sweetness and voila… the essence of Webb.

I wish I could say being with him again is effortless, but there's still so much hanging over my head. I need to tell him about the baby, but every time I have the chance I swallow the words. Everything is going so well and I don't want to burst the bubble we're in. Not yet. I just want to be sure of us before I drop this on him. I want to make sure we finalize things with Violet.

Webb assures me time and again we did the right thing. But I hate the deception. Between the guilt over lying to Lulu and Denny and most of my friends and keeping this one last secret from Webb, my stomach is often in knots. The only time it's not is when he's inside me. Maybe that's why I can't get enough of him.

I tamp down my heavy thoughts and focus on the candy, narrating my moves to Violet. She's too young to understand, but she likes the sound of my voice and she speaks back to me. I pretend to understand what she's saying and answer accordingly. "Why yes it does smell like Daddy in here."

Someone clears their throat. I slide a tray onto a cooling rack and look over my shoulder. Drew leans against the door frame, arms folded across his chest. There are shadows under his eyes and the lines around his mouth are tight. I've never seen him look this rough, not even when he was breaking up with me, and my anxiety immediately ratches up.

"Hey."

"Hey," he says back.

I turn to face him. "How's Mara?"

"She's good." He steps further into the room, shoving his hands in his pockets. He stares over at Violet. "She said the wedding was, uh, nice."

I start clearing my mess. "It was."

He smiles at Violet and holds his pinky out to her. She grasps it in her tiny fist and tries to pull it toward her mouth, spraying bubbles as she babbles. He speaks to her in a light tone. "Hi there, pretty girl. Can you give Uncle Drew a smile?"

Violet obliges, her apple-round cheeks all but swallowing her eyes. She's put on a healthy amount of weight the past few months and I'm loving her soft roundness and all the little dimples.

"So, I heard you talking to her in here," Drew says, his focus on Violet, who's holding her own conversation with him. "You referred to Webb as 'Daddy.' Does that mean it's official?"

I clock the way he said Webb's name, like he was chewing a piece of baker's chocolate, but I'm going to overlook it. "Lulu will probably make a final decision in the next week or so. I'm trying to be more optimistic."

I wash the double boiler, waiting for him to speak. My back stiffens when he sighs and says, "Piper. I still think this is a bad idea."

I drop the pots in the sink with a clatter and whirl around. Violet startles and her big eyes fill. I shush her and set her seat rocking, heading off any emotional outburst.

Can't say the same for me. I attempt to keep the volume down, but I put as much ice and fury into my voice as I can. Drew needs to understand something.

"I didn't ask your opinion, Drew," I seethe. "You've already made it quite clear how stupid you think I am—"

"Piper, I never said that!"

"And I know you don't trust me to take care of myself—"

"It's not you I don't trust—"

I hold up my hand. "I appreciate you're being protective, that you're trying to be a good friend. But what you don't seem to appreciate is that I know exactly what the risks are. I know exactly what I am possibly setting myself up for. And I know exactly how badly this might all turn out."

I gesture to Violet. "But she's worth it. I will do anything for her, even let Webb rip my heart out again if it means, in the end, I still have her. It's a promise I made to Laura and it's a promise I intend to keep."

Drew's glances at Violet, clenching his teeth. "I know she's worth it," he says quietly. "I just don't think he is worth it. I hate that you're letting him back into your life after what happened."

I tighten my ponytail. "Webb gets nothing out of marrying me, and I mean that literally. If anything, it's complicated his life and possibly damaged his already strained relationship with his parents. But he did it to make up for the past. That has to mean something."

I sigh. "And I'm lonely, Drew. I haven't found anyone who

thinks I'm good enough to build a life with and I'm almost forty. Webb says he wants to see where this goes and maybe it'll go the way all my relationships go—with him realizing there's someone better out there, that maybe he was right fifteen years ago. Or maybe, *maybe* I'll finally have someone who thinks I'm enough to stick around. It's a risk, the last one I am ever going to be willing to take. But if it ends up with me having Violet as my family—"

I touch her bare little toe. She's kicked her socks off again. "She's worth any potential heartbreak."

Drew is silent for a long moment, and when he speaks he surprises me. "You were enough, Piper. For me, I mean. When we were together."

I scoff. "Sure I was, Drew. That's why you married Mara barely a year later."

"I wanted to ask you to marry me."

His confession pulls me up short. I shake my head. "But you said our connection was a deep, platonic one."

"It was. It is," he corrects. "But not because of any lack of chemistry on my part. I took my cues from you and the closer we became, the deeper we got into the relationship, the more I started feeling you pull away. It's what you do, Piper. You meet someone and as soon as it starts showing potential for something serious, you put up your walls. It's like your heart is in this lockbox and unless someone has the perfect combination, they're never going to get to it. I think I almost had it, but in the end it wasn't enough. So it wasn't you who wasn't enough for me. I wasn't enough for you to let your guard down."

He steps toward me, his eyes misting and triggering an inconvenient prickliness in mine. I turn to Violet and busy myself looking for her missing sock. "It all worked out, though, didn't it? You and Mara are very obviously soulmates, which means you would've been settling for me if you had proposed and I said yes. It would've been my greatest fear come to life—to have someone choose me and then one day wake up and realize they chose wrong."

"I hate that what Webb did to you hurt you so much you have no faith in love. No trust. Except when it comes to him, ironically, and I don't get it."

I find the sock and rub it between my fingers, the cotton soft and soothing. I give Drew, who's staring at me nonplussed, a wry smile. Because I'm only lately realizing it wasn't Webb who damaged me so badly. "Webb isn't the one who caused me to be like this. It started long before he was ever a part of my life. What happened between us might have solidified this brokenness in me." I shake my head, tears dripping down my cheeks. "But he isn't the cause."

No, that honor goes to my mother. Aria's leaving did a number on my psyche and I've been paying the price my whole life. But no more.

I swipe at my cheeks with the back of my hand and put Violet's socks to right while I speak. "You're right. I didn't see it before. I always took the break-up as inevitable. I had more hope when we were together, but to be honest, when you gave me the whole speech about our friendship being more important to you, I was relieved. For one, I guess I was always waiting for you to go. Especially after I told you about Webb and the baby, and when you didn't, I had a splinter of hope. But it was always overshadowed by impending doom."

I chortle, but there's no humor in it. Only sadness and regret. "But I did love you. The fact you wanted to remain my friend, and become my business partner, meant you'd stay around. So I jumped at it, and I'm really glad I did."

"I wanted to keep you in my life," Drew says. "You're one of the best friends I've ever had."

"Same here."

"I'm sorry for everything I said," he continues. "I hope you know I didn't mean it. I will always be there for you, even if it means helping you pick up the pieces again. But I reserve the right to kick his ass if it comes to that."

I smile. "Whatever happens, it's not going to come to that. I'm stronger than I was before."

He eyes me speculatively. "No. You've always been strong. I'm happy you're finally realizing it."

I wrap my arms around him. He kisses the top of my head. Violet's babbles become louder and I chuckle as I let go of Drew. "Someone jealous?"

He leans over and kisses Violet on the top of her head. Her grin takes up most of her face. "Bye, pretty girl. Be good for Mommy."

My heart aches a bit. I've never referred to myself as "Mommy," holding that sacred title for its rightful owner. But when Drew says it, something right settles over me and I know, it sounds strange, but I feel Laura smile.

THIRTY-FIVE

Piper

It's been a magical, angsty, wonderful, frustrating two weeks of marriage. The sex is mind-blowing, I mean, there's no other word for it. We haven't missed a day since the cabin, even for the five days we had Violet. She's started sleeping through the night, which gives Webb and I ample opportunity for sexcapades. We've christened every room in this bungalow—save the nursery, because ick—and tried almost every position in the Pocket Guide to the Kama Sutra Webb brought home one night. There's a permanent smile on my face, so much so Bette keeps giving me knowing winks every time I go into the cafe. It's bleeding into my work at the confectionery, too. Customers have been raving about the new flavors I've been concocting. All inspired by the loves in my life—Webb and Violet.

I still haven't told Webb the truth yet. I think it's best to wait for everything going on with Violet to settle down. But I am going to tell him. He deserves to know the truth, but I also know he's going to feel hurt. I don't want to add to the stress of waiting on Lulu to make up her mind.

Which has been frustrating, to put it nicely. Violet is still going back and forth between me, Lulu, and Hollis. She's over seven months now, and moving around takes a toll on her. It takes us a good day to get her back into our routine and I imagine the same is true at Lulu's. Webb agrees it isn't good for Violet, and we need to talk to Lulu. Something has to give. I'm worried pushing too hard will push her to Hollis's side, and Tessa hasn't yet found the smoking gun I need to discredit Hollis. Webb says he has something in the works, too, but he hasn't said what. He doesn't want to disappoint me if it doesn't pan out.

Carolynn has been quiet, but Webb's parents are making his professional life difficult. The practice is supposed to open in less than a month, and Webb and his partners are working hard to get it ready, despite some setbacks with construction and equipment delivery. The marketing finally fell into place and combined with the word-of-mouth campaign my SASBO friends organized, they've already booked appointments for every day their first couple of weeks of opening and more keep coming in. It's still not enough to satisfy his mother, though. She's constantly haranguing him about this or that, nitpicking over details and threatening contract breach with every breath. If I could, I would give Webb the money to just buy out of the damn contract and be done with it.

He's late coming home tonight, but Violet and I are still in the kitchen trying to finish dinner. She's suddenly become very particular about her solids. Peas and carrots, which were a favorite last month, are now dramatically despised. I'm wiping pea out of my hair thanks to Violet's violent refusal to swallow the spoonful when Webb walks in.

"Uh oh," he says. "I take it someone is still on an anti-pea crusade."

I'm trying to rub the baby food out of my hair with a dish towel, to no avail. All I'm doing is smearing it worse. I throw the towel down in a huff. "I don't know why I bother. The only thing she'll eat is tapioca and really, is that terrible? It's got vitamins in it."

Webb hugs me. "Why don't you go grab a shower. I'll finish up here."

"Is it that bad?" I hold a piece of my hair out to see.

"Well, you also have some chocolate behind your ear."

"I was dipping truffles today and a tray got away from me."

He chuckles and kisses my temple. "Go. I got this.'

I probably should've taken a shorter shower, but once the hot water sluiced over me, I couldn't move. When I finally pull on my loungewear and head downstairs, Webb and Violet are sitting outside on the back patio. The sliding door is cracked open and I can hear him talking to her.

"Violet, babe, you gotta give Mommy a break," he says to her. She's sitting on his lap while he feeds her—wait, is that, peas? Yes, he's feeding her peas and she's eating them like a champ. She's even smiling at him in between bites. Little traitor.

"She's working really hard to make sure you're healthy and happy, and that means feeding you yummy vegetables like peas. Little girls can't live off tapioca alone, you know."

I watch him spoon a final bite into her mouth, then take a wet cloth and wipe her gums. It makes me smile, he's so conscientious of her oral care even though she has all of two teeth. I take a step to join them when I hear it.

"Dadadadadada," Violet patters, tapping his face.

I freeze and so does Webb. Then he says,"Violet, did you say Dada?"

She gives him a drooly, gummy grin. Then distinctly says, "Dada."

Tears well up in my eyes and I have to swallow hard to keep from bursting out into a sob. Her first word! And it's *Dada*. Wow.

Webb looks equally emotional. He clears his throat. "Well. We should work on Mama now."

Violet looks at him and says Dada again, then giggles. I wipe away the tears that leaked out and step out onto the patio.

"Oh, so she'll eat peas for you. I see how it is," I kid.

Webb looks at me in awe. "She just said—I mean, I think she said—"

I smile, waiting for him to continue. But he doesn't. He just shakes his head. "No, you know, she was just babbling. You know she is."

I catch the baby's attention and pat Webb. "Violet, who is this?"

"Dada!" she squeals. "Dadadadadada."

He narrows his eyes. "You heard?"

I pick up Violet and laugh. "I was standing at the door when she said it. Why didn't you tell me just now?"

He grimaces and rubs the space between his brows. "I didn't want you to feel bad. It doesn't seem fair she calls me Dada first."

He looks so apologetic, I melt a little. "I've done a lot of reading. I know the *da* sound is often easier for babies to say. And you're with her a lot, so it only makes sense."

"Your feelings aren't hurt?"

"No." I kiss the top of Violet's head, then lean down and kiss Webb's cheek. "But it's so sweet you were concerned."

"I'm always concerned for you. I love you, Pip. Don't you know that by now?"

My lips part and I suck in a breath. He stands and puts a finger under my chin, raising my face to his. "You don't have to say it back. You don't even need to feel it, yet. Just need you to know where I stand."

He pecks me on the lips and takes Violet out of my arms. "I'll get this one in a bath. You grab a glass of wine and watch some TV. Relax. There's a new *Fear Thy Neighbor* on tonight."

And with that, my heart trips, flips, and lands right in his hands. The whole damn thing.

THIRTY-SIX

Piper

At Webb's urging, we spoke to Lulu about Violet's routine. She agreed, but the outcome wasn't one I really cared for. "I think we'll keep her with us for the time being, until Denny and I decide what we're going to do," she'd explained. So while Webb and I have been out there on day trips to see her, I haven't had her for an overnight in a while and I miss her. We told Lulu she'd said her first word, calling Webb "Dada," but the stinker hasn't repeated it since that night so I'm not sure she believes us.

Since clearing the air with Drew, things at the shop have been much easier. Hudson signed a contract with us, which means Sugarbreaker Signature Taffy and Truffles will now be available up and down coastal New England. The income will provide us a comfortable income year-round and completely eliminates the financial question surrounding my adopting Violet. I may not be a millionaire, but I will have more than enough. Drew and I already talked about hiring an extra year-round person so he, Mara, and I will have plenty of time for our families.

The day we signed the contract, Webb took me to a fancy

restaurant in Newport. Then, that night, he took me to heaven several times. I think we've managed to make up for the past fifteen years, but Webb disagrees.

"We still have fourteen years and ten months to make up for," he teased, right before he bent me over his desk at the dental office and plunged into me from behind. Thank God we were alone, because being quiet while he rocks my world with his long, thick cock takes a giant feat of strength. And the things that man can do in a dental chair.

Now, it's Friday night, and Tessa is over for our weekly binge. I grab us each a can of soda and settle down next to her on the sofa. "I haven't heard from you all week. What's going on?"

She takes a sip. "Is Webb here?"

"He had to stay late. There's still ten days to go before opening the practice, but they fell behind when they had to rip up all the mislaid flooring and repaint. Then he's going out with his friends."

"Eek. I hope they found someone who can do it right this time."

I laugh. "They did, thanks to me. I strongly suggested they hire local, instead of from the mainland. You can trust locals— we all have to take care of each other, so we're not in the habit of doing shoddy work or screwing each other over."

"Damn straight." She takes another sip, then sets the can aside. Clasping her hands in her lap, she turns to face me. "So. It's preliminary, but I have one of my guys working on getting the details and proof nailed down. Once it happens, I'll package it all up pretty as can be. Then you can present it to the Rosellis and kill Hollis's chances of getting Violet."

My eyes widen. "What did you find?"

She holds up a finger. "First, I want to say I'm only smug about digging up Hollis's dirty little secrets because she's a bitch and it discredits her. But, in actuality, what I discovered is… sad. Disturbing, but also sad."

"Don't keep me in suspense," I groan. "This isn't an ID Channel mystery, so no need for commercial breaks. Spill it."

"Our hunches about the boys were right. They're little delinquents. Mostly things like shoplifting and bullying. Both were kicked out of a school for ganging up on a fellow student who wouldn't let them play with his Switch. It's a handheld video game," she explains at my puzzled look.

"Oh, right." I should probably keep up on these things if I'm going to be raising a child.

"The fire-setting is more problematic. They were caught setting the neighbor's shed on fire after the neighbor, apparently, told their parents they were sneaking into people's backyards. Something about that fire leads them to think it was also them who set two similar fires outside other places where they had previous incidents. And the school that expelled them? A wastebasket in the art room was set on fire. Luckily, the custodian happened to be on that side of the school that night and extinguished it before it could catch the flammable stuff. The whole school could've gone up. They discovered one of the outside doors had been tampered with, the locking mechanism broken."

"Oh my God." My mouth drops in horror. "They did all that?"

Tessa shrugs. "The authorities think so, but the shed fire was the only one they could prove. And Hollis had a good lawyer. That's why the boys are where they are now—a boarding school for troubled youth. But they've been stellar students, so they're expected to return to regular school next fall."

"Wow." I sit back against the cushions. "They need some serious help."

"The oldest one certainly does," Tessa says. "My sources tell me the younger brother is only a follower and probably too scared of his brother to cross him. But the older one, Jensen? My guy and I talked to quite a few people who know them and it sounds like he's an *Evil Lives Here* episode in the making."

I shiver, thinking of how often Violet has been in the same house as him. "She can't go back there."

Tessa nods. "I'll have a formal report for you tomorrow or the next day. You need to take it to Lulu and Denny. There's something else, too. Aaron and Hollis are in marriage counseling."

I raise an eyebrow. "She's led us all to believe she has a perfect marriage."

"Going to marriage counseling isn't a bad thing," Tessa points out. "Except it's not taking. Aaron has reached out to a few divorce lawyers."

"How the hell do you know that?"

Tessa glances away. "I might not have gotten that info in the most legal of ways. But I did get photos of him and someone who isn't Hollis having what was most definitely not a work lunch."

My chest fills. There's no way the pastor can spin a marriage in crisis and on the verge of collapse is a better environment than a single parent household. Even though I'm technically married now, there's much less pressure for us to keep up the charade.

"You know," Tessa says, nudging me with her foot. "Don't take this the wrong way, but you look like you've lost weight. And you didn't need to lose any weight to begin with. What's going on with you?"

"I haven't been eating much," I admit. I try to laugh. "And Webb and I have been burning a lot more calories than I normally do."

Her forehead wrinkles. "Is it a happy loss of appetite or are you worried? Because between your marriage and these revelations about Hollis's family, you've got Violet's adoption in the bag, babe. You're going to win."

I throw my head back against the cushion and stare up at the ceiling. "That's just it, Tessa. A part of me feels like I'm no better than Hollis, presenting myself to be someone I'm not and living a life based on lies. What if Lulu and Denny find out? They'll feel so betrayed. Being Violet's grandparents, they will always be a part of our lives, and I don't know how it will be between us. They might never forgive me. What if they try to invalidate the adoption? What if they sue for custody? I don't know if I want to spend the rest of my life carrying yet another secret."

"What does Webb think?"

"Hah." I sniffle, feeling a lump forming in my throat. "He doesn't see the problem, since what we're doing is for Violet's well-being. He sees this as a second chance for us."

"He loves you," Tessa says softly.

I shake my head. "But he still doesn't know about the baby."

"Piper, you have to tell him."

"I know. But I wanted to wait until we settled everything with Violet first. It's too much to think about all at once. And what if it's better he never knows? It's not like he can do anything now."

"He'll want to know," Tessa insists. "And he can do something now. He can share your grief."

I blow out a breath. "You're right."

She snorts. "I usually am."

"I love him," I confess, staring down at the can in my hand.

"I know," she says softly. "Pretty sure it's why you could never love anyone else. There wasn't room in your heart."

I side-eye her. "You could've told me, you know. I didn't see it."

She shrugs a shoulder. "I didn't know for sure until he came back and I saw the way you reacted."

"Angry, pissed off, and hurt?"

"Yep. Because the flip side of love isn't hate, it's apathy. If you didn't still love him, you wouldn't have felt so much for him." She pats my knee. "And he loves you, he said so. I really think this time he's going to stick around. He's fought too hard to get you back to just let you go again."

I twirl the ends of my hair, pondering what she's said. Webb didn't gain anything by marrying me. If anything, he lost. The estrangement with his parents might be permanent, at least as long as we're together. He's spent almost his entire life trying to earn their love and respect, yet he was willing to throw it all away to help me. Maybe this time he loves me enough to stick.

"Is it annoying always being right?" I ask Tessa.

She laughs. "Not in the least. Now," she picks up the remote and switches to Netflix. "Who's Joe going to kill this week?"

THIRTY-SEVEN

Webb

Carolynn and I were together close to twenty years, but there wasn't a single day with her I felt as happy as I have with Piper over the past couple of weeks. It's not just the sex, although it's even more incredible than I remember. It's the way she laughs at my stupid jokes, the spark in her eyes when she talks about the candy shop, the warmth and love that exudes from her when she's with Violet. She was meant to be a mom and I'm honored to be a part of making it happen. Who knows? Things are going so well between us, maybe she'll be open to the idea of giving Violet a brother or sister next year?

That's a thought I'll keep to myself, though, at least for now. As much as we've been able to put the past behind us, I sense she's still skittish. She hasn't been eating much lately, and I know it's nerves over waiting for the Rosellis to make a decision. It's so obvious to me Piper is the best choice and I'm pissed they're dragging this out. It's not fair to anyone. But Lulu insists Pastor Marty is right that she should take as much time as she needs to give careful consideration. That charlatan has some spell over Lulu and if I could think of a way to break it, I would.

I've already asked a friend of Graeme's to look into him. I didn't want to involve Tessa, she's already doing so much.

Things are moving smoothly at the office, finally. We're back on schedule to open in just under three weeks. I've spoken to Graeme about our contract with DDS and what it would take to buy out of it early. It's a five-year contract and I'd calculated that my partners and I would have enough to operate on our own by the time it ended, but I need to cut ties with my parents now. After speaking with my therapist, I've decided to take his advice and go for a clean break. I'm not the problem, I never have been. I'm not a mistake, even if that's how they see me. Being with Carolynn was my penance, my way of making up to them something that wasn't my fault. But being with Piper is my salvation.

Unfortunately, to get out of the contract will cost a significant amount of money that none of us have, at least not on our own. I have it, if I cash out a portion of the trust I inherited.

It was set up for Philip's benefit by our grandfather, who passed a few months before I was born. Though he never knew me, he set it up to make it untouchable to my parents. In the event more children were born, it would be split evenly. In the case of anyone's death before attaining the age of 18, the funds would be distributed among the remaining heirs. Since I was the only remaining heir, Philip's entire trust was passed on to me. I never felt it was mine and I vowed I'd never touch it. My parents made too many cutting remarks about my *unearned* inheritance and despite Carolynn's attempts to pressure me, I've never claimed it. The dividends it earns are automatically donated to the Dana Farber Cancer and Blood Disorders Center at Boston Children's, but beyond that I never felt it was mine to claim. Until now.

I'm worn out from relief after spending the afternoon on the phone talking to lawyers and brokers about taking out what we'll need to buy out of the contract, plus some extra to seed a trust for Violet, and then using the remaining proceeds to fund an endowment at Dana Farber's. I think both Philip and my grandfather would be happy with my plan. My parents can go to hell.

When I told Pam and Trev at dinner what I'd done and what I proposed about terminating our relationship with DDS, they were stunned. "We'll pay you back," Trev had said.

I waved him away. "We'll figure it all out later. I know you weren't happy about being part of the DDS brand, anyway. This way, we can all get what we want a little sooner than expected."

Pam had expressed some concern for me. "Are you sure you want to do this? You swore you'd never claim that money."

"I never had a good enough reason to before," I'd assured her.

It's after ten when I walk into the bungalow and drop my briefcase by the door, toeing my loafers off. I don't hear Tessa or Piper, and the television is off, so I assume Tessa's gone home. I hope I'm right, because all I want to do right now is drag Piper to the bedroom and make her scream my name.

"Pip, I'm home! Tessa, if you're still here, leave please. I want to get my wife naked." Okay, so I might still be buzzed. Maybe I should have walked home from The Seahorse instead of letting Pam drop me off. No one answers, so I stroll through the house until I find her sitting on the back patio.

"Hey, beautiful. Whatcha doin'?" I ask, closing the French door behind me.

She startles, then smiles. "Thinking and waiting for you to get home."

I lean down to kiss her soft lips. "You and Tess have fun?"

"Yeah. We binged two episodes. Only two more to go, but she's probably traveling next week. You?"

"Today was a good day," I tell her, lounging in the chair beside her. "I made some significant steps in extricating myself and the dental practice from my parents."

"Wow. That's big. Are you sure about it?"

She sounds anxious, so I give her my most reassuring smile. "Very sure. Trev and Pam are on board, too. Trust me, this is all for the best."

"I have big news, too. Tessa found the, quote-end-quote, smoking gun on Hollis."

I sit up, my eyebrows shooting to my hairline. "That's great. What did she find?"

Piper spends the next few minutes giving me the rundown, all while my body goes cold with fear and then hot with anger. There's no way in hell those people will ever see Violet again. I will make damn sure of that, somehow. Now that I've already decided to claim the trust, I have access to enough funds to hire the best family lawyers in the nation if it comes to that.

"What's our next step?" I ask.

"Tessa said she'll have a formal report, with evidence, in the next day or two. I'll take it to Lulu. She'll have to give us custody of Violet after she sees it, no matter what Pastor Marty tries to say."

"That's the best news I've heard all day."

"Did the flooring get fixed?"

"Finally." I sigh. "I think we're ready to open. Just a few small details left."

"I have something for you," she says.

I lean over and waggle my brows at her. "Mmm, I've been thinking about what you have all night."

"Not that," she says with a laugh. She holds up a paper and I recognize the familiar blue backing of a legal document. I squint to read what she's holding. It's a copy of our prenup, confirming that in the event of our divorce, I will retain no legal rights to Violet, and any and all parental obligations will cease.

"Whether we stay together and make a real go of this marriage or we decide it isn't for us, is staying in Violet's life something you would be interested in?" Her voice wavers and it's enough to sober me up and take this seriously. "Would you like to be her father… for real?"

I'm stunned silent, for so long Piper begins to squirm in her seat. "Don't feel obligated."

"Yes." It comes out more of a croak than a word, so I clear my throat and try again. "Yes. I would love to be Violet's father."

She grins and tears the paper in half. "Then you will be. Because I know we're going to get custody. I have such a good feeling about it and I'm not usually all that optimistic. Besides, she already calls you Dada."

I take her hand, stroking the back of it with my thumb, staring at her until the humor slips from her face and she grows serious. She needs to hear what I say next. She needs to feel it. "I know I said we could take it day by day, and we can. But I want to state for the record, right here and now, that I love you Piper Imogene Poincelot Duncan. And I love Violet. And nothing—nothing—would make my life mean more than to spend it taking care of the two of you."

She swallows and blinks, holding back the emotion I can see all over her face. "My middle name isn't Imogene, it's Ingrid."

My mouth curves up. "Doesn't change how much I love you."

She draws in a shaky breath, her eyes reflecting the moonlight. "Webb--I--"

"Shhh." I lean in to brush a soft kiss against her cheek, then drag my lips toward her neck.

She sighs and melts into me. "Take me to bed?"

"Thought you'd never ask."

THIRTY-EIGHT

Webb

Who would've thought sex with your own wife could be this hot? Sure, this was my second marriage, sure, Pip and I have technically been married for about a month now and the sex has been hot. But tonight is the first night we're truly connected. Committed. No more questions, no doubts, only promises between us.

I want to take her bare. Not because I want to get her pregnant, but because I don't want there to be anything else but promises between us. We get to the bedroom and begin stripping each other. I yank off her top and work the bra hooks at her back while her fingers furiously unfasten the buttons on my shirt. My mouth is fused to hers, her tongue plunging inside my mouth, and I back her towards the bed while pushing down on the soft sweats she's wearing. I suck her tongue, moaning at the sweet fizzy taste of her, and when she trips over her pants I've successfully managed to slide over her hips, I catch her behind her back to lower her gently to the mattress.

We break apart, panting like thirsty animals, so I can finish releasing her legs from her bottoms. She turns my belt loose and undoes my fly. I shove them down, boxers included, and kick them away. My cock springs free, flushed, dripping, and hard as steel. Before I can stop her, she lowers her head and sweeps the tip of her tongue across my head. Then she opens and bobs her head down and back up, sucking as she goes, releasing me with an audible pop.

"Mmm," she moans like I'm the tastiest lolly she's ever had, and I know if she does it again I'm going to come all over her face. And I am not ready to end this part of the night just yet.

"Baby, you're killing me," I growl, gently pushing her head away. "Scoot up."

She does as she's told, mischief dancing in those deep, dark eyes of hers. I climb on after her, my eyes fixed on her round, fleshy tits. Seeing my stare, the vixen cups them in her hands and begins playing with her nipples, the dark buds stiffening as hard as my cock. I capture first the right in my mouth as I hover over her, my hot steel sliding against her folds. She writhes underneath me, moaning, and I smile against her as I use my hand to rub the tip of my dick through her wetness to circle her clit.

"Holy fuck, Webb," she hisses through her teeth. "That feels so good. So so good."

I suck on her other nipple while I keep up the work on her pussy. The wet slide, followed by the loop over the most sensitive part of her. My own balls are heavy, aching for release, but I intend to make this good for her.

Her hands roam my chest, then over my back and down to my ass where she squeezes. The bite of her nails makes me grunt and I nip at her stiff peak. She gives a little yowl, then begs me to do it again. I'm not one to deny a lady the pleasure she wants, especially when it gets me off. I nip, then soothe with my tongue.

"I want you inside me. I need to feel you inside me."

I pause and look at her until she's catches my gaze. "I want to feel all of you, Piper. You're on the pill, right? And I'm clean."

She licks her lips, a waver of uncertainty in her eyes. "I'm clean, too. There hasn't been anyone but you in—since my last check up, let's say."

I grin. "Can I ride you bare? I want to claim you and see the evidence run down those sexy legs of yours when you stand up after."

"I—" Her gaze darts away, then back to mine, guilty but resolute. "I'm sorry. I can't. I'm on the pill but, you never know, and I can't—"

"Shh, shh," I say, brushing her hair back off her face. I kiss her temple, then her cheek, then her lips. "It was just a thought and I'm okay if you're not ready for that. I promise."

I slip a finger inside her and she arches into me. "There's so many other ways I can feel you from the inside," I murmur before attacking her throat.

"Webb," she sighs. I suck on the crook of her neck, loving the vibration against my cheek as she says my name. I slick another finger into her and she cries out.

Then she removes my hand from inside her. I draw back enough to see her face. The uncertainty is replaced with lust. She licks her lips as she moves my hand to her ass. "I'm not ready for that, yet, but I am ready and willing to try something... different. Something I've never done before. If you're up for it."

She spreads her legs wider and positions my hand so my finger is at her back entrance. I didn't think it was possible to get even harder than I was, but I could pound nails with my dick right now. "Are you sure?" I breathe.

She nods and gives me a wicked smile. "So I've done a little reading on it. We just need to start slowly."

"God, Pip. You researched this so we could do it?" I groan and press the tip of my finger inside her pucker. "That's so fucking hot."

She grunts and at first there's some resistance, like she's

pushing me out. I remove my finger, not wanting to hurt her, but she puts me back into position. "We just need to do it easy. And I forgot the lube."

I lean over and open the drawer where I know she keeps her toys, finding the bottle we need right on top. I sit back and squeeze some onto my fingers, then massage it onto her, my eyes on her the whole time. Her chest rises and falls with deep, hard breaths. Her pupils are wide, then open even further when my finger slips more easily into her hole. I move it in and out, slowly, going a little further each time.

Beneath me, she gasps. "Oh my G—I didn't know that could feel good."

I smirk. "Babe, there's a million and one ways I can make you feel good."

My mouth is on hers while I swallow her moans, my tongue delving into her mouth in rhythm with my finger. I make a little circle with my finger, stretching her gently. She reaches between us and strokes her nub, imitating the tiny circles back and forth I'm doing inside of her. "That is so hot. Someday I'm going to claim your ass with my cock and watch you touch yourself just like that."

I groan, my dick so painfully hard I can barely take it. But I'll hold on. Until I have her screaming first, he can wait.

I press down and she shudders. "Oh God, do that again."

In, circle, press. I repeat the pattern until she's all but vibrating off the bed, her own hand moving in a furious circle. "That's it, baby. Come for me. Come for me."

I pick up the pace and slide my finger in and out of her, wishing it were my cock, until she shrieks my name, bucking and twisting in my hand.

"Webb, holy shit! Oh my God, oh my God, yesyesyesyesyesyes."

I fist my cock, beginning to lose the battle with my own need for release. "I have to fuck you now."

"Please," she whimpers. I lean over and rummage in the draw for a condom but come up empty. I know they're in there, but damn it, I can't think straight.

"Can you take me down your throat?" I ask, giving up for the moment and shifting up on her body. The words come out in a rasp. Honestly, I'm so fucking turned on I'm afraid I'll blow it all with just one suck. But it's a chance I'm willing to take to feel those lips wrapped around me.

In reply, she opens wide and uses her hand to guide me into that sweet cavern. My head falls back as her lips clamp around me. "Fuuuuuck."

With her tongue swirling around the head of my dick, her lips keeping their steady glide along my shaft, and one hand squeezing my hilt while the other tugs on my balls, I fist her hair. She moans against my shaft but doesn't stop what she's doing. If anything, she's sucking harder, moving faster. When the tip hits the back of her throat, I shout out a warning.

It's going to happen quick and I'm powerless to stop it. Her mouth is a vacuum over my cock, drawing all my power out of it, and I start to shake. My balls draw up and the shock reverberates up my spine as I spill down her throat. Shudders run through me as I gasp, rocking my hips against her face while she takes every drop I give her.

When I finally feel empty, I pull out of her mouth and collapse next to her, my arms wrapping around her. The aftershocks from our orgasms have us both jolting and I squeeze her tighter while we catch our breath. I kiss the side of her head. "You're incredible."

"I think it's you," she pants. "I've never come so hard in my life."

"Me neither."

She presses her lips to my throat. "Maybe it's just us together."

I pull my head so I can look down at her. "Good. Then I'm looking forward to being together. Forever."

⊰⊱

WE WERE TOO EXHAUSTED TO FUCK AGAIN LAST NIGHT, BUT IN the early hours of this morning, I awoke to Piper's gentle touch. We made slow and lazy Sunday love, then got up and shared a simple breakfast and coffee. The gloomy outside didn't match our moods, at least not mine. Piper was more pensive than usual, but I chalked it up to the impending confrontation we were going to have with the Rosellis over Violet. Then I remembered she'd wanted to talk about something today.

"Last night, you said we needed to talk today. What's on your mind?" I ask, taking a sip of my second cup of coffee.

She rolls her shoulders in on herself and starts twisting the end of her ponytail. "Right. We do. Um, there's something I should probably tell you."

Her phone buzzes. She looks at the screen with a frown, then scoots her chair back from the table. "Crap. One of the freezers is on the fritz. I need to go in and check on it."

"I can come with you."

"No." She gulps down the last of her coffee then sets the mug in the sink. "It's okay. I just need to see if it's fixable or if I need to call someone in. Pearl and Ruby are there, so they can help me move everything into one of the other freezers."

She kisses me on the cheek then hurries to get dressed. I take my time finishing my coffee and thinking about Tessa's upcoming report. It can't come soon enough. Violet is going to be ours—I'm going to be a father at last and it's going to happen with the one woman it should've been all these years. There's no stopping the smile lighting up my face. Nothing can knock me off the cloud I'm floating on.

After a shower and a quick jaunt to the store, I'm back in the bungalow's kitchen with my sack of goodies and get to work. It's already a stressful time for Piper and her freezer crapping out on her doesn't help. Tomorrow, if all goes as planned, Tessa will have all the evidence we need to show Lulu how wrong— dangerous, even—it would be to give Hollis and the philanderer she's married to custody of Violet. The baby belongs here, with us.

Us.

A sappy smile graces my face and I'm humming as I put the groceries away. I never could've imagined things would turn out this way. The best I hoped for was she'd forgive me, maybe agree to date me, and I'd spend a few years trying to win her back. After our first meeting, when it was clear she still hated me, I was afraid to hope for more than forgiveness and even that seemed so far out of reach.

Now here I am, little more than a month later. I'm married, a kid on the way—and I have no doubts Violet will end up with us —on the cusp of starting a whole new life on my own. No more Stephen and Eileen to remind me of my failures, no more Carolynn to badger me into being her version of perfect, no more fucking guilt.

Ding dong.

Piper's old fashioned doorbell chimes. Tomorrow, I'll install a video doorbell so we won't have to open the door to see who it is. I swing it open and wish like hell I'd thought to get one before today.

"Carolynn. What the hell are you doing here?"

THIRTY-NINE

Webb

My ex-wife pouts. "Well that's not a welcoming way to greet your wife."

"*Ex*-wife," I grind out. "In case you forgot, which is hard to believe since you crashed the wedding, but I have only one wife and she's not you."

She waves her manicured talons in the air. "For now. After you hear me out, you might feel different."

"There's nothing to hear, Carolynn," I say. "We're through. I gave you everything you wanted in the divorce, including my parents. Leave, now. Before you make a fool of yourself."

I move to close the door but she slaps her hand on it. "I'm not the one who's in danger of being a fool. Will you give me one minute of your precious time? You owe me that much, Webb."

An ache starts throbbing in the center of my forehead. I rub at it with my thumb. I owe her nothing, but sometimes it's easier to let her run her mouth than it is to argue. I step outside and close the door behind her, because she'll get her minute but there's no way she's coming inside.

I hold up a finger. "One minute."

She rolls back her shoulders, the triumphant smirk peeking out from her lips already making me regret it. From her bag, she pulls out a file folder. "I know this marriage is a fraud. You're only doing it to get custody of that baby."

"Ok. We're done." I go to turn around, but her next words stop me.

"I have proof." She opens the folder and begins reading from the top page. "Transcript of recorded call between TW Duncan, party one, and GG St. John, party two."

"What is this?" I ask, dread crawling up my spine.

"The PI that other woman hired came around asking about you. When he told me why, I almost couldn't believe it. Actually, I thought you were doing this so you really could adopt that baby and finally satisfy that paternal urge you have. Then you'd come back to me."

"That wasn't happening," I scoff.

Her eyes narrow. "I know that now. So I made a deal with him—pass along anything he finds that could be useful to me before he gives it to that other woman. I paid him handsomely for it out of our former joint checking account."

"I don't know what you think you found—"

"Shh. I'll skip to the good part," she says, continuing her read.

"Duncan: I have to go through with this. I want to. If I don't marry her, she'll lose any chance of getting to adopt Violet.

St. John: Won't people be suspicious, you marrying again literally days after your divorce is final?

Duncan: Doesn't matter. Besides, we only need to stay married for a few months after the adoption, so it doesn't look too suspicious. I'll just claim she was a rebound and it was a mistake. All that matters is that we make this look real until the papers are filed."

"Stop." I'm clenching my jaw so hard, I'm about to break my molars. "You fucking recorded a private conversation? That's illegal."

"Your mother did, technically."

"Doesn't make it any less illegal, or reprehensible." I stalk away from her, then turn back, not knowing what to do with the fury and fear boiling in my gut.

"Employers can record phone calls between employees."

I bare my teeth at her, but she doesn't even flinch. "I'm not a fucking employee."

She shrugs a shoulder. "You were using a phone paid for by DDS LLC, calling an employee of DDS LLC. Who knows what a court might say? But I know what Louise and Dennis Roselli will say."

There's an evil gleam in those ice blue eyes of hers. "Don't," I warn. The fear is starting to take over the fury. "You can't tell them this, we'll lose the baby. Look, you're pissed at me. I get it. Please don't take it out on Piper or the baby. You don't understand what will happen if you do—"

"I don't give two shits about your precious Piper or some baby I don't know," she interrupts, showing heat for the first time. "You hurt me. You broke my heart, Webb."

Her voice cracks and for the first time, I realize I never considered she'd actually be hurt by my leaving. Angry. Annoyed. Embarrassed. But hurt? It seemed like she loved me as much as I loved her, which wasn't all that much. Maybe at first, there was something there. More on her part, but I did grow to love her. Just not enough. Not the way I love Piper.

"Caro, I'm sorry." I let my arms dangle at my sides and turn my hands so the palms are facing out. I will be submissive, I will beg, grovel, and cry if I have to. Anything to convince her not to hurt me through Piper. "I'm so sorry. I should have been a better husband, a better friend. I know. But you have to admit, sweetheart, we just weren't good for each other. We weren't a match. You deserve better."

She softens at my endearment and I think I have a chance to defuse this situation. She holds the file folder out in front of her like it's a bomb and pushes it toward me. With a sigh of relief, I take it from her hands. But before I can relax, her face hardens again. "Maybe you're right. But the fact is, you took away the future I had dreamed about with you. You left me alone. You hurt me. And now, I'm just repaying the favor."

She nods at the folder. "Those are just copies."

"Carolynn," I plead. But she only gives me her back and her middle finger.

When she reaches her car, she turns around. "Oh, and by the way, you might find what else the PI dug up interesting. I wonder what they'll think when they find out Piper gave up her own baby fifteen years ago. If she couldn't take care of her own baby, what makes her think she can take care of one that's not even hers?"

My brain tries to wrap around this. Piper had a baby? It can't be true. She would've told me.

Carolynn takes pleasure in what she must see on my face, because she broadens her smile before leaving a parting shot. "Wonder if it was even yours."

⁂

I DON'T KNOW HOW LONG I SIT AT PIPER'S TABLE, STARING DOWN at the papers in front of me, trying to make sense of what I was reading. I may not have practiced general medicine since my first year of residency ages ago, but I know how to read a chart. And this one, though a terrible copy of a scan of a facsimile, is legible enough to make out the important pieces of information. They jump out at me as I scan down the page for what must be the hundredth time.

Gravidas 1, Para 0

GA: 15w 5d

BP 160/80

AST 42/ ALT 45

Fetal HB: 150bpm

Discharge notes: After 24h observation, all levels normal. Patient advised to rest, drink more fluids, follow up with regular OB.

Carolynn was telling the truth, at least about Piper being pregnant. According to this, she was about 16 weeks along as of July 4th, which means she was pregnant when we were still together. She was pregnant when I made the dick move to break up with her over text. She was pregnant when I saw her a week later at graduation—and she never said anything.

There's nothing else. Nothing that tells me what happened next. I don't know what I expect exactly. A birth certificate? Adoption papers?

I rub my eyes with the heels of my hands. How could she not tell me? I did an asshole thing, but didn't she know I wasn't the type of guy who would abandon his pregnant girlfriend?

No, you fucking idiot, my conscience reminds me. *You gave her no reason to think you were anything but a heartless prick.*

I jam my hand through my hair and growl. I shift through the papers again, looking for anything. But it's only the transcripts of my calls with Graeme and this one random paper. You know what else I can't find? A reason why she didn't tell me then—or why she hasn't told me now. I thought we were making progress, that we had a second chance. But then why hasn't she told me herself about this? It's been almost two months I've been in town; we've been married for over two weeks now. There's been ample opportunity. Then it hits me—

She was never going to tell me. Not then and apparently not now.

The only reason I can think of why she's kept this a secret from me is that it doesn't have anything to do with me. Maybe it wasn't my baby.

I dismiss the thought as quickly as it comes. Piper wasn't like that. She wouldn't have been sleeping with me and someone else at the same time. No, the baby was mine. She didn't tell me because she didn't trust I'd do the right thing by her, and can I really blame her? I've failed pretty much everyone else in my life. It's who I am and I need to accept it.

My phone buzzes with an incoming text from Piper. *Freezer fixed, crisis averted. Be home soon.*

I grunt and flick the phone away. Little does she know, the real crisis is about to come crashing down on our heads.

FORTY

Piper

It was a long afternoon. We managed to save everything from the broken freezer, but then I had to wait forever for someone to come take a look at it. I suppose I should be grateful, considering it was a Saturday. While I was there, we picked up a steady stream of patrons looking for something sweet on such a clear spring day. By the time I left, the rush had dwindled but I was dead on my feet.

Now, all I can think about as I walk the steps to my front door is how badly I want a shower, a glass of wine, and to lose myself in Webb. A flush heats my cheeks and I smile thinking about all the dirty ways I want him. Maybe starting in the shower. Tomorrow, if Tessa brings us the proof we need, we'll be heading into a fierce battle I have faith we will win. But tonight, I want to focus on us. I should really use the time to tell him everything, but I'm a chicken. And adding that complication to an already-fraught situation —well, one more week won't matter.

The house is quiet when I walk in. I saw Webb's car in the drive, but maybe he's over at Hayes's. I drop my bag and keys on the table by the door and head for the kitchen to pour a glass of wine. I jump when I flip the light on.

"Jesus, Webb," I exclaim, holding my hands to my chest. "You scared the daylights out of me. Why are you sitting here in the dark?"

He doesn't look at me, only continues to stare at the folder on the table in front of him. The muscles in his jaw are working and the vein in his neck strains. What I can see of his expression worries me.

"Webb?" I approach the table until I'm standing on the other side of it. "What's going on? Why do you look like that?"

He raises flat, dull eyes to me. "What do I look like?"

I try to laugh. "Like you've just been given a life sentence."

He scrubs a hand down his face, then flicks the folder toward me. "Sit down, Piper."

It's not a request or a suggestion, but a command. Normally I don't take too kindly to being ordered about, but my instinct tells me to just go along. So I take the chair across from him and slide the folder closer. I flip it open and begin reading. "Did Tessa drop this off?"

"Carolynn did."

My head shoots up at the mention of his ex. "Carolynn, as in your ex-wife? She was here?"

"She wanted to give us a heads up that she's taking the information in that file to the Rosellis. She knows about the adoption and our marriage of convenience. There's proof in there thanks to some creative wiretapping."

I don't understand what he's saying. Wiretapping? "Someone bugged us?"

"Not us. Graeme. My mother has the company phones bugged, apparently—or at least his—and since I've been using a company-supplied cell phone, she recorded our conversations. Including one in which I admit that we're only doing this to gain custody of Violet."

"Oh no. No, no, no." I skim through the papers on top, now understanding what I'm reading is a transcript. It's all right there in black and white—the whole sordid plan. "Wow. You just had to tell him everything."

He grinds his teeth. "He's my best friend. Of course I told him everything. When something important is happening in your life, you tell the people you care about. You tell the people who are affected by it."

My brows knit together, but I drop it. I close the folder and push it to the side. "It doesn't matter. What we have on Hollis is so much worse. When did she say she was giving this to them?"

"She didn't, but if I know her, she'll let us sweat this out for a couple of days. Maybe Monday, Tuesday?" He shrugs. "When they find out we've been lying this whole time, Tessa's report won't make a difference. None of us will get Violet."

"Hey, don't count us out yet."

Fire flashes in his eyes. "You really think this will fly with Lulu and her spiritual advisor?"

"Tomorrow, when we take Tessa's report to them, we'll come clean about this. It'll be better coming from us." I take a deep breath and let it out. "To tell the truth, I'm sort of relieved. I hate lying."

He snorts. "Is that so?"

I frown. "What's that supposed to mean?"

"Seems you might be more comfortable with it than you let on." He nods toward the folder. "There's more in there. The detective Hollis hired is thorough. Dirty, but thorough."

My gaze skirts back to the file, my heart thudding so hard against my chest Webb can surely hear it. I slide the folder back in front of me and open it. "What am I looking for?"

His lips spread in a grim line and he stares at me, his expression inscrutable.

When he doesn't answer, I start leafing through the papers.

Transcripts, notes, copies of Webb's divorce decree and our marriage certificate, a mostly illegible photocopy—

My fingers still on the copy. I lean over to read the smudged print, not understanding what it is at first until I read "South County Emergency Department" at the top. No worries about Webb hearing my heart pounding now because it's seized. I steal a look at Webb and he's as still as my heart, watching me. My hands shake as I skim the contents.

"Webb." His name comes out on a choked breath.

"Tell me I read this wrong, Piper," he says, holding my gaze. "Tell me I didn't read that you were pregnant." His voice breaks and the glimmer in his eyes reminds me of the one I see in the mirror every time I think of what happened.

I swallow back the tears and clear my throat. It was fifteen years ago, it shouldn't still feel like it was only yesterday. "The night you ghosted me, I had planned to tell you. But you didn't show up. And the next time I heard from you was a text saying you're sorry, but you're going back to Carolynn."

"But I saw you the following week at graduation. Why didn't you say something then? Why didn't you tell me?"

His indignation pokes at the rawness in me, slashing open wounds I'd thought long healed. "So I was supposed to march up to you and the woman you chose over me, and say what exactly? 'Gee, Webb, I know you never want to see me again, but surprise! You're going to be a daddy!'"

"Yes." He slams his hand on the table and I jump. "Yes, that's exactly what you should've done."

"Why, so you could reject me and the baby to my face?"

"I would never have turned my back on my child."

"No. Only the woman you claim you loved."

"I did love you," he growls.

I wait a beat for him to continue, to say "I still love you." But it doesn't come. Instead, his face is red, his breathing coming in shallow rasps, and every sinewy muscle of his fine-tuned body is coiled and ready to strike. He jerks from the chair, sending it sliding across the floor. He stabs his finger toward me, unnecessarily punctuating every word.

"You should have told me. What I did was fucked up, I get it. But you don't get to decide if I have a right to know you're pregnant with my child. Unless—"

He presses his lips together and turns away.

"Unless what?" I stand, folding my arms and moving away from the table.

He stares at me with hard eyes. "Was it mine?"

The three words hit me like machine gun fire. I flinch, but I lift my chin and narrow my eyes at him. "Fuck you for thinking that."

He drops his chin to his chest and mutters a half-assed apology. He leans back, gripping the edge of the counter so hard his knuckles whiten. But when he raises his head, any contriteness is gone and his eyes are back to being as hard as jade. "So, are you going to tell me now?"

I blink, unsure what he wants me to say. "You saw the file. You know."

He scoffs. "Right, all I know is from the fucking file. Not from my fucking wife. What happened to the baby, Piper? Do I have a child out there somewhere?"

The pain knifes through me, nearly dropping me to my knees. I hold onto the back of the chair to steady myself. I squeeze my eyes shut as tiny tremors start working their way up my body. I open my mouth to answer, but only a squeak comes out.

"What happened to our baby, Piper?"

His question shatters me into a million little pieces and it's as if I've been transported right back to that time. We'd enjoyed the town's Fourth of July parade and picnic, but right before the fireworks began, I'd had a sudden dizzy spell and a wave of nausea took me down. My dad got me to the hospital on the mainland in record time by borrowing a friend's cabin cruiser and arranging a taxi on the other side. My blood pressure was high and my liver wasn't functioning right, but after an overnight stay everything came back normal and I was discharged with instructions for rest, fluids, and immediate follow up after the holiday weekend. This was on a Wednesday. By the following Monday, it was all over.

When I open my eyes, Webb is waiting for my answer with a grimace on his face and I realize with a start that all the falling apart I'm doing is on the inside. Thank God. Maybe he deserves to know the truth, but he doesn't deserve to know my pain. He doesn't get to see me break. I will never let him see that.

"Do you know what HELLP is?"

The lines around his eyes tighten. "Yeah, Hemolysis Elevated Liver enzymes Low Platelet count. It's a condition that can cause liver failure and hypertension in pregnant women. But your chart noted you were discharged the next day, that you were okay."

"That's not the whole chart now is it?" I give a cold laugh. "Wow. For a doctor, you're actually pretty fucking clueless. You want to know what happened to my baby? To our baby, Webb? The only treatment to keep me alive was to end the pregnancy. I was told this normally happens in the third trimester and babies can be delivered early, but safely. I was barely four months along, so there was no delivery. Our baby died, Webb. That's what happened."

All the tension drains from his body. His shoulders slump, his arms droop loosely at his side, and I almost want to laugh at the comical display of horror on his face. Those eyes of his, so flat and hard only a moment ago now glimmer with wetness. "God. Piper. I'm—I didn't know—I thought—"

"You thought what, exactly?" I tighten my arms around my stomach, physically holding back the emotion threatening to erupt out of me.

"I don't know," he says, his voice hoarse. "Carolynn said you'd given a baby up for adoption and I thought—"

"Right, because your ex would magically know what happened to me fifteen years ago."

"Well, I sure as hell didn't," he snaps. "You weren't ever going to tell me, were you? You were going to have the baby and give it up for adoption, and I'd have never known."

"Who said anything about giving the baby up?" I say quietly.

He moves toward me and instinctively I take a step back. Waves of anger and pain radiate off him and I don't want to get pulled under. "You weren't going to give it up?"

"No." I glance to the side. "I was going to keep him. Laura and my dad were going to help."

His sharp intake of breath has me stealing a look. His eyes are shut, the lines around them tight, and the crease between his brows is deeper than I've ever seen. A small part of me wants to reach up and smooth it away. But I hold back. I can't touch him or I'll lose it completely.

"You were never going to tell me, were you?" It's not really a question, because he thinks he knows the answer. But even I don't know the answer.

"I don't know, Webb. Maybe. You didn't give me a good reason to trust you'd be there for us if I did tell you."

"I deserved to know." His voice cracks. "I might not have deserved your forgiveness, but I deserved to know."

He drops into a chair and leans his arms on his thighs, his hands propping up his head. I don't know what to say or what to do, so I stand there, trying to hold on, trying to avoid the memories from swallowing me up.

Suddenly, he stands. "I have to go. I need—I don't know, I need—space or time or…" He stalks to the foyer and picks up his jacket and keys. I lean against the doorway to the kitchen watching one more person leave, helpless to do anything to make him stay.

He opens the door, then turns to me. "You said *he* before. We had a son?"

I nod. "I found out after it was all over."

His breath catches and on a heavy sigh, he walks out closing the door behind him.

The grief has always ridden close to the surface, ready to poke its ugly head at both the most surprising and unsurprising times. But until Webb showed back up in my life, it'd stayed hidden for so long it was more of an ache, like when your knees let you know rain is on the way. Violet helped fill the void in my heart before and after Laura died. She was my second chance. And now I'm losing her, too.

The dam cracks and this time I let it all flow.

FORTY-ONE

Webb

I leave Piper's house and walk right next door to Hayes's. My heart hammers with every step. When he opens the door, he takes one look at me, drags me inside, and sits me on the couch. A glass of whiskey hits my hand immediately.

"Drink it," he commands.

He gets no argument from me. The burn slides down my throat with ease, but doesn't do anything to quell the ache in my chest. It does, however, loosen the tension thrumming through me. I hold out the glass and he dutifully pours another. I cock an eyebrow. "Wild Turkey?"

"You look like you needed something fast and hard. Not going to waste the Macallan on that."

"Fair enough." I sip this glass, wincing.

Hayes takes a seat in the recliner. "I'm guessing the honeymoon is over?"

I snort. "You can say that again."

"I know you've been hoping she'd decide she can't live without you," he says, leaning forward. "She decide she can?"

I turn the glass in my hands. "Did you know?"

"About what?"

"Piper was pregnant when we graduated." I take another sip, hoping the liquor will lube my throat so I can talk about this without choking. "It was mine. We almost had a son."

"Holy shit." Hayes flops back in the chair. "No, I had no idea. I was living in New York until about four years ago and I never heard anything about it. She must have kept it really quiet. What happened?"

"She lost the baby." I finish the last swallow and reach for the bottle left on the coffee table, but Hayes swipes it away. I scowl. "Hey, I'm not done."

"With that shit you are." Hayes takes the glass from me and sets it down, then pulls me up. "You need more than a few glasses of Wild Turkey. I'm taking you out."

I groan. "I don't want to be around people. There's more shit going on, but that just— that's fucked me up."

"I know, man. But that's why we need to go somewhere else. Someplace you can get trashed without bother and that's further than a hundred yards away from her. In case you try to do something stupid. Come on, we're going to The Seahorse."

I follow him out to his car and let him drive me to the little dive bar on the dock. I've only ever been here with Piper. Like with Piper, the bartender and most of the patrons in the place know Hayes by sight, but I'm surprised they remember who I am.

I get a few congratulations on my nuptials, which makes the aching worse. But I offer a wan smile and thanks, grateful when Hayes ushers me to a table in the far dark corner. "Sit here. I'll be right back."

I take the seat with my back to the room. I don't want to see anyone and I don't want anyone to see me. I take out my phone and think about calling Piper. But what would I say? I settle on a text, but it's the same problem. Intellectually, I know she's hurting, too, and that we need to present a united front tomorrow when we argue our case to Lulu and Denny. But I keep wavering between hurt that she kept something so important from me, that she was going to raise my child and not even tell me, and disgust at myself for what I did that put her in that position.

Hayes returns with a pitcher of beer, two pint glasses and two shot glasses on a tray, a bottle of Patron tucked under his arm. He sets it down on the table. "You want to start telling me the whole story now or get numb first?"

"That's a dumb fucking question," I say picking up a shot glass.

I'M TWO BEERS AND THREE SHOTS IN BEFORE MY TONGUE LOOSENS up enough to talk to Hayes. I start with Carolynn showing up at Piper's door this morning and finish with me walking out. Hayes sits there drinking his beer and listening, letting me get it all out. He's a good friend. The best. I tell him so, a few times.

He chuckles and waves over an older woman. "Hey, Sandy, can you get my friend and I some water? And a plate of wings."

"Bleu or Ranch?"

"Bleu." He looks at me. "Or do you want ranch with your buffalo wings?"

"Bleu."

"So, your fake marriage is about to be exposed," Hayes says after she walks away. "Your chances of becoming a father are about to be blown to hell when it is, and you've just discovered that you almost were a father but not only lost the baby, but you almost lost the baby's mother, too. Is that it in a nutshell?"

I work on my third beer. "You forgot the part where my baby's mother didn't tell me she was pregnant. Wait—not only didn't she tell me, she was never going to tell me. Like, ever. Even if she hadn't lost him, she was going to raise him on her own and I'd be none the wiser."

I chase the beer with my fourth shot. "Don't forget that part."

"It's not the most important part."

I scowl. "How do you figure? It's the part I can't get past. You don't keep information like this from someone, no matter how big of an asshole he acted."

"You were a pretty big douche," he muttered, drinking his beer.

"Doesn't give her the right to keep my child from me."

Hayes rocks back in his chair, his lips twisted in a grimace. "I would agree—"

"Thank you."

"Except," he continues, pinning me with a look, "she never really had a chance to tell you, did she? She may think she wouldn't have told you if she had the baby, but you don't know that. She doesn't know that. No one can know what they would do in a situation like that. You're pissed at what she might or might not have done fifteen years ago."

I chew this over, not quite ready to let my righteous indignation go. "Even if you're right, what about now? She's had more than ample opportunity to say, 'Oh, hey, Webb. By the way, we were almost parents.'"

My voice hitches on that last part. I drink a gulp of my beer to smooth it out. "I told her I didn't want secrets between us and she agreed. At least, I thought she did."

The water and wings come out and Sandy lays them on the table along with a stack of napkins. I take a wing, but I only pick at it while Hayes scarfs down two before he speaks again.

"It sucks."

"Thanks. Your eloquence is touching."

He smirks. "You're not normally a sarcastic prick when you drink."

"You're not usually this annoying."

He shrugs and picks up another wing. "Say she did tell you, would it have changed anything? What if she told you the first day you showed up at her shop? Would you still have offered yourself up as a sacrificial fake husband? Or would you have walked away—again—and never spoken to her?"

I can't picture not having had these last few weeks with Piper. I throw the chicken bone down on the plate. "I don't know. Although maybe Piper would have been better off if I did. Because of my stupid plan, she's going to lose Violet for good."

"You don't know that either. Laura's parents can't be so unreasonable they'd rather their granddaughter be adopted by someone whose own children are arsonists."

"You haven't met them," I huff. "Denny—no. But he's checked out and the decision is up to Laura's mother, who is taking her guidance from a condescending, right-wing religious zealot. One whose corruption, I suspect, would make Jerry Falwell, Jr. look like a candidate for sainthood."

"You got Tessa looking into him, too?"

"My buddy, Graeme, asked a friend of a friend. I didn't want to pull Tessa's focus off Hollis. Waiting to hear back."

We drink in quiet, Hayes polishing off the plate of wings. The alcohol is doing its thing, a peaceful numbness stealing over my nerves. But on the other hand, it's amplifying my self-pity. I can't seem to shake the maudlin veil over me.

"You done being a sad sap yet?" Hayes finally says.

I look up from my fourth—fifth?—pint. "Excuse me?"

He nods at my glass. "You look like you're about to cry into your beer. I was wondering when you were going to stop wallowing and actually do something."

"What would you like me to do, Hayes? I think I've earned a little wallowing."

"A little, sure. But you passed that about two beers and three shots ago. You're entering into whining-like-a-two-year-old-who-doesn't-want-a-nap territory."

"You don't get it." I sway over the table towards him. "I almost had a son, Hayes, one I might not have ever known about even if he lived. Hell, I was about to be a father to a daughter and now that's ruined, too. And it's my fault. Because like with everything else, I fucking failed to be any good for them."

"That's bullshit, and I think you know it," Hayes says, tipping back on his chair. "From an outsider's perspective, you've only made two big mistakes in your life you need to own."

"I think I've made a lot more than that."

"One," he ignores that and sticks out his thumb. "You broke up with Piper, even though you were stupid in love with her."

I grunt in agreement. "Biggest regret of my life."

He adds his pointer finger to the count. "And two, you married Carolynn. Everything else was out of your control, dude, and you have no reason to feel guilt. You can't control wildlife. That deer running out in front of you and causing the accident—not your fault. Your wife fucking some other guy—not your fault, no matter what she says."

He leans forward, eyeing me with an intensely serious gaze. "You can't control biology, so no matter how hard your parents want to blame you because your brother died, that wasn't your fault either."

"I know that," I growl.

"Do you?" He scrutinizes me. "Because I think that's the one big guilt factor that drove you to make those two worst mistakes of your life and is still driving you to make the biggest one of all."

Everything's already fading away... the aching pain, the anger, the regret. But bringing up Philip rubs at the raw, primal pain that won't go away. So I pour myself another shot and knock it back, no longer feeling the burn. No longer feeling much of anything.

"Yeah? So what's my biggest mistake of all? Because it'll be hard to top dumping my pregnant girlfriend over text or guilt-tripping myself into marrying someone I didn't love."

Hayes shakes his head at me, with pity or disgust I can't tell. Maybe both. "The one you're making now by walking out on Piper."

"I didn't—"

"You did the same thing fifteen years ago."

"I just needed a little time."

"Right. The same fucking thing. Fifteen years ago you decided what you needed was to assuage your guilt. You needed to make a grand sacrifice to the universe, like you owed some sort of penance. It was about what you needed to do, not what Piper needed or even what Carolynn needed."

"Go to hell," I spit out, raising my voice. "You don't know—you can't possibly—"

The protest sounds hollow even to my ears, but I persist. "She's had fifteen years to process. I've had fifteen minutes."

"Fine. How long do you need?" he asks quietly.

I guzzle the last of my beer and set the glass down. "Tonight. Grab another pitcher and let me have tonight."

FORTY-TWO

Piper

"Piper? Honey?" Tessa's voice carries up the stairs to my room, where I'm curled up on my bed. My throat is too raw from sobbing to call out. I'd texted her 9-1-1 only minutes ago and here she is. I may not be able to hang on to the love of my life, but I'll always have my friends and that's not bad.

She dashes to my side, dropping her leather satchel on the floor and climbing onto the bed next to me. "Oh God, what happened? Is it Violet?"

I shake my head. "W-W-Webb," I stammer out before more tears cascade down my cheeks.

"What did that motherfucker do?" The expression on Tessa's face is so fierce, I have to laugh, which, turns into hiccupping then choking. She helps me sit up and hands me the last tissue from the box.

"He found out about the baby," I say, blowing my nose.

Tessa strokes my hair. "You finally told him and he didn't take it well."

I bark out a laugh. "I wasn't the one who told him. His ex-wife did."

I sum up what happened, including the transcripts of the calls between Webb and Graeme, and Carolynn's threat to turn it all over to Hollis's detective. By the time I'm done, I realize I'm all cried out. I take a few shuddering breaths and look to her for help. "What do I do now?"

Tessa reaches into her satchel and pulls out a manilla folder. "You take this to Lulu and Denny's tomorrow, first thing. Before church. You confess everything and then you show them this, and then you ask them to decide which is worse: you lying because you were trying to protect Violet, or lying with no regard to Violet's safety and well-being? They're reasonable people, Piper. And I think they want you to have Violet. It's that preacher guy confusing everything."

"Pastor Marty." I snort. "He's the unknown variable here. I don't think he's really on the up-and-up."

"Me, neither."

I hold the folder in my hands, waving it back and forth. "And Webb?"

She puts an arm around me and pushes my head to her shoulder. "He's hurting. You've had a lot of time to process everything that happened, but he found out he was a father, and then he wasn't a father, all in one afternoon. On top of all this with Violet. He just needs time. He'll be back once he gets a little perspective. He loves you."

I sniff. "I don't think he can forgive me for this."

"You forgave him for dumping you by text."

"But this is a little bigger. I was going to have his child and never tell him."

She squeezes me and makes a noise. "Oh, you would've. You have a strong moral compass, Piper."

"Yeah, well, it's not been working lately. I'm so stupid, Tessa. What was I thinking?"

"You were thinking you would honor your promise to Laura, whatever it took. You were thinking about protecting Violet. I'd say your moral compass is pointing in exactly the right direction."

I lift my head and give her a wry look. She chuckles. "All right, well, maybe it's pointing a degree or two off-course. Still no biggie. You were doing the wrong thing for the right reason and that's what matters."

The ends justify the means. That was Webb's argument.

"What happens if, by some miracle, Lulu and Denny do agree to let me adopt Violet? What do I do about Webb? I tore up that stupid prenup. I told him I would share Violet with him, that he could be her dad. They adore each other."

"Then that's what you do."

"What if he doesn't want to anymore? What if—what if he doesn't love me the way he thought and he can't get past this?"

I sit up so I can see Tessa's face. She's thoughtful, weighing out her words, and just when I think she's going to impart some wisdom, she just shrugs. "I don't know, Piper. What I do know is that you can't even begin to think about *what if* until the adoption issue is settled. Which isn't going to happen tonight."

She slides off the bed and takes my wrist, dragging me up with her. "Come on. There's Ben & Jerry's melting on the counter downstairs and a new season of Murder in the Heart-land just dropped. You know murder always makes things better." She grins at me.

I smile back. "Murder, ice cream, and best friends."

THE NEXT MORNING, I WAKE AT SIX AND TAKE A QUICK SHOWER, leaving Tessa snoring on the couch. I'm out the door and on the ferry within the hour, pulling into the Rosellis' drive shortly after. I check my phone one more time and swallow down the disappointment of finding no messages from Webb before climbing the porch steps and ringing the bell.

Lulu opens the door, her eyes lifted in surprise and then confusion. "Piper! We weren't expecting you."

"I know. I'm sorry, I should've called first. But this couldn't wait."

She ushers me in. "Is something wrong?"

I take a deep breath. "Is Denny here? There's something I need to talk to the two of you about. It concerns Violet."

"Sit here in the sunroom," she says, leading me through the kitchen. "I'll get Denny. He's out back."

I take a seat at the table just as Lulu and Denny come back in. Denny leans over and kisses my cheek. "Good morning, Mrs. Duncan. This is a lovely surprise. No Mr. Duncan today?"

I wince. "No. Uh, that's one of the things I came to talk to you about."

I lick my lips, trying to muster the courage to begin, then decide it's best to rip the bandage off. "I have a confession to make. I've been lying to you."

They spare a glance at one another. Lulu tilts her head, her lips pursed in concern. "Lying? About what?"

I'm staring at the tabletop, trying hard not to fidget. It's difficult to look at them, but I have to. It's time to tell the truth. Lulu's eyes flash with concern, while Denny's are so full of warmth and humor I almost gasp. I haven't seen anything but shadows in his eyes since Laura died and I hate myself, because I'm about to ruin everything.

"That first day, when you told me you were going to let Hollis adopt Violet instead of me, I told you I was seeing someone seriously and that we were planning to marry. That we would be willing to move the wedding up if it made a difference. But the truth is, I wasn't seeing anyone."

Denny folds his hands on top of the table and watches me, while Lulu scoffs. "But you were seeing Webb."

I draw in another breath and let it go slowly. "Not at the time, no. I panicked. I didn't want to lose Violet and the lie just came spilling out. I only intended for it to buy me a little bit of time, so I could have a chance to convince you that giving Violet to Hollis would be a mistake. Violet belongs to me. Laura was her birth mother, but I'm the mother of her heart. I love that girl with everything I am and I would do anything for her."

I bite my lip then press forward. "Including agreeing to marry a man just so you'd let me adopt her."

In the stunned silence of the moment, I can hear footsteps in the other room. I look up to see a smirking Hollis standing in the doorway. "I knew it. Didn't I tell you, Aunt Louise? It was all a show."

Lulu draws into herself. "Oh, Piper. This is a joke, right? It has to be. A belated April Fools?"

I shake my head. Tears blur my vision and I blink them back. "It's not."

Hollis snorts. "What were you planning on doing? Splitting up as soon as the ink was dry on the adoption papers? Real nice."

"You're one to talk," I snap. "How's that marriage counseling going for you? Not well, I'd guess, considering your husband is sleeping with one of his colleagues."

Her face turns red, her lips twisted in rage, though in the depths of those icy blues of hers I see real fear. I slide the folder I brought with me and its contents over to Lulu and Denny. Denny gives it a brief glance before returning his attention to his hands, still folded in front of him. Lulu draws back like it's a rattlesnake. "What is this?" she asks.

"You know Tessa is a private investigator," I explain. "She volunteered to do a background check on Hollis and her family. If you open it, you'll find proof that Hollis's marriage is on the rocks. And not only that, but her children are so starved for attention, they've taken to setting fires."

"How dare you," Hollis seethes. She snatches the folder off

the table and tears through it. "You're making all this up. You faked these photos, wrote up these phony reports."

She throws the folder back on the table, its contents spilling out. Lulu hurries to cover the photo sticking out, the one depicting a scantily clad woman kissing Aaron outside a condo door.

"I didn't." My eyes are on Lulu, who's paled underneath her spring tan. "I'm sorry it's come to this, but you didn't leave me a choice when you and Pastor Marty insisted Violet would be better off with Hollis because she's married and already has kids. You weren't giving me a fair chance."

"So you lied?" Lulu's voice isn't much above a whisper.

I squeeze my lips together and nod. "It was wrong. But please, believe me, I was only thinking of Violet and her best interests."

Hollis snorts and I dart a glare in her direction. Lulu stands from the table. "This is all too much. I don't know what to think anymore."

The disappointment in her voice is a knife to my chest. "I'm so sorry and I know you might never forgive me, but please, I only wanted to protect Violet."

"You were looking out for yourself," Hollis says. "You were trying to redeem yourself for what you did all those years ago, like adopting an orphaned child could possibly make up for the abortion you had."

Lulu gasps. Her hand goes to her throat and she sways on her feet. Denny grabs her arm to steady her and helps her back into the chair. "My Lord. Piper—is that—is that true?"

I curl my hands into fists, shooting daggers at Hollis. "You don't know what you're saying."

"It's all in my detective's report," she sneers. "You weren't the only one trying to protect Violet, though I'm the one who had good reason. She needs to be brought up in a loving, Christian home."

I push back the chair and stand, drawing my shoulders back and my chin up. "I'm not going to debate you on what loving and Christian means, because from what I can see, you wouldn't know Jesus if he was wearing a name tag. If that's what your detective told you, Hollis, then he's incompetent."

I turn to face Lulu and Denny, flinching at the horror on Lulu's face, the heartbreak on Denny's. "It's true I was pregnant fifteen years ago. But I did not have an abortion, not like she means. When I was about 16 weeks along, I developed a life-threatening condition that required termination of the pregnancy. I was unconscious at the time, so my dad made the decision. To save my life, he had to end the pregnancy. We both would have died if he hadn't."

I glare at Hollis. "Everyone makes mistakes. My mistake was falling in love with someone who it turns out wasn't worthy of me. I paid the consequences for it. I'm still paying."

Lulu makes a noise and there's no judgment when they look at me. Only pity, which I hate just as much. I lift my chin and say my final piece, even though I know it could end up costing me everything.

"But to be completely transparent with you, I did consider not keeping the baby. I changed my mind, but not because I came to the conclusion abortion is wrong. I came to the conclusion it was wrong for me. The same way Laura did a year ago. And none of that should matter now, because I'm not a scared, lonely 22-year-old girl anymore. I'm a grown woman, fully capable of taking care of myself and a child. I'm not rich, but I do well, and I have more love to give Violet than anyone on this earth can ever have. I don't need a husband to prove I would be a damn good mom. You know my father raised me pretty much alone. My mother wasn't—isn't—capable of being a parent. But not once did I ever lack for anything—not financially, not emotionally. I was loved. And Violet will be, too."

I hold my breath, waiting for a reaction and I get the one I half-expected.

Lulu's head hangs lows as she grasps Denny's hand. "I think you need to leave."

There's a mountain sitting on my lungs, making it impossible for me to draw in more than shallow breaths. My voice strains when I ask as politely, as calmly as possible, if I could look in on Violet first.

"I don't think that would be a good idea," Lulu says.

I give a curt nod, push my chair in, and slowly make my way around the table. I pause when I reach the doorway where Hollis stands and turn around. "Regardless of whether you think I'm moral enough to raise your granddaughter," I clear my throat, "I need you to know that everything in that file is true. You can have it checked out on your own, but it's true."

I bare my teeth at Hollis, who's shrinking away from me. Wise idea. "And you know it," I hiss.

"Aunt Louise—"

Lulu holds up a hand. "Hollis, I think you should leave, too."

Her painted mouth drops open. "But we're meeting Pastor Marty after church for brunch."

"I need both of you to leave."

Hollis is still spluttering when I shut the door behind me. I stand on the porch and raise my face to the sky, allowing the tears to fall. "Laura, I'm so sorry I messed this up."

When I reach my car, there's a cardinal sitting on the hood. It tilts its tiny head to one side and then the other before flying off. I watch it vanish into the trees, hearing a whisper in my head telling me it's all going to be okay. I want so much to believe it.

FORTY-THREE

Webb

My mouth is dry as sand and my tongue as furry as a peach, though definitely not as sweet tasting. I roll over and land on the floor. It takes me a minute, but I remember crashing on Hayes's couch.

I groan and rub my eyes, yesterday's events coming back to me in a punch to the stomach. Twenty-four hours ago, I was enjoying a lazy morning with Piper underneath me. Now, here I am hungover, reeking of despair and—well, just reeking, and the only thing underneath me is Hayes's Persian rug. I check the clock over the flatscreen, since God only knows where my watch is. It's after eight in the morning. Shit. I never called Piper or texted to let her know I wasn't coming home. I really am an asshole.

Snoring from down the hall tells me Hayes is still asleep, so I don't bother to wake him. I gather my shoes, wallet, and keys and let myself out quietly as much for the sake of my headache as for the sake of his sleep. He said a lot of hard things to me last night, things I needed to hear. Luckily, he said them long before I drank my brain cells away.

I slowly walk home and open the door, listening for Piper. There's a noise in the living room, so I head there. "Pip?"

Tessa lets out a little scream and drops the Afghan she'd been folding. "Christmas on a cracker, Webb! Do you need to wear a bell so people can hear you approaching?"

"Sorry, I'm not wearing shoes."

She looks down at my feet and frowns, taking in the rest of my disheveled appearance. "I can see that."

"Is Piper here?" I point my thumb at the stairs. "She still asleep?"

Tessa's eyes narrow. She lays the blanket on the back of the sofa, then turns to me with her arms folded and lips curled back. "No, dickhead. She's gone to see Lulu and Denny and tell them everything. If you'd bothered to come home last night, maybe you'd be with her."

The blood drains from my face. Headache forgotten, I dash for the stairs. If I hurry, maybe I can catch up with her.

"She left over an hour ago. She's already there," Tessa calls after me.

I stop at the landing and spin around, catching sight of her at the bottom of the stairway. "She still needs me."

"Are you sure about that?" Tessa's voice has a razor-sharp edge. "She's been making do without you for fifteen years."

I grimace. "Right. Well. I still need her."

Tessa stares at me one more long minute then backs up a step. "Good luck with that."

"Thanks." Although I think I'll need more than luck at this point. I'll need some divine intervention.

⊹

I'M SURE I CAN SWIM FASTER THAN THIS FUCKING FERRY, BUT THE rational side of me is still working, thank God, so I'm standing at the bow of the boat instead of in the water watching the dock

280

getting closer and closer. As soon as we're only a minute out, I jump into my car and prepare to disembark. Five minutes later, I'm on the road to the Roselli's only ten minutes out. Twenty minutes later, I arrive with my heart on my sleeve and a speeding ticket in my glovebox.

Denny is the one who opens the door. He looks startled to see me, his brows knitting together as he takes in my agitated state. "Webb? What are you doing here?"

"Is Piper here? Has she been here?" I ask, my words tumbling out in a rush.

He straightens to his full height, still putting him a few inches below me but the command in his presence makes me feel like the smaller one. "She was. Now she's gone. Back home, I think, but she didn't say."

I press my thumb to my forehead, trying to quell the throbbing tension there. "Did she—tell you about, er—"

"That the two of got married in order to trick us into signing custody of Violet over to Piper? Yeah, she might've mentioned something like that."

His voice is hard, but there's a glimmer of something in his eyes that isn't contempt or anger. "If that's all she told you, that's not all of it—can I come in?"

Denny nods to the chairs on the porch. "Why don't we have a seat out here?"

"Is Lulu here?" I take one of the porch rockers while he takes the other.

"She brought the baby to church. Needed to talk to Marty." He grunts as he lowers himself down. "Piper also told us about the situation with Hollis, if that's what else you mean. I have to say, I'm only slightly surprised. Hollis has always been a selfish brat, and I never much cared for that husband of hers. But I had no idea her boys were such trouble."

"I hope she gets them counseling."

"She has to admit there's a problem first." Denny scoffs. "Denial tends to run deep in this family."

"Uh, was there anything else Piper said?" I'm fishing and he knows it, but I don't want to come right out and ask in case she didn't reveal anything about the baby. Who knows, maybe the Rosellis don't need to find out? It's not really their business anyway.

"What do you really want to know, Webb?" Denny stares at me with an unflinching gaze. I decide to return it with an unflinching one of my own.

"I want to know if you'll still consider letting us adopt Violet, or—" I swallow hard, "at least letting Piper adopt her. You should know that this wasn't her idea, the whole pretending to be engaged and then getting married. I talked her into it. She wanted to tell the truth right from the start, admit she panicked when she told Lulu she had a man, but I convinced her that if we married, it would all but seal the deal for her to adopt Violet."

"I see," he says, a slight quirk of his brow encouraging me to continue.

"Please don't be angry with Piper. And please don't punish her or the baby for my stupidity. If you saw the PI report on Hollis, then you know she has trouble in her life she needs to fix before she'd ever be fit enough to raise Violet. But, Piper--" I give a half-hearted smile. "I'm the only trouble in her life right now and I will happily go away if that would make any difference. She loves that baby, and she would give her a great life."

Denny considers this, rubbing at his lip with his finger. "And you? Do you love her?"

I don't know if he's talking about Piper or Violet, but it doesn't matter because the answer is the same. "With all my heart. Which is why I'm willing to give them both up. Because what I need isn't nearly as important as what they need, and they need each other."

"Hm." Denny peers at me and I wish I could tell what he's thinking, but the man is inscrutable. Finally, he stands. "I'll tell Lulu you stopped by."

"Is there anything I can do that would convince you to let Piper adopt Violet?" I plead.

"You know, I told Piper that I was taking myself out of the equation when it came to who would raise Violet."

"She told me."

"Then she probably told you why." He let out a sigh as he looked across the front yard. "I doted on my daughter. Laura was the world to me. Sure, I disciplined when it was necessary, but unless it was something really bad, I was the one who let it go. I didn't try to shove values down her throat or police her choices or force her to church if she didn't feel like it. She didn't choose the path for herself her mother and I wanted for her, and I tried to accept it. I figured in time she'd get a more respectable job, meet a nice man, settle down, give us grandchildren. When she came to us to tell us she was having a baby and there was no husband, no father even, I was so disappointed. But not in her. I blamed myself for not being more strict with her, for not doing a better job imparting our values to her. If I had done a better job as a father, then maybe her life would've turned out differently. And in that different life, maybe she would still be alive.

"But something Piper said to me after the wedding has been playing over and over in my head. She said, 'Laura was a great person, a great friend, a great mom. If you think that's because you got it wrong, then I'm glad as hell you didn't get it right.'"

I laugh despite myself. "Yeah, sounds like Piper."

Denny shakes his head, smiling. "She's right. My girl was pretty great. Maybe I didn't do such a bad job after all."

I clap a hand to his shoulder. "I knew Laura, too, so you can believe me when I say you did a great job. When we were in college, everyone loved her. You couldn't find someone more kind."

He clears his throat. "I don't know what's going to happen, Webb. All I can tell you is, I think it's time I put myself back into the equation."

He holds out his rough hand and I take it, feeling a sprout of hope for Piper. I have one more thing I need to do, though, to try to make things right for all of us.

FORTY-FOUR

Webb

I call Graeme on my way to Weston and arrange to stop by his house on my way into town. The luxury townhome he and Tish own is almost a duplicate of the one I shared with Carolynn, only they've made theirs a home with lots of soft textures and family photos. Mine was a monument to minimalist industrial design, sleek and elegant but completely impersonal. Much like my marriage was.

Hayes had one thing wrong. It was partly my fault Carolynn cheated on me. She was trying to get my attention. Had I been honest with her earlier, if I hadn't shut her out, she might not have felt compelled to go to such drastic measures as letting me catch her getting nailed across our kitchen island. Someday, I should apologize for my role in our demise. But she's just had her pound of flesh from me and I'm not feeling that magnanimous today.

"I can't believe your mother has been tapping my phone." Graeme says. "Not only mine, but all the executives—junior and senior. I don't know what her game is, but I've been to the company attorneys and I will also be notifying the Board."

"Graeme, you're risking your whole career," I warn him.

285

"Maybe," he says with a shrug. "But I have a feeling it's Eileen who'll have to worry. There've been grumblings about making a leadership change. Your parents may have built the company, but it's publicly traded now. They don't own it outright anymore and she needs to answer to more than just herself."

"Can't argue with that," I say.

"But hey, you came for this." He hands me a manilla envelope. I shake out the papers inside and scan through them. "I was able to get it through legal without tipping off your mother."

I blow out a breath and one of the dozen knots in my stomach unravels. "So, this is it. Seaside Dental is now free and clear of Duncan Dental Services."

Graeme's smile spreads across his face. "We received the cashier's check from the trust on Friday."

"I can't thank you enough," I say.

He sobers. "So what's going on with you and Piper? Did you talk?"

I tap the envelope against my palm. "Yeah, yeah, we talked. It's—I fucked up. Big. But, I'm hoping we can get through this."

"So it's true, then?" His voice is filled with concern. "Did she give your child up for adoption like Carolynn said?"

"No, not exactly." I look over Graeme's shoulder and see Tish through the open doorway. She gives me a smile and waves. I smile back, but it fades away when something occurs to me. "Graeme, did you tell Tish about Piper and me, about the adoption?"

His brows lift and a spot of color rises on his cheeks. He opens his mouth, then closes it again with a sigh. My heart sinks. "She's my wife, man. She was asking a lot of questions and I couldn't lie to her."

My shoulders slump. "I get it, I do. It's all right."

"She promised not to tell Carolynn," he insists.

I give him a sad smile. "How do you think Carolynn knew to look for recordings of our calls that particular week?"

He closes his eyes and utters a curse. When he opens them, they're filled with apology. "Webb, man, I'm so sorry. I don't know what to say."

I pat him on the shoulder. "Hey, I put you in an untenable position. You shouldn't have to lie to your wife, not even for your best friend."

"She shouldn't have opened her damn mouth." He casts an irritated glance back at the house. "We're going to have words."

"Carolynn's a close friend."

But I'm her husband." He sighs and shakes his head. "For what it's worth, I don't think she spilled the beans intentionally or out of malice. She likes Piper. She just has trouble thinking before speaking."

"That's probably good for you. If she thought about it before saying yes, she might not have married you."

He laughs, relief playing across his features. "I'm still going to talk to her. I expect she's going to shower you with apologies, so get ready."

"If one of those apologies is accompanied by Sox tickets, I won't complain." I open my car door but Graeme stops me before I climb in.

"One more thing. In the envelope is a report of finances about that preacher. My guy could get more detailed with more time, but I think what he found out should be helpful."

"That's great. We can use all the help we can get."

We say our goodbyes and a few minutes later, I roll through the gates and up the drive to my parents' estate. I'd already called ahead to make sure they'd be home and found them sitting outside by the pool.

"Thomas," my mother says by way of greeting, gesturing to the fruit salad and croissants on the patio table. "How nice of you to join us for brunch. Help yourself. There's champagne and orange juice on the cart if you want a mimosa."

My father is reading the paper and doesn't bother to look up from it, but I get a grunt of acknowledgment. Seeing the champagne makes my stomach roll, so I opt for plain OJ and take a seat between the two of them.

"I assume you came here to apologize." My mother takes a dainty bite of fruit, her lips painted the same shade as the raspberry on her fork. Her eyes are hidden behind an oversized pair of sunglasses, a sunhat with a ridiculous brim topping her head.

I take a croissant off the plate and bite into it. It's okay, but it's not Bette's. "I came to talk to you," I say, brushing the crumbs off my fingers. "But I'm not sure it's what you want to hear."

My father folds the paper in half and tosses it to the side, picking up his cup of coffee and taking a drink. He's in his Sunday uniform—chinos and a Ralph Lauren polo, the gold Rolex he was given at his retirement glinting in the sun. "Carolynn told us about the fraud you and that woman are perpetuating with this sham marriage. Are you continuing with the charade?"

I bristle at his tone but bite my tongue. I won't engage until it's on my terms. "I don't know, nor do I care, what Carolynn has told you. Whatever reasons Piper and I had for getting married aren't anyone's business but our own. But I will say, with no equivocation, I plan to stay married to her for as long as she'll have me. I love her."

"You loved Carolynn, once, too," my mother reminds me. "And she was a much better match."

I don't bother correcting my mother, but I challenge her. "Better match for whom? Me or you?"

My mother's mouth tightens. "For our family."

"Right. I know. And it's exactly why I married her," I

concede, hiding a smile at my mother's surprise. "It's also why I divorced her."

"You divorced her because you got a hair up your ass," my father says dryly. "It's a mid-life crisis. Everyone has one, though most of us just buy a sports car or take up a ridiculous hobby. We don't ruin our lives."

"I think I've improved my life," I retort.

My mother looks at her watch. "Why are you here, Thomas?"

I look from my mother to my father and back, identical expressions of wearisome on both their faces. It's always been like this. I tire them. I bore them. I disappoint them. Other parents might be happy if their son, who lives hours away, paid them a visit. Mine are inconvenienced. I search myself for the hurt feelings I normally have when I come to such realizations, but I don't find any. What I find is a vision of the way Piper lights up when I come home from work. A memory of Violet's morning giggles when I swoop her out of her crib and into my arms. A remembrance of how the bartender, a man I barely know, greeted me with a warm and genuine smile last night. There are people in my life happy to see me, who aren't burdened by my existence. It's a shame I can't count my parents as part of that group.

I sit back in the chair and take and release a quick breath. Best to get this over with, I have things to do. People worth spending my time with. "I love you both. I do. You gave me a privileged upbringing not available to most people. I never lacked for anything—except your love.

"I know you only had me to save Philip, a job I failed to do." I wince and hold up my hand. "Wait, scratch that. I didn't fail. It was a matter of biology and as a good friend pointed out to me, I am not responsible for that. I'm sorry I couldn't save Philip. I'm sorry that having me was a waste of your time and energy."

My mother starts to speak, but I cut her off. "No, it's my turn. I've tried to make up for what I thought were my shortcomings, namely that I wasn't Philip. You loved him. He was your Golden Boy, and I understand. I don't begrudge that, not at all. I loved him, too. He was an amazing big brother, and I wish I could've had him for longer than five years. So, I tried to be who I thought you wanted me to be. I tried everything, including abandoning a woman I loved to marry a woman I didn't because I knew it would make you happy. I married her for other misguided reasons, too, but your approval was probably the main catalyst. And it shouldn't have been. Love should have been."

"Thomas," my father began, his stern tone indicating a lecture was about to begin. But I'm done with the lectures and I tell him that.

"I'm done trying to win your approval. I'm done trying to get you to love me for just being me. I don't think you have room for anyone but Philip and each other in your hearts. That's okay. I mean, it's not okay, but I accept it. You will no longer have to worry about me or go through the motions of pretending you care about anything I do. Carolynn and I may have split up, but she's kept the family name. You always liked her best. Let her be your daughter."

"You're being dramatic," my father says.

My mother clicks her tongue. "If this is about your dental practice—"

"It's not about that," I assure her. "In fact, when you go into work on Monday, you'll find I've taken care of dissolving the partnership between DDS and Seaside Dental. My partners and I are going to go out on our own."

"What?" My mother whips off her sunglasses, her grass green eyes flashing. "You can't do that. You don't have the money to buy out the contract and pay the penalty for early dissolution."

"He's not really doing it, Eileen," my father says, putting his hand on her arm. "He's doing all this because he wants to negotiate a better deal. Because he's our son, he thinks he should get better terms."

My laugh is completely without warmth or humor. "Hate to burst your bubble, Dad, but I do have the money and I've already done it. The paperwork is in my car."

"But how?"

"I claimed the trust." I dropped the statement and waited for the fireworks. I didn't have to wait long.

"You what?" my father snapped. His face reddens, the veins on his neck pulsing. "You took Philip's trust money?"

"It's not Philip's," I bite back. "The terms of grandpa's will were clear. The trust became mine when Philip died. Since I never intended to touch it myself, it's sat collecting interest all these years. I thought I'd let it pass on to my child—," my voice sticks in my throat, "but Carolynn never wanted children. Well, now I'm about to have a child, one I refuse to subject to this family's dysfunction. So I'm using a portion to sever ties professionally, a portion to start a trust for her, and the remainder to start an endowment at Dana Farber's in Philip's name."

That stuns them into silence. I use the ensuing quiet to finish my juice and stand. "I've said all I needed to say. You won't be hearing from me again. Unless"--I turn to my mother--"I'm needed for a deposition in any lawsuit that might be brought against you for illegal wiretapping of your employees."

My mother's face turns ashen. "I—what?"

I wave my hand. "More you'll find out about tomorrow. It's going to be a pretty busy Monday for you, Mom."

I turn to walk away, my father's voice stopping me before I get to the house.

"It should've been you," he calls out.

My spine stiffens. Slowly, I turn back around. His words

don't hurt me because I've always suspected the truth. That they wish it had been me, not Philip. "I know."

I walk out of my childhood house and get into my car, putting it and my past firmly in the rearview mirror where they belong.

FORTY-FIVE

Piper

I didn't go straight home from Lulu and Denny's. Instead, I went to the shop and immersed myself in treat-making. Drew and Mara checked in on me, Tessa having told them the bare bones of what was happening. But I assured them, with a tight smile, I was fine and just needed to release my anxiety. Making taffy and truffles and cake pops was my favorite method for doing just that. So for hours, I worked like a fiend in the kitchen. Every so often, my water bottle would disappear and reappear with fresh, cold water. Once, I found a chicken salad sandwich and an apple waiting for me, which I gratefully scarfed down while I waited for my hazelnut brittle to set.

"Hey." Mara stands in the kitchen doorway, Drew at her back. "We've closed up out front and we're going to head home. Want to come with us? We can get some dinner. I'm craving a peanut butter pizza. Gina makes it special for me."

My eyes widen, horrified at the sacrilege, making Mara laugh. "You and Drew can split a normal pizza. I never share."

"Thank God," Drew mutters under his breath. Mara elbows him, then gives him a smile so full of adoration my heart twitches. I look away, focusing on the taffy I'm pulling.

"Thanks," I say. "But I'm going to finish up here and then go home, take a hot bath, and fall asleep to a *Friends* marathon."

"You can stay over at our place, you know," Drew offers. "I love a good *Friends* marathon."

"He really does," Mara says.

"I appreciate the offer, but I'm fine." I wave my hands at them, shooing them away. "You go and enjoy your abomination."

"Don't stay too long," Drew says.

"And our door is open if you change your mind," Mara adds as Drew guides her away.

"Good night," I yell out one last time. I hear the back door open and shut, and then I'm left in silence. I spend a few more minutes stretching the taffy until it becomes too hard to pull, then I divide it into four even balls. I start working on the first ball, rolling it into a long rope, when there's a banging on the back door. Assuming it's Drew or Mara, I take off my plastic gloves and go to open the door.

"Forget your key?" The words die on my lips when I discover Webb standing in the doorway. The sun is setting behind him, outlining him in a golden glow, and my breath catches in my throat. "Webb."

"Hi, beautiful," he says, a tentative smile on a face. "You weren't home, so I thought I'd check here. Are you still working?"

"Yeah, I'm pulling taffy right now."

He raises his brows, his smile turning shyly hopeful. "Need help?"

"You hate taffy."

"Don't care to eat it but doesn't preclude me from helping with it."

I tug on the end of my ponytail. "Why are you here, Webb?"

"I hoped we could talk."

"I think we talked enough yesterday, don't you? I'm not sure there's much else to say."

He sighs, running his fingers through his thick hair. It's sticking up in several places, like he's been doing that all day. "Pip—"

"Piper."

"We're back to that again?" He gives a short chuckle. I look to the side so I don't have to stare into those big green eyes of his. I'm afraid of what I'll see, or more so what I won't see.

"Okay. Piper. I'm sorry for being such an idiot. I shouldn't have walked out last night and I should've been with you this morning. I was hurt and I didn't handle the revelation well."

My throbbing heart is stuck in my throat and I rub at the hollow at the base in a futile effort to dislodge it. But the thick, burning sensation won't give and I'm in danger of drowning in more tears. I'm so fucking tired of all the tears. "Go away, Webb," I manage to croak out.

"Please," he says softly. He touches my cheek with the back of his hand and I fight the urge to lean into him. This needs to be over, and it won't be if I keep letting myself fall back into his orbit.

I jerk away and look him in the eye. "Go."

He puts his foot on the threshold, preventing me from slamming the door closed on him. "Please don't shut me out, Piper. We took vows—for better or for worse—and it doesn't matter why we said them. All that matters is that we did. I told you at the start I intended to honor them, and I do. We can work this out, if you'll please let me in."

I let out a harsh laugh that's dangerously close to being a sob. "I did let you in. And you walked right back out. You didn't call or text, just ghosted away. It felt like fifteen years ago all over again."

I swipe at my eyes, which are wet and burning. "What I did

was wrong. You had a right to know about the baby, then and now, and I should've told you sooner. But the way you reacted is exactly what I'd been afraid of. Did you even try to understand where I was coming from? How hard it is for me to even think about what happened, let alone talk about it? Webb, I was devastated for months after I lost our baby. I couldn't sleep, I barely ate. If it weren't for Laura and my dad, I don't know how I would've made it through. It's how I started making candy."

"I didn't know that."

I look down at the ground and smile at the memory of the first time I tried my hand at candy. "Mrs. Klein, who used to own this place, invited me to help her make taffy one day. Her arthritis kept her from doing some tasks, like pulling taffy. It's very repetitive… a lot of pulling and stretching and rolling. It's so easy to lose yourself and that's what happened to me. There was this peace in the routine and it gave me what I needed to heal. Pretty soon, I was coming back here every day, pulling taffy for her. Eventually, I learned how to make the other treats she sold and when she retired, Drew and I put together our savings and bought her out."

I meet his gaze again and the shadows in those beautiful eyes stop my heart. "Watching you with Violet broke my heart at first, because it was a glimpse of what might have been."

"If I hadn't thrown it away," he says in a watery whisper.

My lower lip quivers. "It was a risk to let you back in, to make you a part of the family I wanted to build with Violet. I knew if I did, I'd have to tell you the truth, and you might hate me for what happened. When I finally realized that I'd never really stopped loving you, despite how much pain you caused, I decided it was worth trying to see if we could be something real. I was going to tell you this morning before I was called away. I never meant for you to find out from someone else, let alone your ex-wife, and I am so sorry I wasn't honest sooner."

"Then I did exactly what you feared," he says. He clears his throat a couple of times. "I wanted to be angry at you for keeping this from me and I spent a good part of the night stuck on the possibility you might never have told me I was a father, even if you had the baby. Until Hayes finally got sick of my shit."

He gives a small laugh. "But I was being selfish. It was easier to hang on to false outrage than allow myself to feel legitimate pain and guilt. You didn't keep anything from me, Piper. I kept myself from you. I don't want to do that anymore. I want to give all of myself to you. I want us. I want us to fight for Violet and I want us to be a real family. You gave me a second chance already; please tell me I didn't blow it. Please tell me we can move on together. I love you."

I bite down into my trembling lip and let his words fill all the cracks in my heart. Reaching out, I touch his cheek and he turns his face to plant a kiss to my palm. Slowly, I pull it away and steel myself. "I love you, too, Webb. I'm not sure I'll ever stop."

"Pip." He breathes out my name and tries to move in, but I put my hand on his chest.

"But I have to try. I'm hurt again, but I'm not broken, not like I was the first time around. I gambled that you wouldn't break my heart again, and I convinced myself that even if you did, I could handle it now because my eyes are open and I'm older and wiser and—and I was fooling myself. The things is, Webb, I don't know that my candy making will be enough this time around to heal me if you break me again."

His lips part as panic flits over his features. "What about Violet? What about our marriage?"

"I said my piece to Lulu and Denny. It's up to them now. But however it works out, it'll be okay."

My hand is still on his chest and I rub the spot over his heart. "All of this will be okay, you'll see. Maybe someday we can be friends again. Maybe I can even convince you to try my taffy."

Leaning over, I kiss the corner of his mouth and breathe him in one last time. "But for now, it has to be this way. Goodbye, Webb."

I close the door and lean against it, my heart beating once again. Even though I can't keep doing this with him, I do believe he loves me and it's enough. For the first time in possibly my whole life, I know I am enough.

FORTY-SIX

Piper

Webb cleared most of his things out of the house before I got back from the shop. I don't see or hear from him for the next few days, though Hayes—through Tessa—has intimated he isn't doing so well. "Are you sure you don't want to go to him?" she asks me one night as I'm closing up the shop.

"It's best if we give each other space."

"What's going to happen with the marriage?"

I shrug. "An annulment, I guess? I don't know. I'll worry about it soon as I figure out what's happening with Violet."

She steals a piece of fudge. I bat at her hand, but she laughs. "Consider it payment for my detective work. Speaking of, what is happening with the adoption?"

This time I let myself smile for real. "Lulu reached out. She and Denny are coming here this weekend and they're bringing Violet."

"Oh my God!" Tessa's face lights up. "Does that mean they're giving her to you?"

"Maybe," I hedge. "Maybe not. I guess I'll find out. But I'm just happy because I haven't seen Violet in almost two weeks and I miss her."

"If they don't, I don't know if I'll forgive them."

"Tessa, they really were trying to do their best by their granddaughter. They don't deserve our judgment just because their values don't necessarily line up with ours."

"Isn't that exactly what they've been doing to you?"

I give her a side-eye. "Two wrongs don't make a right. A little lesson I've learned this past spring."

The hard way, I add silently.

On Friday morning, Lulu and Denny arrive with Violet in tow. They haven't visited since Laura died and the emotion on their faces is clear when they walk into the house. Denny holds Violet, something I haven't seen in a long time, and I almost cry at the heartwarming sight. A collage of photos hangs on the wall in the foyer and Laura's smiling face shines out from most of them. Denny points her out to Violet. "That's your mama, Laura. See how beautiful she was? Just like you, my little flower girl."

I look to Lulu, eyebrows raised. She smiles and shrugs, eyes shining. When Denny and Violet move to the other room, she whispers to me, "Something changed. I don't know what, but he's his old self again. Still tinkering, but this time he's building toys for Violet."

"Wow," I whisper back. "That's wonderful. Violet needs her grandpa."

I gesture to the sofa and they sit. "Would you like anything to drink? Coffee, tea, water?" Whiskey Sour? I could use one of those right about now, my nerves are bouncing all over the place.

"Coffee, please." Lulu says. Denny nods.

I make us each a cup and in a few minutes, return to the living room. Violet is playing on the floor and as I watch, she scoots her diaper butt across the floor toward the little toy box I keep nearby. My mouth drops in astonishment. She wasn't doing that two weeks ago.

"When did she start scooting?" I ask.

Lulu thanks me for the coffee and chuckles. "A few days ago. Her grandpa is now trying to teach her to army crawl. I had to hurry and baby-proof the downstairs."

Webb took care of that here. Soft rubber edge guards protect her from table edges and all the outlets are covered. I take a seat on the floor near her and watch in amazement. Tears fill my eyes. I missed so much in two weeks; how much more will I miss?

I draw in a breath, shaking away the thought and reminding myself it's all going to be okay. "So, um, how have you been?"

Lulu puts her mug down. "Not that well at first. Finding out the truth about everything was a shock."

"Can I say again how sorry I am?"

"You can, but your apology has been accepted." She leans across the coffee table and puts a hand on my arm. "Now we need to apologize to you."

She looks back at Denny, who nods in encouragement. "I never should've let Pastor Marty talk us out of our agreement to allow you to adopt Violet. We know what a strong, loving, capable person you are. You and Laura were like sisters and of course Violet would thrive with you."

The lump in my throat keeps me from doing more than just giving her a small smile. I turn my attention to Violet playing with a rattle but continue to listen to Lulu.

"I—we," she grasps Denny's hand, "got so caught up in trying to make sure we didn't make the same mistakes with Violet we did with Laura. I let Pastor Marty convince me that we had failed Laura by not providing a more solid, moral foundation in our family. I was afraid of failing Violet in that way, so I let myself be swayed into thinking only a traditional, two-parent home could give Violet the best life.

"I was wrong. So wrong. I think in my heart, I knew she would be better off with you and that's why I let this drag on for so long. When you said you were seeing someone and that you would be getting married, a part of me understood it was a lie told in the heat of the moment. But I wanted to believe it was true, because I wanted you to have Violet."

"You doubted we were for real," I say. "But you threw us a beautiful wedding. Why?"

She looks at Denny and they smile at each other. "Because while you two may have thought you were putting on a show, Denny and I saw it differently. It was obvious to us and I think anyone who looked at you that there was something there."

"I thought Lulu should've signed the papers that day." Denny grimaces. "But I was being a stupid fool, letting her shoulder all the burden and leaving Pastor Marty to advise her when it should've been a decision between the two of us."

I touch Violet's hair. She blows bubbles at me and scoots over, holding a cloth book in her chubby little hand. I lift her into my lap and gather my courage. "And the other thing I kept a secret?"

"You were right that it had nothing to do with Violet," Lulu says. "But I do wish you'd told us when it happened, so we could have given you our support. I'm so sorry you had to go through something like that. And then for Hollis to bring it up like that…" She clicks her tongue. "That's unconscionable and she owes you an apology."

"Thank you for saying that." Violet drops the book in favor of squeezing my fingers. She puts one in her mouth and I can feel a tiny, sharp nub. Her first tooth! Webb would get a kick out of this. The thought crosses my mind before I can filter it out and a cloud of regret descends over me. I turn back to Lulu and Denny. "So what changed your mind about all this?"

"Something you said," Denny answers. "About how Laura

turned out to be a great person. We didn't fail in raising her, but we were failing her daughter."

Lulu continues. "It took a lot of courage to confess the truth to us. And to put us in our place. Everything you said the other day was hard to hear, but it was true. Who you are as a person is what counts, not whether or not you have a husband or wealth, or even whether you share our values exactly. You're a good person and you'll be a good mother."

I sniff, unable to hold back, and turn my watery gaze on them. "Do you mean it?"

They share a smile. "We want you to adopt Violet," Denny says.

"Laura would want that," Lulu adds.

I kiss the top of Violet's sable curls to help contain the squeal I want to release. "What about Hollis? And Pastor Marty?"

"We had a long talk with Hollis," Lulu says, frowning. "Hollis isn't a terrible person, Piper. She was desperate to save her marriage, and she thought bringing a new baby into the fold would help bring her and Aaron closer. But we convinced her that she needed to focus on getting her boys the help they need. I also told her she needed to decide if she wanted to continue to be a doormat to Aaron or a strong mother for her sons."

I raise any eyebrow. "And Marty?"

"We're leaving the church," Denny says. "And so is Marty. Thanks to Webb, we learned he'd accepted a large payout from Aaron to persuade Lulu to grant Hollis custody. Apparently, while Hollis thought a baby would save their marriage, Aaron thought a new baby would distract her enough to stay off his back."

Lulu's mouth twists in disgust. "Webb also had discovered he'd been siphoning money out of some of the ministry accounts to cover his gambling debts."

"Holy sh-shnikies," I say, catching myself. If Violet's going to be around permanently from now on, I'll need to curb my saltier speech. "Wait, Webb brought that to you? When?"

"Earlier this week. After he'd stopped by on Sunday, shortly after you left," Denny says.

I'm trying to make sense of the timeline here. "Webb went to see you Sunday?"

"He and I had a nice chat," Denny says with a knowing grin. "He took responsibility for everything that happened, said he had to talk you into the whole scheme. He even offered to take himself completely out of the picture if that was going to be a dealbreaker."

"I didn't know that," I murmur.

"What are you going to do about Webb?" Lulu asks. "We understand if it's not going to work out between you two and we'll start adoption proceedings with only you, if that's what you want."

I look at her helplessly. "I don't know what to do, to tell you the truth. He really does love Violet so much already."

"I don't think Violet is the only one he loves." She pats my hand. "But if you don't want to stay married to Webb, that's okay. Nothing in the law says you have to be married for you both to adopt her."

She reaches into her bag and extracts two documents. "Our lawyer drew up these preliminary agreements to get the ball rolling. They grant you conditional custody of Violet while the adoption is finalized. You alone—or you and Webb together."

I glance over the papers, identical except one names only me and the other includes mine and Webb's names. My heart races. Here is everything I wanted laid out before me. All I need to do is take it. But what if it doesn't work out?

Then it'll be okay. Because no matter what's happened between us, there is one indisputable fact and that's how good a dad Webb will be.

"Think about it and send the signed one back to us."

"I'm overwhelmed, Lulu. Denny. Thank you for trusting me with Violet."

"Thank you," Lulu says, her voice thick and throaty, "for loving Laura and for loving her daughter."

When they leave a few hours later, without Violet, I've made up my mind. I make a quick phone call, bundle up Violet and a few special items, and head out the door. I kiss her on the head as I strap her in the car seat. "Let's go get your Daddy."

FORTY-SEVEN

Webb

The office opened its doors this week and I should be riding a high. We're not crazy busy, but we welcome a steady stream of new patients through the doors. All mention of Duncan Dental Services LLC has been removed from our literature and website, a last-minute edit that cost a pretty penny but was necessary. When I informed Bette about the change so she could pass it on to the rest of the SASBO members, she was surprised and delighted. Being part of a larger health franchise operation had been a big sticking point, but now it was a moot point. I didn't know if I should mention Piper, if news about what happened had made the rounds. But she answered that question for me.

"Heard you and Piper are having some troubles," she'd said, not bothering to be coy.

"We might have rushed things a bit," I admitted.

"Oh bull. You love her, don't you?"

I'd swallowed down the lump that formed every time I thought of her and the bleakness in her eyes the last time I saw her. "With everything I am."

"Then stop dicking around and get her back."

I laugh now thinking about her advice. So on brand for Bette. "If only I could figure out how to win her back," I mumble to myself. I'd just have to give her time and space and hope one day she would let herself love me again.

I'm working on the computer when our receptionist, Amy, knocks on the door. "We had a last-minute appointment come in, but Trev and Pam are already with patients. I know you don't do general dentistry—"

"But I can," I finish, smiling at her. "What room are they in?"

"Two."

"Be there in a minute."

I save my document and close out, sliding my white coat on before I leave. I walk down the hall to Room Two. "Good afternoon, I'm Dr. Duncan. How are y—"

The words freeze on my lips. Perched on the edge of the dental chair in the center of the room are my girls. I blink, but the vision doesn't go away. Then it starts making noise.

"Dadadadadada." Violet is kicking her little legs and flashing a gummy smile at me. Not entirely gummy, I notice. Another two tiny white specks dot her pink gums. Has it been so long since I've seen her that she's grown more teeth?

My gaze moves to the woman holding her. Piper looks lovelier than ever, her hazelnut locks lying loose around her shoulders, coral lips tilted upward in a hesitant smile. Her eyes are the color of wet earth and spark with promise. She chuckles while I stand there, mesmerized, praying this isn't a mirage.

"Um, hello Dr. Duncan." Piper's voice jolts me out of my trance.

"Piper." I want to say more, but her name is all I can manage right now. I crouch down so I'm eye-level with Violet. "Hey there, baby girl. Long time no see."

She answers me back with a stream of intense nonsense, spraying me with drool in the process. I laugh. "Is that so? Well, I'm glad you're here, too."

Violet propels herself forward off Piper's lap, and I catch her in my arms. "*Oof.* Someone's been growing."

"Just wait." Piper laughs. "She's already butt-scootin'. She'll be crawling before you can blink."

I kiss the baby's temple and settle back against the cabinet that holds the x-ray camera. "So Lulu and Denny finally came to their senses. You're adopting Violet?"

When she doesn't answer right away, my heart sinks. I scowl. "Or is this more auditioning for you? I swear, those people—"

"Those people are letting me adopt Violet," Piper interrupts. "Sorry, I was trying to figure out how to answer you—hang on. I have something to show you."

She riffles through the diaper bag, muttering to herself. I use the opportunity of her distraction to drink her in. Her honey-gold skin glows against the white denim jacket she wears over a T-shirt, her jeans hugging the supple curves of her hips and holding her firm ass high. A sugary sweetness fills the air, the kind that only comes from Piper, and it mingles with the fresh, powdery scent of Violet to make a heady combination. It's enough to bring a man to his knees.

"Ah-ha, here it is." She pulls out a thin, folded stack of papers and brandishes it like it's the Golden Ticket. She's radiant, though behind the smile in her eyes is a shadow of uncertainty. "I can adopt Violet, by myself. They realize it was ridiculous to require me to have a husband to prove I'm fit to be Violet's mother."

"That's great, Piper. It's about frigging time." My smile is genuine, and every piece of my heart is jumping for joy for her. But as I snuggle Violet, I can't help the sting of disappointment in my chest. She was almost mine. They both were.

"Yeah, they gave me the choice. All I have to do to get things started is sign these papers, and I can sign them as sole petitioner or," she steps closer, "we can sign them together."

I dart my eyes from the papers in her hand to her face to

Violet and back again. My heart starts skipping in triple time while my brain struggles to catch up to what she's saying. I don't dare hope. "Together. You want to sign them with me?"

Piper lifts one shoulder. "She needs a father, and it seems she's taken quite a liking to you. Uh, and your ties."

I look down and my little imp has my silk tie clamped between her fists and is shoving it into her mouth. I laugh and bounce her in my arms. "You already owe me one tie, kid. What's another?"

"Mmbrrrfpthh."

"My sentiments exactly." I catch Piper's gaze, still not entirely sure what this means for us, but grateful to be included in her life in some way. If not lover and husband, I'll take friend and co-parent. "Are you sure about this?"

She nods. "You're great with her. You love her. You'll protect her. It's probably the easiest decision I've had to make in a long time."

I hold Violet close and attempt to keep my emotions at bay. Wouldn't be too professional to be caught crying at work. "Thank you, Piper. I—just, thank you."

It's then I notice the shirt she's wearing. It's the tee Gina gave her, the one that matches mine. I breathe in sharply. I don't dare to hope.

Or do I?

"You're wearing the shirt."

She purses her lips as she looks down at it. "So it seems."

She raises her head and reaches back into the diaper bag, pulling out the mate to the shirt and handing it to me. The last time I saw it, it was at the bottom of the hamper at Piper's house. "Only, it doesn't make much sense by itself. Kind of like me. I've figured out I don't make much sense without you."

She steps closer and I shift the baby to the side so I can meet her halfway when she rises on her tiptoes. Our mouths touch, her lips warm and tender. She gives me an opening and I slide my tongue inside for a tiny taste. "Mm," I murmur when we break apart. "You've been eating chocolate."

She holds a hand to her mouth and laughs. "I might've stopped by the shop on the way here for some fudge."

I swing the t-shirt over my shoulder. "Should I stop by the grocery store for some chocolate sauce?"

"Why would you do that?"

"If your mouth tastes that good, imagine how other parts of you will taste with chocolate on them." I waggle my brows.

She swats at my arm. "Webb, you can't say things like when you're holding our child."

My smile impossibly grows. "Our child," I repeat.

"Ours," Piper emphasizes. "Just like I'm yours and you're mine, she's ours."

She presses another sweet kiss to my lips and wrangles Violet out of my arms. "We should let you get back to work."

I stare at my beautiful girls, my heart so full, so complete it just might burst out of my chest. Which would make a terrible mess of this newly painted exam room and all the fancy equipment in it, but I honestly wouldn't care. "I love you, Piper."

She slings the strap of the diaper bag over her shoulder and beams at me. Amy pokes her head in at that moment. "Dr. Duncan, I'm sorry to interrupt, but Dr. Glass needs a consult in exam four."

"I'll be there in a minute."

She casts a questioning glance at Piper and the baby, flashing a smile at Violet, who's trying hard to climb out of Piper's arms so she can play with the shiny metal instruments I move out of her way. "Who's this little one? She's adorable," Amy coos. She's from the mainland and doesn't know everyone on the Isle... yet.

"This is Violet, my daughter," I say, stroking the top of her head. "And this is—"

"Hi, I'm Piper." Piper cuts in and sticks out her hand to shake Amy's. "I'm Webb's wife."

"Nice to meet you Mrs. Duncan. I'll tell Dr. Glass you're on the way."

When Amy leaves us alone, I walk Piper out to the front. Before she can walk out the door, however, I wrap my around her waist and spin her and Violet into my arms. I rest my forehead against hers. "My wife, huh? Does that mean you love me, too, and you want to try forever with me?"

"Why not?" she smirks. She uses her free hand to bend my head to her and plants a full-on, toe-curling, lip-smacking kiss on me.

Why not indeed.

Epilogue

By the time the anniversary of Laura's death comes around, Violet is officially ours. She's walking and talking up a storm, but at fourteen months she has yet to say "Mama." I try not to let it bother me, but I can't help feeling jealous over all the "Dada" action Webb gets. Maybe it's a sign, a reminder that Laura is really her mom. I've just been entrusted to care for her. If she can say "Pip", I can be content with that.

We received the news that Pastor Marty has plead guilty to embezzlement; I hear he'll be doing time in Danbury Federal. Hey, Martha Stewart survived doing time. Too bad the same can't be said of his church. It folded, its members scattering to other places of worship. Lulu and Denny took some time finding a new place for themselves, and I think they made a wise choice. The new church is much more welcoming than judgmental, and since it's on the Isle, it gives them a good reason to visit for Sunday lunch. Denny always brings a new toy for Violet, usually something he's made himself. But on her first birthday, the gift he gave her wasn't homemade. It was a worn, much-loved stuffed moose. It'd been Laura's when she was little.

I don't know whether it's because her PopPop gave it to her or because it's soft, but Violet won't go anywhere without that moose. I like to think she feels a connection to Laura with it. Who knows. Stranger things have happened.

Take Webb's parents, for example. After the Board learned about Eileen's recording of executives' calls, she was unanimously voted out. It was ugly at first, and Webb was afraid he'd get drawn into the legal quagmire. But in the end, Eileen chose to take a lucrative early retirement. Graeme was voted in as CEO and the Duncans put their estate up for sale so they could travel the world by yacht.

The sea air must be good for them, because it seems like they've done a lot of soul searching. Webb gets postcards from them from the ports of call they anchor at, and they even sent Violet a small birthday gift along with a card signed Grandma and Grandpa Duncan. None of their correspondence has contained an apology thus far, but I think one will eventually come.

Webb says he doesn't care, that he meant it when he said they were out of his life. But sometimes I catch him re-reading one of the postcards, studying it like he's searching for a clue or an answer to a question only he knows. I can see the sad little boy he used to be, so eager for any morsel of love from his parents, and it breaks my heart. I can usually cheer him up, not that it takes much. I've stopped investing in sexy lingerie since it's rarely on my body for more than a millisecond.

My mother still can't believe I'm married and raising a child, but she did make an effort to come to Violet's first birthday. I think she even enjoyed herself. I caught her giving advice to Violet and among the little nuggets she imparted was to "never say yes to the first offer." I think about that a lot. I told Webb about it and he pointed out that I didn't say yes to his first offer, and look how happy we are. So maybe Aria is a genius after all.

As we gather around Laura's grave—Webb, Violet, and me;

Lulu and Denny; Tessa and Hayes; and Drew and Mara with their three-month-old, Casey—my heart is full. Some tears are shed, understandably. But there are more smiles and laughter today, even from the Rosellis. We trade funny and sweet memories, we express our love for her, we remember the amazing, wonderful daughter, friend, and mother she was. And then we lay down our flowers and say our goodbyes. I don't know that this will become a yearly tradition, but I do know each of us will be back again.

After everyone is gone, I stand at her grave marveling at all the changes that have happened in the past year and mourning the fact I couldn't share them with Laura. An arm comes around my shoulder and Webb pulls me in close, Violet asleep on his other shoulder.

"I wish she could see us, see how much Violet has grown, see how much I've grown." I let loose a little laugh. "She'd be knocked on her ass to see us together."

"Do you think she'd be happy about us?" Webb asks.

"Yeah, I do. She always told me I needed to forgive you and move on. I'm not sure she imagined us getting back together, but she was right about the forgiveness. Kind of wish I had listened to her sooner."

"It happened when it was meant to happen." Webb kisses the side of my head. "And I thank God for that. You know what else?"

"What?"

"I think she does see us. I think she's watching over Violet every day. Nothing can beat having her here on earth with us, I know, but it's pretty damn incredible to think about having her up there in our corner. Can you think of a better guardian angel?"

I laugh, dashing away the tear that escaped. "No, I can't."

We stand there in silence a few more minutes, then Violet stirs. "Guess that's our cue to go."

She lets out a little cry and lunges for me. "Mama."

We go very still and look at each other in complete astonishment. "Did she just—"

"Yeah, I think she did," Webb answers, a huge smile taking over his face.

Violet is still struggling in his arms, reaching out to me. I hold out my arms to take her. "Mama," she repeats, followed by "juice", "home", and "moosey."

"All right baby girl," I say, unable to contain my own smile. If I thought my heart was full before, then its cup runneth over now.

I look over my shoulder at the grave and catch a familiar sight. A cardinal sits on top of the headstone, but before I can call Webb's attention to it, it flies away. I whisper, "Thank you, Laura."

Webb takes my hand and the three of us head home.

Acknowledgments

The pandemic really sucked the creative energy out of me. I thought having no obligations for several months—with school, sports, skate lessons, etc. being canceled—would give me the opportunity to write my little heart out. Instead, I was physically and creatively drained. I had about half a book written when I contracted COVID and couldn't even get back to it for months after I recovered. At which I point I completely scrapped it and started all over.

So I have to first and foremost thank my writing partners, that Damned Mob of Scribbling Women, for their support and encouragement. JL Lora, Laralyn Doran, Shadow Leitner, Audrey Couloumbis, and Katie Baldwin... I wouldn't be here without you. Love you girls!

To my friends in the former Central PA Chapter of RWA, thank you, too, for helping me stay connected even when isolated. Especially Jennifer Bonds, Carrie Jacobs, Alyssa Black, Andrew Grey, and Misty Simon. Without Misty's writing retreats, Piper and Webb's story may still be locked in my head. Special thanks to Michelle Haring and the gang at Cupboard Maker Books. If you're in the Enola, PA area, you MUST visit and say hello to the kitties!

I'd be remiss if I didn't mention the amazing team at Yellow Springs Dental, especially Dr. Maples and Susan. Not sure if they knew why I was asking certain questions, but it was for this.

To my bff and copyeditor, Katie Testa—thank you, thank

you, thank you! You're always there for me and I love you for it. Virgos rule!

To my editor Eli Peters, I'm so grateful for your patience with me. Thank you for assuring me I didn't suck!

To Wendy Poincelot Ott for allowing me the use of her name. Thanks, friend!

And finally, my infinite gratitude and appreciation for my husband and my kids, who are my constant cheerleaders. Without your love and support, I'd never have the courage to keep chasing my dreams. I love you guys!

Special shoutout to my youngest and her passion for figure skating. The bulk of this book was written during her almost-daily 5am skate lessons. Who knew writing in a chilly ice rink could be so productive?

About the Author

Cate Tayler is a beach baby, born and raised on the Connecticut coastline. She met the love of her life while serving in the US Air Force, and after extensive overseas travel, they are now raising their four children and two rescue pups in the wild suburbs of Maryland. When she's not living her own happily-ever-after, she's creating them in her small-town romances. In addition to writing, her passions include cooking (not baking!), everything 80s, sappy Hallmark movies, the Hershey Bears, and the Miami Dolphins. You can connect with her online at Cate-Tayler.com.

Also by Cate Tayler

Mystic Point Series

Love Me Once More: A Mystic Point Novella

Love Me Now

Love Me Like You Do

Love Me Harder

Love Me Like a Song: A Mystic Point Novella

Lacrosse My Heart

Body Check

Standalones

Mistletoe Wish

Mistletoe Miracle

www.ingramcontent.com/pod-product-compliance
Lightning Source LLC
Chambersburg PA
CBHW071355300726

48976CB00006B/1891